New Beginnings at Glendale Hall

New Beginnings at Glendale Hall

Victoria Walters

hera

First published in the United Kingdom in 2020 by Hera

Hera Books
28b Cricketfield Road
London, E5 8NS
United Kingdom

A CIP catalogue record for this book is available from the British Library.

Print ISBN 978 1 78863 968 2
Ebook ISBN 978 1 912973 26 2

Printed and bound in Great Britain by Clays Ltd, Elcograf S.p.A.

To Harry — thank you for inspiring the cake scene!

Prologue

Twelve Years Ago

The buzzer rang out and I jumped up to answer it, telling Beth Williams to come on up. Biting my lip, I glanced around my tiny flat, part of my catering college's accommodation, hoping we'd be able to navigate the tiny space together. It wouldn't be easy but how could I have said no to her coming to stay?

There was a tentative knock at the door, and I pulled it open. 'Hi, Beth,' I said, giving her my warmest smile. She looked like a wreck, poor thing. Exhausted and pale, her eyes red and puffy from crying, and just one bag clutched to her chest.

'Thanks so much for this, Emily,' she said, walking in when I stepped back to let her through. I closed the door behind us, and she let her bag drop to the floor as she took in her new surroundings.

'It's so good to see you,' I said, pulling her into a quick, tight hug. It had been six years since we had last seen each other after I had left our hometown of Glendale, nestled in the Scottish Highlands, and moved with my parents down to London. 'Have a seat, you must be exhausted. How was your journey down?' I asked, wondering if that was a stupid question. I had no idea how she had

had the strength to walk out of her family home, the grand Glendale Hall, and make the long journey down to Brixton all alone like she had. I thought of the frantic phone call I'd received from my Aunt Sally, housekeeper at Glendale Hall, asking me if I could help. Beth was devastated that her family didn't want to support her but she was determined to make it on her own, and when my aunt asked if she could stay with me until she could get herself sorted, I had naturally said yes.

'Pretty tiring,' she admitted. 'But I made it.' Her eyes were wide but she looked relieved. It struck me how much more grown up she seemed since we had last met, but I supposed with everything that had happened to her that was only natural. At sixteen, she was four years younger than me but didn't seem it. I couldn't begin to imagine what she had gone through.

'I'm sorry it's so small. I did tell my aunt to warn you. But this pulls out into a bed,' I said, patting the edge of the sofa where I hovered. 'So, it'll be fine. It's college accommodation and they allow friends to stay over but obviously not long term so we need to be careful.' I realised I was babbling a little like I always did when nervous. I glanced at her arms folded in her lap, covering her stomach. 'How about we have some tea and cake?' I asked, knowing that always made me feel better. 'I just baked it,' I added, walking over to the open-plan kitchen.

She visibly brightened. 'I never say no to cake. I remember how much you loved to cook, just like Sally.'

'Baking, mostly. I'm going to own my own bakery one day,' I said, pulling out a cake knife and reaching for the lemon drizzle that filled the flat with a yummy scent. I glanced at Beth. She looked as if she needed a big slice. 'It'll be okay, you know,' I said then, softly, 'I promise.'

'I hope so,' she replied. 'I won't have to stay for too long.'

'You can stay for as long as you need,' I replied as I cut two slices for us. 'Don't worry, okay? The hard part is over. You're here.'

My aunt had said that Beth's grandmother had been furious with her, that the argument they had had forced Beth to run away. I knew Beth's family weren't easy, they expected a lot from Beth, and she had always rebelled against them but even I had been surprised that they had turned against her so fiercely. It felt old-fashioned to me, but then my family weren't pillars of the community like the Williams family were up in Glendale. All I knew was that I was happy to help Beth as much as I could. Not just for my aunt's sake, who loved her like family, or for our childhood friendship when I would often go to the hall and play with her while Aunt Sally worked, but because it was the right thing to do. I wanted a family of my own one day so I understood why she had gone against her family's wishes. I might have even done the same thing although I knew my parents would always be there for me, like they always had been.

Beth touched her stomach then, where her unborn baby grew; the baby that her family had told her she shouldn't keep. 'I'm here,' she repeated, and finally a slow, small smile spread across her face.

Part One

Chapter One

I stared at the cream and gold embossed invitation with a mixture of disbelief and pride. The day Beth came to stay with me in London all those years ago flashed through my mind. Who would have thought that scared teenage girl would be inviting me to her wedding twelve years later?

The sun pooled on the kitchen floor as I sipped my coffee, smiling at the words on the card. I was thrilled that Beth was finally marrying her first and only love, Drew – the father of her daughter, Izzy – at her family home in Scotland. The one she had run from when she had come to live with me at sixteen. She really had got her happily ever after.

I glanced at the ring-free finger on my left hand and tried to not let a prickle of jealousy seep into my skin. It really wasn't my style, especially as I knew how much Beth deserved this. But my boyfriend Greg had always told me he didn't believe in marriage and even after three years together, I still harboured a secret hope that he might one day change his mind about that.

'Any left in the pot for me?' Greg called as he strode into the kitchen wearing his uniform. That uniform had made me swoon when we had first met. I had been at the bakery where I still worked when a new member of staff had set the kitchen alight and Greg had been the first fireman on the scene. It was pretty much love at first sight for me. All the clichés had been present and correct – he was tall, broad and strapping, with dark hair and a dimple in his cheek when he grinned. After he had put the fire out, he strode over to me, full of confidence, and handed me a piece of paper with his phone number on. The epitome of charming, you just couldn't help but warm to Greg when you met him. Even now, when we were far away from those first heady, love-struck weeks, he could still make me melt if he tried.

The problem was, he just didn't bother trying as much any more.

Perhaps that's what happened to every couple who lived together but it was starting to worry me.

'Plenty,' I replied, watching him go to pour himself a large cup of coffee. He was working day shifts this week so we actually got to see one another in the morning. 'I can't believe the wedding is only a couple of weeks away now,' I said, sliding the invitation across the kitchen table towards him. He leaned against the counter to sip his coffee, giving it a cursory glance. 'It's come around so quickly,' I added, as he didn't seem to be studying it at all closely.

'I don't think I'll be able to get the time off now,' he said with a shrug.

'I thought you had it all booked?' I asked, surprised. Beth had given us months' notice of their intended date, and he was well aware of how important it was for me to be there. Not only as the long-time family friend I was, but because Beth had asked me to be one of her bridesmaids (even though I said I was too old to be called that) and had also asked me to bake their wedding cake.

'I did, but the chief says I'm needed at work now. There's not much I can do, babe.' He gulped down the rest of his coffee. 'But you'll have so much to do there, it's not like we'd have any fun.'

'It's a wedding, of course we would!' I cried, annoyed that something which meant so much to me could mean so little to him.

He strode over to plant a quick kiss on my cheek. 'I'm sorry, babe, but you know what the chief is like,' he said, walking out as briskly as he had entered. 'See you later!' he called back, whistling as he left our house, not seeming to have noticed that I hadn't replied.

I sighed, the sound echoing in the empty room. I couldn't believe he was only telling me now that he wouldn't be coming, just a couple of weeks before we were meant to be up in Scotland. Not only had I been really looking forward to the wedding, I had also been hoping it would be an opportunity for us to reconnect. That it would have been romantic to be there together, snuggled up at Glendale Hall, watching two people in love make their vows.

But now it looked like I'd be going up there alone.

Looking at the clock on the wall, I jumped up. There was no time to wallow in self-pity, I had to get to work myself. I pulled my long, blonde hair up into a ponytail, grabbed my jacket and bag and locked up our house. It was a small but pretty property in Clapham. I loved it – not only because I still couldn't quite believe we owned our own home in the city, but because it was cosy and homely, and only a twenty-minute walk to work.

June was already starting to warm up the city nicely and once midday came around, I knew I wouldn't need my jacket any longer. I enjoyed my walk to work; it took me through a park that made you forget you were in London, reminding me of the countryside I had grown up surrounded by. Thanks to the sunshine and blue sky, I had cheered up considerably by the time I opened the door to the bakery.

I had worked at Molly's Bakery for five years. Molly, the owner, was a lovely lady – she had run the bakery for forty years and I loved her like a second mother. The problem with that was it had so far proved impossible for me to think about leaving her. The prospect of opening my own bakery one day still hung dangling like a carrot for a future Emily to grab hold of, but present Emily just couldn't quite grasp it. I didn't have the money yet either. So, it had been easy to keep putting off thinking about it.

The delicious smell of freshly baked bread filled my nostrils as I headed for the back. The place always smelled wonderful and had a slightly old-fashioned feel to it, somewhat out of place with the trendier shops and eateries nearby, but even more beloved by the locals because of that fact. Molly would never gentrify her bakery. And woe betide anyone who even dared to mention the word.

'Emily, darling,' Molly said, beaming as I went to hang up my jacket and put on an apron. She was a petite, pretty woman with white hair that was always carefully pinned back. 'You must try one of these!' She thrust a pastry at me. 'Now, tell me what you think and be honest…'

I took it with a grin. This was the reason I was what you'd call 'curvy'. No one could be skinny with Molly around. That is, apart from our new girl Steph, who was built like a rake and made me feel like I should try to cut down the amount of cake I ate. It was just so hard to resist everything, though. I took a bite of the pastry and let out a moan. 'That's so good, Molly!'

'Apple and cinnamon. Just so warming, isn't it? Shall I add them to the menu?'

'Definitely!' I polished the rest of it off. 'And make sure you give me the recipe.'

'Naturally, my dear. Now, I need to tackle the dreaded books. Will you be okay out the front on your own until Steph gets here?'

'Sure thing,' I replied. Steph was there to help with the morning and lunch time rush. Once that was over, Molly and I could start baking out the back while keeping an ear out for any late customers until everything had been sold for the day. Molly usually shut up by four p.m. as she had to be up so early to bake bread in the morning. I still didn't know where she got her energy from.

I opened up the doors and all thoughts of Beth's wedding and Greg's disappointing absence from it faded away as I dealt with people desperate for one of Molly's treats on the way to work. Steph arrived half an hour later and we were rushed off our feet until lunch time.

'I'm exhausted!' Steph cried when at last the queue had gone. She looked at the counter. 'There's barely anything left.'

'Everyone was walking to work today as it's such a nice morning and had to stop off on the way,' I guessed. I leant against the counter. 'We've made a killing, though.'

Steph pulled out her phone. 'I have, like, fifty WhatsApp messages!' she cried, scrolling through. Any spare moment she got, she was glued to her iPhone. She was studying at a local uni and working at the bakery to help fund her studies. I sometimes envied her being at the start of her journey. I glanced over at her as she smiled, her cheeks flushing a little.

'New fella on the scene?' I asked, cringing at myself for using the word 'fella'. Sometimes she made me feel twenty years older than her, and not ten.

'Oh, no,' she said, quickly, putting her phone back into her apron pocket. 'Just arranging to meet some friends later. We're going to a club.'

'Oh, right,' I said, thinking that I couldn't even remember the last time I'd set foot in a club. Greg and I had a great social life when we first got together but then all our friends started getting married and having babies, so not only had nights out been traded for coffee mornings and soft play areas, it had become more and more painful to spend much time with them. 'I'm going to check on Molly,' I said to Steph, needing to stop comparing myself to someone whose life was so different to mine. Different, I reminded myself, not necessarily better.

'It was manic out there!' I told Molly as I walked into the back, sitting down on one of the office chairs, relieved to be off my feet for a bit.

'That's good. Look what I spotted at the wholesaler… I thought you could use it for your friend's wedding cake, maybe?' Molly showed me the white and silver pack of iced roses.

'Oh, thanks. I'm still debating on what colour scheme to do. But they are lovely.'

'What about the sponge? Have you decided on that yet?'

I groaned. 'I don't know why I'm being so indecisive about it. It doesn't help that Beth isn't around to taste anything. She just wants to leave it all up to me but I'm scared it won't be right.'

'Well, of course you want it to be perfect but she trusts you so don't worry too much.'

'I just want to make sure it's extra special.' I tried not to think the reason I was so desperate to make Beth's wedding cake perfect was because I was worried I'd never have one of my own.

Molly gave me a sympathetic look. 'It will be special because you will make it with love. Are you getting excited for your trip back to Scotland? Greg must be eager to finally see where you grew up?'

I had been so excited to show him the village of Glendale, nestled in the Scottish Highlands, after trying to persuade him to come up there with me for as long as we'd been together but there had never been a 'good' time, and now I was worried there never would be. I couldn't stop the cloud from falling over my face. 'Well, Greg now says that he can't have the time off work so it looks like I'll be going alone.' I looked away, afraid that the pity on Molly's face would make me cry.

'That's a shame, love.' She gave my hand a gentle squeeze. 'How are things now between the two of you?'

I sighed. Molly knew all about our problems; she was the first person I turned to for advice after my own mother. 'Not great, which was why I had been so excited to go away with him. But that's not happening now. I know it's not his fault but I am disappointed, you know?'

'Of course you are!'

'Anyway, why don't I get a batch of cupcakes started? We can put them in the window to tempt the kids on the way home from school.' I got up and headed for the kitchen area, knowing that I needed to do something or I would definitely start crying on her shoulder. It wasn't just the fact that Greg wouldn't be coming away with me that had upset me so much, it was the fact that he didn't seem to care less about it. And I couldn't help but wonder if it was just one more sign that things were going from bad to worse with us. Signs I'd been trying desperately to hide from for months but which were becoming impossible to ignore.

Chapter Two

I cursed myself for not cancelling, but I was running out of excuses, or outright lies, to avoid social occasions. So, I stood on Hazel's doorstep and took a deep breath before ringing the bell. I'd met Hazel through her husband Johnny, one of Greg's workmates, and when we'd first got together the four of us had double-dated a lot. Hazel and Johnny had been a lot of fun, the kind of couple always pressing you to stay for one more drink, always ready with a funny anecdote or an idea for something to do, like the time we had champagne at the top of The Shard, or the time we'd run off to Paris for the weekend on a whim.

That had all changed though when they got married and very quickly had a baby.

'Em!' Hazel opened the door with a wide smile, her toddler balanced on her hip. 'We were worried you wouldn't make it,' she said, still smiling but with an edge to her words. I was almost an hour late.

'I'm sorry, we had to make cakes for this work do so I had to stay on to help Molly finish them,' I said, walking in when she gestured for me to do so. It wasn't a lie exactly, we had finished on time but I had cleaned up much more carefully than needed and walked to Hazel's slowly, aware that the later I arrived, the earlier it would finish. Was I a terrible person? I *felt* like a terrible person. I had never been like this before but it had just become harder and harder to be around my happy friends and their perfect families.

'Happy birthday, Amy,' I said to the little girl wrapped around Hazel. 'Here you go.' I handed Hazel a gift bag, one of the presents on the extensive approved gift list she had emailed everyone last month.

'Oh, thank you! I'll just pop it on the present table. Go on through,' Hazel said, pointing to the living room as she disappeared with Amy. I walked on through and looked at the room full of people, balloons, and pink bunting. It was a mixture of faces I knew and unfamiliar ones – Hazel's friends from nursery, all of them either bouncing a baby on their knee, or calling out to older children taking too many sweets from the food table. I stared at them and felt the all-too-familiar ache in the pit of my stomach.

'Emily, come and sit down here!' Rachel waved me over to the sofa where she was holding her baby, just a month old. 'How mad is it in here, huh?'

Rachel had been my closest friend of our group. Again, we'd met through our partners, but we would often spend time just the two of us, having a glass of wine and putting the world to rights, until she got pregnant. She had drifted closer to Hazel and the other mothers she knew, and now I couldn't remember the last time the two of us had been out alone. I knew things had to change but I had been surprised by how *much* they had changed.

'How was work today?' she asked. She had given up her corporate job after she and Paul had got married, which surprised me at the time as she had seemed ambitious, but she had wanted to focus on having a family. And she certainly seemed to have embraced motherhood. She was positively glowing.

'Really busy. I don't know where Molly gets her energy from, I'm knackered,' I said, looking out of the corner of my eye to see if there was any alcohol anywhere but I couldn't see any, worse luck.

'I couldn't imagine spending all day on my feet,' Rachel said, shaking her head. 'But you're off to Scotland soon, aren't you?'

'That's right. My friend's wedding is just a couple of weeks away now,' I replied. 'I can't wait to see Glendale again.' I couldn't believe it had been three years since I'd seen my hometown. My parents and I had gone back a few times since we'd moved to London when I was fourteen but after I'd met Greg, I hadn't joined their trips. At Christmas my Aunt Sally, still working as the housekeeper at Beth's home Glendale Hall, would come down to London to see us. I had really missed it but now the excitement about the trip had been dulled a little by Greg cancelling on me.

'Your accent comes back when you say "Glendale",' she noted with a smile. 'I'm so jealous. I doubt I'll have a holiday for ages with this one around,' she said but I could tell she didn't really mean it. The love for her baby overrode everything, and rightly so. 'And I bet Greg can't wait for a romantic trip away either.'

'He couldn't but now he's been told he has to work,' I said with a grimace.

Rachel frowned. 'Really? I'm surprised because Paul asked for a couple of days off so we can visit his parents last minute and was given it by the chief,' she said.

I stared at her. If Paul had been given time off at the last minute how come Greg couldn't have his long-booked trip then? 'That's strange,' I said, trying to hide how annoyed I was. My heart had plummeted inside my chest. Had Greg just made that up? To get out of coming away with me?

'Maybe I've got it wrong though,' Rachel said, quickly. 'Paul said I've got such a baby brain at the moment. You know what it's like.' Her face fell as I looked at her, her cheeks turning pink when she realised what she'd said. 'Oh, Em, I'm so sorry, I...' Thankfully, her flustered apology was cut off by the sudden chorus of 'Happy Birthday' as Hazel's husband carried in a cake lit with a number two candle. I looked away from Rachel and her expression of pity, and watched as Hazel and Johnny sung to their little girl and helped her blow out the candles, tears welling up in my eyes.

I left Hazel's as soon as I politely could and walked home in a daze, thinking about how far apart Greg and I seemed now. Far apart enough that he appeared to have made up an excuse to get out of going away with me. There was a time when we would have done anything to go away together.

Back at home, I went into the kitchen and started to go through the motions of making us dinner. I didn't want to get into an argument about Scotland but I just didn't understand why he wouldn't want to come. He seemed to be signing up for more and more shifts at work, especially night ones, so times together were few and far between, and I thought that, like me, he was eager for us to get away. I had to find out what was going on.

Pouring a large glass of red wine, I prepared his favourite meal – spaghetti bolognaise – hoping we could at least have some quality time together tonight, and then maybe I could get him to re-think this trip. I really thought we needed it. Hopefully he would too. I put a salad on the table and lit two candles, before turning on some soft music, hoping to set a romantic mood.

'In here!' I called, as I heard the front door open then close. 'I'm cooking!'

It was a moment before Greg appeared. 'I'm just going to have a quick shower and change,' he said. He seemed to realise then what I had said. 'Oh, I'm going out, didn't I say? Mike's got lady troubles once again.'

I turned from the cooker. 'No, you didn't. I made your favourite.' I gestured lamely to the simmering pan behind me, willing him with my eyes to cancel his plans, willing him to *want* to cancel them. For me.

He sighed heavily. 'Okay, I'll eat quickly and then go out. Right – back in a min.' He paused then threw on one of his charming grins. 'You're the best,' he said, before ducking back out of the room.

I picked up my wine and took a long gulp. I hated to think that this distance between us was my fault. Everything had been so good at the start but once we started trying for a baby… that's when things had changed. It had been fun before that. We were head over heels in love, full of plans for the future; our main one being that we wanted to have a big family. We were both only children so we wanted a big brood of our own. Greg might not have been on board with marriage but babies were a different matter and that proved his commitment to me as far as I was concerned. I soon came off the pill but nothing happened. Maybe we should have kept it just the two of us for longer, but we were excited, we couldn't wait for our future to begin.

Only then it didn't. And it still hadn't.

I wanted us to go and see a doctor but Greg kept saying it was too soon for all that. He hated doctors so the thought of tests made him nervous, I knew, but it seemed crazy that after over two years of trying we hadn't got pregnant once. We were now stuck in this limbo of saying it was bound to happen soon on one hand, and on the other, rolling over in bed, a huge gap between us, not even wanting to try any more. We hadn't had sex in six weeks. And that time had only been because we'd both drunk a lot of wine one evening.

I kept thinking there must have been something wrong with me and I knew that I could get checked out without Greg – rule out any problems on my side, at least – but I was scared. Scared it was my fault. Scared that he'd run off and leave me if I couldn't have children.

And that made me annoyed at myself for being so pathetic.

So, we kept on as we were. With me resenting our friends more and more for their perfect families, events like today piercing another hole in my heart, and resenting Greg for not wanting to help me fix our problems. And Greg burying his head in the sand about it – working more and more but pretending that we were fine. As a result, we had grown further and further apart, neither willing to address the giant baby-pink elephant in the room.

'Smells good, babe,' he said then, coming back in, his hair still wet, aftershave floating into the room. He had put on tight black jeans and a dark shirt. He grabbed his glass of wine and sat down at the table.

'You're dressed up,' I said, before I could stop myself. I drained the pasta, the steam turning my cheeks even pinker. I knew my tone was whiny but I didn't understand why he was making such an effort for Mike, and not for me.

'Don't be silly,' he replied, dismissively. 'I'd rather be curled up with you watching Netflix, you know that,' he said then, in a softer tone. I dished up and carried over two steaming plates of spag bol. 'This looks amazing. You're such a brilliant cook. This is the best part of not having to work nights.' He tucked in instantly, and I had to smile at the way he devoured my food. That hadn't changed, at least.

'What's up with Mike this time then?' I asked, trying to take an interest in his workmate. Mike was always having women trouble, mainly because he couldn't seem to grasp the fact that he should just see one woman at a time.

'God knows, but at least he's buying the drinks,' Greg replied.

There was a short silence. I really didn't want to start a fight but I had to say something. 'So, I went to the birthday party at Hazel's today,' I said as Greg ate his food as quickly as he could. 'Rachel was there. She said that Paul had been given some time off at the last minute so they could go away,' I continued, watching Greg's reaction. 'Which made me think it was strange that they hadn't allowed your holiday.'

Greg took a long gulp of his red wine before finally meeting my eyes. 'Babe…' he began. I winced inwardly. He had always called me that but sometimes it felt patronising, like it was a way to appease me. 'I need these extra shifts – we need these shifts. I forgot I'd volunteered for them when we were supposed to be away but now I've said yes, I can't let them down. You understand that, don't you? And I'll bet you'll have lots more fun with your friends up there without me.'

'I just wish you'd been honest with me,' I said, not really sure why we needed him to do so many more shifts. I was about to ask when he checked the time and groaned.

He stood up and came around the table to kiss me on the cheek. 'I'm sorry, but I'm late now. Leave the clearing up for me, okay? And don't wait up; you know what Mike's like once he starts talking.'

'Try not to be too late,' I said but he was already walking out of the room. I sighed, knowing full well Greg would stumble in off his face some time in the early hours and end up passing out on the sofa as he always did after their nights out. I didn't mind exactly, of course he needed to go out with his friends sometimes, but it annoyed me that he hadn't thought to check with me first. And that he still had a single friend to go out and get drunk with while I waited at home for him. I didn't want him to see me as a nagging girlfriend, which it felt like he did a lot of the time, but was I really overreacting or was Greg being unfair?

I leaned back in my chair, putting my cutlery down, not sure I could face finishing the meal by myself, although I had become more and more used to eating alone. I really needed to make some decisions about Beth's wedding cake so I started looking at my phone, googling wedding cakes but it was hard to put my heart into it. In the end, I abandoned the images of layers and iced flowers and cleared up the dinner. Despite what he had promised, I knew better than to trust that Greg would be in a fit state to do any of it later.

Retreating into our cosy living room, I drew the curtains and lit the lamps, curling up on the sofa. I found myself on Facebook, clicking through our photos. It was difficult not to keep thinking about our relationship when my head was filled with Beth's impending happy ever after. I zoomed in on my favourite picture of the two of us, the one I had enlarged, framed and hung on the wall in our hallway – a black and white shot of us kissing. Greg had dipped me back on the dance floor at his friend's wedding and the photographer had caught our passion in that moment. I was wearing a cocktail dress, Greg a tux, and we looked like a golden Hollywood couple.

I couldn't help but wonder where all that passion had gone. Had real life extinguished it like a breeze blowing out a flame, or had we been too caught up in our whirl-wind romance to realise that we wouldn't be able to keep hold of it long term? I was sure it was inevitable that a relationship had to shift from the heady days of first love into something more comfortable, more stable, something that lasted but I wasn't sure that was what had happened to us. We didn't feel comfortable or secure. If anything, I was more insecure than when we were first dating. It felt as if things were changing, shifting, like the wind blowing in a new direction, and there was nothing I could do to stop it.

Chapter Three

The sound of the front door slamming woke me with a jump.

I sat up in the dark, my heart racing, glancing at the illuminated clock beside me. It was three in the morning, and my boyfriend was crashing about downstairs as if there were five of him. I groaned into the silence, sleep having been snatched away from me. I climbed out of bed and went downstairs to find him with his head stuck in the fridge, searching for food.

'Greg, it's three a.m.!' I cried, leaning against the doorway and folding my arms across my chest. I hated it when he made me feel like I was his mother telling him off.

Greg leaned back out of the fridge. 'Sorry, babe,' he said with a grin. 'We got a bit carried away,' he added, slurring his words a little.

'Yeah, I can see that. Don't you think you should come to bed?'

'In a minute. Got to line my stomach,' he said, leaning back into the fridge.

I sighed, and turned away. I hated dealing with drunk Greg.

'Pass me my phone, would you?' He called out after me, finally shutting the fridge and carrying his food over to the table.

I saw his phone lying on the table by the door. It usually never left his hands. Obviously, it was only because he was drunk that he was even trusting me to touch it. I felt like throwing it at him. As I grabbed it, it lit up in my hands with a message.

> Tonight was amazing. I wish you hadn't had to leave. My bed feels really lonely without you xxx

The room spun. I dropped the phone with a thud onto the carpet. It felt as if someone had poured cold water over me. Despite the warm night, goosebumps trailed down my arms as the words from the message swam in front of my eyes.

'What's taking so long?' Greg called out then, his mouth clearly full of food.

Sucking in a deep breath, I picked up the phone and walked slowly back into the kitchen. I held it up. 'It's here. Complete with a message from the woman you're clearly shagging,' I said, spitting out the words. I could barely get them out, I was so furious.

Greg dropped the fork he was holding on the plate he had piled up with cake. Cake I had baked. The blood drained from his face. 'What are you talking about?' he asked, throwing on his charming smile as if he thought he could somehow talk his way out of it.

23

I threw the phone at him. He ducked and it fell against the wall.

'Em!' He cried, jumping up, rushing to it. 'You've cracked the screen,' he wailed at me.

'That is seriously what you want to say to me right now?' I asked him.

Cradling the phone, he stepped closer. 'Look, I'm sorry you read that. But, babe, it doesn't mean anything, okay? It was just a one-night thing. I didn't mean to... she means nothing to me. It was just sex, I swear.'

'And what? That makes it okay?' I gaped at him.

'You're the one I love,' he pleaded. 'It was a mistake. A big, drunken mistake. Look at the state of me! I would never have done that sober,' he said, reaching for me.

I shook his hand from my arm. 'So because you're drunk, I should just be okay with the fact that you've just cheated on me? Jesus, Greg!' I threw my hands up in despair. I knew things weren't great between us but I had honestly never expected that he'd cheat on me.

'I'm sorry, Emily, so sorry,' he said, looking down at the floor, his face full of shame.

'Have you done this before?' I asked him quietly, my pulse racing.

He looked up. 'No! Of course not. I swear it.'

I sucked in a breath. 'Who was she?' I asked, even though I wasn't sure I really wanted to hear the answer.

'Just someone we met in the club tonight,' he said, not meeting my eyes. He sank down into the chair, dropping the phone on the table. 'She means nothing to me. Nothing, I swear it.'

Staring at him, I wondered why he kept saying that. If she was just a random girl in the club then why would she mean anything to him? I swiped the phone up into my hands before he could stop me.

'Babe, no! What are you doing? Emily, please…'

I had already called the number the text had come from. I turned away from his begging to listen as a sleepy female voice answered. He jumped up and tried to take the phone from me. I twisted out of his reach.

'Greg? Is that you?'

'Who is this?' I demanded but the voice had already sounded familiar. I had a sudden thought. But no. Please no, not her…

'Emily, is that you?' she squeaked, panic replacing tiredness in her voice.

Greg succeeded in grabbing the phone out of my stunned hands then, cancelling the call and stuffing the phone in his pocket. He took both of my hands in his and forced me to look at him. 'I promise you it meant nothing; she was just there tonight. We bumped into one another and she was all over me. I know that I should have walked away but… It meant nothing. I love you.'

I felt sick. The man sat in front of me suddenly felt like a stranger in my house. How was this someone I had given my heart to?

'You slept with Steph,' I said, slowly, as I tried to fathom the truth in my mind. Younger, prettier, Steph, who I had to work with, who I saw every day, who had slept with my boyfriend! 'Bloody hell, Greg, did you just want to hurt me as much as you could?' I made for the door.

'No, please!' He grabbed my arm again. 'I never wanted you to find out. As soon as it was over, I was disgusted with myself. It's been such a shit week… I was so drunk. I just wanted to forget about everything, just for one night.'

I met his eyes. 'You mean you wanted to forget about me?'

'Never,' he said, fiercely. 'Never. I promise you.'

Moving my arm from him, I just shook my head. I felt almost numb. I couldn't take in what he was saying. How could he have touched another woman? How could he have done that to me… to us? 'Have you been having an affair with her?' I asked him then, dreading the answer.

He shook his head. 'No, I promise. It was just tonight. You know how much you mean to me,' he said in a quiet voice then, as if he was far away. And he was, wasn't he? He had never felt so far away from me. It was as if there were a million miles between us. When had they appeared? Why couldn't we have stopped them?

'Do I? When was the last time you told me that? Or showed me? What are we doing, Greg?' My question hung in the air. He looked helplessly back at me. We stared at one another, both exhausted suddenly. Words wouldn't come. I was shell-shocked, not knowing what to say or think, or do. All I knew was, I couldn't bear to look at him any longer. 'I'm going to bed. Please don't follow me, okay? Please do that for me.' I left him then, going back to bed alone, the tears coming as soon as I closed the door.

The sun was already climbing up into the sky when I finally fell asleep, my pillow soaking wet.

Chapter Four

Greg had gone to work when I finally went downstairs. He had left a note on the kitchen table along with a croissant and coffee bought from the café down the road.

I really am sorry. I can't believe I did that. I really wasn't thinking straight. Please forgive me. You have to. We're forever, you and me. I love you.

I stared at it, my heart aching. Were we still forever? I thought about what would happen when he came home. He would be charming and apologetic, he would remind me why I fell for him, and I would find it harder and harder to think clearly, to know what I really wanted. I realised then that I didn't want to be there when he came home. I needed to think about everything by myself. To know what I wanted to do next without him telling me.

Usually I thought through everything carefully but something snapped inside me, and I knew I needed to do something right now. Pulling out my phone, I rang Beth.

She answered quickly. 'Hi, Emily, what's up?'

'I've been thinking… I think it would be better if I made your cake up there. I'm worried about travelling with it. Would it be okay if I came to stay sooner? Would you have room for me?'

'Of course! When were—'

'Can I come now? Like, today?'

There was a short silence. I imagined her frowning with confusion, trying to work out why I suddenly wanted to come over two weeks before the wedding. 'Is everything all right, Em?'

I cleared my throat. 'Yes, it's just I need to get away and I need time to make the cake and everything. But, don't worry, if you—'

'Don't be silly,' she cut in as I felt my voice break. 'You're welcome here any time, you know that. I'll get your room ready. You come whenever you like, okay?'

I squeezed my eyes, a tear rolling down my cheek. 'Thanks, Beth. I really appreciate it.'

'No thanks needed. Ever. You know that.'

We said goodbye then and I let out a relieved breath. I knew Beth would be wondering just what was going on but I couldn't face telling anyone yet. Saying the words out loud that my boyfriend had slept with someone else would be just too humiliating for me right now. I didn't know how I was going to deal with it yet. I just knew that I had to get away from him, from the situation, from the relationship I suddenly felt trapped in. I needed a break from it all and this wedding was the perfect opportunity. I tried not to think about how it would feel to plant myself smack bang in the middle of celebrating someone else's happy love life but I wouldn't let Beth down even if it hurt.

I swung into action and went back upstairs to shower, dress and pack. I needed to talk to Molly and then I was going to get on the first train I could to Scotland. I knew I would be leaving her somewhat in the lurch but she would understand, I was sure of it.

When I was ready, I carried my two bags downstairs and went back into the kitchen. Next to Greg's words, I added my own.

I've gone to stay with Beth early. I need time to think. Please give me the space to do that, okay?

Looking around our house, I felt the tears start to well up again so I shook my head and exited quickly. I couldn't get sentimental about going away. It was only for a couple of weeks and if our relationship was ever going to repair itself after this then I had to go. Right now, I wanted to kill Greg, to tear down our life with my bare hands, but I knew that making a rash decision in anger wasn't something I should do. I loved him still and the future we had planned, the family we both desperately wanted, was something I couldn't just let go of in a moment.

When I arrived at the bakery, I paused by the back door. In my hurry I hadn't thought about Steph. But then my body sagged with relief. It was her day at uni; she wouldn't be there. I knew that I needed to talk to her. But I couldn't right now – I would have started crying, and I didn't want her to see my tears. I didn't want her to know that she had broken me. When I faced her, I wanted to have the upper hand.

Pushing open the door, I walked in to find Molly kneading dough in the kitchen. 'What's wrong?' Molly cried when she saw me. I must have looked terrible. I dropped the bags I was holding, and she pulled me into a tight hug.

When we finally drew apart, I met her worried gaze. 'Molly, I'm really sorry to do this to you but I need to get away. I've asked Beth if I can come up to Glendale early, and she's said yes. I was hoping to go today but I won't if you need me.'

'You wouldn't be going if it wasn't something important. I know that.'

'I hate letting you down.' I bit my lip, hoping I could stop myself from crumbling in front of her.

'You have never let me down,' she replied fiercely. 'Is it... is it Greg?'

I nodded once.

'Well, I think this a good idea. You deserve a break. But make sure you call me, okay? Let me know you're all right.' She patted my arm. 'Do you need anything?'

I shook my head. 'I was hoping to stay there until the wedding but if you can't spare me...'

'We'll be fine here. My daughter-in-law can step in, you know that. And Steph can do more hours, I'm sure. Don't you worry.'

The mention of Steph was like a knife to my heart, but she wasn't to know. She only meant to be kind. I swallowed hard. 'Are you sure?'

'I'm sure,' she replied, firmly. 'You take as long as you need.'

'Thank you. I'm going to get the train now. I'm so sorry,' I repeated again.

Molly pulled me to her again, giving me a warm hug. I let out a sob into her chest. 'No apologies needed, I promise. You just take care of yourself. Emily, I hope you know how special you are.' She pulled back to brush away a tear from my face. 'It'll be okay, I promise.'

I nodded, hoping that she was right.

Chapter Five

I didn't relax until I was seated on the train to Inverness. I leaned back against the seat and looked out of my window. London rolled past, fading into the background. I felt relieved as the train headed North; I had made it out of the city in one piece.

Pulling out my phone, I left a voicemail on my parents' landline to ensure I didn't have to talk to either of them. I knew I'd break down if I heard their voices. I told them I was heading to Glendale Hall to help with the wedding, leaving out Greg's name altogether. They would likely assume we had gone up together for a holiday, and to be honest that's what I implied, not wanting to give them any sign that something was amiss. I needed to decide what I wanted to do about Greg before I involved anyone else. I knew they'd be furious with him if they knew and if (and it was a very big if) I did want to work things out with him then I didn't want them to have already turned against him.

Mum and Dad lived close by, in the same house we'd moved to when we left Scotland, so Mum could take on the Head of Department role at a school there – she was now the headmistress. It had been a big change for all of us leaving our small-town life in Scotland for inner-city living, but Mum had wanted to take on a challenging school, one that really needed her, and there was no doubt she had single-handedly turned that school around. My father was a PE teacher at a local school and had been passionate about children from lower income families being given more opportunity in sport, so it had been a perfect move for them. And it had given me the chance to study at one of the best colleges for baking in the country but I had missed the community and countryside of Glendale over the years, I couldn't deny it.

It was a long journey up to Scotland, and I tried to catch up on the sleep I had missed last night, but my mind was racing too much. I hadn't thought to bring a book and I didn't want to go on social media and risk posting a vague 'everything sucks' update anywhere so I was left to look out of the window and think things over, and over again. I broke the journey up halfway through by buying a sandwich and a cup of tea, wishing it was a glass of wine instead. But I couldn't finish it. I couldn't stop thinking about what had happened. The thought of Greg being with another woman made me feel physically sick. How could I ever erase the image of the two of them from my mind?

When the train finally pulled into Inverness station, I jumped up, eager to get away from my own thoughts. I yanked my bags off the train with me and headed towards the taxi rank outside.

'Emily!' a voice called out and I turned in surprise to see Drew, Beth's fiancé, waving to me as he leant against his car.

'Drew, what are you doing here?' I asked, when I walked up to him.

'Beth called to say your train was due in any minute and I've just left work. I'm heading to the Hall so thought I'd wait and take you with me,' he replied, taking the bags from my hand and loading them into his boot. Drew was a doctor at the hospital in Inverness. He smiled warmly at me. 'How was your journey up?'

'Long but okay. Thanks, Drew,' I replied, touched that he had come to pick me up. I had only met him once before, when he and Beth had come down to London with their daughter Izzy last summer.

'I'm excited to see the Hall again,' I said as we climbed into his car.

'You'll barely recognise the place. It's been turned into wedding central,' he replied with a chuckle. 'Caroline is our unofficial wedding planner. It's like she's running a military operation.'

'I can only imagine,' I replied, remembering Beth's rather formidable mother. 'And how are you guys feeling? Just two weeks to go...' I forced myself to smile and keep my tone light, interested, happy for what was to come, and not reveal my shattered heart. It was hard to know if I was pulling it off or not but I hoped with Drew I could just about manage to do that. Beth, I feared, would be another matter entirely.

'Just really excited. I can't wait to get married. I probably should be nervous but...' he shrugged. 'I'm with the right person, so there doesn't seem to be anything to be nervous about.' He glanced at me. 'You know what I mean.'

I looked away, wondering if I did. I had thought Greg was the right person for me, that we'd be together forever, but was that just a fairy tale now? The wild Scottish

33

landscape rolled past the window, a world away from the urban view I now saw every day. It was strange thinking back to when I lived up here. 'I can't believe it's been three years since I set foot in Glendale.'

'So much has changed,' Drew replied. 'I'm under strict instructions not to show you the village, though,' he added, turning down an even smaller country lane. 'Beth wants to take you there herself to show you everything she's done,' he explained, the pride unmistakable in his voice.

The last time I saw Glendale, I had been struck by the change in the village – the shops had closed down, people avoided going there, and the council had wanted to sell it all to developers. The thriving village and strong community that I had known seemed all but gone. That was until Beth had moved back and decided that she wanted to turn it all around. And using her inheritance from her grandmother, she had reportedly done just that. 'I can't wait to see it,' I said, eager to see what it looked like now.

'How's everything in London then? How's Greg doing?' Drew asked. We had all gone out for a drink when they had come down, and Drew and Greg had got on pretty well talking about their work, which they were both passionate about, despite being very different people. Drew was quiet and steady, and I certainly couldn't imagine him ever breaking Beth's heart. But then again, I wouldn't have believed Greg capable of breaking mine either.

'Oh, fine. The same, you know...' I answered as vaguely as I could get away with. Drew glanced at me but didn't say anything.

We turned down another lane, and I sat up in my seat as we passed the sign for Glendale. Despite everything, I felt a fizzle of excitement. I may have lived in London for eighteen years but my heart still called Glendale 'home'. We reached Glendale Hall itself then, sweeping through the open large iron gates and turning into the wide gravel drive of Beth's family home. It was more like an estate, though. The house was impressive, tall and wide, rising up ahead in cream-coloured stone, pretty ivy climbing over the oak front door, which was flung open as soon as Drew parked outside.

Beth rushed out of the house to greet us, her long, dark wavy hair flying out behind her. 'You're here!' Beth cried as I climbed out of the car, pulling me into a tight hug that lifted my feet from the ground.

'Hi, Beth,' I said, laughing. 'You look amazing,' I told her, honestly when she released me. She had always been pretty with an enviable willowy figure but moving back to Glendale had really brought the light back into her eyes. She was wearing skinny jeans and a white shirt, her hair loose over her shoulders, and her skin tanned from all the gardening she did. I had never met anyone who ate as much as Beth and her daughter did and yet stayed so slim.

'I'm so happy you've come to stay,' she said, pulling back to look at me. A small frown appeared. 'Was your journey up okay? Are you tired?'

I wondered how I looked to her. If it was as bad as I felt then I really wouldn't be able to hide anything from her at all. 'It was a long journey, I guess,' I said, stepping back and looking away from her piercing gaze.

'Well, let's get you in and settled and you can rest before dinner. We're having a barbeque to celebrate you being here. Sally will be home from the shop soon, she's so excited to have you back,' Beth said, slipping her arm through mine.

I was looking forward to seeing my aunt again, I had really missed her. She was still their housekeeper but also helped out in the new Glendale Hall shop in the High Street, which she had told me she loved.

Drew followed us, carrying my bags despite my protests as we walked inside the Hall. It was as grand as I remembered but it felt more welcoming. Beth was now the owner of the Hall and vases of wild flowers were dotted all around, adding brightness and a gorgeous scent to the house. We walked up the wide, ornate staircase and down the corridor to one of the many guest rooms.

'I put you in this one, which is next to Izzy's room. I hope you like it,' Beth said, opening the door. I followed her inside, smiling despite myself at the pretty room. It offered a lovely view of the stunning grounds, the sun streaming through the wide window. Decorated in soft cream, there was a large four-poster bed that looked instantly inviting, and a vase of lavender by the bed emitted a relaxing fragrance all around us.

'It has its own bathroom too,' Beth added, pointing to the en suite.

The whole effect was calming, relaxing me despite all that had happened over the past twenty-four hours. 'It's lovely, Beth. Thank you,' I said, already feeling like I had made a very good decision in coming to the Hall.

'Okay, well, we'll let you get settled in. We're going to start up the barbeque. Dinner starts at seven, if that's okay? Do you need anything else?' Beth's eyes were searching and I knew that she would be grilling me about everything once we were alone. Drew put my bags on the floor by the bed and wrapped his arm around Beth's waist. I had to look away from them, pretending to take in the view from the window.

'It's all perfect. I'll be down for dinner,' I promised. I watched them go and then, when I was alone, I flopped down on the bed, throwing off my shoes, exhaustion washing over me all at once. I rested against the comfortable pillows and before I knew it, my eyes had closed and I had fallen into a deep sleep.

Chapter Six

When I woke, the sun was dipping in the sky and I sat up suddenly, wondering where I was for a moment. My phone vibrated with a message. I glanced at it and smiled; it was Beth telling me to hurry up. I checked the time; it was past seven. I couldn't remember the last time I had napped like that. Climbing off the bed, I went into the en suite and splashed my face with water. Glancing in the mirror, I saw that I still looked exhausted but I knew I couldn't hide up here all night, when everyone was downstairs ready to welcome me.

Sucking in a deep breath, I left the bathroom and changed quickly into one of my maxi summer dresses, pulling on flip-flops, and letting down my hair loose over my shoulders. I was about to grab my phone but then I decided it was better left in the room. Greg would be home soon from work and would discover I was gone, and I really didn't want to have to deal with him quite yet.

I hurried downstairs and walked into the kitchen. The doors had been flung open to the garden and a delicious smell was coming from a gas barbeque just outside; the patio area full of people. Laughter and voices greeted me as I stepped outside. The evening was warm although there was a welcoming cool breeze, reminding me I was a long way from the city.

'There you are,' Beth said, coming over to me. She handed me a tall glass. 'We made Pimm's and lemonade,' she said, passing it to me.

'Emily!' My aunt Sally hurried away from the group to come up to me, wrapping her arms around me. I stiffened, trying to swallow down the lump that quickly rose up in my throat at the sight of her. 'I'm so happy you decided to come up early and stay with us,' she said. Sally was older than my mother, her hair greying but her eyes still twinkling. She looked me over as Beth had. 'Is everything okay?' she said, more quietly.

I nodded, taking a long gulp of my drink. 'I just thought it was better to make the cake here, and I was owed holiday anyway…' I mumbled, unconvincing even to my own ears. 'So, this is quite a party,' I said, walking towards everyone, hoping I could shift their focus away from me. I said hello to the rest of party guests. As well as Drew and Beth, their twelve-year-old daughter Izzy was there, with her pretty, long red hair and freckles. Her cat, Ginny, sat happily on her lap so I had to give her a one-armed hug. The rest of the group were Caroline, Beth's mother, and the Hall's gardener, John, along with Drew's brother Rory, and his girlfriend and Beth's oldest friend, Heather, who was cradling their five-month-old baby, Harry. I swallowed another lump in my throat when I saw him.

'It's lovely to see you again,' Caroline Williams said, giving me a kiss on each cheek. Beth's mother was elegant and polished and I'd always been a little nervous of her, particularly because when Beth had run away to come and live with me in London, she had deprived Caroline of being with her granddaughter while I had seen them almost every day. I worried Caroline resented me for that but her welcoming smile was genuine, and I was relieved that she seemed okay with me being here.

'Right, food's up, folks,' Drew called then, waving a spatula in the air.

The long, wooden table was already piled with food and he added all the cooked meat to it, everyone forming a line, carrying plates over to it. I was surprisingly hungry and I filled my plate with salad – much of it grown in the gardens of the Hall – new potatoes, cold pasta and rice, and the tasty looking kebabs from the barbecue. Beth refilled my glass with Pimm's and I sat down next to Izzy, who had shifted her cat off her lap so she could eat.

'Are you excited for the wedding?' I asked Izzy as we tucked in. Everything tasted amazing. My aunt had always been a great cook and with all the fresh, home-grown produce, it really put the packaged supermarket food we had at home to shame.

'I can't wait,' Izzy replied, her red hair bouncing as she talked. 'My bridesmaid dress is so pretty!'

'I'm looking forward to seeing it,' I told her. I was Izzy's godmother in anything but name as Beth had never had her christened, and had known her all her life. She had blossomed since moving to Scotland. She had always been shy, awkward even, her head stuck in a book all the time, but she seemed so much more confident and happier now.

'Mum said you're going to bake the cake here. Can I help, do you think?' she asked me, hopefully.

'I would love your help,' I said. 'I still need to come up with the perfect idea. I'm hoping once I see what you have for the wedding already, I can make sure that the cake complements everything.'

'I'll show you the gazebo after dinner,' Izzy said. 'That will help you.' She leant in closer. 'My dress is pale yellow,' she whispered, glancing at her dad to make sure he couldn't hear her. 'I told Mum she should have Harry Potter colours for the wedding, yellow and maroon, so that's what we've done. Well, kind of. The yellow is lighter than it should be because Mum said it's a summer wedding so everything needs to look summery.' She shrugged, as if she didn't really understand that reasoning.

I laughed at the idea of a Harry Potter themed wedding. I knew it was Izzy's favourite book series and could well believe she had worn down her mother to choose that colour scheme. 'Well, we need to make sure the cake matches that, then,' I said.

After dinner, Sally brought out strawberries and cream for dessert, followed by coffee. The sun started to set. I gazed out at the grounds, watching as the clear sky turned burnt orange above us. I hadn't sat and watch the sun set for a long time. It really was beautiful in Glendale. I glanced at Beth and Drew watching the sky together, Beth leaning her head on his shoulder. They looked so content, it made my heart ache. But they deserved to be.

When Beth had come to stay with me, pregnant at sixteen, Drew had gone to America to study to be a doctor, not knowing he had a daughter. Beth hadn't wanted him to give up his dreams so she had raised Izzy alone. When her grandmother got sick, she and Izzy had finally come home to Glendale and Drew had come back to stay with his brother for Christmas, discovering he had a ten-year-old daughter. Beth and Drew had fallen back in love, and they had all decided to return to Glendale for good, and were now a happy family.

Theirs was a story that could make even the coldest heart believe in true love but I had to look away from the happiness that radiated from them then. Greg interrupted my thoughts once again. Had he seen my note yet? Was he sad? Or relieved that I had gone?

'Come on, let's go and see where the wedding is going to be,' Izzy said, bored of watching the sunset. She grabbed my hand to pull me out of my chair, and Beth gave me a little wave as I followed her, chuckling at her eagerness, grateful that she was saving me from my painful thoughts.

The grounds of Glendale Hall stretched out for acres. We walked across the grass towards the stream, which glittered under the setting sun. Just by the stream was the area ear-marked for the wedding. The gazebo had already been constructed of painted white wood, there were steps leading up to it and an archway stretched across it. The view behind it was stunning. 'We're going to wrap flowers all over the arch but Mum said it's too early to put them up in the heat,' she said. I could just imagine how pretty it would look covered in coloured blooms. Beth really had an excellent eye for flowers.

Izzy pointed to where white chairs would be laid out for the guests to watch the ceremony. They had created a path down the middle and she explained there would be flowers lining that too, to match the archway. 'Dad was worried about it raining but I don't think it will, do you?'

'I really hope not,' I replied. It would be such a stunning wedding ceremony. 'And then the meal will be nearer the house?'

'Yes. We've hired a big tent. It's called something fancy but I can't remember what. We've got picnic tables coming and Mum's making flower centrepieces for each one, and we're going to have jars with fairy lights in and lanterns as well.'

'Sounds like it will be magical,' I said as we started to stroll back towards the house. My mind was already whirring with cake ideas. It sounded like Beth was really going for a summery outdoors wedding with lots of wild flowers and craft touches; a 'rustic wedding' I supposed people in London would say, to complement the stunning location. I just had to make sure the cake would come up scratch.

'Right, you,' Beth said when we went back to the group. 'It's time to get ready for bed,' she told Izzy who groaned. Rory and Heather had already taken Harry home and everyone was clearing away the dinner things. The sun had set properly then, and candles had been lit along the table, casting a pretty glow to the garden.

'I think I'm ready for my bed too, to be honest,' I said, feeling exhausted suddenly.

'How about tomorrow we walk into Glendale together?' Beth suggested. 'I really want to show you what we've done to the High Street and what we'd still like to do. Plus, I need to pop into the church to speak to our minister.'

I nodded. 'Sounds good.' I knew she was looking for an opportunity to talk to me alone and I needed to decide how honest to be with her. I couldn't lie outright to Beth but the thought of admitting what Greg had done filled me with horror. I knew how upset and angry she'd be for me... plus, it was embarrassing. Humiliating, even.

Especially when I could see how happy she and Drew were. Could I bear her inevitable pity right now? But we'd been through so much over the years, and I knew she'd always have my back like I had hers, and I needed a good friend right now, that was for sure. She had left a hole when she moved back to Scotland, and I really missed our friendship. She was the only one, beside my mum and Molly, who knew how much I longed for a baby, and how hard it had been to keep failing to get pregnant.

I said goodnight to everyone and walked slowly up to my room. Closing the door, I stepped out of my flip-flops and walked to the bed, reaching for my phone, my heart floating up to my throat as I prepared myself to face it. There was a voicemail from Greg. I took a deep breath as I pressed play.

Em, I've just come home and seen your note. I can't believe you've just gone off like this. I really think we need to talk about what happened last night, don't you? Please call me back. I… I hope this is just a holiday. You are coming back, aren't you? Call me, babe. I love you.

I played the message twice, not knowing how I felt about it or how I wanted to respond. I couldn't face speaking to him. Not yet. I put my phone down and got undressed slowly. Greg's voice had sobered me up, and my lovely evening had come crashing back down to reality. I had run from him but I couldn't hide, even this far away. I knew I would have to face it all in the morning. I hoped a new day would bring with it the knowledge of what I wanted to say to him… but what could I say? He had cheated on me, he had broken my trust and the future we had planned together. He said he loved me, and I knew

44

my heart still belonged to him – as much as I wished right now it didn't – but was love enough now?

I'd always thought that I'd never accept cheating from anyone. I remembered telling friends in the past who had been cheated on that they should leave, that if their partner had done it once then they would just do it all over again, but now it had happened to me. Now it was my Greg who had done it. I had pretended for too long that things were still okay between us. I couldn't do that any longer. I had to face the fact that my relationship had not turned out the way I hoped it would.

But what I should do about that fact, I still hadn't got a clue.

You are coming back, aren't you?

Greg's question repeated itself on a loop as I climbed into bed, wishing I had an answer, both for him and for myself.

Chapter Seven

I went down to the kitchen early the next day still wearing the shorts and vest I had slept in. I found Aunt Sally laying the table for breakfast, Beth and Caroline already there drinking coffee. Izzy rushed past me in her school uniform telling her mum she had lost her PE kit. Drew was making tea in the kitchen and attempting to keep Izzy's cat away from the milk as he poured it out.

'Yes, it's always like this,' Beth said, smiling at me as she got up. 'I know where it is, Iz. You have something to eat and I'll find it, okay? And get Emily some coffee, please. She's like me – not human until she has a cup.' She dropped me a wink as she left to find the missing PE kit.

I chuckled, remembering how Beth was annoyed when I'd told her she needed to limit her coffee when she was pregnant. I took a mug of strong coffee gratefully from Izzy.

'Did you sleep well?' Aunt Sally asked me as she laid the table with warm pastries and muffins, a stack of toast and homemade jams and marmalade. There was a basket of fruit and several containers of cereal and milk on there as well.

'I did. The bed is super comfortable,' I replied, taking a long sip of coffee. I had thought I would lay awake until the early hours thinking of Greg but I had slipped into a deep sleep, and felt so much better for it. I winced, staring at the coffee. It tasted too bitter. I liked my coffee strong usually but this felt just too strong. I put it down, disappointed. I kept quiet about that though, not wanting to seem ungrateful. My stomach rumbled loudly, and I reached for a croissant.

'Here we go,' Beth said, returning with the kit as Drew came to the table and grabbed a slice of toast. 'You off in a minute?'

He nodded, his mouth full. 'I'll be back in two days,' he said, eating quickly. When he had to put in long shifts at the hospital, he stayed over in Inverness as it was too far to go back and forth to the Hall. He glanced at me as he sipped his tea. 'I hope you like the new and improved Glendale.' He gave Beth a kiss and Izzy a hug. 'Right, guys, see you soon!' We all chorused goodbye to him. I reached for another pastry and poured myself an orange juice, which was wonderfully refreshing.

'Are you still okay to go to the garden centre?' Beth asked her mother who nodded. She turned to me. 'We want to buy some ceramic pots to decorate and sell in the shop. Ready-made for people's gardens.' Beth had always wanted to be a gardener, and since returning to Glendale had gone back to college to study, and now worked closely with John to look after the grounds, and supply their shop with produce.

'Sounds like a great idea,' I replied. 'I hope the Glendale shop is doing well, then?'

'It is,' Caroline answered. 'You'll see; we've themed the shop all around the wedding at the moment,' she added, pushing her chair back. 'Izzy, I'll drive you to school on the way. Let's go and drag John out of his cottage. See you all later,' she said, hurrying Izzy along.

'My mother has finally accepted that she and John are courting now,' Beth said with a smile when they had gone. 'They are so sweet together.' Her parents had recently divorced, but her mother was only just admitting how close she had become to their gardener through the years.

'I still hold out hope that my aunt might find someone,' I said in a low voice as Sally cleared away Caroline and Izzy's plates. My uncle had passed away a long time ago and she had remained resolutely single.

'I guess once you find The One it's hard to ever imagine being with anyone else,' Beth said, clearly thinking of Drew. She smiled at me. 'And how is your One?'

'Oh, fine, you know,' I replied, stuffing my mouth with a muffin. 'He couldn't get out of work to come to the wedding in the end, though. He's really sorry about it,' I said, when I'd swallowed the muffin down.

Beth frowned. She had been in London still when I had met Greg, and had witnessed just how quickly and deeply I had fallen for him. I still remember her warning me to take things slowly. I had been a little annoyed with her at the time, but now she could well have the right to say, 'I told you so'. Not that Beth ever would, of course.

'That's a shame, I know how much you were looking forward to showing him Glendale,' she said. She paused and then tilted her head. 'Are things okay at home, Em? I mean, you sounded kind of frantic on the phone, and rushing up here like this... I'm not trying to pry, I'm just saying if you want to talk about anything, or tell me anything, then you know you can, right?'

I took a long gulp of juice as I thought about how to respond. I had been right about how hard it would be to hide my troubles from her. We had known each other for too long. 'I was upset that he couldn't come to the wedding,' I admitted. 'Things haven't been that great between us lately. I think this break will do us good.'

'That's a shame. I'm sorry, Em.' She touched my hand gently. 'I know how much you love him, I'm sure things will work out. And he does have an important job. Like Drew. They can't help but put that first sometimes, can they?'

I nodded, not able to bring myself to tell her about the cheating. Not yet anyway. I didn't want to bring the mood down any more. She was looking forward to her wedding, I didn't want my problems to get in the way of that. 'Gives me more time to work on your cake, though,' I said, trying to smile, and turn the conversation.

'I'm so excited about it. I still miss your cake. And popping in to Molly's. How is everything at the bakery?'

I tried not to think about Steph. 'Still the same. Molly is an institution,' I replied. I didn't want what Steph had done to sully the place for me but I had no idea how I could ever bear to work side-by-side with her again.

'Well,' Beth said, brightly. 'I'm glad you came up early; it's been too long since we spent proper time together.'

'I've missed it too,' I said with a smile.

'My God,' she cried then, staring down at my mug. 'You've left coffee! Are you really feeling all right?' She laughed as she got up, carrying her plate over to the kitchen.

I stared at the full mug of coffee. It was weird that I didn't even want to attempt to finish it. I shrugged. Must just be too used to my own coffee. 'I'm fine,' I called after her, hoping that I would be. 'I'd better jump in the shower,' I added, standing up.

'Come down whenever you're ready and we'll head off to the village,' Beth called back to me.

I walked back to my bedroom and closed the door. I knew that before I could have a shower and go out I really needed to return Greg's call. I didn't think I'd ever left it that long without getting back to him, even in the early days of our relationship, and if the shoe had been on the other foot, I would have been worried about him. I needed to check in with him at the very least.

Flopping on the bed, I crossed my legs and put my phone on speaker to call him, closing my eyes and willing myself to stay strong.

'Babe,' he answered straight away. 'Thank God, I was worried. Are you okay?'

My heart betrayed me by melting a little at his obvious concern for me. 'I'm fine, I'm here in Glendale. Safe and sound,' I replied, hoping my voice was steady.

'Well, that's good. I wondered if you were ever going to call me back,' he added in a soft voice.

'Me too, if I'm honest,' I replied. There was no point in keeping from him how hurt I was. He needed to know that.

Greg sighed. 'Em, I really am sorry. I've been thinking about it… I am so ashamed about what happened. I can't defend myself. I was drunk but I should have known better. I think, though, I was lonely.' His voice dropped. 'Things haven't been great between us, have they? I haven't felt close to you for so long. It's been so hard for us, not getting pregnant, you know? Sex became this painful thing for us as nothing was happening, so I think maybe I couldn't deal with that, but instead of talking to you and telling you how I felt, I... I did this disgusting thing. I hurt you. I hurt us.' He sniffed then. 'And I never meant to. I wish I could go back and change it. I feel so bad, I really do.'

I closed my eyes, squeezing out a tear. I didn't think he would admit to being upset about us not having a baby. I thought it was mostly me that was finding that hard. Could I accept that as a reason to cheat? I wasn't sure about that, but perhaps his admission did make me understand it just a little bit more. 'I've found it so hard trying for a baby and getting nowhere. You know I think we should talk to a doctor about it but—'

'I know,' he interjected quickly. 'But I've felt scared, like I'm not enough of a man if I can't... but it's different now. I can't lose you, Em. Let's go. As soon as you're back. Let's get help. Let's make our baby.'

God, it was so hard not to be swayed by his words. The promise of my longed-for baby. I didn't know what to say. He was offering me everything I had wanted twenty-four hours ago but was it all too little and late?

'Please think about it,' he continued, perhaps sensing that I was wavering. 'I swear to you I'll never do anything like this ever again. Coming home and finding you gone... it was like my world had come crashing down.'

'That's how I felt when I saw *that* text,' I said then, my voice firmer. 'You're the reason I'm here.'

'I know, I know. I'm so sorry.'

I knew I had to hang up before I gave in. 'Let me go now. I need to think things through, okay? Give me some space, please.'

'Can I still call you, though? Please. I can't go for weeks without talking to you!'

I sighed. 'Of course we can speak, but I need to catch my breath. I never thought that you could do this. It's made me unsure, of everything.'

'God, don't say that. Never be unsure of how much I love you. I know that things haven't been great but we can change that, can't we? This can be fixed, I know it.'

I swallowed. I knew we should have dealt with our problems sooner instead of hiding from them, and now we had ended up like this. It wasn't all his fault, I knew that, but even so, I never would have cheated on him, despite all our problems. I still loved him and I was so hurt by what he had done. Could we fix us? I wished I was as certain as he seemed to be. 'I really need to go now. Beth needs me,' I said, ducking the question for now.

Greg sighed, defeated. 'Okay. Well, I'll call you tomorrow, then? Please don't make any rash decisions. Just know that I love you and I know that we can work this out.'

I said goodbye and hung up quickly. Hearing his voice made it so hard to think clearly. My head said he was wrong but my heart hoped that he was right. I got up slowly and headed for the shower, hoping the hot water might help to clear my head because I felt more confused than I had ever felt in my whole life.

Chapter Eight

Glendale village was about a twenty-minute walk from the Hall and the summer sun was out in full swing when we reached it. Walking into the High Street, my eye was immediately caught by the colourful hanging baskets above each shop. When I had last been in Glendale, it had felt like a ghost town with most of the shops boarded up, and no one in sight. But today, all the shops were open, bar one, and there were lots of people making use of them.

'Morning, Beth,' a man said, nodding his head as he passed us, walking into the farm shop, which I knew was run by Drew's brother Rory, and his partner, and Beth's best friend, Heather.

'Hi, Mr Walker,' she replied. 'Glad your leg is doing better.' She waved then to a woman walking past us. It seemed like she knew everyone here.

'There's so much more life in the village,' I said as we made our way towards the Glendale Hall shop. We passed the library that Beth and Heather had helped keep open, and I glanced at Beth, who beamed with pride. She had worked hard to make all of this possible. Obviously, she had had her grandmother's money but people had given up on the village and she had rallied the community, and rebuilt it. 'You've done an amazing job,' I added with a smile. 'Who would have thought the girl who had run away all those years ago would now be the saviour of the community?'

Beth chuckled. 'Quite the turn around, huh? But, seriously, it hasn't all been down to me. The community has really got behind it.' I knew though that she and her mother had offered discounted rents in a profit-share scheme so local businesses could return to the shops. As well as the farm shop, and the Glendale Hall shop, there was also a small convenience store, a florist and a butcher's. I looked down the road and saw Glendale Arms, the village pub at the end, the steeple of the church rising up high in the distance behind it.

'We are hoping to open up a café here again,' Beth said then as we passed the one premises still vacant. 'We think that would be the final, perfect addition but with all the wedding planning, it's been put on hold for the summer,' she explained as she led me to the Glendale Hall shop. All the family helped make or buy things for it, and they all served in there, although they had a full-time manager as well.

'I think that sounds great. Cake always cheers a place up,' I replied as we walked into the shop. I smiled at the pretty wedding display Caroline had created. 'Is the whole town involved in this wedding?'

Beth rolled her eyes. 'Yes! Don't get me started. My mother has roped pretty much everyone into it and she decided we should stock all sorts of wedding things in here but they have been selling well so I think she was right, unfortunately. I leave that to her. This is my baby...' Beth showed me the gardening area of the shop, the passion and pride in her voice clear as she talked me through everything.

'These are really cute,' I said, picking up one of a pink watering can that had been filled with pretty flowers.

'Would you like one for your garden?' Beth asked.

'I don't know...' I looked up at her, and the room seemed to tilt around us. I felt a little unsteady suddenly, the colour draining from my face.

'What's wrong?' she asked, looking at me in alarm. She took the watering can from me and then took my hand, and led me outside back into the sunshine. 'Are you okay?'

I just shook my head. My legs were shaky, and I really wanted to sink down into a chair.

'Right, we need to talk,' she said, firmly, steering me towards the pub. Seating me in the pretty beer garden, she ducked inside and returned with two cold orange juices. I was relieved it wasn't coffee. 'Now, I know you, and I know that you like to help everyone else but yourself but you've come up here so suddenly... I know there's something wrong and I'm not going to let you carry the burden of it all by yourself,' she said firmly, reaching for my hand and squeezing it. 'What's going on, Emily?'

I took a sip of juice to gather my strength. The cool sweetness made me feel less faint than I had a moment ago. I had actually been worried I was going to pass out in her shop. I took a deep breath. 'I found out that Greg's cheated on me. He slept with the girl I work with at the bakery,' I told her all in a rush, only letting out a breath at the end. I stared at my glass unable to bring myself to look up and see the pity that was undoubtedly on her face.

'Oh my God,' she said slowly. 'I'm so sorry, Em.' She squeezed my hand again. When I finally had the courage to look up, her face was twisted in anger, not pity. 'I can't believe he would do that to you!'

'I can't get my head around it,' I agreed.

'What did he have to say for himself?' she demanded.

'That he's sorry, that it will never happen again. All the right words. And things haven't been great between us for a while, which isn't only his fault,' I told her.

'That doesn't excuse cheating!' she cried.

'I know, I agree. But it makes it more complicated, you know? All the issues we've had with conceiving… it's taken its toll.'

'I know,' she said, softly. 'But he should never have done that to you.'

'I still love him. I don't know what to do.'

Beth sighed. 'I think you did the right thing in coming up here, giving yourself some time and space to think it all over. I wish I could help but only you can decide what you want to do.'

I met her gaze. 'But do you think I should leave him?' I was certain that Beth would never put up with a man cheating on her.

Beth's face gave into the pity then. 'I can't answer that. Only you know how you feel, and what your relationship is like. But I do know that you deserve someone who loves you and respects you and treats you well. Okay?'

I could feel myself start to well up again. 'Thanks, Beth,' I said, grateful that I had someone I could turn to. 'Please don't say anything to Aunt Sally, will you? I'll tell her… I just need time to get my head around it all. Decide what I want to do, you know, before I tell my family?'

She nodded. 'Of course.' She checked the time on her phone. 'Now, I need to meet the minister but do you want to wait for me here?'

'No, I'll come. Anything to take my mind off things,' I replied, feeling better for having told someone what was going on. It was horrible to admit the truth about Greg but I did feel lighter for having done it, and I knew that Beth was the last person to judge anyone.

'Everything will work out okay, I promise,' she said, standing up and holding out a hand. I took it and she pulled me up with her, tucking her arm through mine as we strolled towards the church. 'Neither Drew nor I are particularly religious but my family have always felt that you should get married in church. I used to imagine Drew and I getting married here when I was younger but when we started planning, we both really wanted to get married at the Hall. So, the minister has agreed to give us a blessing after the civil ceremony. He's been really nice about it, actually. He was quite close with my grandmother before she died. I think she confessed a lot of her sins to him,' Beth said with a wry smile. She and her grandmother had had a difficult relationship but were able to make peace with one another before she died last Christmas. She pushed open the heavy door to the church. Inside, it was dark and cool and it was empty, save for the minister who was up at the altar, with his back to us. 'Prepare yourself,' Beth added in a whisper to me. She had one of her wicked grins on her face and I was immediately intrigued. I followed her up the aisle.

'Brodie,' Beth called up ahead.

The minster turned around with a wide smile. He was tall and was wearing jeans with a black shirt and clerical collar, trainers on his feet. I raised my eyebrows as we reached him, realising why Beth had been grinning – he was really good-looking. He had short, sandy-coloured hair and big, blue eyes, and broad shoulders with arms that suggested he worked out in the gym. He also looked like he was around my age. Not what I was expecting at all. 'Beth, it's lovely to see you again,' he said, giving her hand a firm shake.

'This is Emily Prescott – she's come to stay from London,' Beth said, gesturing to me. 'This is Reverend Stewart – or Brodie, as he likes us all to call him.'

'Pleased to meet you, Emily,' Brodie said, holding out his hand. I shook it, feeling the warmth of his skin spread into my own. He met my eyes with a steady gaze and gave me a warm smile. 'One of the bridesmaids, I seem to recall?'

'That's right, although she won't let me call her that,' Beth said.

'When you reach your thirties, I don't think you can let yourself be called a bridesmaid,' I replied with a laugh.

'I take it she won't be in a long pink dress either, then?' Brodie let out a deep laugh, which echoed around the church. 'Come through and let's go over some of the details for the service, okay?' He held out his arm to let us pass. We walked out of the back of the church into a small room, which housed a kitchenette, and a table. Brodie told us to take a seat and asked if we wanted tea or coffee. Beth had a coffee, of course, and Brodie tea, but I couldn't face anything.

Once he had made their drinks, Brodie joined us at the table. 'Have you thought any more about your vows?' Brodie asked, pulling out a file and picking up a pen.

'We're going to write our own vows. The registrar said it's best to finish the civil service and then have your blessing straight after that.'

He nodded. 'That's usually the way we do it, yes. This is what I would plan to say.' He passed over a card with the prayer written on it. 'But let me know if there's anything there that you might want to tweak. Show it to Drew as well.'

'It's lovely,' Beth said, looking down at it, moving it so I could read it too. 'And the choir were happy with our choices?' she asked him. Glancing back at me, she explained, 'The church choir have kindly agreed to come and sing during the ceremony. We're not allowed any religious content during the civil ceremony so they're going to sing some love songs then once it's over and we have the blessing, we'll have a couple of hymns. Family favourites.'

'Yes, that was all fine with them,' Brodie replied. 'So I think we are all on track now.'

Beth beamed. 'Perfect. I'm so grateful for all your help. It's going to be a beautiful ceremony. We just need the sun to stay out for it.'

'I'll have a word,' Brodie replied with a wink.

I glanced at him, surprised again. He saw my face. 'I don't think I've ever met such a young minister.' I found myself blurting out the thought in my head without thinking and felt myself blush immediately afterwards.

He chuckled. 'Well, we all have to start somewhere, don't we?'

'Of course, yes. I just meant…'

'He's teasing you,' Beth said. 'He caused quite a stir in Glendale when he arrived three years ago. The last vicar died on the job.'

I gasped and looked at her in horror.

'I'm not making that up,' she promised. 'He had a heart attack just outside the church.'

'Oh my God,' I said, then I looked at Brodie in horror. 'Oh no! I didn't mean…'

He held up a hand. 'It's fine, relax, Emily. You won't get struck down for saying that. I don't think, anyway.' He laughed at my face. 'I don't think your friend has met a minister who has a sense of humour before.'

Beth laughed too. 'No, I don't think she has. Right, we shall leave you in peace. But you're coming to the party on Saturday, right?' she asked, standing up. I jumped up too, eager to escape my embarrassment.

'I'll be there,' he promised before turning to me. 'It was lovely meeting you, Emily.'

'You too,' I said, quickly, unable to meet his gaze. I felt his eyes on me as I followed Beth out of the side door, the sunshine brilliant after the dimness inside.

Beth burst out laughing as soon as we were alone.

'Shut up!' I said, elbowing her in the side.

'Don't worry, I don't blame you. He's so good-looking it's sometimes hard to think clearly. Just don't tell Drew I said that,' she said, trying to calm down.

'As long as you swear not to tell anyone what a moron I was back there.'

'I'll take it to my grave.' She saluted me and then started laughing again. Despite everything that had happened, I burst out laughing too, and we were hiccupping as we started off back in the direction of the Hall.

Chapter Nine

Sitting at the kitchen table of Glendale Hall, surrounded by cookbooks and my phone full of internet tabs open, I started sketching out ideas for the wedding cake. In the oven, a sponge was baking, emitting a delicious smell around me, even if I did say so myself.

Adding food colouring to the shopping list that was growing by the minute, I looked up as the French doors opened and in skipped Izzy, followed by her grandmother.

'What smells so good?' Izzy asked, as she bounded over, pulling off her school tie eagerly.

'I'm trying out a recipe for your mum's wedding cake,' I explained, smiling at her.

'Ooh, that's exciting! Gran, can we have some lemonade please? I think that would go really well with cake.'

'How do you know you'll be allowed any cake?' Caroline replied with a roll of her eyes as she went to the fridge.

'Emily said I was chief cake taster, didn't you?' she said, widening her eyes to try to make me agree with her.

'I do need a taster,' I replied. 'We need to make sure this cake is just right so we'll have to try a lot. Are you sure you're up to the job, Izzy?' I asked her with mock seriousness.

Izzy stood a little bit straighter. 'I won't let you down,' she replied, solemnly.

Caroline laughed as she brought over two tall glasses of my aunt's homemade lemonade. 'Well, I'll leave you two to your tasting then. I definitely won't fit into my wedding outfit if I stay, plus I need to check in with the florist.'

'How was school?' I asked Izzy as I sipped the lemonade. It tasted as good as I remembered from my childhood.

She sat down opposite me at the table. 'Well, English was good and it was fun playing rounders, but this afternoon we had a double maths lesson.'

I groaned sympathetically. 'I hated maths at school too.'

She held up her glass and I clinked it with a chuckle.

'Right, I think it might be ready to come out of the oven now.' I got up and went over to the Aga, which Aunt Sally had shown me how to use, and pulled out the perfectly browned sponge. Placing it on a wire rack to cool, I showed Izzy the flowers I had sketched in my notebook. 'I want to make these out of icing to decorate the cake. Hopefully they will match the flowers that will be climbing over the gazebo arch at the ceremony. I'd like the icing of the tiers to match but it's going to be tricky to get the right lemon and maroon food colouring, I think.'

'They're so pretty,' she said, leaning over to look. 'Will you put anything on top of the cake?'

'Well, I think a bride and groom is a bit old-fashioned for this wedding but I've had a few ideas. I might leave that as a surprise for everyone, though,' I replied. She sighed, making me smile. 'Now that we're on our own, you can be honest with me. Your mum has gone to pick up my dress for the wedding. She's been so secretive about it. Am I going to like it?'

'You'll love it,' Izzy replied. 'As soon as we saw it, she said it was the perfect dress for you.'

'Well then, I can't wait to see it.' I had protested about Beth making me a bridesmaid ever since she had phoned me to tell me that she was engaged. She had Izzy, after all, and her best friend up here, Heather, was going to be maid of honour but Beth had insisted she wanted me in the bridal party, and that I had to wear a dress along with Izzy and Heather. I still thought I was too old to be a bridesmaid but I was touched she had wanted me to be part of it all and she did have amazing taste so I was hopeful the dress wouldn't be a hideous meringue or anything.

'Is it cool enough to try yet?' Izzy asked, looking over at the cake.

'I doubt it but never mind, let's try it anyway.' I cut up two slices and brought them back to the table. 'Okay, you go first and be honest with me about what you think,' I said, handing her one.

She took a big bite and chewed it thoughtfully. 'Ooh, it's so good. Lemon-y but then also a bit floral. It smells nice... And it's really light. What is it?'

'It's lemon and lavender. I thought Beth would approve of that,' I said, cutting myself a bit to try. 'I'm really happy with that. I think we might need a touch more lemon rind in there to give it a real kick,' I said, jotting that down in my recipe notebook. 'And I'm going to try dark chocolate buttercream between it and the next layer. What do you think?'

Izzy grinned. 'Chocolate is always a good idea.'

'My thoughts exactly.'

I perched on the bed in my room at the Hall as Beth hung up the big plastic bag containing my dress on the full-length mirror.

'Okay, drum roll please…' she said to Izzy, who sat on the window seat. She started drumming her fingers on the windowsill. Beth reached up and did a dramatically slow pulling down of the zip, shedding the bag from the dress. 'Ta-da!' she cried, holding out her hands like a magician's assistant as the dress was finally revealed.

I leaned forward. It was a knee-length pretty tea dress, pale lemon with tiny flowers throughout. 'Oh, it's really pretty,' I said, smiling as I realised she had noted my love of floral dresses and simple looks and come up with the perfect dress.

'I think it will look lovely with Izzy's prom style dress, and Heather's – which is a long one, all in lemon shades,' Beth said. 'And your bouquets will be lemon and maroon too… do you really like it?' she asked, looking at me anxiously.

'I really do. Let me try it on.' I jumped up and pulled off my cropped jeans and t-shirt, slipping into it easily. It was a little bit snug on my boobs but that often happened with dresses thanks to my hour-glass figure. I stood in front of the mirror. The colour looked lovely against my light hair and I was starting to get a summer glow to my skin, which set it off nicely.

'We just need the perfect shoes,' Beth said, smiling from behind me. 'What do you think, Iz?'

'You look lovely, Emily. Really pretty.'

'Thank you, darling. It's such a great find, Beth.'

'It's from a vintage shop that Heather knows in town; we got all the bridesmaid dresses there. Mine is being made but I'm keeping it as a surprise from all of you,' she said with a grin. 'Which my mother is constantly moaning about.' Her eyes twinkled, making it clear that she was quite enjoying winding her mum up even though they were much closer now than they had been when she was growing up. 'It's all coming together,' she said. 'I can't believe it's almost here.'

'We're finally going to be a family,' Izzy said. 'I can't wait.'

Beth went over and sat with her, draping an arm around her. 'Me neither.' Izzy leaned against her, and I found myself looking away, my heart squeezing a little inside my chest. I couldn't help but look at their closeness and think of the family I so desperately wanted.

'I'd better get this off,' I said, giving my reflection one last glance. It really did suit me. I wished that Greg could see it on me but I knew that one pretty dress wasn't about to solve our problems. Still, I could imagine the wolf-whistle he would have let out if he had been with me. He was always saying I should show off my figure, telling me that my curves were the thing that he loved the most about my looks. I tried really hard not to think about slim, leggy Steph but it was impossible not to. She was younger and prettier than me. That hurt. I couldn't deny it. It made me angry all over again with him that he had chosen to leave our bed for hers.

'Are you okay?' Beth asked me as I turned abruptly from the mirror.

'I'm fine,' I assured her as I stepped out of the dress, hating that I couldn't be as excited about her wedding as

I so desperately wanted to be. Greg really did have a lot to answer for.

Chapter Ten

A couple of days later, Beth and Izzy had left the Hall to have dinner with Rory and Heather at their farm, and Caroline was with John at his cottage in the grounds, so Aunt Sally and I decided to go to the pub in Glendale village together for food.

It was such a lovely summer's evening so we walked there. The sun was still high in the sky despite it being early evening. 'How did you know that you and my uncle belonged together?' I found myself blurting out. The sun warmed my back and the birds were noisy in the trees above us. It felt like a world away from London. I found that I was starting to have that relaxed holiday feeling, which was impressive considering how stressed I was about me and Greg.

Aunt Sally glanced across at me but she thought my question over for a moment. She was my mum's older sister and had been a constant through my childhood. She was kind and sensible and I had definitely inherited my love of baking from her. My mum couldn't cook at all so Aunt Sally had taught me. 'Alec was the first and only man I ever loved. We were at school together but when we were young, I didn't like him at all,' she replied, smiling at the memory. 'He was loud and boisterous, always playing football. He had brothers and they would shout and play-fight all the time. I think he intimidated me a little. Then, when we were fifteen, we had a school dance and this girl who I had never got on with started saying mean things to me and my friend. Suddenly, Alec was there telling her to back off. He asked me to dance. He was really popular at school, always joking and laughing, whereas I was the quiet, studious one in the corner, so it was a big deal, you know?' I nodded. 'When he put his arms around me, I had never felt braver or safer all at once. After the dance, he walked me home and asked if he could kiss me. After that, we were inseparable. We married when I was eighteen, and he was nineteen. He told me once that we were complete opposites and that's what made us a perfect fit. I think he was right.'

I let out a little sigh. It was so hard for my aunt when Alec passed away far too young. They had planned on growing old together but that had been cruelly taken away from them. He'd had a sudden heart attack in his forties, and Sally had been devastated. 'I'm so sorry that you had to lose him like you did.'

'I know. And it was the hardest thing but I know how lucky we were. Not many people find someone they belong with like we did. That has always been enough for me. Why, may I ask, has Alec come to your mind tonight?'

'I suppose I've been thinking about the future, you know? Whether Greg and I are the right fit... I thought we were but now I'm not as sure.' I not only had Sally's one true love to live up to, but my own parents had been happily married for years, a true strong partnership, and one that I had always assumed I'd find for myself. And when Greg crashed into my life, I had thought case closed, but now everything felt uncertain.

'Is that why you've come up here without him?'

I glanced at the shrewd look my aunt gave me. 'I suppose so, yes.'

'I know that nowadays people give up on relationships a lot quicker than they did in my day. We knew that you had to work at marriage for it to last happily. Now, I don't know, you can walk away so easily… but that doesn't mean I'd ever advocate staying with someone because you feel you have to. A true, lasting relationship is a choice you both make every day. Does that make sense?'

I nodded slowly. 'I think so. Even when it gets hard, and you have disagreements, if they're the right person then you still want to be with them, you want to work it out, and so do they.'

'Exactly. And if you're not sure they're worth fighting for then that might mean that they're not. Only you know the answer to that, Emily.' She gave me a reassuring smile. We reached the pub then and found a table in the beer garden. I went to order us drinks and food inside, thinking about what Aunt Sally had said. She had never considered leaving Glendale, even when she lost Alec; she loved this place so much that even my parents, and me, being in London hadn't changed her mind about staying here. I admired how strong she had always been about what she wanted to do. I wished I was as decisive about my own life. I felt as if I was always thinking and worrying more about what other people thought or felt so I didn't always consider my own heart in things. Aunt Sally wasn't like that.

Take Greg, for example. After we had fallen in love and started talking about the future, I had told him how I wanted to get married and have a family but he had claimed marriage was just a piece of paper, something we didn't need, a waste of money, old-fashioned even, and because he had been excited about trying for a baby, I had let it go. I had gone along with him and we'd moved in together, with no prospect of getting married. Now, I wondered if that had been the real start of our problems. If you didn't both want the same things in life, could you really make a life together?

I shook myself out of my thoughts to take the drinks the barman handed me, and I walked outside and joined Aunt Sally at the table.

'How is everything at Molly's?' Sally asked, taking a sip of her wine.

'It's really busy. I felt bad leaving her but her family are around to help. I get the feeling they wish she would start leaving the everyday running of the bakery to someone else, you know? I don't know what I'd do if Molly wasn't there, though. I love working with her.'

'Do you not still want to have your own bakery one day?' she asked, raising an eyebrow.

'I would still love that, yes, but it would take so much work, and money – especially in London – to set it all up. And I suppose I put it off because I thought Greg and I would be having a family.' I looked down at my wine, and wiped at the condensation on the glass with my fingertips. That felt even further away than ever.

'I suppose you do sometimes have to think about your priorities and focus on them,' Sally said. 'Alec and I were never blessed with children so I was very glad of my work at the Hall when he passed, and now helping with the shop has been a lot of fun; it's been wonderful to have been there building it up from the start with Beth and Caroline.'

'I think you guys have done a great job with it,' I said, pleased she had found a project to bring her joy. She was right – I had prioritised Greg over my bakery dream. It was impossible now not to worry that had been a bad idea. 'I do envy the fact that you guys created something of your own. I love Molly and her bakery is a wonderful place to work but it's all hers.'

'You'll figure out what you want to do. I know you, Emily, you often take the long way around in life but that's just you. You've always had to weigh things up carefully, consider what you want before doing it. That's no bad thing.'

I thought that I was like that with most things, but not with Greg. I hadn't carefully considered that at all. When he asked me to move in with him just three months into dating, I had ignored my usual pros and cons list, and jumped in heart first. He had made me feel like I was fearless but perhaps I had leapt just a bit too quickly. 'Except when I just follow my heart, that's when it all goes wrong.'

She shook her head. 'Even if things aren't working out between you and Greg, and I'm not going to ask for the ins and outs of that, it's up to you what you want to tell me, but that doesn't mean you were wrong to take that chance then. Everyone brings something to our lives when we let them in. They all change us in some way, for better or worse. Greg was meant to come into your life, you just need to decide if he's meant to be in it for keeps or not.

Sometimes it's not always clear why things happen until you get some distance from them. One day, you'll know what you want, I'm sure of that.'

'Aunt Sally, what would I do without you?' I asked her as our food was brought over.

She chuckled. 'You know very well you would be fine, I'm not really telling you anything you don't know yourself. Right in here.' She put her hand over her heart and then picked up her cutlery. 'Well, this looks tasty, doesn't it?'

I smiled. 'It does.' Even though I still had no answers to my questions, she had made me feel better if only for her faith that one day I would be able to answer them.

Chapter Eleven

'A garden party sounds very fancy,' I said, over breakfast at the Hall on Saturday morning. I still didn't fancy coffee for some reason so I was drinking orange juice with my scrambled eggs and bacon. Everyone was up and about early to prepare for the party that afternoon.

Beth smiled. 'My grandmother used to hold them here when my mum was young. She thought we should rein-state them,' she said, looking affectionately at Caroline who was going through the list of food and drink with Aunt Sally. 'We now have the Christmas trail of lights in December, and this in June. We thought we could use it to help the village, and it worked really well last summer.'

People paid for tickets to the garden party, Beth told me, and the money went back to the community – helping to keep things like the library open, the High Street clean and tidy, the hanging baskets there in the summer, and fairy lights in winter, the large Christmas tree in the middle of the village, and services that were voluntarily run, such as providing lunch for the elderly in the church hall, or a kids' club in the school holidays. 'I think it sounds like a great idea, and I'm sure everyone appreciates you still having it with the wedding so close. Can I help at all?'

'We want to serve summer punch and that needs mixing, if you're okay to do that?' Aunt Sally asked.

'Of course,' I said, standing up, ready to pitch in.

'I'm off to help John and Drew put out the tables and chairs,' Beth said, jumping up. 'Izzy, can you help your grandmother put up the sign outside? Not everyone can see the entrance until it's too late otherwise.'

I followed Aunt Sally into the kitchen. The French doors had been thrown open to let in the breeze. It promised to be a long, hot summer's day. I could see why my aunt loved living and working at the Hall so much, there always seemed to be something to do, no idle days to think of long-lost loves, you could always be busy here, and there were always people around to stave off any feeling of loneliness. I had only been at the Hall for a few days but London, and Greg, felt as if they were in another world entirely. It was only when he phoned or sent me a message that thoughts of him came flooding back, otherwise it would have been easy to shut our problems away in a box and not think about them at all while I was here. I tried not to think about what I'd have to face once the wedding was over, and I had to go back home.

'This sounds delicious,' I said, looking at Sally's recipe for the punch. 'And potent, too.'

'Your grandmother used to make it on special occasions so it's a long-held family recipe.' She passed me two large glass bowls, and two ladles. She was icing cupcakes that she had baked yesterday, and we worked side-by-side in comfortable silence. It was how Molly and I worked at her bakery. I tried not to think about how returning there would mean coming face-to-face with Steph again. She belonged in the London box, sealed shut while I was in Glendale. If only I never had to open it up.

After I had made the punch, I started to make two large bowls of salad using fresh produce from the Hall grounds. Most events at the Hall were catered, including the forthcoming wedding, Aunt Sally told me, but the garden party was all about mucking in so they could raise as much money as possible. And that was fine with me. The morning passed by in a blur.

As lunch time approached, I ducked out of the kitchen to see what was happening in the garden. The long picnic table was covered in a pretty floral tablecloth, with glasses, plates and napkins all ready on it. Across the lawn were coloured deckchairs for people to sit on. Balloons had been draped around the trees and fairy lights strung between them, ready for sunset. Everyone was bustling around getting everything ready.

'I understand now why you never came back to London,' I said to Beth as she carried over two watering cans full of flowers to use as centre pieces on the table. 'This is pretty spectacular.'

'The only thing we missed there was you,' she replied, touching my shoulder as she straightened the flowers up. 'I didn't want to come here when my grandmother was sick, as you know, but once I did, it just felt like it was time to come home again. The community here just refused to let me go. And, of course, there was my family and Drew... Honestly, it was the best decision I ever made.'

I didn't begrudge Beth one second of her happiness but it was hard not to feel a little bit envious, I was only human after all. I yawned then and found myself sagging against the table. It had been a busy morning.

She noticed. 'Why don't you go and get some rest? We're almost done anyway, and we all need to get changed. Everyone will be turning up at three so you have time for a nap.'

'God, when did I get old enough to need a nap?' I said with a laugh, but I couldn't pretend that the prospect wasn't appealing. I checked Aunt Sally didn't need me and then I retreated to my room.

As I lay down on the bed, I saw my phone light up. It was a message from Greg.

> **I just got off my shift – what are you up to?**

I typed out a brief response.

> **The Hall is throwing a charity garden party later so we've been getting ready for that.**

> **I wish I was there with you, babe.**

Sighing, I let my phone fall on to the bed. Honestly, I wasn't sure what to say. Did I wish he was here? I missed what we had had, that was certain, but what we had been for the past few months I didn't miss. I closed my eyes, exhausted by my thoughts and the busy morning, lulled by the gentle breeze floating though the open window and the sun streaming on my face, and soon I was fast asleep.

–

'Feeling better?' Beth found me when I walked into the kitchen that afternoon.

'Much, thank you.' I had had a long, cool shower after my nap, and felt refreshed, and ready for the party. I had put on a midi floral pleated skirt with sandals and a blouse, my hair loose over my shoulders, sunglasses and lip gloss completing the look. Glancing in the mirror before I came out, I had to admit I had a glow that had definitely been missing in London.

Beth and I stepped outside and I broke into a smile. Guests had already started to stream into the garden. Local teenagers had been hired to serve the drinks and help put out the buffet, and they weaved around the guests, in black trousers and white shirts. A local band was playing soft guitar music at one end of the garden.

'There you two are,' Drew said, appearing by our side. He held out two glasses of punch. 'I need to borrow Beth, please. My boss and his wife are here.'

'I'll be fine,' I replied, waving them off. I took my glass from him, and walked out onto the lawn, looking around to see if there was anyone I knew in sight.

'I must warn you,' a deep voice with a strong Scottish lilt to it said suddenly by my side. 'I'm a minister who drinks, as well as being young with a cracking sense of humour.'

I turned to see Brodie, smiling as he raised a glass of punch up for me to see. I laughed. 'Thank you for warning me. I have readjusted my views on ministers since we met so I will no longer be shocked by anything you do,' I told him.

He raised an eyebrow. 'Oh, really? I feel like you might regret saying that.'

I shook my head. 'Just don't drink too many of those and I'm sure we'll be fine.'

'Deal. I'm not a big drinker anyway but someone thrust this at me when I came in.' He shrugged and looked around.

'You'd better put it down then, I made the punch, and I have to confess I added more alcohol than the recipe said to.'

'Well, now I'm the one who's shocked.' We looked at one another and smiled. Brodie walked over to the nearby table and put the glass down. 'Fancy a stroll around, Emily?'

'Sure.' I put my glass down too, feeling like I wasn't too keen on drinking today either. First coffee, then booze, what was Scotland doing to me? We set off towards where the band were playing.

'So, where do you live in London?' Brodie asked me.

'Clapham.'

'I'm afraid I don't know London well, I've only been there a couple of times.'

'I grew up in Glendale, and it's a very different way of life. We don't have anything like this,' I said, gesturing around me. 'But you're not from here, are you?' I felt sure I would have remembered Brodie growing up, there was no one as good-looking as him at my school, that's for sure.

He shook his head. 'No. I actually grew up in Inverness so more of a city boy but I really love it here. The community has been wonderful, they made me feel at home even though I was very different to the last minister, and now I couldn't imagine living anywhere else.'

'Did you always want to be a minister?' I couldn't quite get over how unlike a minister he seemed to me.

'Well, I grew up in a very religious family. I went to church, Sunday school, all of it but as I moved into my teens, I became… disillusioned, you could say.' We walked further down the lawn, side-by-side, Brodie nodding at a family who passed us. He, like Beth, seemed to know everyone here. He glanced at me with a wry smile. 'I rebelled, refused to go to church, turned from God, made some new friends, what you'd call a "bad crowd" I suppose.' He sighed. 'I wasn't happy but I told myself that I was cool so that was okay.'

'Sounds like most teenagers,' I said. 'It's not easy at that age.'

'No, it's not. I did some things that I'm not particularly proud of but I can't change it. All I can do is try to be better now.'

'How did you find your way back?' I asked, finding his story fascinating. I wasn't used to a man being this open and honest with me when we'd only just met.

'My sister,' Brodie said. 'She was in a car accident. She almost died. She was in a coma and I sat by her bedside gripped by this fear I'd never had before. And I prayed. I told God I'd do anything if He would just save her.' He smiled. 'I didn't expect for this conversation to become so heavy on such a lovely day. Needless to say, my sister pulled through, and I made good on my promise. I studied theology at university and then began training to be a minster. As soon as she opened her eyes, I just knew.'

'Wow.' Goosebumps travelled down my bare arms despite the sun beating down on us. 'That's amazing, Brodie. Your family must be really proud of you.'

'They are. My sister is in Edinburgh, she stayed on after university, and my parents still live in Inverness. We try to see each other as often as we can. What about your family?' He lifted his hand to wave to a child running in front of us.

'I'm close with my parents; it's just us three. They don't live too far from me in London. We moved down when I was a teenager. I think they always plan to retire back up here. I think we all miss Glendale sometimes.'

He nodded. 'I can well imagine that.' We turned then and walked towards where the band were playing. Some people were dancing on the grass in front of them, making it feel like we were at a music festival. 'When I moved here, I was nervous that I wouldn't make friends but it's such a strong community. I have to turn down invitations or I'd never be at the vicarage.'

I smiled to myself. I bet he was the talk of the village when he arrived. Surely every eligible woman in the surrounding areas had their eye on him? He saw me smile. 'It must be that sense of humour of yours,' I said.

He chuckled. 'Indeed. You're staying at the Hall by yourself then?' He gave me a quick look before turning to wave at another family passing us.

'That's right. I'm staying until the wedding,' I replied, not quite meeting his eyes and hoping he wouldn't notice. I didn't want to sully our nice chat by bringing up Greg and having to explain why he wasn't with me.

'London's loss is our gain then,' he said.

I wished I could blame the warm sun on my face for its sudden flush but I knew that wasn't the case at all.

Chapter Twelve

It slowly came to our notice that the lawn had emptied around us and when we turned around, we realised everyone had moved up closer to the house where the food was being served. With sheepish smiles at how long we had walked and talked, we made our way back up the garden to the massive buffet laid out on the tables. I was surprised by how much we had lost track of both the time, and other people. Brodie really was easy to talk to.

As we reached everyone, Brodie was intercepted by some of his parishioners so I left him to it, and piled up my plate with the gorgeous food, making my way over to where Beth's friend, and maid-of-honour, Heather and her partner Rory, Drew's brother, were sitting with Izzy, their baby asleep in the pram beside them. 'Can I join you?' I asked them.

'Of course, Emily,' Heather said, smiling at me warmly.

'This looks amazing,' I said, sinking into a deckchair next to them. I was definitely going to put on weight staying at the Hall. I tucked into my plateful with relish. 'This pasta salad is so good. I'd better ask my aunt for her recipe.'

'I helped make that,' Izzy said, waving her fork excitedly.

'You did a great job,' I told her.

'So, I see you're already acquainted with our minister,' Heather said, leaning across Rory to speak to me. 'Be careful, you'll have all the single ladies here after you with their pitchforks. He's the most eligible bachelor I think Glendale has ever had,' she added with a laugh.

'Hey!' Rory protested. 'I was an eligible bachelor, I'll have you know.'

She rolled her eyes. 'Yes, of course you were, love, but I snapped you up. Brodie, however, is very much still available.'

I shook my head but I couldn't forget the spark I had felt between us when he had smiled at me, and how much I had enjoyed talking to him. Should I be feeling guilty about that? I looked at him stood talking to two ladies, one of whom was touching his arm every time she said anything. 'He's certainly very popular for a minister,' I commented. And good-looking too, I added silently to myself. I wondered if he'd be able to escape to get any food, poor bloke.

'I can't say I blame them,' Heather replied with a sigh as she followed my gaze to him.

'Seriously, I'm right here!' Rory said, waving his hands to get her attention.

'What's got Rory's knickers in a twist again?' Drew asked, approaching us then, hand-in-hand with Beth.

'He's annoyed that we've been lusting over Reverend Stewart,' Heather told them with a grin.

'That sounds so wrong when you call him that,' I said with a shake of my head.

'No one would blame you,' Beth said. 'I think every woman in the village is lusting after him. We're only human.' She shrugged.

83

'Now I feel like I should be upset too,' Drew complained.

Beth gazed up at him. 'Hey, you know that you're the only one for me but it doesn't hurt to look, does it?'

'Why can't you reassure me like that?' Rory demanded, glaring at Heather.

'I'm not sure you're The One yet,' she replied but she was grinning.

Rory leaned back in his chair and crossed his arms. 'Well, maybe I'm not sure either,' he said, sulking.

'We both know that's not true,' Heather replied. Everyone laughed at them. I joined in but I did feel a pang in my heart. It was obvious that both Beth and Drew, and Heather and Rory, had found their perfect partners. Their relationships were stable in a way that mine just wasn't.

'Speaking of…' Beth muttered under her breath, and we turned to see Brodie coming towards us, hands in his pockets. I tried not to watch but it was hard not to. I could well understand why the ladies of Glendale were taken with him.

'I was starting to think I'd never make it to the food table,' he said, running a hand through his hair and looking a little shell-shocked by all the attention. He glanced at my plate. 'Want to refill?'

I looked down in surprise at my empty plate. I couldn't get enough of the food at Glendale Hall, it seemed. I got up and followed him to the food table, trying to ignore the feeling of eyes on my back from the others. 'You must be the most popular minister Glendale has had,' I found myself blurting out as we reached the buffet. I seemed to be unable to filter my thoughts around him.

Brodie chuckled, his laugh deep and rumbling. 'I must admit I was pleasantly surprised myself at how well church services were attended here until I had my first dinner invitation, and then my housekeeper clued me in on why suddenly so many single women seemed to have found faith.' He shrugged. 'I'm not complaining, though. If anyone wants to help out the church, I'm not going to turn them away.'

I shook my head. 'I can't believe you're actually admitting to knowing the real reason why women are suddenly becoming believers around here, and using it to your own advantage. Is that really Christian of you?'

'Of course I'm hoping that they come for me and stay for Him,' he replied, pausing in putting potato salad on his plate to point a fork to the sky. 'And it wouldn't be Christian to turn them away now, would it?'

I chuckled then. 'Shameless. Completely shameless. But what will they all do when they realise they have no chance of becoming Mrs Stewart?' I wondered, adding a sausage roll to my plate and putting one on his too.

'I didn't say they have no chance. I'm a single man, after all.' He grinned, looking boyish and most un-minister-like. Then he looked a little more serious. 'I hope to get married one day.'

'So, you're just waiting for Miss Right then?' I asked, genuinely interested. It was clear he could have the pick of the village; I was surprised that he didn't seem to be dating anyone.

'I don't exactly believe in right or wrong... marriage takes hard work and compromise as well as compatibility. I know that when I do get married it will be forever so I want to make sure that I don't rush into anything. When you feel you need to set an example to your parish, you don't want to make any mistakes.'

'I understand that,' I replied. He definitely took marriage more seriously than I had seen any man do, apart from Drew, maybe. 'I think it's admirable actually.'

He looked surprised then. 'Really?'

'Sure. I don't like rushing into anything, either. In fact, my Aunt Sally always tells me that I could do with being more impulsive but to be honest, when I have been, it hasn't really worked out.' I thought of how hard and fast I fell for Greg. It had been out of character for me. In hindsight, maybe that was my warning sign.

'You have to do what feels right for you,' Brodie said. 'I'm always being asked by my family when I'm going to settle down but I'll know when the time is right, I'm sure of that.'

'I wish I had the same conviction,' I replied, thinking that I could do with some sort of sign about what to do about my relationship with Greg.

'You just need a little faith, Emily,' he said, passing me the bread basket.

I smiled. 'Maybe I do.'

'There you are, Brodie,' a small, grey-haired lady suddenly appeared by his side, looking cross. 'I wanted to speak to you about the bake sale tomorrow. We still don't have a Victoria sponge, and you can't have a bake sale without one!' She looked aghast at the thought.

'Oh, well, no. Of course not,' Brodie replied, looking taken aback. 'Um...'

'I could bake one,' I found myself offering. I glanced at him. 'I work at a bakery.'

'Thank you, dear,' the woman said with a brisk nod, leaving as quickly as she had appeared.

Brodie turned to me. 'Are you sure? You're on holiday, I wouldn't want to force you to work.'

'It's fine. It won't take long. I could bake one in my sleep I think.'

He broke into a warm smile. 'Well, that's very kind of you. It starts at two o'clock in the church hall tomorrow.'

'I'll bring it by before then,' I promised. I looked at my plate, piled high again. 'I'm going to be huge if I keep this up.'

'Don't be silly, you have the perfect figure.' Then he realised what he had said, spluttered a little, and turned bright red.

'And I thought it was just me that said inappropriate things to you,' I said, bursting out laughing.

'It seems to be catching,' he replied dryly but he joined in with my laughter, and I felt another burst of warmth in the air between us.

Chapter Thirteen

I got up before the rest of the household the following morning and pulled on jeans and a t-shirt. Sunday had dawned grey and cooler so it wasn't a hardship to be in the kitchen baking. I put on the radio and made myself a cup of tea, humming along to the music as I started to cream the butter and sugar.

It had been a lovely garden party yesterday with people staying long into the evening – it had been well past midnight when all the guests had finally left the Hall. I had fallen asleep as soon as my head had touched the pillow and had woken up with lots of energy, ready to get baking. I was also going to be helping Aunt Sally in the Glendale Hall shop so I was looking forward to a busy day ahead.

My phone rang in my pocket as I sifted the flour. I looked down at it and saw Greg's picture lighting up the screen. I knew I couldn't keep dodging his calls. 'Hey,' I said as I put it on speaker and kept on stirring the mixture, nerves flooding through me at talking to him.

'Em,' he greeted me, sounding relieved. 'I was worried you weren't going to answer again. What are you doing?'

'Making a cake for the church bake sale.'

He chuckled. 'Of course you are,' he said. 'I'm just getting ready for work, I took some extra shifts. It's so quiet here without you.'

I stopped stirring, affected by his words. 'It's so strange being away from you,' I told him, honestly. I wasn't sure if it was good or bad but it was definitely weird. I was so used to being around him. I looked at the mixture in the bowl and knew that if he had been with me, he would have been trying to steal a bit of it. He often said that my baking was one of the reasons he fell in love with me.

'I really want you to miss me as much as I'm missing you,' he said then. 'You do miss me, don't you, babe?'

I sighed. 'Of course, I do. But that's not really the point. I love you but I don't know if that's enough any more.' It was almost a relief to say the words aloud, to finally tell him I was no longer sure we had a future together. The thought of him being with Steph still hurt like hell.

'Don't say that,' he said, his voice trembling a little. 'We belong together. We both knew it that first day we met, didn't we?'

'I did feel like that…'

'Because you knew it was something special. And it is. We can't just throw this all away, can we?'

'We? I'm not the one—' I began, anger shooting quickly through my veins as if he had injected me with it.

'I know, I know!' he said, quickly. 'I'm sorry. I know this is all my fault. I just wish you'd tell me what I can do to fix it.'

'Honestly, I don't know. I wish I did.'

'At least you wish you did.' He sighed then. 'I guess I have to go to work now. All I can do is swear I'll never hurt you again. I hate the thought of losing you, of losing us. We can fix this. I know we can. Please just tell me that you hope we can fix it? Em?'

'I hope so,' I whispered, not sure if I was telling the truth or not. He said goodbye and I started to stir the cake mixture again, furiously. I felt torn. I loved him, I really did, but could I ever trust him again?

'You're up early,' Beth said, shuffling into the kitchen. She was still in her pjs. 'I need coffee and painkillers.'

'Too much wine last night?' I said, forcing a smile.

'And the fact that I have really bad period pain today.' She came over to put the coffee machine on and glanced at the bowl. 'I've missed your cakes.'

I spooned the mixture into two cake tins as she poured out a coffee for herself and shook my head when she offered me one. 'Right, that's all done,' I said, sliding the tins into the oven. 'Shall I make us some breakfast?'

Beth grimaced. 'I can't face it. I'll just go and have a shower, I think.' She glanced at me. 'You're very bright-eyed and bushy-tailed this morning. Anything to do with seeing Brodie later?'

I threw the tea towel at her, and she giggled. I watched her leave and leaned against the counter. I did feel full of energy that morning. I felt bad for her suffering with her period, I was always grumpy on the first day of mine. But I hadn't felt like that for a while. Izzy's cat came in then, brushing against me as she went to her food bowl. I frowned as I watched her, wondering why I hadn't felt period pain for a while. I shook my head. Probably my last one had been easier than usual, which was why I couldn't remember.

'Ready for a day in the shop?' Aunt Sally asked then as she came in, dressed and ready. 'How about some pancakes before we go?'

'I heard that!' Izzy cried from behind her, bouncing into the kitchen. 'And I say yes to pancakes!'

Sally laughed. 'Of course you do.'

'Let's see who can toss them the highest,' I suggested, my worries fading with their enthusiasm. My stomach instantly rumbled on cue. I was definitely in the mood for pancakes.

–

The Glendale Hall shop was quiet until it was almost lunch time, and then suddenly the High Street seemed to wake up all at once.

'Everyone leaving the church,' Aunt Sally said when I made my observation. We had been watering the plants but had to abandon that to help the influx of customers. So, Brodie hadn't been lying about his well-attended services then. We spent the next hour without being able to take a breath.

'Ooh, we'd better get to the bake sale,' a woman said to her friend as they queued up with their purchases.

I glanced at the clock behind me. 'Me too,' I said to them. 'I baked a Victoria sponge. Someone said it was the one thing missing.'

'It's going to be the best turnout for a bake sale ever,' her friend replied with a shake of her head. 'Not that I can blame them. If I wasn't married...'

The other woman rolled her eyes. 'Everyone needs to get a grip. Seriously, if he's that good-looking and single at thirty, there must be something wrong with him. See you there!' she added to me as they hurried out.

I watched them go, wondering if they were right. It did annoy me how people assumed that single people were desperate for love but Brodie had seemed keen to make a commitment one day soon. And it was surprising he hadn't found anyone special. Or perhaps he had, but his heart had been broken, like mine. I knew that I shouldn't be so interested but there was something about Brodie that intrigued me. I turned to Aunt Sally. 'Right, I'd better take my cake along then. Will you be okay on your own, though?'

'I'll be closing in a minute anyway,' she replied. 'And it sounds like everyone has gone to the bake sale.'

I went out the back and grabbed my bag and the cake and strolled towards the church. It was still cloudy outside and I was pleased I'd put on a cardigan. There were people milling around the back of the church so I followed the crowd and walked into the hall, which was a separate building behind the church. It was a long room with a wooden floor; tables were lined up along one wall, and people were arranging their cakes on them.

'That looks delicious,' a voice behind me said. 'I might have to buy that myself.'

I turned and smiled at Brodie, who was behind the table. 'Made with Glendale Hall jam too,' I said, putting it down.

'Well, then, how can I resist? Do you need to get off or do you want to stay and help us unload all of these on the village?' He gestured to the cakes. There were a lot to sell. The whole village must have baked something.

'I can help,' I replied, slipping behind the table to join him.

'I'm hoping we might raise enough to buy a new organ for the church, we've been fundraising all year and we're almost there,' he said, rolling up the sleeves of his long-sleeved shirt. I tried not to look at his muscular arms as he did so.

'We can definitely sell all of these. We've got this,' I replied. He held out his fist and I laughed as I bumped it with mine. People started to file in to look at the cakes. Brodie priced mine at five pounds, and then promptly hid it behind the table for himself. I couldn't help but feel good about that.

As I suspected, the hall quickly sold out of cakes. It felt as if most of the village had turned up to buy something. Even Heather and Harry dropped by and left with cupcakes. I hung back to help Brodie wipe down the tables, and soon the hall had completely emptied out.

'Let me walk you home,' he said, as he locked up the money in the cashbox.

'Oh, no need,' I said, quickly, shrugging my cardigan back on.

'I need to stretch my legs after being here all day, and to be honest, all that's waiting for me at the vicarage is a ready meal and a box set so I can put that off a little bit longer.'

I thought how that would have been the case for me too if we were in London, Greg almost certainly working, so I nodded. 'Okay then, thank you.'

Chapter Fourteen

We stepped out of the hall and Brodie locked up behind us. There was a cool breeze in the air but I didn't mind. The village was beautiful even on a grey day. People passed us in the High Street, all either waving or stopping to say a quick hello. It was something that I still wasn't used to, having lived for so long in London.

We strolled side-by-side as we turned towards Glendale Hall, the trees above us rustling in the breeze. The road to Glendale was empty. Sunday was drawing to a close and everyone was heading home for their evening meals. Growing up, Sunday had always been a family day – my parents and I sitting down for a roast dinner then curling up to watch a film, my dad always falling asleep in his armchair. I had always wanted that one day with my own family. I wondered now if that would ever be on the cards.

When we could see Glendale Hall ahead of us, I asked Brodie about what he had said before we left the church. 'Are you all alone at the vicarage, then?'

He glanced across at me. 'I have a housekeeper, Gloria, but she has Sundays off, and she doesn't live with me – she lives in the village with her husband. What about you?'

I looked away, knowing that I had to 'fess up. 'I live with my boyfriend, Greg. Well, I'm not sure if he's still my...' I paused in my babbling to take a breath. I met

Brodie's steady gaze. 'I just found out he cheated on me. He slept with someone else. That's why I came up here, really, without him,' I added, alarmed at how easy it was to confess things to Brodie.

'I'm sorry, Emily,' he replied. 'That happened to me. Before I came to Glendale. Part of the reason I moved here, I suppose you could say.' He shrugged. 'It's not easy – all that broken trust.'

I nodded vigorously. 'So, you couldn't forgive her?' It was becoming clearer why Brodie was single, and not in any hurry to change that fact.

'I was ready to but she didn't want me any more. She left me for the man she'd been seeing. My mother told me they're married now.'

'I'm sorry,' I told him. That was heart-breaking. 'But you thought you could forgive her? That you should, I mean?'

He thought for a moment before answering. 'I would never say you *should* forgive someone. But forgiveness is something I do believe in. It's far easier to say than do, though. And there are so many things it depends on, of course. I suppose you need to consider the future of the relationship. Is it something you still want? Do you think you'd be able to trust him if you do go back to him?'

'That's the million-dollar question. He has been full of regret and apologies. Says how much he misses me. It's just so hard to get my head around. I love him but I can't believe he put what we have at risk like that. Maybe it shows he doesn't see the same future that I do? Well, did.'

'Maybe. You'd need to ask him that. There are so many reasons why people look elsewhere. I blamed myself; too focused on work, not giving enough commitment to our relationship. But what happened next… I don't know. She fell in love with someone else. How could I have done anything to have stopped that? Does that say more about her than me?' He smiled then. 'I still haven't found the answers to all my questions. But I do know in my heart we weren't meant to be. I believe that and it helps. Even when I get lonely or sad.'

'You're very honest, for a—'

'Minister?' He grinned.

I shook my head as we reached the gates of the Hall. 'For a man, I was going to say.'

He chuckled. 'Perhaps I am. I definitely do believe in honesty.' He paused. 'Well, we're here. Thank you again for your help today.'

'Any time. And thank you for your advice.' I stopped too, and faced him. 'Is it easier? Relationships, and well, life, I suppose, when you have faith like you do?'

'Sometimes. Sometimes it's harder. But I wouldn't be without it.'

I nodded. I shifted my feet. I knew I should turn away and go into the Hall but I wasn't sure when I'd see him again, and that made me blurt out: 'I need to go into Inverness tomorrow to find some things for the wedding cake. I don't suppose you have any free time? I mean, I'd like the company…' Why did my cheeks always have to turn red in his presence?

'Sure. I have a prayer meeting but I'd be free around midday. I could drive us?'

'That would be great. Right, then, I'll see you tomorrow.'

'Goodnight, Emily.' He put his hands in his pockets as he started walking back to Glendale. I watched him go, unable to help smiling. There was something calming about his presence, something that made me want to spend time with him. And now he knew about Greg so there was no harm in doing just that.

Was there?

Walking through the gates, I let myself in to the Hall. It was quiet and I headed upstairs, wanting to sit alone for a few minutes. I knew there would be a family tea soon. I slipped into my room and closed the door, flopping down on the bed. The evening was becoming chillier so I thought I should change before I went down to the kitchen. Yawning, I realised how tired I felt suddenly. It had been a busy day but I was knackered. I laid down on the bed just to close my eyes for a few minutes.

When I opened my eyes, the light outside was fading. I sat up with a start. I'd been asleep for an hour. Why was I suddenly napping like an old woman? I had been sleeping so well since coming to Scotland but I was definitely lacking energy. Perhaps I was coming down with something?

Then my eyes snapped to my reflection in the full-length mirror. Not only had I been sleeping a lot, even napping a couple of times, and yet was still tired, I had also weirdly gone off coffee. I was hungry too, eating as much as I could get my hands on. And then Beth kept saying I was glowing. Plus, I hadn't wanted the punch at the garden party either.

I shook my head at myself. There was no way, was there? Thinking hard, I tried to remember my last period but I hadn't had one for six weeks. And usually I was never late. 'Oh God,' I said, aloud, as it all clicked into place.

But surely, it couldn't be.

Could it?

My hand flew to my stomach as I told myself not to be silly.

But even as I tried to deny it, I knew it was possible.

I hadn't been on the pill for years, after all. And Greg and I had slept together seven weeks ago. It was so rare now that I remembered it clearly. But the timing. The universe would really have a sick sense of humour if after all this time trying… had I finally fallen pregnant?

And if I was, what the hell was I was going to do?

Chapter Fifteen

'So, all ready for school tomorrow?' Caroline asked Izzy at dinner. I had hurried down after my impromptu nap to find it almost ready but everyone had assumed I'd only just come back from the bake sale, and I didn't contradict them. I wasn't sure if anyone had noticed that I was quiet, or just picking at Aunt Sally's delicious pasta bake. I was trying to pay attention to the conversation but it wasn't easy when all I could think about was the fact that there could be a baby growing inside me.

Izzy launched into an enthusiastic story about the book she was reading for English, but I found myself tuning out until I suddenly heard my name.

'Huh?' I asked, looking up in confusion.

'I said – do you fancy lunch out tomorrow?' Beth asked me from across the table, giving me a small smile. She had clearly noticed my preoccupation.

'Actually, I can't,' I admitted. 'I need to go into Inverness for some cake supplies… and Brodie offered to drive me.' I found myself blushing a little as I told them, and I wasn't quite sure why. I wondered if I should cancel as I very much doubted I would be good company for him, but then I realised that I could go into Boots there, and pick up a pregnancy test. There was no way I could do that in Glendale village without someone telling someone in the family, I was sure of that. I knew what the small town could be like.

Beth raised an eyebrow. 'Ah, I see.'

I shook my head. 'He's just being nice...' I said, a little flustered. Especially because I didn't deserve the sly looks everyone was giving me. Even if I did find Brodie attractive, I could well be pregnant with another man's child. Not that they all knew that, of course, and I wanted to keep it very quiet until I knew for sure.

'Maybe Tuesday then,' Beth said, taking a sip of her wine and exchanging a look with her mum.

I sighed into my glass of water.

Drew came in then from work. 'What a day,' he said, giving Beth a kiss and going over to hug Izzy. He looked exhausted, and slumped into the chair next to Izzy.

'Here you go.' Beth slid him a glass of wine and then spooned out some of the bake onto a plate for him. 'Everything okay?' she asked as she passed it to him. Their eyes met, and I knew that they were trying to keep Drew's hard day from Izzy. Perhaps someone had died at the hospital; he looked quite shaken. He nodded and assured her that he was fine but I saw her bite her lip and watch him anxiously as he took a long gulp of wine.

I knew it was wrong to feel jealous in that moment but somehow Beth's concern was more touching than the times I'd seen them kissing or hugging. There was real love and care for the other person between them.

And it reminded me that I was far away from Greg. Any other time, I would have told him that I was late, and we could have done the pregnancy test together. Our first test! And I was alone, miles from him, for it. It was so complicated. I really could have done with a hug from him and for him to tell me that everything was going to be okay. Because I really wasn't at all sure that it would be.

When dinner was finally over, Caroline took Izzy upstairs and Beth and Drew retreated into the living room together, talking in hushed tones. It was clear they wanted to be alone, and I couldn't blame them. I followed Aunt Sally into the kitchen to help her clear everything away.

As I passed her things for the dishwasher, she studied me through her steady brown eyes.

'Are you sure you're okay, Emily? You don't seem your usual self. Is it Greg?'

I nodded, unable to tell her more than that.

'Is there anything I can do to help?'

'No, honestly, I just have to sort things out for myself.' I leaned against the counter. I had no idea how I was going to do that, though.

'You know that there are so many people you can ask for help. Remember that.' She touched my arm as she passed by, carrying a saucepan to the sink to wash. 'And you should look after yourself. Go up to bed, you look exhausted. I can do all this.' She saw me about to argue. 'Don't make me put my foot down,' she added, sternly. I instantly flashed back to being a kid and smiled, despite myself. There really was no point in arguing with her.

'Okay, thank you.' I gave her a quick kiss on the cheek, to her surprise, and I hurried out, suddenly afraid I might start crying. I wanted to tell her everything, I really did, but I was scared. Scared to say the words out loud in case I was wrong. I had to know myself first. Before I could do as she suggested and ask for help.

–

Brodie picked me up the next day as promised, and I hurried out to his car, avoiding anyone at the Hall. I couldn't take any of their teasing this morning. The sun was out at least, promising a warm day. I had flung on a long skirt and strappy top with my trusty flip-flops, and a large pair of sunglasses to hide the bags under my eyes after my restless, anxious night. Brodie gave me a wide smile when I climbed in beside him. He was wearing a short-sleeved shirt and jeans, one tanned arm leaning out of the open window. 'Right, then, let's go cake shopping,' he said with a chuckle, pulling away and driving out through the gates.

'We're not actually shopping for cake,' I replied. 'Just things I can use to make the cake…'

'I stand corrected,' he replied, throwing me his trade-mark grin. We drove through winding lanes, the Scottish countryside either side of the car providing a stunning accompaniment to the journey. The radio was on softly, and Brodie hummed along. I envied how content with life he seemed.

After a while, he glanced at me. 'You're quiet this morning. You didn't even comment on whether my car is suitable for a minister or not.'

Despite myself, I smiled and turned to him. 'Doesn't everyone in Glendale drive a Range Rover?'

'I suppose so. What about my radio station choice, though?' He asked.

'Very middle of the road. Very minister-like.'

'Hey! Middle of the road! Right…' He pressed a button and a dance song filled the car. He turned it up loud, the bassline vibrating. 'How about this?' he half-shouted over it.

I started to laugh. 'I don't believe you like this!'

He pretended to nod along for a minute then winced and turned it down, and back to the previous station. 'Fine. You got me but I have to conform in some areas, right? Otherwise you'd have me kicked out of the church.'

Shaking my head, I smiled and turned back to the window. It was hard not to feel cheerful with Brodie, especially on a lovely day and on such a pretty drive but my thoughts couldn't stay on trivial things for long. I found myself touching my stomach. If this had happened before, I would have been thrilled and so would Greg. Now, everything had turned grey and I wasn't sure how I was supposed to feel about any of it. I felt like I was losing control of my life, and I didn't like it one little bit.

'How did you start baking?' Brodie asked me then, drawing me back out of myself and back into the car with him.

'It was all down to my Aunt Sally, really. She taught me, and I've loved it since I was little. I suppose I decided to go to college and actually make it my career when I was a teenager. One of my friends was really upset after her boyfriend dumped her so I baked her a cake, and it seemed to cheer her up, and I realised that I could make people just a little bit happier with my cakes and that seemed like a pretty good job to me.' I shrugged. I still loved to see people's little smiles when they bought themselves a sweet treat. I hoped the cake I was going to make Beth would put a smile on her and Drew's faces, too. 'I know it sounds a little silly,' I added, feeling a little embarrassed at revealing my thoughts about cake.

Brodie shook his head. 'Not silly at all. When anyone is upset, you straight away think of sitting down with them and having a cup of tea and a slice of cake.'

I smiled, pleased he hadn't laughed at me. 'What do you like about being a minster then?'

'Much the same as you... I like helping people. My faith guides me, and I want to help guide others in the same way, I suppose. People say becoming a minster is a calling from God. But for me, it was also a calling to people as well.' He glanced at me when I didn't any anything. 'No jokes about that?'

'No, I think it's a beautiful thought,' I replied, swallowing the lump in my throat down as hard as I could. I turned back to the window, and we drove the rest of the way in companionable silence.

Chapter Sixteen

We parked the car and walked towards the shops, which were quite quiet, thanks to it being both a weekday and a sunny one. There was a craft shop that had been in Inverness ever since I was a kid that I wanted to go to. I suggested I meet Brodie in an hour or so for coffee so he wouldn't need to come in with me, and so I could nip into Boots alone. He readily agreed, sloping off with his hands in his pockets to the supermarket as he needed a few bits, he said. I pulled out my list as I walked into the shop, its bell jangling merrily as I did so. With how full my mind was at the moment, I knew I would forget everything if I didn't write it down.

Picking up a basket, I slipped my sunglasses onto my head and strolled down the aisles, adding everything I needed. I paused in the cake-decorating space, getting as excited as I was able to in my current state about choosing things. Despite what was going on with me, I still wanted to make Beth the best cake that I could. I frowned as I concentrated, and let out a little gasp when I found the perfect things. Instead of putting a bride and groom on the top of the cake, I wanted something to symbolise them as a couple. Neither Beth nor Drew were traditional and I wanted the cake to showcase that. I leaned down to look at the plastic figurines they had, mostly men and women. Then I spotted a selection of Highland cows.

I giggled as I remembered Beth telling me about how she and Drew were chased by a cow when they were teenagers. Apparently, they had been laying in the grass, kissing, in one of Rory's fields, and the cow had suddenly appeared and made a very loud, disapproving noise. They had been so startled, they had jumped up, started to run, and the cow had followed them until they reached the gate, and managed to escape. I hadn't been able to stop laughing, and I loved the idea of choosing something that would be significant for them. I picked up a brown and white one, and hoped it would make them smile too when they saw it.

I added food colouring and plastic flowers to my basket, planning to mix them in with the other flowers I designed out of icing, and arrange them around the bottom of the cake too. Then I paused, my eyes falling on a bride and groom in front of me. The man was dressed as a fireman, holding hands with his bride-to-be. And it was stupid but immediately I pictured them as Greg and me. She even had long, blonde hair. I picked them up. I couldn't help it – even after everything, I still fantasied about marrying Greg. And when I thought about the fact that I might be carrying his baby, that longing went deeper than ever. But even if he hadn't cheated, even if I was pregnant, I knew that marriage wasn't something he had ever wanted. A sob rose up in my throat.

Stumbling to the till, I paid for everything in a daze, not understanding anything the shop assistant said to me. I mumbled a thank you and grabbed the shopping bag, rushing out of the shop. I gulped in the fresh air when it hit me and leaned against the wall outside, trying to breathe. I didn't know if it was hormones or everything catching up with me but seeing that bride and groom figurine and knowing that it might never be me and Greg made me burst into tears.

I put my head in my hands to try to hide my crying from passers-by.

And that's how Brodie found me five minutes later.

'Emily, what's happened?' he asked, gently. I just looked at him, and he pulled me into his arms. I was too upset to protest and I let him hold me tightly. 'It's going to be okay,' he said, soothingly, rubbing my back. Some people are good huggers and Brodie was an excellent one.

After a minute, I pulled back, sniffing and wiping at my eyes. Brodie wordlessly passed me a tissue and I dabbed my eyes and then blew my nose. I pulled my sunglasses back on and managed a small smile. 'Thank you. I'm sorry.'

'How about we get some tea and cake, huh?'

I nodded. Brodie scooped up my bag and I followed him to a small café nearby where he found us a table in the corner and ordered a pot of tea and two slices of lemon drizzle cake, despite me telling him I wasn't hungry. 'You need the sugar,' he told me, firmly.

When the waitress left us, I found the courage to take my sunglasses off again. 'How bad is it?' I asked him, knowing my eyes would be as red as anything. I had never been one to cry pretty, that was for sure.

'Oh my God,' he replied, eyes wide. Then he touched my hand. 'Sorry, I couldn't help it. You can't tell, I promise.'

I smiled, feeling the loss of his hand when he took it away. 'How did you get so good at dealing with crying women?'

'My younger sister. I have made many a Ben & Jerry's run when she had boy trouble.' He stopped speaking as the waitress returned with our tea and cake. He poured me a cup and then one for himself, waiting for me to take a sip. 'You don't have to tell me anything, obviously we've only just met, but if there's anything I can do to help, please ask,' he said then, before tucking into his cake with gusto.

I almost cried again because of how kind he was being to me. I took another sip of tea. Why was tea so soothing in times of trouble? 'I really am embarrassed,' I said. 'Honestly, I don't know why I broke down like that. It was so silly… I saw something in the shop that reminded me of Greg. And then I got to thinking about us, and what's happened. And I didn't sleep well last night…' I trailed off, aware that I really wasn't making much sense.

'Have some cake, it's really good,' Brodie said, giving me a warm smile. He watched me try a bit of it. He was right – it was delicious. 'You don't need to worry. We all have moments like that. You're only human. You don't need to pretend everything is okay, especially with me.'

Somehow, I knew he was right. There was something so honest and open about him, he made you feel like you could be like that too. Part of it might have been his job but mostly, I thought it was just Brodie. 'I think it all just got on top of me a bit.'

'Well, it can't be easy. You may have come up here for a break to think about your boyfriend but you're surrounded by people getting ready for a wedding.'

I nodded. 'Exactly. And I don't know if I'll ever have one of my own.'

'Is that what you want?' he asked, gently. 'For you and your boyfriend? Greg, isn't it?'

'Yes, Greg.' It felt strange to be talking about him with Brodie. 'I honestly don't know. It's all so complicated. It *was* what I wanted, though. He was never keen on the idea. He never wanted to get married, to anyone. So he says.'

'You're not sure whether to believe him?'

'Well, believe is a strong word – it's more I'm not sure whether to trust it. What if he actually means he just doesn't want to marry *me*? Maybe the next girl he meets will make him think completely differently.' I sighed then. 'God, I can actually hear myself and how pathetic I sound! He cheated on me but I'm worried about him not wanting to marry me. He should be the one begging me! It's just that...' I bit my lip, stopping myself from telling him that I thought I could be pregnant. It was one step too personal. Even if he was a minister. 'I don't know,' I mumbled to try to cover up my sudden pause.

'It's hard but it sounds like you really need to talk to him. If getting married is what you want, you need to tell him that. You might think you already have but sometimes people don't really hear what they don't want to.'

I nodded, chewing on the cake absently. I knew he was right. I had accepted what Greg wanted and hadn't been clear that it was very different from what I wanted. If I was pregnant then I would want us to all have the same surname. It was old-fashioned maybe to think like that, but that was what I felt in my heart. And Greg would need to know that. I just had no idea what he would say. 'Thanks, Brodie,' I said.

He smiled. 'So, what set you off in that shop anyway? You said something reminded you of Greg?'

I explained about the plastic bride and groom who I thought looked like me and Greg. Brodie watched me for a moment and then he suddenly started laughing. 'I'm sorry... but a plastic bride and groom made you cry...' he said, gasping between laughs.

I chuckled. 'You're right, it's crazy,' I said, shaking my head that I let something so trivial set me off. 'Seriously, it's not that funny!' I said as Brodie couldn't stop laughing and then I gave in, and laughed along with him, and whether it was the laughter or the tea and cake or Brodie being kind and listening to me, or the fact that I had cried all my worries out, I felt a lot better by the time we left the café.

Chapter Seventeen

Glendale Hall was quiet when I returned after lunch. The house was shady and cool compared to outside and I slipped up to my room, clutching my bags to my chest, relieved that I didn't have to make any excuses to anyone. After Brodie and I had left the café, I had sent him on ahead to the car and nipped into Boots to pick up my first pregnancy test.

I put down my bag and the craft supplies and slipped off my shoes, sinking into the soft carpet. Padding through to the bathroom with the test, I glanced at my reflection. My eyes looked red and puffy despite Brodie's assurances to the contrary so I splashed some cold water on my face. I was scared, I realised. More than the nervous excitement I had always imagined I would feel at this moment. I didn't know what to root for, I supposed, which was beyond confusing. My much-longed-for baby was suddenly within real, attainable reach, and I wasn't sure how to feel about it.

'Don't be a chicken,' I whispered sternly to myself. I couldn't put it off. I had to know either way. Sucking in a deep breath, I ripped open the packet and read the instructions. I went to the loo, taking a bit of time to get the stick under me properly, but I got there, and then it was done. I carried it to the sink and laid it down, walking away to check the time on my phone. I set the timer and sat down on the edge of the bed, my leg bouncing with nerves.

It was the longest two minutes of my life.

Finally, my phone beeped and I got up, walking slowly towards the bathroom. 'Please,' I whispered aloud, not entirely sure what I was asking the universe for. The result that was best for me, perhaps?

I tried to be sneaky and stood on my tiptoes from the doorway to try to see it but it was no use. I had to walk up to it and pick it up.

And once I did, I gasped.

There was no doubt with the expensive one I had bought. It spelled out simply and clearly. No line to try to see under the light. This one clearly said in bold, black letters, 'pregnant'.

'Emily!'

I jumped out of my skin, and rushed out of the bathroom to see Izzy bouncing through the bedroom door followed by Beth.

'Sorry, I told her to knock,' Beth said, stopping short when she saw my face. She looked from me to the stick in my hand, which I left too late to move behind my back. 'Um… Izzy, actually, I need to speak to Emily about something. Go on down to the kitchen and we'll follow you in a minute.'

'But, Mum…'

'Now, please,' Beth added, more sharply. Izzy went off in a sulk. Beth took my arm and gently led me to the bed. I let her pull me down next to her. She held out her hand and wordlessly, numbly, I passed the test to her. 'Oh, Em, I know how much you wanted—' she began when she saw it then she looked at me. 'But it's complicated, huh?' I nodded. 'Come here.' She wrapped her arms around me, pulling me in for a tight hug. I leaned against her, grateful to her for knowing what I needed. I suddenly felt terribly alone, which was crazy as I had just discovered I wasn't alone at all.

'I can't believe it,' I whispered when we finally leaned back from one another. She handed me back the test and I stared down at it, the word still not sinking in. I had no idea how to feel. Instead, I looked at Beth, hoping that she could tell me. 'What am I going to do?'

'What do you want to do?'

'Speak to Greg,' I replied, without thinking. My eyes widened in surprise at what I had said.

She smiled. 'Then do that. I'll go down and have the kettle on ready. Listen, whatever happens, I'm here for whatever you need. You know that, right?'

I nodded. 'I do. Thank you.'

'No thanks needed. It wasn't that long ago you looked after me when I was the one who was pregnant,' she reminded me as she left.

That felt like a lifetime ago. I picked up my phone and called Greg, the only person who could help me make sense of this now.

'Hey, babe.'

'Hi, listen, can you talk for a minute? Where are you?'

'Yeah, I'm at home. What's up? You sound serious.'

I could hear the worry in his voice. 'I need to tell you something…'

'What is it?' He sounded as nervous as I felt.

'I just took a pregnancy test.' There was silence. 'Greg?'

He cleared his throat. 'And?'

'It's positive.'

The breath caught in his throat. 'Seriously?'

'Yes.' I nodded even though he couldn't see me. 'I'm pregnant.'

'Put me on FaceTime!'

I did as he asked and showed him the test.

He beamed. 'Em, I can't believe it! After all this time!'

I felt a tear roll down my cheek. 'I know. It's crazy.'

'It's what we always wanted. How far along are you?'

'It was the night we drank all that wine. So about seven weeks I think,' I said, remembering the last time we had slept together, and that I'd been in Glendale for a week.

'Wow.' He frowned. 'Are you okay? You don't seem excited.'

'I think I'm still in shock. And it's so strange me being up here, and you down there...'

'Well, we can change that. Let me come up to see you.'

'What about work?'

'I have this weekend off anyway so I can get the train up on Saturday, and we'll take it from there. I need to see you.' He paused and looked at me. 'You do want me to come and see you, don't you?'

I hesitated but I knew that I couldn't deal with this on my own. This was our baby, no matter what else had happened, and that had to come first now. 'Yes, please,' I said, at which a big grin spread across his face.

After we had hung up, with Greg saying he'd book a train ticket for first thing on Saturday morning, I started to cry again. I stared at the test until my eyes were too blurry to see it, then I wrapped it in tissue and stored it in the bathroom to wait until Greg could see it himself. I knew I'd done the right thing in telling him to come.

This was our baby. The one we had wanted for so long. Yes, we weren't in the place I would have wanted us to be but it had happened. Finally.

I looked up at my reflection again. 'I'm going to be a mother,' I said, and I smiled at myself through my tears.

Chapter Eighteen

In their spirit of being firmly a non-traditional bride and groom, Beth and Drew hadn't wanted big stag and hen dos. Instead, they had decided to hold a joint one, that Izzy and Harry could be part of as well. With all my life drama, I had completely forgotten that they had booked for everyone to go to Loch Ness for a couple of days.

Originally, Greg and I had said we couldn't make it as it was too much time to have off work for that and the wedding too, which was a week away. But now I could be part of it. Beth and Drew had booked three log cabins in woodlands close to the Loch and arranged a host of activities for the group. Beth told me I could stay at the Hall if I wasn't up to it, although I wasn't sure how we'd explain that to everyone, but I decided it would be better to go and take my mind off everything. I hadn't been to Loch Ness since I was a little girl and I was excited to see it again.

We set off early on Wednesday morning, a minibus arriving at the Hall to pick us up. We then made a stop in the village to collect the others joining us. The group consisted of Drew and Beth, Izzy, who was excited to have been allowed the time off school, Caroline and John, Heather and Rory with baby Harry, Brodie, Aunt Sally, Drew's friend Mike who I vaguely remembered from school, Beth and Heather's friend Kate from their college, and me. It was a gorgeous summer's morning and everyone was in good spirits ready for the trip.

I was feeling much better. The news was starting to slowly sink in and despite the nagging issue of Greg and what our future was going to be, I had wanted a baby for so long so I was determined to be happy about it. And there were three days before Greg would arrive at the Hall and I needed to make any sort of decisions about our future. Plus, I had excellent company and sunny weather to further boost my good mood. I was keeping it quiet from everyone else, and I knew Beth wouldn't tell a soul, as it was still early days. I wondered though if they could see how much I was smiling.

'Aren't you missing evening prayers tonight to be here?' I asked Brodie who sat in front of me on the bus next to Drew.

He twisted around in his seat to look at me. I had already noticed he was wearing knee-length shorts, and tried not to notice his legs under them but it wasn't easy. 'Let me guess, you don't believe that ministers deserve any time off? I thought I'd already shaken your long-held views...'

'Just making sure you aren't leaving your congregation in desperate need or anything.'

Drew turned around then. 'I bet the ladies of the congregation won't be happy.' He winked at me.

Brodie shook his head. 'I think they will cope just fine.' Drew snorted, and I hid a smile. I was sure Brodie's absence would be very much noticed but it was nice that he had come. I felt like I was with a bus full of friends.

'Shall we sing something?' Izzy suggested next to me to a chorus of groans but she started a song anyway and soon we were all joining in. It was a lively journey to Loch Ness and the bus began to wind higher and higher as we left behind civilisation and entered the woods. The scenery took my breath away. I had become so used to city living that I had forgotten how alive you could feel in such a stunning place.

The bus soon pulled up outside the cabins and I looked out of the window in awe. Perched high above the Loch, we had a spectacular view of the crystal water below, stretching out for what seemed like forever. We all jumped out of the van, grabbing our bags, and looked around.

'How fab is this place?' Heather said from beside me. She was carrying Harry as Rory unpacked the pram from the van. 'Where did you find it, Beth?'

'John recommended it,' she said, over her shoulder, as she held Izzy's hand and walked towards one of the cabins.

John shrugged in his usual casual way. 'Guy I know owns it. Gave us a good deal.'

'Well, it definitely beats camping, which was Beth's original idea,' Caroline said, handing him her large bag. She looked horrified at the thought, and I hid a smile. Not that I could blame her – I wasn't really the camping type either. Beth was much more outdoorsy than I had ever been. This seemed like a perfect compromise though, thankfully.

'Right, cabin one is Drew, Rory, Brodie and Mike. Cabin two is me, Kate, Heather, Izzy and Emily. And not forgetting baby Harry. And because they are old, Sally, John and my mother get cabin three to themselves,' Beth called out with a wicked grin at her mother. She came over to me. 'I asked my dad but, you know, it would have been a bit awkward so he's taking us out for dinner next week instead.' She leaned in closer. 'Are you doing okay today?'

'I'm fine, thanks. I'm glad I'm here.'

She smiled. 'Me too.' She turned back to the others. 'Right, race each other for the best beds!' she shouted, and then there was laughter, and scrambling to get inside the cabins. I followed slowly, not caring which bed I ended up with, letting Izzy pick the one she wanted first. She chose the largest room which she would share with Beth and Heather. She was thrilled she could sleep in a bunk bed. There were two small single rooms left for me and Kate.

I dumped my bag on the bed and looked out of the window of my room, which faced the forest. It was so peaceful I could already feel some of the tension of the past few days sliding out of me. Picking up my phone, I snapped a photo of the view and messaged Greg to say I had arrived. He had already begged me not to overdo things and look after myself, which was sweet. He was as excited about the baby as I had always hoped he would be, and it was infectious.

Beth knocked on the door and poked her head around it. 'We've booked canoeing in half an hour but you can just hang around the cabin until we come back for the picnic lunch we're having?'

'I'm pregnant, not ill,' I replied. 'I'm coming!'

'Okay but just don't capsize the boat with your extra weight,' she replied, leaving with a wicked grin on her face before I had time to throw the pillow I had grabbed from the bed at her. I wondered how much my figure would change. Looking at the mirror, I couldn't see much difference yet although I felt fuller from all the good food I'd been eating up here. I changed out of the maxi-dress I was wearing into denim shorts and a t-shirt, applied suncream, popped on my sunglasses and slipped into my Converse before heading out of the cabin to join the others minus Caroline, Aunt Sally, and Heather who were sat at one of the picnic benches with Harry. He was obviously too young to join in, Aunt Sally declared she was too old, and Caroline would clearly not be seen dead in a canoe so we waved to them and walked down the long, winding track to the Loch.

'What if the monster knocks us out of our canoes?' Izzy asked her dad in front of me. 'My friend Daisy said that can happen.'

Drew wrapped an arm around her. 'Daisy is wrong. Nessie likes canoes, she'd never knock us out. I promise. I can't guarantee your mother won't do it though, she's not the best driver.'

'I heard that!' Beth shouted from ahead.

I smiled at their family banter, it was cute. And I felt better about witnessing it now I knew about what I had growing inside me.

'I'd never heard of a joint hen and stag until they invited me,' Brodie said, hanging back to fall into step with me. I was at the back of the group, walking a little slower than I would usually, just making sure I didn't slip or anything.

'It's getting more popular, especially in London. I've been to a couple there already,' I told him, thinking back to how I'd had to grin and bear all those days out and weekends away, Greg not seeming to care that we'd never have one of our own.

'It's a nice idea. Means they could make it a family thing. Plus us, of course.'

'I definitely like the idea of doing this if I ever get married,' I said, thinking that I wouldn't be sure whether I could trust Greg and his firefighting mates alone on a stag night, which was an awful thing to admit to myself, but understandable based on what happened between him and Steph. I couldn't help but wonder if this baby might be the thing that could finally change his feelings on weddings, although I warned myself not to get my hopes up too much. He had already disappointed me more than I had ever thought possible.

Brodie smiled across at me. 'Me too.'

'Well, as a minister, you definitely couldn't have a stripper, could you?'

Brodie let out a bark of laughter. Loud enough that Beth glanced back at us curiously. 'What would my bishop say, huh?'

I smiled along with him. 'Exactly.'

'And would your boss approve of you having a stripper?'

'Molly would definitely approve of making naughty cakes for it; I've seen what she can create with her icing skills, and dirty mind,' I said, remembering a batch of hen-themed cupcakes we'd made together once. I blushed the whole time, whereas Molly couldn't stop laughing. She had a wicked sense of humour, which I loved, and seemed to only get worse as she got older. She had sent me a couple of messages to check on how I was and I owed her a phone call. I missed seeing her every day.

'I'm not sure whether to be impressed or worried about that,' Brodie replied. 'It does make me look forward to seeing your wedding cake though.'

'I just hope I can do a good job,' I said, knowing I needed to get baking it next week, and hoping Greg would be able to amuse himself at the Hall while I did just that.

'Of course you will.' Brodie gave me a confident smile. I liked that he seemed to think I could do anything, it made me think that maybe I could. He leaned in closer. 'Can I admit that I'm nervous about this? I do not have good balance, which feels like something you need to have in a canoe.'

'Just make sure you wear a life jacket,' I told him with a laugh. He looked at me in mild terror. 'Where's your faith, minister?'

'It only works on dry land,' he replied.

Chapter Nineteen

We reached the Loch itself and were greeted by two guides and a stack of canoes ready and waiting for us. The sun danced on top of the clear water, creating sparkles of light. It was easy to let all my worries slide away as I gazed out to the water. I suspected that at places like the Loch, Brodie's faith was in easy reach; even I wondered if there was something higher than ourselves creating such beauty.

We had to stop looking at it though as the guides explained where we would be going and went through some safety advice. Then we had to pull on life jackets and helmets despite the rapidly warming day before following the guides to the water where they helped us, one by one, into canoes, holding them still on the water as we climbed into them. I stepped gingerly into mine, remembering my promise to Greg to take care.

Once in the water, the canoe bobbed a little as I took the oar handed to me by one of the guides. He gave me a little push so he could help Beth into hers and I drifted out into the water a little. It was so peaceful on the Loch. I watched the others getting into their canoes and then the guides got into theirs, one at the start of our group, and one at the rear.

'Use your oars to propel you forwards!' The guide at the front, a strapping teenage boy yelled back to us as if it was the easiest thing in the world. I did as he said and was surprised that I got my canoe moving pretty easily. I looked over at Brodie and stifled a laugh to see him twirling in a circle, not going anywhere.

'Here,' I said, floating alongside him. I reached out and gave his canoe a little push, holding up an oar to show him how to dip it into the water and use it to make the boat move. He copied me and followed a little bit slower behind me but was now going in the right direction. I smiled when he gave me a thumbs-up.

Once everyone was canoeing in the same direction we moved along the edge of the Loch. The sun was beating down on my shoulders and I was glad I had put suncream on. The day was proof that Scotland did sometimes get very hot. I hoped my baby could feel what a lovely day it was tucked up inside me but I knew that was silly; it was probably only the size of a nut. Still, it was comforting to know it was in there with me. Perhaps one day I would even tell it about the time I sailed pregnant on Loch Ness.

'Any sign of Nessie?' Drew called from beside me, twisting around to see Izzy. She was doing brilliantly, speeding alongside her mum who was adding canoeing to the long list of outdoor activities she already excelled at. I was just happy to be keeping myself upright and out of the water.

'She keeps to the bottom on a hot day like this,' the guide from the back, a slightly older man, called out with no hint of any sarcasm.

I found myself looking over the edge of the canoe. The water went so far down you couldn't even begin to fathom where it ended. All I could see was my reflection and the deep, dark water below. I shivered and sat back up quickly.

Perhaps there could really be something at the bottom that we didn't know was there. I quite liked the idea of us not knowing everything that existed in the world besides us.

'You doing okay?' Beth asked in a low voice as she appeared beside me.

'It's lovely out here,' I said back.

'Oh, look out!' she cried. As I had been looking at her, I'd missed the fact that I was heading straight for Brodie's canoe. Mine crashed right into his. He managed to steady himself but the surprise meant I dropped my oar, and I couldn't get my balance before my canoe turned right over and I was plunged into the cold water. Kicking out my legs, I rose to the surface with a loud splutter as I tried and failed to grab hold of my upside-down canoe.

'Here,' Brodie called, managing to hold on to the end and pull it over towards me. I flopped on it gratefully, trying to catch my breath, coughing up some water. 'Are you all right?'

'Take hold of mine and I'll pull you back to the edge,' the teenage guide said, suddenly with us. I did as he said and we moved quickly through the water towards dry land. I climbed out of the Loch and wobbled unsteadily. I sat down as he got out of his canoe and came over. He put a hand on my back to ask how I was and suddenly I leaned over and was sick.

'Jesus,' the guide said, jumping back away from me.

'Emily, are you okay?' Drew was climbing out of his canoe and rushing over to me. 'Did you hit your head?' he asked, kneeling down beside me, worried. I could hear the others saying things, everyone abandoning the Loch to rush to my side. 'She's been sick, she might have concussion,' Drew was saying as Beth joined us.

I shook my head. 'I didn't hit my head.'

'Maybe it was just swallowing the water,' the older guide suggested, reaching us then.

I sat up on my knees weakly, embarrassment washing over me.

'I think we should take her to hospital,' Drew said.

Oh, God. 'No, seriously,' I said, firmly. 'I'm fine. It's just…' My eyes met Beth's. She was biting her lip. I really didn't want to go to hospital so, despite the fact it was far earlier than I planned to tell people, I found myself blurting out the words, 'I'm pregnant'. My eyes found Brodie's and although he looked away quickly, I didn't mistake the disappointed look on his face.

–

'Drew, I'm fine,' I repeated for the hundredth time. We were back at the cabin site and I had been planted on one of the picnic benches with a glass of cold water as Drew checked my blood pressure and pulse next to me. The others were either changing or getting the picnic ready, bustling about around us, trying not to keep checking on me but failing.

Aunt Sally sat opposite me, nursing a cup of tea and an anxious expression. 'Let him check you over, Emily. It's better to be safe than sorry.'

Drew leaned back. 'Everything looks normal but I still think you should take it easy for the rest of the weekend – no more outdoor sports unless it's gentle walking. Okay?'

'Yes, doctor,' I said. He gave me a stern look at my sarcasm. 'I promise,' I added quickly. He got up to carry his bag back into his cabin and I relaxed on the seat, glad he had stopped fussing. To be honest I wasn't used to it at all, and it made me feel uncomfortable. 'See, all okay?'

Aunt Sally smiled. 'When did you find out?'

'Only on Sunday when I did a test. That's why Greg is coming up at the weekend.' When I had told everyone Greg would be joining me, I hadn't missed the looks shared between them. Only Beth was supportive but that's because she knew the reason why. Now Sally nodded as if it all made sense. 'He's so happy. I mean, I am too, of course. It's just things are so weird right now.'

'Things never come along when we want them to, do they? For what it's worth, I'm thrilled for you. I know how much you've wanted to be a mother, and you will be an amazing one. If you take care of yourself.'

'I didn't know I was going to fall into the Loch, did I? Anyway, it wasn't the fall… it was all that bacon I had for breakfast that did it I think. Mostly, I feel fine though. It's just surreal to know there's someone growing in there.' I felt my gaze fall on Brodie. He was carrying a big bowl of potato salad outside and gave me a small smile. He hadn't really said anything to me yet. I knew it was a shock for him to hear the news. And I understood why. There was no denying there was chemistry between us but we both knew that we couldn't be anything more than friends. I hoped he would want to be that anyway. I couldn't imagine him fading from my life now but perhaps I was being too optimistic.

Caroline called Aunt Sally over as they needed her to make her special salad dressing so I took the opportunity to slide over closer to where Brodie was placing the potatoes down. 'I wish they'd let me help,' I said.

He glanced over at me. 'No need. It's almost all done now. We'd much rather you rest.'

'I'm embarrassed, to be honest.'

He stopped what he was doing and came to sit beside me. 'Why?'

'I don't like people fussing. I'm used to looking after myself, I guess. Plus, I threw up in front of everyone, which was pretty gross.'

He grinned. 'It was but you couldn't help it. And everyone here cares about you so just let them fuss, it makes them feel better.'

I nodded. 'True.' I really wanted to ask if he cared about me too but I knew that was inappropriate considering what had just happened. 'I hadn't planned for everyone to know quite so soon. I'm only just getting my head around it myself. But at least we know why I cried when I saw those bride and groom figurines.'

'Oh, yes. It's good to know it was hormones and not that you're crazy.'

'Hey!' I elbowed him as he chuckled. 'I guess things will be different with Greg coming up here,' I mused then. The dynamic of the group would inevitably have to change. Greg and I would have so much to talk about but I wanted to still be part of the wedding celebrations too.

'Is he excited?'

'We were trying for a long time so it's a shock for both of us. But a good one,' I added with a smile. 'I just wish things were better between us, you know?'

'Of course. You'll work it out, Emily. You just need to have a little faith.'

'That's your department, not mine,' I reminded him.

'I'm not talking about God, I mean faith in yourself.' He patted my hand once before getting up and going back towards the cabin.

I watched him go, wondering when I had lost faith in myself. I used to be so certain of things. That I wanted to run my own bakery. That Greg and I would get married and have a family and live happily ever after. But things got muddled along the way. I touched my stomach as the others came out with the picnic, hoping that I could get that faith back as Brodie seemed to think I would. My baby needed me to have it not just for myself again, but for it as well.

Chapter Twenty

After the enormous picnic had been demolished, our group split off into two. The first group went off to a nearby archery centre for a lesson booked by Beth, and the rest of us decided to take a stroll through the woods, following one of the marked trails.

Brodie, Aunt Sally, Caroline and John and I set off on the walk. I knew that Brodie was there to keep an eye on me after spotting him and Drew having a quiet chat but it was hard to mind when we were surrounded by such beauty. In the woods, the trees blocked the sun, keeping us cool, and a slight breeze floated up from the lake rustling the leaves. Apart from our footsteps and birdsong; that was the only sound we could hear.

'This place is idyllic,' Aunt Sally said, beside me. She kept shooting concerned looks at me but I pretended not to notice. I felt fine now that I was back on dry land and had eaten lunch. The sun warmed my shoulders and the gentle pace we moved at was perfect.

'Do you remember us coming here with Mum and Dad when I was little? We got so lost, we only ended up spending like an hour here before we had to drive home again.'

She smiled. 'Your father was always hopeless with directions. I think that's why he moved you all down to London – so he wouldn't need to drive anywhere again!'

'That wouldn't surprise me,' I said, shaking my head. 'I can't wait to tell Mum and Dad about the baby. I think I'll wait until I can do it face-to-face though – make it more special.'

'Good idea. They will be so excited.'

I smiled. She was right – they would be. Especially because I hadn't given them any hint that things were anything but rosy between me and Greg.

Caroline called Sally over then to show her some pine cones that she thought they could do something with at the Glendale shop so I wandered over to where Brodie was.

'Look,' he whispered. I followed his gaze to where a deer stood in a gap between the trees, watching us warily, the sun beaming down on top of it. My breath caught in my throat as we watched. There was a rustling sound to our left and the deer's head spun around and it was gone in an instant.

'Wow,' I said, feeling privileged to have seen it.

'Nature is amazing, isn't it?' We began walking again. 'I'm so glad Drew persuaded me to come.'

'You weren't sure?'

Brodie looked down as he navigated around a tree stump. 'I have the type of job that makes it difficult to make friends. Sometimes people are wary of having a minister come along to things for fear that it'll put everyone on their best behaviour or something.'

'Well, you know that wouldn't happen with me.' I smile. 'I wouldn't have thought of that. I suppose you work so closely with people, you can't always know when they cross over from parishioners to friends.'

'Exactly. But Drew even moved it mid-week so I wouldn't have to miss Sunday service.'

'I don't have that trouble working in a bakery – I know that everyone is just being nice to get cakes out of me,' I joked.

'People really will do anything for free baked products.' We walked on for a bit in silence, moving further away from the others. 'How are you feeling really – after earlier?'

'I'm fine.' I felt him look at me. 'Really, I promise. I must say I prefer this to trying archery though.'

'Me too. I was never very good at things involving hand-eye co-ordination.'

I snorted and he raised an eyebrow. 'Sorry. My mind went to the gutter then.' He looked away but not before I caught a slight blush to his cheeks. I hid a grin. Brodie was so easy to tease, it was becoming one of my favourite things to do. 'Can you hear that?' I asked then, pausing. I could hear the sound of running water.

'This way,' Brodie said, heading off to the side. I followed him eagerly and we found ourselves in a small clearing, in front of a waterfall trickling down rocks into a stream that wound itself through the forest. We walked over to it, stunned into silence by its beauty. 'Here.' Brodie got out two pennies from his pocket. 'This is definitely a wishing waterfall.'

'Isn't that wells or fountains?' I asked, taking one of the pennies sceptically.

He shrugged. 'Worth a shot, right?' He flipped his penny in, closing his eyes for a moment. I found myself longing to know what he had wished for.

I hesitated, feeling a little silly, but he told me to go for it. I closed my eyes and threw my own penny in. 'I wish for everything to work out the way it's supposed to,' I thought as hard as I could. It seemed to be the safest wish for me to make right now. We watched our pennies float down to the bottom, and I hoped our wishes would come true.

'There you two are!' Aunt Sally emerged from the trees followed by John and Caroline and, weirdly, it felt like some kind of spell had been broken.

–

The sun was only just starting to set over the Loch despite the fact that we were well into the evening. Drew and John had built a fire and we sat around it on the overturned logs left there for cabin users, watching the sky turn orange above the water below us. We had gorged ourselves on barbeque food for dinner and now were toasting marsh-mallows like we were kids again.

I had grabbed a blanket from my room and wrapped it around my shoulders as the air turned chilly around us. I was a little jealous of the others drinking whisky and wine, apart from Izzy of course, who sipped lemonade and little Harry who was fast asleep in his pram off to one side. My contentment floundered a little when I tuned back into the conversation around me, and I heard Caroline snap at her daughter.

'I just don't see why he has to stay. He doesn't live far away, he can get a taxi home, surely.'

'He's my dad. He's family. I want us all to stay in the Hall and have a breakfast together before we go on our honeymoon,' Beth replied, her voice quiet and calm, unlike her mother's.

'I don't mind him but the fact that he's insisting that *she* stays too…'

I looked away, embarrassed to be witnessing this argument. Caroline's husband had left her for another woman but Beth always maintained that their marriage hadn't worked for a long time and they were both a lot happier now that they were apart. I could understand though why Caroline didn't want to embrace her ex's new love.

'Why are you getting so bothered?' John asked her then, mildly, from the other log. 'They already live together, this isn't news to you, love.'

'Don't patronise me,' Caroline flung back at him. 'I know my husband ran off with another woman, the divorce is almost all signed, sealed and delivered but does that mean I have to accept him bringing her into my home, our home, and rubbing it in my face?'

I glanced at Brodie who was studying the marshmallow he was toasting very closely. It was so awkward being present for this family row. Kate and Heather started talking loudly to Izzy to try to distract her but we could all clearly hear every word. I felt bad for John. Beth had told me he had loved Caroline for many years even when she was still happily married to David so this couldn't have been easy for him. I supposed that even though Caroline was happy with John, she was still angry with her ex, and his betrayal. And I could completely understand that. Why did relationships have to be so complicated?

'Mum, you're overreacting. Why is it upsetting you this much? Dad is happy with Cathy, and you're happy…'

'It's the principle of it, Beth. It's my house and I don't see why I should have to put up with his fancy woman staying there.'

'God forbid we all actually move on or something,' John said then, standing up abruptly and walking away from the group.

'John!' Caroline called out after him but he disappeared into the trees. 'For goodness' sake. Now look what you've done!' she snapped at Beth before hurrying after John, disappearing from view.

Beth sighed. 'It's still always my fault despite how much progress I think we've made,' she hissed to Drew.

'You said we could tell stories,' Izzy piped up, going to sit between her parents. 'That would be more fun than all this arguing.'

'I'm sorry, love, you're right,' Beth said, stroking back her daughter's hair. She sighed. 'Sorry, everyone.'

'I have a good campfire story,' Brodie said loudly, clearing his throat. 'And I promise it isn't Bible-related,' he added, throwing me a little grin. I relaxed back on my log, glad he was trying to defuse the tension. We all turned to him to listen. 'It was a dark, and stormy night…'

I pulled my blanket closer around my shoulders as Brodie told us his ghost story, expertly making us all forget the argument. I could see why he was a popular minister – he told a story well and held everyone's attention in the palm of his hands. The sun set fully as he talked, the glow of the fire becoming our only light, and a delicious shiver ran down my spine.

Chapter Twenty-One

Beth let me borrow her car to pick up Greg from the train station on Saturday. My couple of days at the Loch felt suddenly far away as I battled the traffic in Inverness city centre, showing how used to peace and quiet I had become already. It was nowhere near as hectic as London, of course, but it was still a shock to my system.

I was nervous to see him. It was only my second weekend in Scotland, but so much had changed. So, coupled with the traffic, I was feeling quite frazzled when I finally made it to the station and pulled into a free parking space. Checking the time, I jumped out and hurried into the station. Greg's train should have already come in. I stopped in the doorway spotting him standing with a suitcase beside him, searching the crowd.

'Greg!' I called and waved and I saw his face light up, which relieved some of the tension I was feeling.

'There you are!' He reached out for me and pulled me in for a long, tight hug. I relaxed into his warm arms. He picked me up then and spun me around, making me squeak, before rubbing a hand across my stomach. 'You are positively glowing, you've never looked more beautiful,' he whispered into my ear.

I couldn't stop the smile his words brought to my face. I pulled back to look at him. He had stubble across his chin just how I liked it, and he smelled like home. 'How was the journey?'

'Long and boring. I'm starving. How about we find somewhere for lunch?'

'We can go into the village before we go home,' I agreed, leading him out of the station.

'Home? Forgotten all about me and London already?' He said it teasingly but his look was more serious.

'Of course not. You know what I meant,' I told him as we reached Beth's car.

'I've just missed you, that's all.' He threw the case into the boot and climbed in beside me. 'I even went to Molly's the other day for a brownie, I missed you so much.'

I looked at him, my tension returning instantly. 'And saw Steph?'

He sighed. 'No, of course not. I went in on her day off. I haven't seen her since you left, I swear. You know I wouldn't do that again. Especially not now.' He gazed at my tummy. 'You're blooming, really, babe. You look gorgeous. There's something about you... you're sexy. Really sexy.' He stroked his hand along my thigh. I was glad I had worn a long skirt and not a short one.

'We have a lot to talk about,' I replied pointedly. I didn't want him to think all was forgiven now I was carrying his baby or that we'd fall into bed together as soon as we got back to the Hall. It was annoying that he looked so good though and that pregnancy did seem to make me feel sexier. I shook my head to clear away the thought.

'I know.' He removed his hand and settled back in his seat. 'I'm not going to apologise for fancying my girlfriend like hell though, okay?' He grinned and it was impossible not to smile back at him. 'I'm going to take that smile as a sign that you still fancy me too.'

I rolled my eyes. So much for my absence having dented his ego. And yet his attitude was almost comforting in its familiarity. Something that had attracted me to him in the first place. He hadn't been like any of my exes. His confidence had made me feel confident in return. I wasn't quite sure when or how I had lost that.

We drove to Glendale village and I parked outside the pub. It was another sunny day albeit with a chill in the air. Greg took my hand as we walked in and I found myself glancing around to make sure no one I knew was there. I wasn't quite sure why. We found a table in the beer garden and Greg brought over a beer for himself and an elderflower cordial for me.

'I bet you're missing the wine already,' he said as he sat down across the table from me.

'Some men would stop drinking in solidarity,' I replied, giving him a look over my sunglasses. He just snorted and took a big gulp of the beer, draining half of it in one go. I raised my eyebrows. 'I take it you've been going out a lot since I came up here?'

'What else was there to do?'

I sipped my drink, hating that I immediately wondered if any women had been involved in these nights out of his. I never worried before, even when he was out with his work mates – although they were a rowdy lot when they were off duty and women were attracted to a group of firemen like honey to bees, I had trusted him. Now I wondered if I had just been naïve and it had always been a case of when, and not if.

'Do you know what you want to eat and I'll order when I get another beer?' Greg asked then, having already finished the pint.

'I'll have the fish and chips, please,' I replied, trying not to look surprised that he already needed a second drink. At this rate, we'd arrive at the Hall with him pissed. He sloped off inside and I tilted my face towards the sun, hoping that I was just overreacting because I couldn't have alcohol myself any more.

Over lunch, Greg asked about what I'd been doing at the Hall. I told him all about the Loch Ness trip, leaving out my fall and sickness as I didn't want him to worry, and about the wedding preparations. 'Unfortunately, I'm going to have to get baking when we get back but there's so much to do, you won't be bored.'

'I don't care as long as we're together,' he replied, making my heart melt a little bit. He finished his burger and put his cutlery down. 'You've mentioned this Brodie a lot?' The question was asked casually but I didn't miss the slight edge to his tone. A small part of me, one that I didn't like to foster, was a little bit pleased that he seemed jealous. I knew I had nothing to feel guilty about so where was the harm in letting him feel some of what I had felt after finding out about Steph?

'He's the minister, he's around a lot, what with the wedding and everything… you'll like him, I'm sure.' I took a sip of my drink.

'Ah, the minister.' He looked pleased and I hid a smile. When he saw Brodie for himself, he would definitely look a little less smug. I was certain of it. 'I'm so glad I'm here to be with you and look after you. I can't wait to take you back home after the wedding. The house has felt really weird without you.'

I chewed on a chip to refrain from having to answer. The wedding was on Wednesday, and then my extended holiday would have to be over. There was Molly and the bakery to think of, and just normal life to get back to. Which meant Greg was right – I'd be going back to London with him then. And I really wasn't sure how I felt about that. 'Can you stay up until then?' I asked, realising what he had just said. 'I thought you were needed at work?'

He shifted in his seat a little bit. 'Well… I spoke to the chief and explained that I needed to be up here after all. He was okay about it actually.' He shrugged. 'Anyway… once we're home, we can start getting everything ready for the baby. You'll need a scan, won't you, and we'll need to decorate the spare room. Turn it into the baby's room.' Greg reached for my hand and squeezed it. 'This is the best thing to happen to us, Em. You are excited, aren't you?' He seemed to notice I had gone quiet.

I was trying to take in everything he was saying. It was strange that he could suddenly stay for the wedding but I guessed he'd told his boss it was an emergency. And he had been working extra shifts for ages. I realised he was frowning at me so I threw on a smile. 'Of course I am.' Why did it feel like I had just lied to him? The thought of a baby's room… it was all happening so quickly; one minute I wasn't sure that we should be together, the next we were becoming a family. I felt like I was playing catch up with my own life.

Greg leaned across the table and I met him halfway, brushing my lips with his. He leaned back, grinning at me, pleased, as if everything that had gone wrong between us had been swept away. I was pregnant and to him that meant we had no problems any more. If he had his way, in just over a week's time, we'd soon be back to our old life together as if nothing had happened. As if he hadn't cheated on me. As if I hadn't run away to Scotland without him. Like the pregnancy test was a magic wand that had been waved over us.

The problem was, I just wasn't sure I believed in magic any more.

Chapter Twenty-Two

'You weren't kidding – this place is huge,' Greg said when we stepped into Glendale Hall that afternoon. He'd had three beers at the pub and was in a buoyant mood. I led him upstairs to my room so he could dump his bag. Beth had offered another spare room if I wanted him to sleep there but I knew that would cause a huge argument – plus she'd be needing the room for her wedding guests anyway. 'I can see why you've been in no hurry to come home now,' he said, looking out at the view from the window and then sinking down onto the bed. 'Come here,' he added, patting beside him as he stretched out on his back. 'Please, babe,' he pleaded when he saw me hesitate.

Resigned, I walked over and climbed onto the bed next to him. He held an arm out so I nestled in against his chest as I had done so many times before. His nook felt warm, familiar and safe and I felt more confused than ever. 'I know you're really excited about the baby, and I am too, but I'm nervous about… us,' I said, closing my eyes as I spoke.

'Why?' he whispered, brushing back my hair.

'You cheated on me and I'm scared you'll do it again,' I replied honestly. 'I don't know if I can trust you.'

'I promise I wouldn't do that. We're going to be a family like we always wanted.' He pulled me closer and kissed my hair. 'I'll never hurt you again.'

I wanted to believe him. So badly. I lifted up my head to look at him but his eyes were closed and then I heard a gentle snore. He had fallen asleep. 'Seriously?' I said, out loud. I ducked out of his arms but he didn't stir so I climbed off the bed. So much for us having an honest chat. He seemed so sure that everything was now sorted out because I was carrying his child. But why was I still so uncertain?

I shuffled out of the room and headed downstairs, leaving him sleeping, so I could get on with my baking.

'There you are,' Beth said from the kitchen table when I wandered in. She was nursing a cup of coffee, Izzy reading next to her. 'Did you not pick Greg up?'

'I did. He's fallen asleep,' I replied with a roll of my eyes.

'Oh, well, train journeys are tiring, I guess.'

'So are three beers over lunch.'

Beth chuckled. 'Well, at least he's here safe and sound.'

'I'm going to do some baking. You can stay over here as long as you don't peek at what I'm doing,' I said, sternly.

'Yes, ma'am,' she said with a giggle. 'I need to ring the florist actually. I can't believe the big rehearsal is the day after tomorrow. There still seems to be so much to organise. Remind me not to get married ever again!'

I walked over to the kitchen, nerves prickling down my back. That meant Brodie would soon be at the Hall, at the same time as Greg. I was worried about the two of them meeting and was not quite sure why. Perhaps I wanted Brodie to like Greg, to think well of him, to believe I was doing the right thing in going back to him. Somehow his opinion had become important to me in such a short space of time.

'Can we bake something to have now?' Izzy called over, putting her book down at the hint of baked goods coming her way.

'You can, I'll supervise,' I called back. Izzy rushed straight over, rolling up her sleeves, and pulling on her apron eagerly. I helped her gather the ingredients for shortbread as I started to mix up a cake mixture. It was still too early to bake the sponge layers properly but I decided to make up one just so I could be sure I had the recipe exactly right for the real thing. Izzy turned on the radio and I relaxed straight away as we started mixing ingredients. I loved how baking made me forget everything that was going on and let me just focus on it instead. I needed the distraction.

'All ready for the oven,' Izzy said then, oblivious to my inner turmoil. I slid her tray of shortbread in the oven and put my sponge in. 'I'll grab my book to read while we wait,' she said, hurrying out of the kitchen.

Beth finished her call with the florist so I took over a cup of coffee for her, and tea for me. 'How are things with Caroline and John?' I asked her. I hadn't seen them since we returned from the Loch.

'Not great. Mum can't understand why her still being angry with Dad and Cathy hurts John, and John can't understand why she can't move on from what happened and just be happy for them. It's complicated, I guess. Mum was married to Dad for so long, she's hurt by what he did but she really loves John, I know she does. The problem is, they hid how they felt for so long that now they don't have to, I'm not sure they quite know what to do. I feel like banging their hands together to be honest!'

'I can see why. No one can tell you how you're supposed to feel though, can they? I don't blame your mum for not wanting to spend time with Cathy. Even if she is happier without your dad, it was a betrayal and she'll always remember that.'

Beth gave me a sympathetic look. 'The difference between forgiving and forgetting?'

'Maybe you can't ever really do both.' I was, of course, thinking of Greg sleeping upstairs. If I did forgive him for Steph and focused on raising our baby together, I wasn't sure I'd ever fully forget what he did. It would always be there between us, our relationship forever changed by it however hard we worked to get past it. He cheated on me and we would never be able to erase that fact.

When Izzy returned, I mixed up the dark chocolate buttercream I wanted to use for the cake and took it over to the table to give her some on a spoon to try. 'What do you think?'

'That is so good, Emily,' she said as she swallowed.

'Can I have a taste?' Beth asked. 'Pretty please?' she begged me.

I shook my head. 'Okay then.'

She grabbed a spoon. 'Oh wow, that's delicious. And the sponge is lemon?'

'With a hint of lavender,' I confirmed.

She squeezed me around the waist. 'It's just perfect, thank you!'

'Wait till you see the finished cake,' I said, smiling. I couldn't wait for her to see it.

'You really are a baking genius,' she said. I took a bow, and Izzy clapped me. I really hoped the cake would be perfect for Beth and Drew – they deserved it.

When the sponge and biscuits were done, we pulled them out of the oven and waited for them to cool. Izzy went back to her book as I sat at the table with her and Beth and sipped a cup of tea. The afternoon had turned grey and cloudy outside. I wondered how long Greg would sleep for. We were meant to have a family dinner tonight and I wanted him to be in a good mood for it so I left him up there.

'Oh no, Ginny!' Izzy said, suddenly, jumping up. I craned my neck to see Izzy's cat jumping up on the kitchen counter. I rushed after Izzy who managed to grab the cat before she took a bite out of anything.

'That cat is a menace,' Beth said as Izzy opened the kitchen door and shooed her outside. 'I never believed that a cat could have a sweet tooth until we got her.'

'That was a close call,' I said, as I touched the sponge. 'I think we're all ready over here.' I put the cut-up shortbread onto a plate and Izzy carried them to the table to ice them with Beth. I poured buttercream over the sponge and then cut off a slice. I took a bite and let out a moan. It was delicious. I beamed at it. With all the complications in my life, at least this cake was a triumph.

Taking a photo of it, I sent a message to Molly to tell her what I had made.

Her response came through almost immediately:

> **We are so making this at the bakery when you get back! We'll call it Emily's Excellent Cake xxx**

I smiled and typed a reply back.

> **Only if I get fifty per cent of the profits! Xxx**

> **Twenty-five per cent and you've got yourself a deal! ;)**

I shook my head – always the negotiator. But that was how she had made the bakery such a success. I tried not to feel a prickle of jealousy. My cake would be sold at her bakery and not at one of my own. But now I had a baby on the way, how could I ever make the bakery dream come true anyway? I had always loved working at Molly's, I needed to be happy with what I had.

'Emily, come and have a biscuit with your tea,' Izzy called to me. I slipped my phone in my pocket and joined them, trying to ignore the sudden sinking feeling in the pit of my stomach.

Chapter Twenty-Three

When I went back to my room, Greg was finally stirring.

'Hey, lazy bones. I'm the pregnant one, not you – I should be the one napping the day away,' I teased, going over to perch on the edge of the bed.

'Obviously, seeing you made me so content I fell asleep,' he replied, yawning and stretching as he sat up.

'More like it was all that beer at lunch.'

He frowned. 'Don't start nagging me.'

I raised an eyebrow. 'I wasn't. I was joking,' I told him, surprised that he looked so annoyed. Although then I wondered if I was really joking. With a sigh, I got up, hating that things always descended into an argument with us now. 'It'll be dinnertime soon so let's get ready.'

'I have to change for dinner? Is the queen coming?' He grinned though and climbed off the bed.

'Wear whatever you like,' I replied. 'I'm just covered in flour and butter.' I went into the bathroom. 'Oh God, I forgot! I saved this for you to see.' I came back out holding my pregnancy test.

'I love you but I don't really want to touch that,' he said, coming over. He wrapped an arm around my waist. 'I can't believe it's really true.'

I looked at him, and how happy he was, and felt my earlier tension leave me a little. 'It's what we always wanted.'

He leaned in and kissed me gently, pulling me closer and deepening the kiss when I didn't pull away. My body responded to him automatically. 'Let's just stay up here,' he pleaded, burrowing his face in my hair.

'Everyone is excited to see you,' I lied, ducking out of his arms and heading for the shower. I wasn't ready to lose myself in his embrace quite just yet.

'Room for two?' He asked, trying to follow me.

'You mean three,' I replied, touching my stomach, smiling as I closed the door firmly on him. I sank against it and sucked in a breath. It would be so easy to settle back into our relationship and I didn't know why I was holding back. I mean, we were having a baby, I owed it to all three of us to fix things, to make it work again. Didn't I? It was what I wanted, wasn't it?

I let the questions drift over me as I turned on the shower and stepped into the steam.

As I got dressed afterwards, my phone beeped with a text. I looked at it and sighed. It was Hazel. To be honest, all thoughts of our London friends had drifted away since I had been up here. I didn't feel like I had to compete with anyone in Glendale, unlike how I often felt with them.

> Hey lovely, I just heard what happened! OMG are you okay? I'm here if you need to talk! Xxx

I stared at it in confusion. What did she mean? 'What is Hazel on about?' I asked, showing Greg my phone so he could read the message. He was buttoning up a clean shirt, having decided to make an effort for dinner, I was pleased to see.

His expression darkened. He thrust the phone back at me. 'God, you know what she's like.'

'Yeah, but…' Then I realised. 'She knows about Steph?'

'What?' Greg asked, getting up and walking to the window, suddenly finding something interesting to look at outside.

'She knows about you and Steph?'

He took a moment to answer. 'Oh, God. I'm sorry, yeah. I went round to theirs when you'd gone. I had one too many beers with Johnny, and ended up spilling my guts to them,' he replied, slowly.

I sighed. Great – not only had I been feeling second best to them for months, but now they knew Greg had cheated on me.

'I'm sorry,' Greg repeated, coming over to slip an arm around me. 'But we'll have great news to tell them soon, won't we? Come on, let's go down and show me off to your friends. I need a drink,' he said, going to the door.

Weirdly, the thought that I'd now be part of their mummy group, that I wouldn't feel left out, that I could hang out with them as much as I wanted to back in London now, didn't make me as happy as I once thought it would have done.

–

We went into the formal dining room for dinner as there was so many of us. Beth, Drew and Izzy, of course,

Caroline, John and Aunt Sally, along with me and Greg perched around the long, mahogany table for Aunt Sally's pasta bake. There was a big basket of fresh bread and bowl of salad plus ample wine and beer, and soft drinks for me and Izzy. Everyone was in high spirits now that we were so close to the wedding, although I detected a slight stiffness between Caroline and John still after their tension at the Loch.

'How's work, Greg?' Drew asked, passing him a beer across the table.

Greg took a long swig of the beer before answering. Aunt Sally handed me a plate loaded with pasta, and my stomach growled in hunger. 'Manic, as usual.'

'I'm surprised they let you have time off,' Drew replied with a smile.

'Some things are more important than work,' Greg replied, rubbing my knee.

'Definitely. It's not easy though, is it? I had to fight to get the wedding and honeymoon off,' Drew said, smiling at Beth. 'Good job you didn't want two weeks in the Maldives or something.'

'God, the whole wedding and honeymoon thing is just such a waste of money, isn't it?' Greg said, buttering a piece of bread and rolling his eyes.

'I wouldn't say waste,' Beth said, glancing at me. 'It just depends on your priorities.'

'I think people who spend a fortune on their wedding are trying to compensate for something,' Greg added, draining his beer and grabbing another one.

'Like what?' Drew asked, interested.

I was fast losing my appetite. It was mortifying that he was airing all his views on marriage to our friends who were about to walk down the aisle, not to mention he seemed to have completely missed how his own girlfriend felt about the subject. Had he always been this clueless?

'If you're really happy together then why do you need to spend thousands just to show off to your friends and family?' Greg asked, oblivious to my incredulous look.

'Maybe you want to share your happiness with them,' I said, unable to keep the bitterness out of my voice. I glanced at the wine on the table, wishing I could drink some and erase his words.

'Then you'd just go to a registry office and down the pub,' Greg said with a shrug. 'I'm lucky you don't care about any of that stuff. We're happy just the way we are,' he said, throwing me a grin before going back to his food.

I leaned back in my chair, wondering how he could know me so little.

'Well, I'm glad you didn't want to do that, Beth,' Caroline cut in, looking at her daughter.

'You'd never have forgiven me,' Beth replied with a grin. She turned to Drew. 'Our wedding is going to perfect, right?'

He leaned in to give her a kiss. 'Definitely.'

'I can't wait!' Izzy called from the end of the table.

Conversation turned to wedding preparations and I picked up my fork and tried to carry on eating but Greg's words rang in my ears. Had I just been kidding myself to think that he might want to get married now we were having a baby? I glanced at him; he was already close to finishing another beer. I was sure he didn't used to drink this much. What was going on?

Chapter Twenty-Four

Rain greeted us on Monday morning for Beth and Drew's wedding rehearsal.

'A bad dress rehearsal always means a good show,' Aunt Sally said, briskly, carrying a basket of muffins over to the table as I walked in with Greg. We had spent Sunday wandering around Glendale, me showing him the sights before eating at the pub, and then we'd had a movie night with everyone so we hadn't had much time to talk about things. I supposed I kept putting it off and Greg certainly seemed happy to never mention our problems ever again. It was as if our not talking about struggling to have a baby had been replaced by not talking about his cheating. We appeared not to have learnt from the past at all.

'I hope so. I keep checking the weather forecast,' Beth replied, biting her lip. 'Wednesday says cloudy at the moment. Warm but cloudy. I knew I was too optimistic about the bloody Scottish weather!' She glared at Aunt Sally. 'And you said Wednesday was the luckiest day to get married on.'

'It is,' Sally assured her. 'Don't fret.'

'It says it's sunny in London this morning on my phone,' Greg said, sitting down. Beth threw him a glare but he didn't notice as he poured himself a coffee.

'It's better for it to rain today,' I said, joining them at the table. 'Gets it out of the way so the wedding day will be dry.' I reached for the rack of toast and glanced at Greg who was loading eggs and bacon onto his plate as if he hadn't eaten in a week. 'Save the rest of us some,' I said, but he just laughed. He really could be annoyingly oblivious. 'How long will the rehearsal take? I need to bake the cake today.' I'd left it as long as possible to make it to keep it fresh but we had just two days to go so it was time.

'Only an hour or so hopefully,' Beth said. 'We'll go through the ceremony with the registrar and with Brodie and where we need to be for everything. We'll be showing everyone the gazebo and the florist will be putting some of the flowers out there today. I'm having my final dress fitting this afternoon so it'll all be over by then, I promise.'

'Sounds like I'd better make myself scarce for a while,' Greg said, chewing on Sally's breakfast happily.

'That's probably a good idea,' I agreed, glancing at Beth who looked away quickly.

'Ah, Brodie is here,' Drew said as the doorbell rang. He jumped up to let him in the front door. I studied my plate, hoping my cheeks hadn't turned as pink as I thought they had. I hadn't seen him since Greg had arrived; he'd been working yesterday, obviously. Drew returned with Brodie in tow a minute later. He was wearing his dog collar with jeans and waved at us all cheerfully. 'Join us for breakfast and then we'll get started,' Drew said, bringing him over to the table.

Although the table was large, Brodie had to squeeze in next to me as we were all there, our arms brushing as he sat down. He smiled at me, and my cheeks turned pinker. 'You know everyone apart from Greg,' Drew said, gesturing to him.

'I'm Brodie, Glendale's minister,' he said, reaching around me to hold out a hand to Greg.

'Emily's boyfriend,' Greg said, shortly, giving his hand the briefest of shakes. He glanced at me but I swallowed a big gulp of orange juice to refrain from having to say anything. 'You're… young to be a minister, aren't you?' I felt Greg's glare, I was too embarrassed to look up to actually see it.

'Emily has already told me that I'm not what a minister should be like at all,' Brodie replied with a grin at me. 'Yet they let me wear the collar and everything.' He took a bite of his muffin, oblivious to Greg turning his glare on to me.

I picked up my juice and drank a big gulp. It went down the wrong way and I coughed and spluttered. Greg reached out and thumped my back. Once I had stopped coughing, I gave him a weak smile, my face now red and hot akin to a lobster's. Brodie tried to hide his grin as he poured himself some coffee but I didn't miss it. Great. Their introduction could not have gone worse.

'Right, if Emily is okay now,' Caroline said, looking at me. I nodded, wishing I could hide under the table. 'Why don't we head out to the gazebo and make a start? Sally, are you okay to show the registrar out when she gets here, please?'

I pushed back my chair, scraping it on the tiles, and jumped up. I hurried out of the kitchen, sensing Greg hot on my heels as I walked out into the hall. 'Are you sure you don't want to join the rehearsal?' I asked him.

'Well, now I'm wondering if I should,' he replied. He took my arm, stopping me in my tracks. 'You kept it very quiet that this minister you've been spending so much time with is young and... and looks like that!'

He clearly couldn't quite bring himself to call Brodie good-looking but even Greg wasn't blind to the fact that he was. 'Greg, don't be silly. He's a minister, for goodness' sake! You think he goes around preying on women who not only have a boyfriend but are also carrying that boyfriend's baby?!'

'Oh, unlike firemen. Is that what you mean?'

I pursed my lips and took a breath. 'That's not what I meant,' I said quietly, although I wasn't sure I was being entirely honest.

Greg sighed. 'You used to tell me everything. Now, I have no idea what you're thinking.' I knew part of his hostility was that I had been avoiding his touch since he got here, and it was becoming obvious to us both. He knew I was holding back but could he really blame me after what he had done?

'I'm sorry you feel like that. I'm not thinking anything. I'm going to go and help Beth with her wedding rehearsal and then bake her a wedding cake, which is what I came here to do.'

'I thought you came here to get away from me.' We stood watching one another, both suddenly weary, not sure where this argument was even going.

The doorbell rung behind Greg.

'That'll be the registrar,' Caroline said, sweeping past us through the hall.

'Right,' Greg said, stepping back from me. 'I'll head off then.'

'Where are you going?' I asked him, not wanting him to leave like this.

He shrugged and turned away. 'I'll be back later.'

'Greg, come on, please...' I reached for him but he walked past Caroline and the woman she was letting in, and slipped out of the front door. I hated it when Greg walked off like a toddler having a tantrum but I knew it was better to let him go and cool off. There was too much to do for me to worry about it so I shook off our argument and headed outside.

—

I pulled my hoodie up as we gathered by the gazebo, the rain still drizzling down on top of us. The registrar, an older lady in a smart suit, addressed the group and took us through how the ceremony would run. My attention dropped a few times, wondering where Greg had gone off to, and trying to ignore the rain plastering my clothes to my skin.

We practised walking down the aisle of chairs up to the gazebo and I watched Beth and Drew grinning at one another when they stood up there, holding each other's hands, the registrar explaining how they would say their vows. I found myself looking away. I caught Brodie's gaze below as he waited for them to finish. He gave me a small smile but I couldn't quite return it. After the initial happy feeling that accompanied my pregnancy test result, my emotions had been steadily sliding downwards and I didn't like feeling so worried and glum, it just wasn't like me.

'And that will be the end. We will sign the papers on the table you're going to set up over here while the band play, and then you'll be man and wife,' she finished up, drawing me back to what was going on.

'Are you going to catch Mum's bouquet?' Izzy asked me. 'I'd rather not do it, I don't want to get married until I'm forty.'

I couldn't not smile at that. 'I'm not sure I want to catch it either.'

'Don't you want to marry Greg?' she asked in surprise.

I coughed instead of replying as Brodie stepped up to the gazebo.

'I'll then take us through a short blessing of your marriage,' Brodie said. 'You'll stand like this...' He arranged them in front of him and brought their hands back together, giving them a brief outline of what he would be saying. He spoke softly but I had no doubt we'd all be able to hear him on the day.

'And then we can finally get a drink,' Drew said when Brodie had finished, making us all laugh. I knew he was nervous about being in front of everyone, it wasn't something that came naturally to him but I also knew on the day it wouldn't be a problem, he would only have eyes for Beth anyway. The florist jumped up then to look at the archway and we all walked down the steps back down into the garden.

The rain started to really come down then.

'Right, I think we had better all go back to the house,' Caroline said, frowning up at the sky. 'A cup of tea for everyone, I think.'

Gratefully, we all trooped back to the house, eager to get into the dry. 'Can I take over the kitchen for a bit?' I asked Aunt Sally who already had the kettle on for us all.

'Just don't make too much of a mess, I remember what you're like when you're baking,' she replied with a stern look.

'Are you free to help?' I asked, hopefully.

'As if you need my help. But, anyway, no, I'm due at the shop in a bit, I'm afraid,' she said.

'Can I help?' Izzy jumped in.

'If your mum doesn't need you.'

'Don't you want to come to my fitting?' Beth asked, to which she got a scowl. 'Fine, stay with Emily. Mum can take me.'

'I'm off to work.' Drew dropped them both a kiss before hurrying out, followed by the florist and registrar, and then Caroline and Beth left to pick up the wedding dress.

'What about the tea?' Aunt Sally spun around, hands on her hips as she stood with a tray of cups.

'I'll take one off your hands before I have to walk back to the vicarage in this rain,' Brodie replied. He leaned against the counter as she passed him one before walking off, muttering about everyone.

'I'll just tie my hair up,' Izzy said, rushing off out of the kitchen.

'So, you finally got to see me minister-ing,' Brodie said when we were alone. I took a sip of my tea, leaning opposite him, wrapping my hands around the mug to warm them up. I was happy I'd be in the kitchen for the rest of the day after that.

'Minister-ing? Is that a word?' I smiled over my mug. 'Maybe I should come and see you in action properly doing a service.'

'When was the last time you went to church?'

'A few months ago for a wedding in London. But I'd be supporting a friend so it's different.'

'Well, you'd be very welcome.'

'Right, I'm ready to bake!' Izzy cried then, hurrying back in. 'Are you helping too, Brodie?'

'I should head off,' he replied, grimacing at the rain that was now pelting down the window in thick sheets.

'Stay until the rain eases or someone can give you a lift at least, you'll get soaked,' I said. 'Right, what do we need? Eggs, butter, and what else?' I asked Izzy who rushed to the fridge to gather the ingredients.

'I warn you, I'm not much of a baker,' Brodie said, rolling up his sleeves gallantly. 'I'm usually just an eater.'

'We'll make a baker out of him, won't we, Izzy? I said, giving him a smile.

'We can try,' she replied, doubtfully, making Brodie laugh.

Chapter Twenty-Five

We were stacking the three layers of Beth and Drew's wedding cake when Greg finally resurfaced. The rain was still pounding against the kitchen roof and Brodie was still at the Hall, the afternoon drifting by without us noticing as we baked and talked. Brodie and Izzy watched as I balanced the sponges on top of one another, trying to prevent the buttercream from oozing everywhere as I did so.

'This looks cosy,' Greg said as he banged open the kitchen door on his entry, making us jump.

'Oh,' I gasped, just about managing to steady the top of the cake quickly. 'You're lucky I didn't just drop this on the floor!'

'Oops,' Greg said, walking over. I could tell immediately that he was drunk. He swayed, grabbing hold of the counter as he leered at us and the cake. 'We can't have the precious Beth and the amazing Drew's cake ruined now, can we?'

I could feel Brodie's concerned gaze on me and my cheeks started to burn. I righted the cake and stood back from it, turning to Greg. 'No. The people who have been kind enough to let us stay in their house, who are celebrating their wedding in two days, do not deserve to have anything ruined. Especially by you.'

Greg held both hands up. 'Well, excuuuuse me. I just came in for a drink anyway.'

'Don't you think you've had enough?'

The back door opened then and in walked Caroline and Beth, their cheerful chatter fading when they saw our faces. 'Everything okay?' Beth asked, tentatively, trying to work out what was going on.

'Fine. Until everyone invaded the kitchen. I'm doing the cake, everyone out,' I said, trying to keep my tone light and teasing although my patience was fast evaporating. I turned to block the cake from Beth's view.

'Of course, of course,' Caroline said, hurrying past. 'We'll stay out of your way. Come on, Beth, don't ruin the surprise now. Greg, Brodie, why don't you join us too? And Izzy, we need you anyway to try your dress on again...'

'But I was helping,' Izzy started to protest.

'Emily has had enough help for today,' Caroline told her, firmly.

Greg looked at me but I turned away so he let himself be led out by Caroline, who was a hard woman to argue with at the best of times. She successfully ushered everyone out of the kitchen in record time, leaving me alone with the cake. I sagged against the counter. I was beginning to regret Greg coming to stay. I thought he was excited about the baby so why was he acting like this? And drinking so much? I was sure he hadn't drunk that much at home. Or had he? He certainly had been going out more than ever before. I had put it down to the strain in our relationship but maybe I shouldn't have been so accepting of it. Especially now that I knew he'd cheated on me on one of those nights out. I had been in denial about a lot of things regarding our relationship, and I knew I needed to stop that now.

Trying to take my mind off our problems, I started to spread the icing over the sponge, wishing life was as easy to make pretty as decorating a cake was. Time passed as I worked and I managed to calm myself down somewhat, until there was a knock and Caroline popped her head in. 'We're going to order pizza for everyone. Why don't you join us when you've finished in here?' she said, kindly.

'Thanks.' I smiled at her. 'I won't be long.'

'Ah, Greg, I don't think…' Caroline stepped back as the door swung open fully and Greg reappeared.

'It's okay,' I reassured her. She threw Greg a warning look before leaving us alone.

Greg shuffled over to me. 'Babe, I'm sorry. I know you want the cake to be special,' he said, glancing at it. 'It looks great. Really.'

'Thank you,' I replied, picking up a flower to place on it. 'I'll be in soon, okay?'

'Good, because I don't want to be with them, I want to be with you. And it's pretty insufferable in there with all the wedding talk. Even that minister is at it.'

'Some people are excited about the wedding,' I said, trying to keep my tone light but anger was bubbling up inside me again. Why did he have to be quite so down on weddings?

'I just can't wait for it to be over and to have you home, that's all.' He tried to wrap an arm around my waist but I pulled away and went to the fridge for more iced flowers. He sighed but I ignored that. 'Em, why are you being like this?'

I shut the fridge and faced him. 'Like what? Greg, you're acting all over the place. You're drunk, for one thing, and for the other, you're acting like a spoiled child. I'm baking a wedding cake, for goodness' sake! Why is that such a problem for you?'

'Because everything is more important to you than us!'

'That's not true but I can't just pretend the past two weeks didn't happen like you seem able to do. You cheated on me. You broke my heart,' I told him, feeling a lump rise up in my throat.

'God, you're going to throw this back in my face forever, aren't you!' He turned and started to stomp out of the kitchen.

I followed him. 'What the hell do you expect? I can't just move on like that. We need to talk, to work at this…'

Greg spun around. 'I'm sick of talking. That's all we do.'

'So, what then? We just pretend that everything is okay? You think that will really work?'

He looked defeated for a moment. 'I don't know what will work. I thought we loved one another.'

'Sometimes love isn't enough.'

Greg opened his mouth to say something but then I heard a noise behind me. I spun around to see a streak of fur as Izzy's cat jumped up on the counter.

'Ginny, no!' I screamed, rushing over to see the cat lick the top of the cake. I tried to grab her but she bolted in fear, kicking her back legs out as she jumped down, knocking the cake. I watched in horror as time seemed to slow down into painful slow-motion and the top layer of the cake slid off the others and crashed to the floor, smashing on the tiles into a gloopy mess.

'Shit,' Greg said, from behind me.

Sinking down onto the floor, I knelt beside the ruined cake. 'You let the cat in,' I said, my voice shaking. 'You let the bloody cat in.'

'Hey, I didn't know,' Greg said, on the defensive immediately.

'Just go. Please. Just leave me alone.'

'Fine by me,' he spat out, and marched out of the kitchen, leaving me to burst into tears.

Chapter Twenty-Six

'Are you sure?' I wiped the fallen tears from my cheeks. Beth and Brodie had come rushing into the kitchen after hearing what had happened from Greg. Brodie immediately offered to help me redo the top layer so I could get it done before bed.

'Of course! Nowhere else I'd rather be,' he replied, rolling up his sleeves again. 'Just please bring us some pizza when it comes,' he added to Beth.

'We could all help?' Beth asked me.

I shook my head. 'Honestly, too many cooks and all that… plus I want it to be a surprise still. Thanks, Brodie, it would be great to have a hand.' I glanced at Beth. 'Where's Greg?'

'Sinking down whisky,' she replied. 'Don't worry, we'll keep an eye on him, and the cat too.' She touched my arm. 'Are you sure you're okay? Can't you rest now and finish it tomorrow?'

'I'll just get the sponge done and finish decorating it in the morning. I won't be able to relax until that's done; it's getting tight timewise. I'm fine, I promise.' I forced a smile for her. I was exhausted but it was mostly emotional fatigue. Beth left us alone and we worked in silence, the rain easing as the evening drew on.

'Do you want to talk about it?' Brodie asked as I slid the new layer we had mixed together into the oven. Beth had brought in a large pizza for the two of us so we went over to the table and opened the box up. I supposed we could have gone to join the others while the cake was in the oven but I was scared to leave it alone and really didn't want to have to make conversation with everyone, especially Greg, so I was relieved that Brodie hadn't suggested it. We both put two slices on a plate and poured a glass of Coke out. I sank into the chair, grateful to finally sit down, the smell of the pizza mixed with cake making my stomach rumble loudly.

I took a bite of the cheesy pizza before answering him. 'Honestly I don't know what to say about anything right now. I like knowing what I'm doing. I'm not used to being so… uncertain. To have my life feeling so up in the air.'

'You could look at it as an opportunity – a chance to take stock, to decide what you want, and change direction accordingly. I like the fact that life isn't all mapped out exactly to plan, otherwise what's the point in even living it?'

'That all sounds good until everything starts going wrong and you kind of wish you knew that it would all be okay in the end.' I sighed. 'I'm sorry. I feel like I'm always dumping problems on you.'

'I'm used to it,' he teased. 'Honestly, Emily, I'm here for you. You know that, don't you?'

I met his gaze and nodded. I did. Which was strange, as we still didn't know each other all that well but I knew I could trust him. With anything. Reaching across the table, I found myself touching his hand. Looking into his eye, I knew he felt the warmth that I did as our fingers touched. 'Thank you,' I told him, sincerely.

'You're welcome.' He smiled and moved his hand away to reach for his drink but I didn't miss the fact. I drew back from him, trying not to feel disappointed. 'I suppose I should be heading back to the vicarage, I've been here much longer than I planned. Which I don't mind at all,' he added, quickly. 'But there's always a lot to do so...'

'Sure, you should head back,' I agreed. 'Thank you so much for staying to help me.'

He stood up and held up a hand when he saw me start to get up as well. 'Stay and finish your meal. You need the rest. I'll see myself out. I hope the cake turns out well.'

'See you at the wedding,' I said, watching him go with a weird feeling in my chest. He gave me a cheerful wave as he left, as if he wasn't bolting from me but I knew that he was. I shouldn't have touched him like that. I groaned aloud into the now empty kitchen. I seemed to be getting everything wrong.

After I finished off the pizza, the cake was ready so I took it from the oven and moved it, and the finished layers, into the utility room for which Beth had given me a key. I locked the cake up safe and sound so no one could destroy it again and then I slipped out. I heard the others still in the living room but I was too tired to go in.

I went to my room and wasn't surprised to find Greg already there, fast asleep on the bed. Relieved that there wouldn't be any more arguments tonight, I put on pyjamas and climbed in beside him. My whole body ached with tiredness. What a day. Rolling over away from Greg, I curled up into a ball and closed my eyes, hoping things would be better tomorrow.

'Emily?'

I woke up to Greg whispering my name. Opening my eyes, I saw him lying next to me, facing me in bed, sun streaming into the room behind him. 'Hmmm?' I replied, sleepily.

'We need to talk. Please.' He brushed back the hair that had fallen over my face. I nodded, trying to wake up when I saw how serious he looked. 'I think I need help,' he whispered. He put his hand over mine, which rested on the pillow.

'Help?' I was trying to catch up with him after my night of tossing and turning.

'My drinking. I think I need help.' He let out a small sob and instinctively, I pulled him into my arms.

'What's going on?' I asked him as he cried, wide awake now.

'It's all got out of control. Not only did I end up cheating on you but...' He sobbed again. 'I've been suspended from work for two weeks for coming into work pissed. I don't even remember how I got there.'

Oh, God. 'Greg... how... why are you drinking so much?'

'I just wanted to forget, I suppose.' He lifted up so we were face-to-face. 'There's more.'

My heart sank. 'What is it?'

'I'm in a lot of debt. I borrowed, and I'm struggling to pay it all back. Drinking helps me, I don't know, forget about it all. And I suppose after you left, I just couldn't cope. I wanted to numb everything. And now I don't think I can stop.'

'Why are you in debt, though? Why did you have to borrow money?' I was confused. It wasn't like he'd been splashing out money lately. We hadn't been on holiday for a year and hadn't done anything major to the house. Neither of us earned a fortune, of course, but we'd never struggled before and he'd been working all those extra shifts too.

'I've been gambling. I think I might be addicted,' he burst out with a sob and buried his head back down onto my chest.

'Shhh,' I said, my heart dropping. I stroked his hair as he broke down completely. Suddenly, it all made sense. Why things had been so rubbish between us the past few months, the cheating, his working more and more shifts, and going out so much... And that text from Hazel. She had obviously known what had happened at work from Johnny. I wasn't sure what I felt most in that moment. Disappointment. Anger. Pity. Fear. A tear rolled down my own cheek.

'What are we going to do?' he asked me when he'd managed to quieten his tears.

And I had no idea how to answer him.

Chapter Twenty-Seven

Beth and Drew's wedding dawned dry and sunny. I woke up early after another fitful night's sleep and looked over at Greg who was thankfully still dreaming. He was shattered. As was I. We had spent the past day talking everything over, and it had been exhausting for us both.

Greg came clean about everything. He said he had always enjoyed a gamble and a drink but it had got completely out of control. He said he had felt hopeless about not being able to give me a family so he had gone to the casino one night with his workmates and he had become addicted to the thrill of it all, always thinking he could make back what he lost, and then of course never doing that. He had borrowed money to pay his debt to the casino from some loan shark who charged ridiculous interest, and was now struggling to pay him back. Drink had become his way to bury his head in the sand. And, naturally, that had led to even worse decisions like hooking up with Steph in the club, and turning up drunk to work.

In a weird way, Greg seemed better now he had told me everything, as if a weight had been lifted from his chest, and he seemed to think that together we could solve it all and get back to how things were before. I was less sure of that. Obviously, we needed to work out how we were going to sort out the debts he had got us in, and find him help for both his drinking and gambling problems, but that was easier said than done. I was even less eager to leave the comfort of Glendale Hall for London now but I couldn't be like Greg and stick my head in the sand. We had to sort it all now before it got any worse. Once the wedding was over, I would have to leave with him.

Climbing quietly out of bed, I slipped out of our room, needing some time alone before the big day took over. Today wasn't about our problems, I wanted it to be a happy day for my friends, and to be honest I needed a day of being normal and happy myself before real life took over again.

Walking downstairs, I went into the empty kitchen and made myself a cup of tea. Carrying the mug, I let myself out of the back door and stepped out into the garden. It was already warming up and the sun beat down on me from the cloudless blue sky. Aunt Sally had been right about Beth having weather luck today. It looked like it was going to be a beautiful summer's day.

I went to one of the benches and sat down with my tea, looking out into the grounds that would soon be filled with well-wishers.

Sipping my tea, I thought over the past twenty-four hours. My head hurt with it all but at least I knew everything now. I touched my stomach. I hadn't even thought about the baby since Greg's confession. It felt like my happiness over being pregnant had been snatched away. Greg still saw it as our saving grace though. The thing that was going to pull us through it all. I didn't know that I agreed with him about that, but he needed my help and I would give him that.

'What are you doing up?'

I turned to see Aunt Sally coming out to join me. 'It's just so peaceful out here.'

'Would you rather be alone?'

'No. Sit down, please.'

Aunt Sally sat down and sipped her coffee. She smiled as she looked out at the grounds. 'I've always loved this garden. I don't think I could bear to ever leave it.'

'Why are you thinking about leaving it?'

'I suppose I'm feeling retirement calling me a little bit. It's getting harder to do all the jobs in the house. Caroline has hired a girl from the village to do some cleaning and ironing twice a week but I feel like they need a more capable housekeeper. Not that she would ever say that though, bless her.'

'They'd never let you leave. I'm sure of that.'

Aunt Sally smiled. 'I'm just an employee at the end of the day. I'm not family.' She touched my hand. 'And how are you feeling about leaving Glendale again?'

I sighed as I swirled the tea around in my mug. 'Like you, I'd happily stay here. It feels like we're in a bubble up here, like you could shut yourself away from the world, and right now, I want to do that more than anything.'

'Sadly, the real world will always find its way in. Even here. You've come to stay when things are the happiest they've been in a long time but not that long ago, things were tough here too. Beth was estranged from the family, and then old Mrs Williams passed away... plus Caroline and David's marriage was on the rocks. It was a hard time but we all got through it. As will you.'

'The problems with Greg... they're worse than I thought,' I admitted. 'He's in real trouble. When we go back to London, I need to help him sort everything out. If I can.' I sighed. 'I just don't know if we have a future now.'

'I'm sorry, Emily. But you need to think about you and this baby you're carrying. You need to do what's right for the two of you.'

I nodded. 'I know. That doesn't make it easy though, does it?'

Aunt Sally smiled. 'No. No, it doesn't. Are you going to talk to your parents?'

'When I get back, I'll go and see them, and tell them what's going on. I really didn't see any of this coming.' I smiled wryly. There was so much I wanted to talk to them about, and I wasn't sure quite where I would start. 'I used to have everything all planned out, and now I have no idea what's going to happen.'

'Life happens when you're busy making plans.'

'You can say that again.'

The door behind us opened again and out came the bride-to-be, holding a mug of coffee in her hands. 'Room for one more?' she asked with a smile.

'Of course,' Aunt Sally replied as I waved her over.

She sat down opposite us. Like us, she was still in her pyjamas, her long, dark hair tied up in a ponytail. 'I couldn't sleep,' Beth admitted. 'I didn't think I'd be nervous. After all, this day is something I've fantasied about since I was sixteen and met Drew, but I'm terrified.'

'It's only natural,' Aunt Sally reassured her. 'When I married Alec, I was actually sick with nerves and look how happy we were.'

'God, I'd better not eat much then,' Beth said with a laugh. 'At least the Scottish weather is playing ball, huh?'

'It's going to be perfect,' I told her. I didn't feel envious any more. Beth and Drew were special people and they deserved a special day.

'Are you really leaving us on Friday?' Beth asked, grimacing.

'I have to but I can't thank you enough for having me here. I needed this trip more than I even knew.'

'Well, you're always welcome here, you know that. We're all going to miss you. Especially someone whose name I won't mention.' The glint was back in Beth's eyes.

I shook my head. 'You're shameless, Beth Williams.'

'I won't be a Williams for much longer,' she replied, cheerfully.

'You'll still be shameless,' I said.

'Just promise me you won't leave it so long next time. That you'll be back soon?' she said then, more seriously.

I thought of all that awaited me back in the city. I wasn't sure when I would even be able to think of Glendale again but I nodded. 'I promise,' I said. I knew that I wanted to come back soon. Glendale was hard not to love, after all. I just hoped I would be able to keep my promise.

'What are you all doing out here? We need to start getting ready!' Caroline called, flinging open the back door. 'The hairdresser will be here soon. You need a shower, Beth. Now!'

Beth shook her head. 'I'm about to become a married woman but some things never change,' she said under her breath to us. 'Okay, Mum, I'm coming!' she called back to her mother. 'We'd better be having champagne soon,' she added to us as she climbed off the bench. We both chuckled as we watched her go inside, and then there was no more time for peace, we had a wedding to get ready for.

Chapter Twenty-Eight

'You look lovely.'

I stepped in front of the full-length mirror, Greg behind me doing up his tie. And I smiled. The dress Beth had found me was so pretty and I did feel good in it. I had had my hair curled so it fell gently over my shoulders, and my make-up had been done for me so my skin glowed. I had no sign of a bump yet but I did think I'd put on a couple of pounds, probably mostly due to Aunt Sally's food. The tea dress skimmed my stomach perfectly though. I looked really well. I could get used to this pregnancy thing. I turned around and despite myself, I smiled. 'And you look very handsome.' I helped him straighten up his tie. I had always loved Greg in a suit. 'We scrub up well.'

'You'll keep an eye on me today, won't you?' Greg asked me then, a little nervously. 'Make sure I don't drink?'

I nodded. 'Of course. We will both stay away from drinks today. It's going to be a lovely day. Try to relax if you can. Let's enjoy ourselves, okay?'

He smiled a little. 'Okay, babe.' I wasn't used to him being so agreeable but he was trying hard not to rock our delicate boat any further and I appreciated that.

'Right, let's go.' We walked downstairs together where Greg gave me a quick kiss on the cheek. I watched as he went out into the garden. Guests were starting to arrive – a sea of suits and pretty summer dresses walking across the lawn towards the stream where the ceremony would take place. I turned into the living room where the wedding party was assembling for our walk down the aisle.

Stopping in the doorway, I broke into a smile. Beth stood in the centre of the room, the make-up artists finishing off her red lipstick. Her hair was up in an elegant chignon, and clipped to it was a lace veil. Her dress was stunning: a long, off-the-shoulder delicate lace white gown. Like the lemon bridesmaid's dresses, it had a vintage feel to it, and she looked so beautiful in it. Izzy stood by her in her pretty dress, and Heather was in her long one, sitting on the sofa with a glass of champagne. 'Beth, that dress is so gorgeous,' I said, walking into the room.

Caroline was dabbing her eyes. 'I thought she was going to wear some sort of black dress or a really short one or basically something weird,' she said, between sobs.

Beth grinned. 'I have no idea why.' She winked at me. 'So, I'll do then?'

'Mum, you're like a princess!' Izzy declared, answering for all of us.

Someone cleared their throat in the doorway. We turned to see Beth's father, David, standing there in a grey suit as all the men in the wedding party were wearing, a lemon rose in his buttonhole. 'Is it safe to come in?' he asked. He went over and kissed his daughter. 'I couldn't be prouder,' he told her. 'You all look lovely too!' His eyes fell on Caroline in her cream suit and he gave her a small smile. She didn't quite return it but nodded at him, evidently trying to be on her best behaviour today. It must be so strange to be in the same room as someone you were married to for so long but were now estranged from.

'Here we are!' the florist swept in then with our bouquets. The bridesmaids' bouquets were made up of lemon and white flowers with dark red roses, some of which had been grown in the grounds, and Beth's was a more dramatic version with flowers trailing down the front of her dress. She took it from the florist with a big smile. She couldn't stop smiling. It was so lovely to see.

'Time to go I think,' Beth said then. She looked at us. 'Thank you for being part of our day. It means the world to us.'

'Oh God,' I said, reaching for one of the tissues on the coffee table.

'Don't ruin your make-up yet!' the make-up artist cried out frantically, rushing over to me to check my eyeliner hadn't run.

'I'm sorry. No more speeches,' Beth promised. 'Let's go.'

We left the Hall and started our procession down to the stream together. Glendale Hall watched us go, seemingly giving us its blessing as we left it, the sun high in the sky above. It felt really special to be in the place Beth had grown up in and loved so much for her wedding. It was the perfect choice of venue for her and Drew. Beth walked in front, her arm through her father's, followed by Caroline and Izzy holding hands, and then me and Heather walking side-by-side, smiling across at one another.

As we approached the stream, we saw all the guests sitting on the white chairs in front of the gazebo where the registrar and Drew stood waiting. Rory was, of course, by his brother's side, both in sharp grey suits. Yellow, white and dark red flowers were draped everywhere, and the archway where they would stand to say their vows was covered in flowers, the scent and sight of which were breath-taking. The choir were lined up to one side, the stream behind them glistening in the sunshine, singing as we reached the makeshift aisle. My eyes found Greg first, sitting near the front, twisting around to look at us, and then I saw Brodie right at the front ready for his blessing, smiling happily, and my heart started to speed up.

The choir began to hum the 'Wedding March' as Beth reached the aisle. We followed slowly, the guests beaming at our party. I looked up then and saw Drew's face as he saw Beth for the first time. Happiness spread across it, and I felt another lump rise up in my throat. They were such special people, it was wonderful to see them look so happy. I couldn't help but hope that one day, I would get my own happy ending as well. I just had to decide what I wanted it to look like.

Beth stepped up onto the gazebo and Drew took both of her hands in his. 'I love you,' I saw him mouth to her.

'Forever,' Beth mouthed back.

We sat down in the front row and the registrar stepped forward to welcome us to the ceremony. Beth and Drew said their vows, both unable to take their eyes off one another and the choir sang again as they stepped to the side to sign the marriage certificate. I glanced back then at Greg who gave me a little wave. When I turned back, I met Brodie's gaze. He quickly looked away.

Once Beth and Drew were officially married, they returned to the gazebo where Brodie gave them his blessing.

'Marriage is something that takes hard work. You are starting off on a long journey together today, one that will be filled with joy and laughter but one that will likely be tested a lot as well. Your commitment today is that you will make it through those tests together, side-by-side, partners through the good and the bad, looking after one another, and always remembering the vows you made today. Love is special, and you should both cherish that love. Not everyone finds such a love in their lives so I hope you both appreciate the blessing that your love is, for the rest of your lives,' Brodie said. 'And now we pray...'

I bowed my head as he prayed for Beth and Drew, his words echoing in my mind. Love was special and it was a gift when you found it but how many tests were too many to come back from? Love was worth fighting for, I believed that, but it also shouldn't only be about fighting either. How did you know when you had found the love that you would never give up on? Perhaps if you even had to ask the question then you hadn't found it after all?

Beth and Drew kissed then to an enthusiastic round of applause from everyone. We all stood as they walked hand-in-hand down the aisle as a married couple. I glanced at Brodie who watched them with an almost wistful look on his face. I turned back to Greg who was looking out to the stream, not paying them any attention.

The rest of us filed out of our seats to make the short walk to the marquee for the reception. Greg waited for me and took my hand as we followed the guests across the lawn. 'I saw you dabbing your eyes,' he teased me.

'I couldn't help it, I'm really happy for them.'

He leaned in closer. 'Maybe that will be us one day.'

I was so stunned, I couldn't form a response. Thankfully, Izzy bounced over to lead us to the top table inside the marquee, and I didn't have to.

Chapter Twenty-Nine

The wedding marquee was full of life.

Everyone was talking while a pianist on the small stage played background music, and servers dished out the wedding meal of bruschetta, followed by salmon and new potatoes and chocolate brownie and ice cream for dessert. I kept looking at the wedding cake on the table close to where we sat, proud of what I had created. Beth and Drew had already told me how much they loved it, and it fitted in with the lemon and maroon theme in the tent perfectly. More flowers were inside, lending their lovely colour and scent to the proceedings and fairy lights were draped all across the ceiling ready for sunset. I watched Greg closely, relieved to see that he was sticking as promised to soft drinks like I was.

And then it was time for the speeches. A waiter brought round glasses of champagne ready for toasting, and I failed to prevent him from putting a glass in front of both of us.

'Greg...'

'Relax. We have to take a sip for the toast,' he said, squeezing my thigh. 'I'm doing okay, I promise.'

I couldn't say anything else because Rory had stood up and was clinking his glass for silence. I was unconvinced that Greg would be able to handle it but I didn't want to cause a scene, which me taking the glass from him would inevitably create.

'I wish I could stand up here and regale you with hilarious stories of my brother's exploits but annoyingly, he has always been too sensible for that. Unless you count the time that he came home to the farm drunk when he was a teenager and managed to open the gate where the pigs were. We woke up to pigs in the kitchen eating all our food. And Drew tried to convince me they must have managed to open the pen themselves!'

We all laughed as Drew shook his head. 'But, seriously,' Rory continued. 'My brother has always been hard-working, kind, and fiercely loyal. I missed him a lot when he was in America studying to become a doctor so having him back in Scotland has been great. And that's all thanks to Beth and Izzy. I don't think many people end up marrying someone they have loved since they were teenagers but Beth and Drew both like to do everything differently to the rest of us. And that's why they are perfect for one another! Raise those glasses then to my kid brother who has gone and married the love of his life, and I couldn't be happier for them both. To Drew and Beth!'

We all stood and echoed the toast. I took a sip of my champagne and out of the side of my eye, saw Greg throw his back and drain it in one go. My heart dropped down to my stomach.

Drew stood up then, grinning at his brother. 'I think I got away remarkably unscathed by that speech, I think Heather must have edited it!' We laughed but Heather nodded so I thought he wasn't far off the truth. Drew went on to thank everyone involved in the wedding including me, and then turned to his bride and daughter sat next to him. 'I can't believe that just a couple of years ago I had no idea that I had a daughter. Everyone knows that Beth and I were apart for a long time but I don't think that either of us ever stopped loving the other one. To finally be a family with Beth and Izzy is a dream come true. I love these two with all of my heart and I want to be the best father and husband that I can for them.'

I watched as Beth dabbed at her eyes, pulling Izzy close to her.

'We have made mistakes in the past but the love we have for each other has got us through all of them and I know that will always be the case whatever happens in the future. So, please raise your glasses again to true love!' Drew leaned in to give Beth a long kiss and then he hugged their daughter tightly, and I had to wipe away another tear. This wedding was one of the most emotional I had ever been to. Beth's father and mother then both gave speeches of their own, talking about Beth growing up and how proud of her they were now. I knew that the family had had their troubles but it was lovely to see that they were all close now. That the past could be forgiven.

Greg signalled the waiter, who refilled his champagne glass as Beth stood for the final speech. I moved my leg so that Greg's hand fell off it as I kept my gaze fixed on her.

'Don't worry, this will be short and sweet so we can get the party started,' Beth said, smiling at the room. 'I just wanted to say thank you to you all for coming today to celebrate with us. Glendale has welcomed me back with open arms. I still can't believe that I spent ten years away from this place. I did a lot of things that I wish I could change in the past but I also feel like if I could, I wouldn't change any of it because everything that happened brought me here today. And today has been perfect.' She smiled at Drew and Izzy. 'There is one person missing today and she is the reason that all of this was possible. So, please raise your glasses for the final toast.' She turned back to the room and raised her glass. 'To my grandmother Margaret Williams, who believed in forgiveness and family, two things that I plan to carry with me always.'

'Forgiveness and family!' we all echoed, raising our glasses. I took another sip of mine as Greg knocked back his second glass.

I turned to say something to him but then Beth came over and touched my arm. 'We're going to cut the cake, please come with us,' she said, holding out my hand. I followed her, glancing back to see Greg sitting down and grabbing hold of my glass to finish it. Dread settled in me. I perhaps hadn't fully believed he had a real problem but now I could see it with my own eyes.

'This cake was designed by my friend Emily,' Beth said as everyone gathered around. Greg remained at our table. I looked up to see Brodie smiling at me and I smiled back, remembering his help with it all. 'It looks so good,' she said, squeezing my hand. 'Oh my God, cows!' she added when she realised what were sat on top of the cake. 'You remember?' she asked Drew.

'I'm still scared of them,' he replied, with a shudder. I smiled, pleased they had got my joke. She and Drew wrapped their hands around the knife, everyone taking photos as they cut into the cake. We all clapped and they pulled out a slice and both took a bite, laughing as the buttercream oozed out. 'Oh my God, it's so good!' Beth declared. Drew kissed her and everyone cheered.

'Now I can add wedding cake baking to my CV, right?' Brodie said, coming over to me.

'You'll be watching *Bake Off* next,' I replied with a laugh. 'I'm glad they liked it.'

'Are you kidding? It's gorgeous. I can't wait to taste it,' he said, watching as a server started to carve it up for the guests. The band began playing then, and Drew led Beth onto the dance floor. I smiled as I realised that they were going to dance to 'Isabelle' – the song that Beth named their daughter after. The song they listened to when they fell in love as teenagers. Drew spun Beth around and then pulled her close, moving in a well-practised dance that had begun when they were so young. They had been through a lot, of course, but it had all worked out somehow. I thought Brodie was right – love was a gift to cherish, and Beth and Drew were doing just that.

'Are you okay?' Brodie asked me. My eyes had filled with tears.

'Weddings, you know,' I said with a laugh, trying to brush away my tears. I glanced back at Greg who now had a beer in front of him as he leaned back in his chair.

We watched as John led Caroline onto the dance floor followed by Rory and Heather, other guests joining them. I looked over at Greg again, he was talking animatedly to David about something. 'Want to dance?' I asked Brodie, as casually as I could. My heart began to beat hard inside my chest.

'Are you sure?' he asked, one eyebrow raised.

'Please?' I held out my hand and Brodie took it without saying anything else.

We walked onto the dance floor as the band shifted into another slow song. Brodie's arm wrapped around my waist and I lifted my arms onto his shoulders. I looked at him and he met my gaze steadily. We spun slowly around in silence, and everyone around me seemed to fade into the background. All I could really hear was my heartbeat. All I could see were Brodie's eyes looking at me.

'I'm sorry,' I said, finally.

'For what?' he asked softly.

I took a moment to answer, to think of the words that would explain how complicated everything felt. I knew I had to, though. It might be my last chance. I would be back in London soon, far away from him. And that thought hurt me more than I cared to admit, even to myself. 'For not being free,' I replied, finally, opening up my heart to him for the first time.

Brodie exhaled. He looked away for a moment. We slowed then, barely moving to the music. Finally, he looked back into my eyes. 'I'm sorry for that too.'

Chapter Thirty

'Mind if I cut in, minister?'

Brodie and I stopped moving immediately, dropping our arms from one another as if we had been burned. Greg stood by us, his face stony, almost spitting out his words. Without waiting for a response, he took my waist and pulled me into his arms, spinning us away from Brodie. Over Greg's shoulder, I watched as Brodie turned and walked off the dance floor, and felt as if something had been taken away from me.

'What the hell, Em?' Greg hissed then, pulling me closer. 'I look over and see you all draped over another man!'

'I'm surprised you even noticed,' I said, coldly. 'I thought you were more interested in the drink in front of you.' I dropped my arms and stepped back out of his embrace. I hated it when couples argued in front of people but I couldn't hold my anger in check. After all his promises to get help, to change, he hadn't even been able to last two days.

'I'm fine,' he insisted. 'I've only had a couple... I can stop at that.'

I shook my head. 'You told me you have a drink problem. That means you won't – you can't – stop at two drinks.'

'You have no faith in me,' he complained, turning away and storming off. I watched him walk straight over to the bar.

Standing by myself on the dance floor, I felt eyes on me. Embarrassment and anger and sadness welled up inside me. I rushed off, needing to get away desperately. Outside the marquee, I gulped in fresh air. The sun was only just starting to slip lower in the sky.

'Emily, are you okay?'

I turned around to see Heather ducking out of the marquee after me. With everything that had been happening since I came up to Scotland, I hadn't gotten to know Heather as much as I wanted to, so I appreciated the look of concern on her face as she came to stand beside me. 'I just needed some air.'

'I couldn't help but see…'

'It's okay,' I reassured her as she trailed off, embarrassed. 'Things aren't going great with Greg. It makes it so much harder when I think of this one,' I admitted, touching my stomach.

She nodded. 'When I got pregnant with Harry, I had only just started seeing Rory. Obviously, I'd known him for a long time but still, we were only just starting out as a couple. I thought he'd run for the hills, actually, but he was even happier about it than I was. What I'm saying is, I'm sure Greg will step up to the mark. I mean, he has to, right?'

'I don't know,' I said. 'I also don't know how long I can wait around for him to do that, do you know what I mean? Can I ask you a really personal question?' I said then, turning to her.

'Uh-oh.' She smiled, though. 'Fire away.'

'Why haven't you and Rory got married? If that's too personal though, just tell me to shut the hell up.'

Heather laughed. 'I mean, you're not the first person to ask me that! Everyone assumes that Rory hasn't asked, that he's scared of the commitment but actually...' She kicked at the grass with her feet. 'It's me who keeps saying I'm not ready.'

I was surprised. I supposed it was usually the man who backed away from commitment. Like Greg. 'Why aren't you ready? Are you worried he's not The One?'

She shook her head vehemently. 'Definitely not. Rory and I are for keeps but I always pictured myself getting married at the local church with my family there. And my mother... she died a few years ago, and I just can't face the day knowing she won't be there. Rory understands but I know it upsets him too. He wants a day like this for us.'

'That must be really hard. But if it's what you want... she would want you to be happy, wouldn't she? Why don't you do it differently? Maybe don't have the massive wedding. Then maybe it won't feel like such a black hole without her.'

Heather nodded. 'Beth suggested the same thing. I'm warming to the idea. But I think I'll get this wedding out of the way first. Why the marriage question? Has Greg proposed?'

'No. I always wanted him to. But he said he didn't believe in marriage and I kind of went along with it but since I found out I was pregnant, I thought maybe he would change his mind. I wanted him to change his mind. But he's been lying to me. And now I'm not sure what I want,' I told her, honestly. 'I need to do the right thing for our baby. I just wish I knew what that was.'

'You will,' Heather promised. 'Give yourself time. It's such an adjustment when you find out you're having a baby. Everything will change. You just need to ride it out. Don't force yourself into making all the decisions now.'

'That's good advice.' I turned around to see Brodie step outside behind us.

'I'd better check on my boys,' Heather said, seeing him. She touched my arm quickly. 'I'll be inside if you need me.'

'Thanks, Heather.' I walked over to sit on one of the benches as she disappeared and Brodie stepped over to me. He stood in front of me, hands in his pockets. 'Where's Greg?' I asked, fearfully.

'At the bar. Drinking.'

'He needs help,' I said with a sigh. 'He needs my help, Brodie. Whatever else, he's the father of this baby.'

'I understand. You know that.' He sat down next to me. We both looked out onto the garden. We were silent for a couple of minutes before Brodie spoke again. 'You're going back to London.'

'I am.'

'I want you to know... I'm here for you, Emily. As I friend, I mean.'

He really was a good man. I smiled. 'Thank you. We'll see each other again. This isn't goodbye.'

'Isn't it?' He stood up. 'Take care of yourself, Emily. And that little one too.'

'Brodie...'

'It's okay,' he said, stopping me with a smile.

'Is it?' I asked, raising an eyebrow.

'It will be,' he promised and then he turned and walked towards the Hall, disappearing out of view. I sighed heavily. It did feel like an ending somehow. One that I didn't really want. But I knew this thing between us, whatever it had been, had to end.

'Em! Get your butt in here, we are dancing!' Beth yelled from the doorway. I shook off my melancholy. It was her wedding. It was a party and, let's face it, it was likely going to be a while before I was in the mood to party again. I jumped up and followed her inside where the band where playing ABBA and everyone was on the dance floor. I joined Beth, Izzy and Heather. I glanced over at the bar where Greg was sullenly drinking a beer but I was determined to put that issue on hold until we were back in London. Tonight, I was going to have fun.

And I did.

We danced until after midnight when people started to drift home. Soon, the band had finished for the night and started to put everything away. The serving staff started to clear up as well. And then it was just our family party left in the marquee. Drew got everyone a glass of the family whisky, minus the kids of course, and me, and we sat in a circle together – Beth, Caroline, John, Aunt Sally, Rory, Heather, Heather's father, David with Cathy, his new partner, and the kids. Greg was slumped in his chair asleep next to me, and I was steadfastly ignoring him.

'I can't believe I'm a married woman,' Beth said, taking a sip of her drink. She had kicked off her shoes and her legs were draped over her husband's lap.

'Nor can I,' her mother replied dryly. We all chuckled.

'Speaking of married women...' John said then, clearing his throat. He stood up and all eyes fell on him. 'I am often accused of being a man of few words. But I have always found action to be stronger than words anyway.' He pulled out a box from his pocket and turned to Caroline who let out a little gasp. 'I've loved you for twenty years. Will you marry me?'

She jumped up out of her seat. 'Of course I will,' she said. He slipped the ring on her finger and she wrapped her arms around him for a tight hug.

'Oh my God!' Beth jumped up and joined in their hug. 'This is just wonderful!'

I glanced at David but he smiled and nodded and squeezed Cathy's hand. It was strange seeing an ex-husband look happy for his ex-wife like that, but I knew that he had found love with Cathy so must have been relieved that Caroline had done the same thing. It was lovely to see John and Caroline get their happy ever after finally.

'Okay, I think we need another toast…' Drew said when the excitement had died down. 'Here's to the future. May it be a happy and healthy one for all of us!'

'To the future,' we echoed.

I looked at Greg, and a shiver ran down my spine.

Part Two

Chapter Thirty-One

I expected London to greet me grey and drizzly to match my mood, but the sun was bright above us in a clear, blue sky when our taxi pulled up outside our house. The journey back down from Scotland had been long and tense. I was still upset that Greg had got so drunk at Beth and Drew's wedding. He had spent the next day hideously hungover, sulking in the corner, as we had a big family breakfast and then waved Drew and Beth off on their honeymoon. We had left Glendale Hall first thing on Friday morning, and I felt like I had left half of my heart there.

'Here you go,' the driver said, lifting our bags out of the boot for us. Greg paid him and we watched him drive off, leaving us alone on our doorstep. I looked up at our house. It was still pretty and welcoming but it didn't lift my spirits as it usually did. I was worried about what awaited me inside.

'Right then.' Greg picked up our bags and gave me a small smile. 'We're home.'

I followed him as he unlocked the door and let us in. The hall was cool and dark. Closing the door behind us, I led the way into the kitchen. 'I need tea,' I said. I noted that at least he hadn't destroyed the house while I was gone. It looked fairly tidy and clean.

'I'll take these upstairs then.' Greg headed up with our bags and I wondered if we were going to be this stilted with one another from now on. We didn't feel like a couple, more like two new roommates. Popping the kettle on, I flung open the back door to let in some air. I stood there for a moment looking out at our small garden which burst with colour. It was a world away from Glendale Hall's grounds but it was all mine. I gazed out at it, feeling sad. Was it still mine? I was scared to find out how deep Greg's money troubles ran for fear that this would be taken away from me. I knew it was just a garden at the end of the day but I had spent many hours out there planting and making it look as good as such a small space could. With a heavy sigh, I turned away to make the tea, knowing that I needed to be logical for now, and not sentimental.

Greg came into the kitchen and sat down at the table as I carried over two mugs of tea. He scratched at the line of stubble on his chin. 'Back to reality then,' he said, trying to smile across at me.

'Hmmm,' I said, wrapping my hands around the mug. It had a big donut and 'Donut Worry, Be Happy' written on it. Greg had bought it for me from a shop in Brighton when we'd spent a weekend there. It had been my favourite mug to use since. Now it seemed to be mocking me. 'I don't even know where to start.'

'I'm sorry about the wedding,' Greg began, unable to meet my eyes. 'I really messed up. I know that. I was so confident I could just stop. Because I want to, I really want to.' He looked up tentatively then.

'I don't think you can do it on your own.'

'I have you…'

'I mean you need professional help. Don't you?'

He looked down again. 'Yeah, I suppose I do.'

'Because it's not just your drinking, is it? The gambling, the lies... I still can't get my head around it all but it's too big for us to handle on our own now. We need help.' I took a breath. 'How bad are our money problems? Give it to me straight. How much do you owe? In total?'

'I haven't worked it out...'

'Let's do it then.' I pulled out my phone and opened up the notes. Greg reluctantly started to list his debts. There was the casino. The loan shark. Credit cards. He'd even borrowed a bit from a couple of his mates too.

'And last month's mortgage payment,' Greg said, finally. 'I didn't pay it.'

My head snapped up. 'What?'

'I had to pay the guy the monthly instalment for the loan. Believe me, I can't miss those.'

'But the house, Greg!'

'Hey, hang on, my money paid for this house after all...' he started to say, on the defensive straight away.

'You may have put down the deposit but we pay the mortgage equally. You should have told me!' Greg's grandmother had left him some money when she passed away, allowing us to buy the house. I couldn't believe he had put it in such jeopardy like this.

'I know. I know.' His voice cracked. 'They sent a letter before I came up to Scotland. I didn't know what to do.'

I looked across at him and couldn't believe that things had got so broken. 'And you've told me everything now? This is all we owe?' He nodded once. In silence, I added it all up. Then I did it again because I couldn't quite believe it. I showed him the figure on the phone. 'How are we even going to begin to pay this back?' I wanted to be strong. I wanted to go into fight mode. To deal with it. But the weight of it all crashed over me in that moment.

Out of the corner of my eye, the £50,000 figure on my phone flashed at me like a neon beacon.

–

Even though I was home again, I was more lost than I had ever been in my life before.

I had to get out of the house and there was only one place that I could think of to go. I walked briskly, trying to enjoy the feel of the sun on my shoulders but they felt too heavy to be lifted by it. The streets were as familiar to me as breathing but they also failed to comfort me. Soon Molly's bakery drifted into view. I paused to look at it. It looked smaller, somehow.

Pushing on, I opened the door with a jangle of the bell. And then I froze.

I had forgotten. I don't know how but I had.

Behind the counter were Molly... and Steph.

Molly looked up and beamed. I gave her a small wave and then I glanced at Steph. Her cheeks turned pink as she concentrated on packing up a bag of cakes, not making eye contact with me. Marching through to the back I did the same and didn't look at her. She was nothing compared to the avalanche of issues that I now faced with Greg but she was still something as well.

'Emily!' Molly followed me into the office soon after and gave me a big hug.

'Can we talk?' I asked.

She frowned 'Well, of course. Sit, sit!' She sat down with me. 'We missed you. How was Scotland?'

'So much has happened since I left, I hardly know where to even begin...' I admitted. I had slowly realised that keeping everything to myself hadn't done anything to change what was wrong. I had always tried to work things out on my own but I knew that there was no way I could this time. I needed people around me more than ever. 'It's all such a mess, Mol.'

'What is? What's wrong?' She reached out and squeezed my hand.

'Everything is falling apart. Greg and I... we're in trouble. He's been gambling and drinking. I don't really know what to do.'

Molly sighed. 'Oh, Em, that's awful.'

'He's kept so much from me. We're in a lot of debt. He even cheated on me. That's why I left for Scotland early, actually. I should have told you but I don't know, I was so shocked and ashamed too. Now, I just can't believe what he's done.'

'My goodness. Now I wish I had poisoned that brownie he came in for while you were away.' She gave me a small smile and I managed a weak one in return.

'When he came in then,' I began, hesitantly. 'Did he speak to Steph at all?' I remembered Greg promising that he hadn't but now I wondered if I could trust anything he told me.

She thought for a moment. 'Not that I recall. Why?'

'She's the one he cheated with.'

'No!' Molly cried. She shook her head. 'Our Steph? How could she do that? Wait until I get my hands on her. But, more importantly, what can I do to help you, Emily?'

'I just needed to talk to someone. There's nothing you can do. I'm not even sure what to do next. I just wanted to see a friendly face I suppose.' I hesitated. 'There's one more thing, actually.'

'I'm scared to ask, what?'

'I'm pregnant.'

Molly leaned over and pulled me into her arms. We sat like that for a moment, neither of us saying anything. I held on tightly to her. I had missed her. 'Whatever happens, you're having a baby. Nothing else matters but you and this baby. You hear me?' Molly said then, sternly, pulling back to look at me.

'I'm scared, Molly.'

'Well, of course you are. But you're not alone even if you feel like you are right now. Okay? Now, I'm going to put the kettle on and get us a cake and then we're going to sort everything out.'

'Thanks, Molly. I knew I'd feel better being back here. Oh, didn't you say you wanted to talk to me about something when I got back?' I asked then, remembering the message she had sent me the other day.

'Oh, that can wait. What are you going to do next then?'

'I need to speak to my mum and dad. They are going to be so disappointed.'

'In Greg. Not in you,' she said, standing up. 'You've done nothing wrong.'

'I fell in love with him, Mol. How can I ever trust myself again, let alone him?' I sighed. 'I just hope we can sort this all out. What if we lose everything?'

'Then you start again.' She switched on the kettle. 'You know what I've always said and I stand by it even in this situation.'

'When life gives you lemons, then just make the best damn lemonade that you can,' we said in unison. And despite it all, I chuckled right along with Molly.

It was a cliché but I knew in my heart it was true. I needed to dust off that lemonade recipe; and fast.

Chapter Thirty-Two

When I left Molly's office full of tea and cake and sympathy, I stepped out into the empty bakery. Steph was wiping down the counter getting ready for closing time but she looked up when I came out. I started to head for the door but I knew that I had to say something. I had been so shocked and ashamed before I had gone to Scotland, I had given her a pass on the whole sleeping with my boyfriend thing but after accusing Greg of sticking his head in the sand, I couldn't let myself do the exact same thing. I spun around to face her. 'Why did you do it, Steph?'

She stood up straight, not trying to deny it. She immediately went on the defensive instead. 'Hey, I'm not the one in a relationship—'

I held up a finger to silence her. 'No, you're not. Greg cheated on me. There's no excusing that. I'm not blaming you more than him, far from it. But you know me. We work together. I thought we were even friends. It doesn't matter that you're single, you knew he wasn't, and not only that but you know me. The person he was cheating on. How could you do that?' I felt strangely calm. I actually wanted to know why she had done it. It was something I knew I could never do to someone. 'You're young, attractive, a lovely girl. You could have anyone.

Why did it have to be him?' I pressed on when it was clear she wasn't going to answer me.

'I was jealous,' she admitted finally, slumping a little against the counter. 'You had everything that I wanted – a lovely man, a lovely home. When I saw him in that club and he started flirting with me, I just wanted to know what it would feel like. Sure, men come on to me, they sleep with me, but they never love me, never want to be with me, to have a life with me.'

'So you thought you'd try to steal mine instead?' I didn't get it. Even if she did feel envious about what I had – which was ironic, given what I had just found out – that didn't give her the right to try to take it from me.

'I am sorry,' she said, quietly. 'I felt so bad… afterwards. And he did too.'

I shook my head. 'I was angry but now I just feel sorry for you. One day someone will do to you what you did to me and break your heart. You should treat others in life how you want to be treated, then maybe you'd get the love you seem to so desperately want.' I suddenly felt tired. I turned and walked out of the shop before she could respond. I had no clue if my words would even have any impact on her but I felt better anyway for saying them. Women had enough to deal with in life without making it harder for one another. I hoped Steph might learn that one day and actually deserve the love she was searching for but that was up to her, and not me.

My phone started to ring in my bag so I pulled it out and nodded at the number on the screen. I had been expecting it after leaving a message on the way to Molly's. 'Hello?'

'Emily, it's Peter returning your call.'

'Thanks, Peter. I was hoping I could set up a time to come to your office to talk about a few things,' I said. Peter was a long-time family friend, and he was also an accountant. I needed some financial advice, and fast, so I had reached out to him. I changed direction. I didn't want to go home yet and I had put off telling my parents what was going on in my life for too long. Peter readily agreed to meet me and found a slot the following day for me to come to his office, for which I was really grateful.

There was one more thing I wanted to arrange. I was doubtful Greg would do it for himself, despite him saying how much he needed help. I dialled another number and set off at a slow pace to my parents' house before I let myself chicken out again. They lived only about a twenty-five-minute walk from my house. I think after such a big move in my teens, I hadn't wanted to go far when Greg and I moved in together.

'Emily, this is a nice surprise,' he answered, cheerfully.

'I am so sorry for calling you on your honeymoon,' I said to Drew. 'I just needed to ask you something really quickly.'

'Of course, it's no problem. We're just on yet another long walk.' I heard Beth say something, and he chuckled. 'Yes, yes, I love walking. So, how can I help, Emily?'

'It's Greg. He needs some help and I'm not sure where's best… who to go to, really,' I said. I was unused to reaching out for help; that was true. I had always preferred to sort things out on my own but I knew that in this situation, I needed all the help I could get, and I trusted Drew. I told him briefly about Greg's drinking and gambling problems. 'It's out of control,' I admitted.

'I'm so sorry, Emily. We're here for anything you need, okay? The best thing to do is encourage him to make an appointment with his GP; they can point him to the best services in your area to help. Or even make the appointment yourself. It may not feel like it right now but that fact that he has admitted he has a problem and asked for help, is a great sign.'

'I guess you're right,' I replied, feeling slightly more positive.

'Let me know how it goes, okay?'

'I will. And thank you. I'm so sorry for calling you.'

'Do not apologise. You've done so much for us! You take care of yourself. And don't forget to make an appointment for yourself too, Emily. You need to tell your GP that you're pregnant, and get a scan booked.'

I paused for a moment. In all honesty, with everything going on with Greg, I hadn't even thought about that. 'You're right. I will.' Beth called out that she sent all her love, and we said goodbye. I felt so much better for having reached out to them. I then made another call to my doctor's surgery, making two appointments.

And by the time I had done all of that, I was standing on the doorstep of my parents' house. It was the home we'd moved to when we left Scotland. They still lived there, and the familiarity of it was a welcome sight with all the change that was going on. I remembered the shock of leaving Glendale for London. I had been young so I adapted quickly but the first night in this house, I had cried for Scotland and I sometimes wondered if I had actually ever really let it go.

'Emily! You're back!' My mum flung open the front door before I reached out to knock. She held out her hands and I tumbled into them. Sometimes, no matter your age, you just needed a hug from your mum. And, of course, I started to cry. 'Oh no, what's going on? Let's get you off the doorstep,' she cried, pulling me into the hall and closing the door behind me. 'Your dad is still at school. Come on, this way,' she said, leading me through to their kitchen. The back door was flung open, letting in the afternoon light from their garden. It was a shame Dad wasn't there. We were more alike and somewhat closer than me and my mum because of that but, then again, he was likely to tell me what I wanted to hear whereas my mum would most definitely not, and perhaps that was what I needed.

She briskly made us a cup of tea as I dried my eyes. I looked out to their small patio garden, which was filled with colourful pots of flowers. My dad was the green-fingered one out of the two of them. He loved being outdoors. He was a PE teacher, after all. And happy to stay one. Whereas my ambitious mother was now head-mistress, my dad was content in his job. 'Now, what's going on? I knew there was more to your sudden flit up to Glendale than you said in that hurried voicemail you left us,' she said, giving me a stern look. She sat down opposite me and slid over a mug to me. Mum had my blonde hair but hers was almost white now, and styled in a sharp bob, and she had blue eyes whereas mine were hazel. She had my curves too but our dress sense was very different – she wore a pencil skirt and blouse from her day at the school, and she loved wearing heels.

I took a deep breath. 'Everything feels like it's falling apart,' I admitted. 'You're right, I went up to Glendale early because things weren't good with Greg. They're still not, and I think we need help.' It was always hard for me to lean on my mum as she always seemed to have everything sorted in her own life.

She reached out and squeezed my hand. 'What has he done?' she asked, certain it was all his fault.

I smiled a little at her loyalty. So, I told her. About the cheating, the gambling and all our debts, and the fact that he had tried to drown his sorrows in booze. 'It just keeps getting worse. I've found out all these things… how could I not know the man I was living with at all?'

Mum shook her head. 'You know that I always thought that you deserved someone better. I didn't like the way he didn't seem to respect you but I would never say I told you so because I really didn't think he'd ever do anything quite like this,' she said, after absorbing it all. Mum was a staunch feminist. She had actually been upset when I told her I had fallen in love. She had wanted a big career for me. She herself hadn't married Dad until she had become head of the English department when I was five. I had been an accident. She had always been open with me that she had wanted to wait until her late thirties to become a mother but she had been happy when I had come along and never let motherhood hold her back in any way.

I think she had known that I wouldn't focus on my career once I found someone. She had been right. I had put Greg ahead of everything. I had just wanted to build a family. Now I couldn't help but feel I would have been better off if I had followed her advice. It was all very well in hindsight, though.

'You need to walk away, Em,' she said then. 'It's great he's trying to get help and by all means, be there for him, but he's lied to you so much. How can you trust him? You need to sell that house and start over again. You can always come back home. You need to put yourself first for once,' she said, firmly, as if she would brook no arguments on the matter.

'If only it was that simple,' I said, shaking my head.

She sighed. 'It can be if you let it, Emily.'

'No, you don't understand, Mum...'

'I know you love him but—'

'Mum!' I snapped, stopping her in mid-sentence. Sometimes it was hard to get her to listen when she was off on a rant but I had to tell her the last piece of the puzzle. Why it was so much more complicated than she thought. Why I still felt so torn and confused about what to do. I looked at her. 'I'm pregnant.'

Chapter Thirty-Three

On Monday morning, I turned up for my first day back at work, and Molly informed me that Steph had handed in her notice, and they'd agreed she'd leave immediately.

'I think she realised there was no way she could face you every day,' Molly said. 'And that I no longer wanted her here. So, I've put a sign up for someone and in the meantime, my daughter-in-law can help on busy days. And we'll muddle through just fine,' she added, cheerfully. I couldn't help but feel relieved, although it would be a lot more work for us now, but at least I wouldn't have to deal with Steph again.

'And how are you feeling?' Molly asked as we opened up. 'I hope you're looking after yourself,' she added, with a stern glance in my direction.

I smiled weakly. 'Baby-wise, I'm fine,' I said. 'If still tired most of the time but the other things, well, there's so much to sort out.' I was saved from having to say more as our first customer came in. My break in Glendale felt almost like a dream as I was very quickly planted back into my London life. Days spent at the bakery, rushed off my feet, and then evenings spent trying to sort everything out with Greg.

I had met with Peter the accountant and he had put us in touch with a debt management service. We had worked out payment plans for Greg's debts and we'd had an estate agent round to value the house. Greg was trying to argue that we should try to keep the house, and I knew part of that was because he was desperately trying to keep hold of our dream of being a family, living there together.

But I knew we had to sell it. There was no way we could pay off the debts otherwise. We had made money on the house luckily so if we did sell it and pay off what Greg owed then there would be a little left to start again. Although technically Greg was entitled to more of that as the deposit had come from him. It very much all depended on whether we were going to start over again together or not. And that was something I just didn't know.

My parents were insistent that I could move back in with them as soon as I wanted.

'I try not to get involved in your life unless you want me to. You're a grown woman and a very capable one but sometimes you lose sight of what you want. So, please focus on that. Do not just go along with what Greg wants, okay? At least promise me that, Emily,' Mum had said, holding me tight after I told her I was having a baby. 'If you want to stay with Greg then I will support you but you are more than capable of raising this baby on your own. Sometimes it's best to try to keep a family together but other times, a child would be happier if their parents were happy. And that might mean you don't stay together. You can do anything that you want to, don't ever forget that.'

The problem was, I just didn't know what I wanted. I had never felt quite so confused. I was proud of Greg for facing his problems and trying to get help. He had met with our GP and had been referred to a local treatment centre to help with his addiction problems. They had suggested rehab might be the best place but Greg had said no so they recommended a mixture of group and one-on-one counselling sessions for him. He didn't want residential treatment because he didn't want to be away from me. But it was so hard; I could see how much he was struggling. He was often moody and irritable and tired all the time, so, coupled with hormonal me, the house was often tense. He was determined though to save us. He kept saying we owed it to our baby.

But was he right about that?

And then there were the nights I lay awake, thinking about everything, and my mind would conjure up the look on Brodie's face when he told me that he wished I was free. Sometimes I even ended up reaching for my phone, wanting to call him, to hear his voice, to ask his advice. But how could I? How could I ask him about what I should do? I couldn't be that selfish. And yet I desperately wanted to be.

The happiness I had felt being up in Scotland with him and our friends had faded into a memory but I didn't want it to. I wanted to be happy. If only I could be sure what would make me happy.

—

I had been back in London for a couple of weeks when I felt I couldn't ignore Rachel any longer. After she and Hazel had heard through Johnny that Greg and I were now back in London, she had sent me two messages begging me to meet with her. We arranged to meet in one of our favourite coffee shops and when I arrived, my heart sank a little to see that she'd also invited Hazel and they were both there already, kids on laps, waiting for me.

I hesitated in the doorway for a moment before sucking in a deep breath and walking over.

'Emily!' Rachel jumped up, rather awkwardly as she was holding the baby, and I leaned in to kiss her on the cheek. 'You look radiant,' she said, unable to hide her surprise. Perhaps they both thought I had crumbled with Greg's fall from grace.

'Your trip away must have done you good,' Hazel agreed, tilting her face up so I had to kiss her too.

I sat down opposite, facing the two women whose lives I had so envied. It all felt rather trivial now.

'So, how are you doing, poor thing? We couldn't believe Greg turned up to work drunk like that,' Hazel said, screwing her face up.

I could have glossed it over perhaps but I was too tired from the past few days trying to sort our lives out and, really, what was the point? Greg had had to tell his boss the truth and he was on sickness leave so no doubt his colleagues would hear all about it anyway and Johnny would pass it all to his wife. 'Greg is an alcoholic,' I said. 'He's getting help, though.'

'Oh my God,' Hazel said, exchanging a look with Rachel. She looked horrified. 'You must be devastated. You're not going to stay with him, are you?'

'Hazel,' Rachel said, with a soft reproach. 'Can we help at all?'

I smiled a little at her more sympathetic response. 'No, but thank you.'

'Well, thank goodness you didn't have a family in the end. I mean, can you imagine?'

I stared at Hazel. I wondered then how I had ever sought this woman's approval. How I had wished so desperately to be her. 'Actually, I'm pregnant,' I found myself saying. We were due to have the first scan next week but I couldn't stop the words from flying out. 'And I can only hope you never have any problems in your life, Hazel, because no one will be at all sympathetic if this is how you treat other people going through a tough time.' I stood up abruptly.

'No, Em, don't go,' Rachel said, quickly. She gave Hazel a stern look. 'I am so happy for you! And now we can all hang out with our babies; it's what we always wanted.'

'So, now I can hang out with you guys again?' I asked, incredulously. 'You basically ditched me as soon as you got pregnant, and you don't know how much that hurt. How much I looked at you both and wished I had your lives. But you know what? Friendship shouldn't be about convenience. I have real friends who are with me through whatever happens in my life because they love me, and I love them, and it's not about what stage of our lives we're at, or how useful we are to one another,' I said, my heart aching for my friends back in Glendale who didn't care if I had a baby or was married or not, but who just cared for me as a person.

'That isn't what I meant,' Rachel said, her cheeks turning pink, looking thoroughly embarrassed.

'This is silly,' Hazel added. 'You need us, Emily. You don't want to turn your back on us right now.'

Suddenly that threat felt like nothing to me. 'I think I'll do just fine actually,' I said, lifting my bag onto my shoulder and striding out of that coffee shop, leaving them staring after me.

For once in my life I didn't feel horrified by the confrontation, or desperate to make amends, I felt like I had just set myself free.

Chapter Thirty-Four

Nerves fluttered in my stomach.

I glanced across at Greg who was walking with a frown, frequently brushing the hair back from his face despite the fact there was no breeze on the air so I knew he was nervous too. We were walking into hospital for our first scan. We were well into July now, and the city had become hot. Almost unbearably so. The sun was scorching, high up in the sky and I longed for the Scottish air. Not only for the cool breeze that you always felt up there, but because I was so nervous, I wanted to run away. I was desperate for everything to be okay with the baby. And I could tell Greg was tense too. So much had gone wrong for us, we were both on tenterhooks, hoping that our baby at least would be fine.

I longed for Brodie's faith as we pushed open the doors to the hospital because if I'd had that, I would have said a little prayer. Instead, I just crossed my fingers in the pocket of my dungarees.

We were soon shown into a room where we met the sonographer. I was asked to get comfortable on the couch and to adjust my clothing. Greg sat down beside me, and patted my leg quickly. I knew he was trying to be fully present with me even though he was struggling, and I did appreciate that. The woman rubbed gel on my tummy and I flinched from the cold. When she moved the probe over me, I realised I was holding my breath.

She smiled as she looked at the screen in front of her. 'There we go.' She moved it a little so I could see and I gasped as the grainy black and white image of my baby appeared on the screen. 'Looking perfect,' she added.

'Really? Everything is okay?' I asked. I glanced at Greg who was smiling. He reached out and took my hand and I let him hold it as we watched our baby.

'Everything is fine. And it looks like you're eleven weeks so it's all progressing nicely.' She went on to talk about the next scan that would check for any abnormalities and where we could find out if it was a boy or a girl but I found myself tuning out her words as I stared at the image on the screen. I hadn't been quite prepared for the feeling that washed over me. A fierce protective feeling. That was *my* baby. It was growing inside me. It only had me to protect it, to nurture it, to love it. For nine months, anyway.

Pulling my hand out from under Greg's so I could wipe away the tear that had rolled down my cheek, it was the first moment that I knew it for sure.

I could look after this baby, with or without Greg.

–

After we left the hospital, we walked to the supermarket and picked up two sandwiches and then headed into a nearby park to sit and eat them on a bench in the sunshine. I was relieved that the scan had gone so well, and now that I was approaching three months, I knew I could no longer hide from this baby, I needed to get everything organised.

We only had six months until a brand new human being came into this world, and there was so much to do.

'I still can't believe our baby is growing in there,' Greg said then, glancing at my stomach. There was just the beginning of something there now. I felt curvier too but softer as well, and the buttons on my jeans were getting a little snug. But I didn't care for the first time in my life. I felt freer than I ever had. I was sure that Greg could see it as he gazed at me, a slight crease in his forehead as if he couldn't quite place me any more. I understood why. I was feeling the same way myself.

'It's amazing,' I agreed. 'After all this time too… although the timing could have been better.'

Greg shook his head. 'The timing is perfect. We need this baby.'

I looked at him. 'A baby can't fix problems, you know that. It just means we need to sort out as much as we can before it arrives. And that means trying to get ourselves out of this debt. We *have* to put the house up for sale.'

'But where will we live with the baby?' His face twisted in confusion.

'Well, I might have to go back to my parents for a while, until there's enough to get my own place again.'

Greg stared at me. 'You mean us, don't you?'

'Well, I was thinking. Your counsellor mentioned a residential place, didn't she? I know that you said you wanted to try day therapy and everything but maybe staying there for a while would be the best thing. You're finding it so hard and they did say it was the best route. I know you want to stay with me but the sooner you can start getting a handle on it all, the better, surely. Especially for this one.' I touched my stomach.

Greg thought about what I had said for a moment. 'But when I came out, then we'd be together, wouldn't we?'

I twisted on the bench to face him and took one of his hands in mine. I hated how scared he looked but although I wanted to do all I could to help him beat his addictions, I didn't think I should lie to him either. 'Seeing our baby on the screen like that just made it all real. Greg, you need to look after yourself right now. You need to try to get better. I really think that the best thing for all of us is for you to go to the centre while I sell up our house and pay off our debts. Do you see that?'

'But I should be with you right now,' he said, his lip trembling. 'You need me.'

'What I need is for you to be ready to be the best father that you can be for him or her, and the only way you can do that is to get the help you need. Battle your addictions and get strong and healthy for them. And you will do that much faster if you go to the treatment centre.'

Greg looked down at our entwined hands. 'I know that I've screwed everything up but I do love you. And this baby. So much.' His eyes filled with unshed tears.

A lump rose up in my throat. 'I know. I'll always love you. And this baby will love you too. I promise you that.'

He drew his hand away as if my words were finally getting through. He nodded once. 'Can I have some time alone? To think?'

I bit my lip. 'I don't want you to—'

'I won't,' he interrupted me. 'I promise I won't go to a pub or casino or anything. I just need to process all of this. I hear you, though. I do hear you.'

'Okay then.' I stood up from the bench. 'See you back home then? For dinner? Maybe we can get a takeaway?'

I knew my words sounded lame but I couldn't think of anything else to say. He gave me a small smile. I really hoped he wasn't going to do anything stupid. I leaned down and kissed him on the cheek and then I walked away.

At the gate at the edge of the park, I glanced back to see him on the bench cutting a forlorn, lonely figure. It hurt to see him like that, so different to the man I fell in love with. And I wanted to be here for him. But I had changed too. Our relationship was no longer what it once was. I think deep down he knew that. There was no way back for us but I hoped he could be a father to our baby, that he would get better, and I would do my best to get him there. But my priority was this baby, and I knew I was doing the right thing in putting it first now.

I walked out of the park and pulled out my phone to call the estate agent. The wallpaper on my screen was now the grainy scan image of my baby and that gave me the strength I needed to make the call.

Chapter Thirty-Five

Greg didn't come home until late. The sun was starting to set outside when I heard the front door finally open. I let out a long exhale of relief. I had picked at leftovers in the fridge, and was sitting in the kitchen with a cup of tea constantly checking the clock and my phone, getting more anxious by the minute that he had relapsed or something. He wasn't picking up his phone or replying to my messages so I was about to call his parents to see if they had heard from him when he walked into the kitchen, looking tired but coherent.

'I'm glad you're not in bed yet,' he said, giving me a small smile.

'I was worried about you,' I said, wearily, trying to subtly check for signs that he'd been drinking.

'Oh, sorry. I didn't think. Can we talk or do you want to wait until the morning?'

'Let's talk,' I said, glad that he seemed to be sober.

Greg went to the fridge and brought over a can of Coke. He had upped his sugar intake since stopping drinking alcohol, I had noticed. 'I've been thinking about what you said. I went to see my parents and talked to them too,' he said, sitting down opposite me. 'You're right. I need to go away to get help. Being here, I'm tempted all the time. My parents are willing to pay for a month's stay at the centre so I can go straight away and don't need to wait or anything,' he said, in a rush. I knew that he found it hard to talk about his problems still.

'That's great, Greg,' I said, touching his hand briefly. 'I really think that's the best thing to do.' I felt like a huge weight had been lifted. He had reached out to his parents and not only had they agreed with me, but had swept in with an excellent solution. 'I know it will be tough but you can do it.'

'I hope you're right.' He sighed. 'I'm... scared,' he admitted then. He took a big gulp from his drink and I saw that his hands were shaking slightly.

'Of course you are. But it will be the best place. You can get better there. You will get better.'

'I have to try at least, for our little one,' he said, looking at my bump. Then he lifted his eyes to look at me. 'I am sorry, you know. More than I can ever explain. I should have told you sooner, got help sooner. The thought that I hurt you in all of this... that's the worst part. I hope you know that.'

I nodded. 'I do. I know that it's an illness, that some of it was out of your control, but it's still hard for me to come to terms with,' I said, honestly. Greg had always seemed so strong and capable. I mean, he was a fireman, for goodness' sake. I had always felt so safe with him. I thought he could handle anything. But he was just human at the end of the day.

'I wish I could take it all back,' Greg went on, looking down at the table. 'Go back to how we were but I see now that it's impossible. I still hoped, I suppose, that we had a future together. Somehow. But that was selfish of me. You deserve so much better.'

'Honestly, I can't think of anything right now except this baby,' I replied, carefully. I wanted him to know that I wanted to support him in getting help, but anything more than that was something I couldn't even think about, with him or anyone.

'I know, I know. You're going to be such a great mother,' he said, looking up then. 'I just hope I'll get to see it.'

'Of course you will! You'll get better and you'll be a great father.' I hoped that I would be proved right about that.

'I'll do the best I can.'

'That's all any of us can do.'

–

An invitation landed on the doormat late one morning. It was a bright, sunny day, and I was putting books into a box when I heard the postman. Opening up the fancy cream envelope, my heart lifted inside my chest at the words inside.

We cordially invite you to the wedding of Caroline Williams and John Thompson at Glendale Hall…

'What's that?' Greg asked from behind me as he carried a box down the stairs. We were trying to sort out all our belongings. The house was up for sale and we had so much to clear through – packing up things for storage and things to sell as well as to keep. It was helping to take our mind off Greg's impending admittance to rehab, at least.

'An invitation to Caroline Williams' wedding. They only got engaged at Beth and Drew's wedding but they've known each other for so long… it's in three weeks' time,' I replied, slipping it into the pocket of my dungarees. I picked my box back up and carried it into the kitchen. I tried to focus on the task in hand but my mind was swimming with thoughts of Glendale. I desperately wanted to go but it was surely impossible. Greg followed me and we added our two boxes to the growing pile to take to the charity shop. It really was amazing what you could accumulate in just a few years.

'Will you go to the wedding?' Greg asked me.

'I can't. There's so much to do here and anyway, you'll be at the centre then. I can't leave you,' I said, shaking my head even though my heart ached with longing.

'I was going to talk to you about that.' He ran a hand through his hair and I was immediately on alert at the nervous action. 'They prefer you to have as little contact with the outside world as possible, especially at the start. I'm not allowed any phone calls or visitors for at least two weeks. My therapist can provide updates but I need to focus on my treatment. After that, I can use the phone at certain times, but as I'm just there for a month, they're recommending no visitors.'

I let that sink in. 'Are you sure you want to do this?' I checked. It was brave of him to go there and to do it all alone. I wasn't sure I could have done it if our roles were reversed. He nodded.

'Will you let me know when I'm allowed to phone you then?'

'I'll call you. I promise,' he replied.

I sank down into one of our chairs. 'It will be the longest we've ever been apart since we met.'

'I know.' He leaned against the counter. 'You know what? I think you should go to that wedding.'

'I couldn't. How could I celebrate and be happy when...' I trailed off, hating how much I wished I could be in Glendale again. It was hardly surprising with everything that had been going on in London, all the stress and worry of the past weeks – the thought of peaceful countryside, Sally's wonderful food, and all my friends up there was incredibly appealing.

'Why sit here and worry all the time though? You love it up there. It'll take your mind off everything. You should go. Our estate agent can show the house to anyone, you don't need to be here. In fact, they prefer us to be out when they come.'

'I don't know. Maybe, I suppose.' I pulled out the invitation again. It was elegant, just like Caroline. They would be getting married in the Glendale church. I couldn't help but think of Brodie. He'd be conducting their ceremony, of course. Did I have the strength to see him again, just as friends? Or would my heart betray me, wanting so much more from him?

Chapter Thirty-Six

After dropping off a couple of boxes at the charity shop, while Greg began to pack a bag for rehab, I took the sunny afternoon as a sign and decided to walk back to the house. I was thinking about what he had said about me going to Glendale, and the pull I felt to go back there. But it still felt strange to be thinking about attending such a joyful occasion while Greg was trying to overcome his demons. Not to mention how much there was still to sort out regarding our money problems and the house sale, although I knew both our parents would step in readily to help if we asked them to.

I walked down the High Street and then through the park. It was full with families as the school holidays had just begun. I couldn't help but wonder if one day that could be me with my own child. Would I still live in this area then, though? The future was so uncertain. After having my life so planned out, it was disconcerting to not be able to picture what it would be like when my child was five.

Leaving the park, I turned down our long road and slowed a little, in no hurry to get back home really. The sight of the church on the corner slowed me down even more. I wondered if Brodie knew I'd been invited to the wedding. He must assume I had. It had been so strange to have no contact with him since I came back to London. But I knew I would have to be the one to reach out; he wanted to let me sort things out down here, he knew I had so much going on. I missed him, though. More than I could have imagined.

Did he ever ask Beth and Drew about me? It was so hard not knowing if he ever thought about me at all. If he missed me too. They knew we were selling the house and that Greg was going to the treatment centre, both of them reminding me that they were there for me if I needed them. Perhaps they had told Brodie that. Or perhaps he hadn't asked about me at all. Neither Beth nor Drew would ever gossip about me, I was certain of that, so it might be that he thought Greg and I were sorting out our problems; that we were back together. I wasn't sure which scenario was better or worse.

The church was drawing me closer to it. I decided to let it, turning off the road and walking through the open, oak door. It was much cooler and dimmer inside. It was quiet, too. My footsteps echoed as I walked.

I slid into a row of pews and sat down, looking up at the gold altar and the stained-glass window above it, through which the sun was shining, creating a rainbow on the tiled floor. Even though I wasn't at all religious, I did feel calmer in there somehow.

The past few weeks washed over me in that moment. I knew that currently I was just reacting to my life. It was hard to do otherwise. Things had literally been thrown at me and I was just trying to keep everything afloat. I would soon have to start thinking about what came next, though. What I wanted to come next. Maybe leaving London again would give me that clarity. I would have space to think about myself again. And my baby. And what we would do next.

But how would I feel seeing Brodie again? And was that a big enough reason not to go?

I had been hoping that the church would give me some sort of sign but I knew deep down that only I could decide what to do. I pulled out the wedding invitation from my bag and a pen. I hovered over the RSVP tab at the bottom. Taking a deep breath, I ticked a box and sat back in the pew.

'Well, if this all goes wrong, I know who to blame,' I murmured, looking up at the altar ahead.

–

Molly invited me to her house for brunch on Sunday. I hadn't wanted to leave Greg on his last day at home but his parents invited him over and I knew that he wanted to spend some time alone with them so I hopped on a bus to Molly's house in Putney. She lived in a large house that had been in her family for generations. She had never wanted to leave and I couldn't blame her. It was lovely and now housed her, her son and daughter-in-law and their two children. Molly loved people around her, at work and at home, and was unfailingly generous.

'Emily, darling!' she cried, flinging the door open and pulling me into her arms. She leaned back to look at me and tutted. 'You look tired. Come on, you need food – you're eating for two, remember!'

'That's a myth,' I replied with a smile as I followed her through her hall and into her large, bright, open-plan kitchen where there was a delicious smell of bacon in the air. 'But when it comes to your food, I'm very happy to oblige.'

'Are you sure you're looking after yourself? Sit, sit!' Molly said, bustling over to the Aga. 'Help yourself to tea or juice, or both,' she added, pointing to the table.

I went over and sat down. 'I'm fine, really,' I insisted as I poured myself a glass of freshly squeezed juice. The table was laid with a gingham cloth. A bowl of croissants sat in the middle with butter and jam, pots of tea and coffee next to it, and a bowl of fruit. A vase of yellow roses completed the set-up. Aunt Sally would have been impressed. 'It's just been a stressful few days, what with putting the house on the market and trying to clear our stuff, and Greg getting ready for rehab. There's so much to do, you know?'

'Well, just don't exhaust yourself. You need to take care of you and that little one.' Molly carried over two plates piled high with bacon and eggs then came back with a stack of toast and a plate of pancakes. 'Dig in, you need to keep your strength up,' she said, sitting down next to me. I smiled and dutifully started to eat. Molly was an excellent cook as well as baker. 'I really am sorry you've got all this going on. How is Greg doing?' she asked after nodding with satisfaction as she watched me take a big bite.

'He's terrified to go into the centre but desperate to go as well. He's been struggling this week trying not to relapse so I'm glad he'll be there tomorrow. But, it's weird. Even after everything, I will miss him when he goes. It feels like the end of something.'

Molly nodded. 'Of course. You've been together a long time and you really loved him. And still do. You can't just turn it off like a tap. Unfortunately. But it's the best place for him right now so you have to focus on that. And do you think the house will sell quickly?'

'We had someone come for a second viewing yesterday. I mean, it's a nice road and we priced it competitively to try to get a quick sale so I hope so. I'll have to go back to my parents' once it sells. I don't know how long for.' I wasn't keen on doing that, it felt like I was going backward but I knew it was more important to get out of our debt than worry about that. 'I'm really grateful to you for giving me more time off of work. I hate leaving you in the lurch,' I added as I buttered another slice of toast.

'You know that Anna loves covering there,' Molly said, waving away my thanks, talking about her daughter-in-law. 'In fact, that's why I asked you over today. I did have an ulterior motive. I wanted to talk to you before but well, with everything that has happened... But I think it might help.' She bit her lip and looked nervous. I watched her, wary after all the bombshells I'd had to deal with already. 'Emily, dear, I've decided the time has come for me to retire.'

Chapter Thirty-Seven

I stared at Molly in shock as her words sank in. 'Retire? But…'

'I know, I'm too young, aren't I?' she said with a laugh but I couldn't raise a smile back. 'But as I said, Anna loves working in the shop and now that her kids are at school, she wants to find something full-time again. I want to hand the running of the bakery over to her while I'm still young enough to go off and do the travelling I always wanted to. I married young, as you know, and had my son young too, and I've worked in the bakery most of my adult life. I would like to stay with my sister in Australia, and see the world. I always planned to and then just didn't do it. But what am I waiting for, you know?'

It felt like the room was spinning a little. I put my knife and fork down. Molly leaving Molly's bakery? Why was everything I knew suddenly changing so much?

'But you can't leave the bakery, you just can't,' I burst out, realising I sounded like a spoilt child.

Molly put her cutlery down and touched my hand. 'It's time. For me. I'm sorry, Emily. I really didn't want to upset you. I thought that you might see this as a good thing.'

'Why would I do that?' I asked, my voice coming out squeaky.

'Well, as I said, Anna will manage the bakery for me so I can do some travelling, and we will be sharing the profits from it. I also have a very good pot of savings so there will be more than enough for me. So, I thought what else could I do to make use of the money I have now while I'm still alive and kicking?' She smiled at me. 'And I've decided that I'd like to give some to you.'

'Me?' I repeated, still spinning from what she was saying. I was glad to be sitting down as I worried I might fall otherwise.

'Yes, you.' She patted my hand and spoke gently, sensing that I was having a hard time taking all of it in. 'I want to give you some money towards setting up your own bakery. When I first met you, fresh out of cookery school, eager to take on the world, you wanted to have your own bakery. I thought you'd be with me two years tops. That you'd go on and be a huge success. And then you met Greg, and I saw that your ambition had faded. Your priorities had changed. Now, there was nothing wrong with that. I wanted a family too, I understood. I was surprised, though. You were happy to stay with me, and I was happy because I loved you like a daughter and you're a brilliant baker but perhaps I should have encouraged you more. Given you a push. I don't know. But it's far from too late. So, here I am, giving you that push.'

'I don't know what to say,' I admitted after a moment's silence.

'That's okay. I know you need to think about it. But I think you could do it. I always have. I want to help you do it, then I can go away knowing you're okay. I mean what

I say about loving you like a daughter.' Her eyes started to mist up.

'I know,' I replied, swallowing the lump in my throat. 'I feel the same. But this is too much. I couldn't accept...'

'Pish posh,' Molly said, cutting through my words. 'If I leave it to you in my will, you'd have to take it but what's the point in that? I want to see you do it. I want to come and have a cup of tea and a slice of cake in your bakery.'

'But it would have to be an investment, I couldn't just let you give it to me.'

She waved her hand. 'Well, we can worry about all that when you have decided to say yes. Which I very much hope you will.'

'Oh, Molly.' I couldn't stop the tears then and wiped at my cheek as they rolled down. 'I honestly don't know what to say.'

'Come here.' Molly pulled me into her arms. 'I know how scared you are. I was terrified when I was having my son and I had my husband and this house and the bakery, so I understand how confused and lost you must be feeling but you'll come out of all this. You have no idea how special you are. Or how capable. I promise that it will all be okay.'

Her words echoed Aunt Sally's. My parents'. Those of everyone around me, really. How could they be so sure? I let out a sob on her shoulder. 'I don't know if I can do it,' I admitted out loud for the first time. I had swept into action and tried to sort everything out but deep down inside, I was lost, and the future felt so uncertain.

'Well, of course you can.' She leaned back to look at me. 'I remember when you walked into my bakery. You were young and full of energy. You told me you wanted to own a chain of bakeries one day. I told you to start with making me a cupcake and we'd see.'

I smiled as I thought back to that day.

'You made me quite possibly the best cupcake I'd ever had, and I knew I couldn't let you get away. That girl is still right here.' She touched my chest. 'Don't ever forget that.'

I nodded and sniffed. 'I wanted to do so much.'

'You're still so young; you have all the time in the world to do it.'

'But what about this one?' I touched my stomach.

'What about them? Do it for him or her. Make your child proud.'

I sniffed hard, worried I'd dissolve into tears all over again. 'You really think I can do it?' I asked, the first stirrings of excitement mixing with the fear inside me.

'I really do,' she promised. 'Now, why don't we start coming up with a plan, but only when you've eaten some more food.' She passed me the stack of pancakes.

'If that's the rule...' I managed a smile as I stuck my fork in and picked up a couple.

-

Greg and I sat side-by-side on the train, watching London roll past the window, slowly being replaced by countryside.

We were on the way to the treatment centre in Surrey as a drizzle of rain blotted out the view. Greg had two cases with him and sat with his hands in his lap, rubbing his fingers together. His parents had wanted to come but he had told them that he wanted me to drop him off. 'How are you feeling?' I asked him, softly, finding our strained silence excruciating after a while.

He turned to me. 'Nervous as hell. I never thought I'd end up here.'

I nodded. Neither had I.

'I was thinking earlier about the day we met. How I saw you standing there in the bakery with all that blonde hair and those curves,' he said in a low voice. 'And I thought that it must be Christmas Day or something.'

I smiled. 'I remember thinking how much I liked a man in uniform,' I said.

'Would you have said yes to a date if I hadn't been in my uniform?'

'Probably not.' I laughed a little. God, that seemed so long ago. 'We were different people then, weren't we?'

Greg thought for a moment. 'I don't think we're all that different. We've had to deal with different things but we're the same people. I've always been impulsive and passionate. I was addicted to you when we first met. I didn't want to leave your side. I think, maybe, I've always drunk just a little bit too much, not known my limits… even choosing to be a fireman, diving into fires even when I was told to hold back, I've always just done things then thought about them later.'

It was so interesting to hear him analyse himself. He was right. 'One of the reasons I fell in love with you was how fearless you were.'

'Maybe sometimes it's okay to let yourself have a little fear. It helps you not take too many risks.'

'I don't want you to change,' I said then, wrapping my arm through his.

'I have to, Em,' he said. 'I have to grow up.' He placed a hand on our baby inside me. 'Then I can help this one to grow up.'

'You're right, I know. I just mean, the things that I love about you, they are what make you special. I wouldn't want you to lose them.'

'I won't, just like you'll never lose how kind and compassionate you are. But if I need to be less fearless then you need to be more fearless,' he added. I'd told him what Molly had offered me. 'This is your chance now. Maybe I held you back.'

I shook my head. 'I don't regret falling for you. Even after the past few weeks,' I said, honestly. I couldn't regret it. He'd made me happy. We had been happy. And now he'd given me a baby. I'd never want to change that.

'I'll always love you,' he promised then, pulling me closer.

'Me too,' I whispered back.

The train pulled into our station then and we pulled apart, getting up and heading out to the waiting taxi. The centre wasn't far from the station, set back from the road behind large gates. It was a long, low building surrounded by trees, all new and white and shiny.

'I think I should go in alone,' Greg said when the taxi stopped outside and a woman in a suit came out, waiting to greet him.

I turned to him in surprise. 'But don't you want me—'

'It'll be harder to say goodbye if you come in. I'll want to run out of the door with you. Please.' He leaned in and kissed me softly on the cheek. 'Thank you, Em. For everything.'

'Why does this feel like the end?' I asked then, feeling myself clinging to him.

'It is the end of something,' he replied with a small smile. 'But hopefully it's the beginning of something too. Right?'

I nodded. 'Right. I'm so proud of you.'

'Save that for when I get out of here. Okay, then.' He opened the door. 'Wish me luck. Is that what you say to someone going into rehab?'

'Good luck,' I replied shaking my head at his attempt at a joke. The taxi driver had brought his bags down and held the door open for him. I watched Greg climb out of the taxi and shake the hand of the woman from the centre. The driver closed the door and went around to get back in. I hastily slid across the seat and pushed the sliding window down. 'I'll see you,' I called out to him.

Greg paused and turned back. He grinned at me, and looked just like the man I fell in love with again for a moment. 'I'll see you, babe,' he called back. And then he followed the woman up the steps and through the door.

'Shall we go?' the taxi driver asked as I sat, frozen, watching the closed door.

I took a deep breath. 'Okay.' I kept my eyes on the centre as we drove away, looking out through the back window as we passed back through the gates, and it got smaller and smaller. Finally, I faced the front again, and what awaited me next, alone.

Chapter Thirty-Eight

I sneezed as I disrupted a pile of dust coating the box I had just opened up in the loft. I really couldn't remember what we'd put up in there apart from the Christmas tree, the only thing we'd ever brought down again since we moved in. On my knees, I leaned over to look inside it. 'Oh,' I said aloud to the empty loft. It was a box of things from my days at catering college. I pulled out a faded pink notebook. It was where I'd written all my recipes. I'd since put my favourite ones on my laptop and mostly worked from memory anyway.

Opening it up, I saw my handwriting all across the pages, recipes written down and crossed-out, notes in the margin with tips like how much to sieve the flour, or to add in more vanilla essence. Turning the page, I stopped at the recipe for red velvet cupcakes. This was the recipe I'd made for Molly when I'd bounced into her bakery and practically demanded that she give me a job.

I jumped up, clutching it to my chest, deciding that I'd done enough sorting for one day. Climbing carefully down the ladder, I walked downstairs to the kitchen, itching to make the cupcakes again. As I re-read the recipe, I realised that I now made them slightly differently, having reworked it through the years and just baking them the way I felt on the day really, but this time I thought I'd make them to the recipe. The one that made Molly give me my job.

Turning on my laptop, I selected my baking playlist and turned it up loud. Rolling up the sleeves of my floral shirt, I wrapped an apron around myself and got to work. The world fell away as it always did and I hummed along to the music as I weighed the ingredients, wanting to make it exactly as I had back at college.

My phone rang as I slid the tray of raw cakes into the oven. 'Hi,' I answered breathlessly, trying not to smear cake mixture all over my phone.

'Hey,' Beth answered, cheerfully. 'Just checking in. How are you?'

I smiled. 'I'm okay. I'm just baking.'

'Ooh, something you're bringing up here?'

'Might do,' I replied, shaking my head. Beth was always thinking about food.

'Well, I just wanted to make sure you're okay with Greg gone. You're not going to spend the night in alone wallowing, are you?'

'I'm having dinner at Mum and Dad's,' I said, sitting down for a much-needed cuppa. 'Are you sure I shouldn't get Caroline and John a wedding gift?' I had taken the plunge and accepted the invitation to their wedding. Greg had been right – I wanted to get back to the fresh air and friendly faces of Glendale. Beth had told me I was welcome to stay for as long as I liked but I knew I couldn't hide in Scotland forever so I had just planned to stay a week. I was hoping it would be the perfect place to come up with a plan about what I was going to do next. I was still getting my head around Molly's offer. I was still very unsure about it but I had faithfully promised to think it over.

'No way. They don't need anything, trust me. They just want the people they love there to celebrate. We're all really excited to have you back.'

I hadn't told Beth about what Molly had said but I wanted to when I got up there – I needed all the advice I could get. 'Me too,' I said. 'And how is it all up there? Is everyone okay?' I couldn't stop myself from wondering if Brodie knew I'd be there again soon.

Beth hesitated for a moment as if she was thinking of him too. 'We're all fine. I just can't wait to give you a big hug. You'll take the journey easy, won't you? I'll be at the station to meet you and Sally is already planning dinner for you.'

I laughed. I liked how nothing seemed to change up there. 'I'll be there soon. Safe and sound, I promise.' We said goodbye and I hung up, letting myself be excited about going back to Glendale. Even if I would soon be coming face-to-face with Brodie again.

When the oven timer went off, I got up and pulled out the tray, smiling at the delicious smell coming from the cupcakes. I put them on a tray to cool and made the buttercream icing. A new song started to play, and I paused. It was a song by a band that I loved, one that Greg had taken me to see on one of our early dates. The song took me right back to that night, dancing and singing along with him in the crowd until my throat was hoarse and my back sweaty. We'd rushed home to his tiny flat, throwing our clothes off, and spending the whole night up talking and kissing, curled up in his single bed. It was so sad that all that was over. But I'd never forget those times.

'I wonder if you'll like this song one day,' I said to my tummy, feeling a little silly doing it. Once the cupcakes were cool enough, I iced them and put one on a plate, the others in an airtight tin for Glendale Hall. Taking a big bite, I let out a moan. 'Oh my God,' I said. They really were so good.

Sitting back down, I pulled out the notebook and spent the rest of the afternoon reading through my recipes and writing down the ones that I loved the most. Slowly, a menu of sorts was forming, and I couldn't ignore the thrum of enthusiasm that ran through my veins as I wrote. 'This is the kind of place I'd love to eat at,' I murmured as I looked down at it.

Maybe, just maybe, one day I might.

—

'There you are, love.' Dad opened the door to me that evening, pulling me in for one of his bear hugs immediately. Dad had grey hair and big, bushy eyebrows that my mum was always trying to get him to let her shape. 'Let's go on through – dinner is almost ready.' Once I left home, Dad became the cook in the family, and my stomach rumbled on cue as I smelt something delicious coming from the kitchen. My mum was sitting at the table, lighting candles, and in the background soft music was playing.

'You look tired,' Mum said as I leaned down to kiss her on the cheek.

'Thanks,' I said with a wry smile as I sat down opposite her.

'I just meant – are you getting enough rest?'

I shrugged. 'I haven't been sleeping all that great. Don't worry,' I added, quickly, when I saw the look of concern on her face, 'I'll be in Glendale tomorrow and there will be plenty of resting there. Although I'm still worried about going when there's so much to do here.'

Mum waved away my worry. 'We're here, and it's the summer holidays so we can do anything that needs doing, I already told you that. Until the house sells there's not much else you can do anyway. Just go and have a nice break.'

'I haven't been back long.'

'But so much has happened and you need the rest. The most important thing is that you and that baby in there take care of yourselves. Everything else will sort itself out.'

'I wish I had your confidence.' I smiled at my dad who handed me a homemade lemonade and gave my mum a glass of wine. 'I'll be happier once we sell the house and get all the debts sorted. It's hard to stop stressing about all of that until it's settled, you know?'

'Of course it is,' Dad said, carrying over a big pot. 'But I'm sure it will happen quickly. Right, here we are.' Mum and I leaned forward as he uncovered the pot and we breathed in the smell of his cottage pie. 'I thought we could all do with a comfort meal even though it's a bit warm really.'

'It's never too warm for your pie,' I replied. He spooned out a plateful for each of us – no small portions on his watch – and passed over a bowl of green veg dripping in butter.

'There's more too… adding to my stress,' I said, passing the veg over to my mum after I'd taken some. I told them about what Molly had offered me. 'So, it feels like everything is changing, like it's all up in the air, and there's so many decisions for me to make.' I took a big bite of pie to help the situation, and moaned appreciatively.

'Well, I think this is great news,' Mum said, clapping her hands together. I raised my eyebrows in surprise. 'Why are you looking at me like that? I remember when you were young and you used to play bakeries with your dolls, feeding them cupcakes and making a mess everywhere, by the way. This has always been your dream, why are you so worried about it?'

'But the timing is completely wrong. I need stability right now, not losing my job – as well as my house, by the way. It's so hard to run your own business anyway, let alone while you're pregnant, and then what happens when the baby comes? I'll be doing it all on my own!'

'No, you won't. You have so many people in your life, Emily. Nothing ever happens at the perfect time. But without a mortgage to pay, and with Molly's money, you can easily do it financially, I'm sure. This is something you've always wanted and someone is willing to give you a massive foot on the ladder, why would you turn that down, for goodness' sake?'

I stared at my mum, impatient and cross that I wasn't excited, then I looked at my dad who shrugged as if to say she was right. I leaned back in my chair. 'I have been writing down recipes that I could make...' I started to say.

'There you go,' Mum said, smugly. 'You know this is the right thing for you.'

'I'm scared though,' I admitted in a small voice. My mother never seemed scared of anything but I just wasn't her.

'The best things in life are scary,' my dad surprised me by answering instead.

I took another bite of pie, their words rolling around in my head. They were right about one thing – Molly was offering me something that most people could only dream of. I had, in fact, dreamed of it. Whether I could make that dream come true was still up for debate though.

'You'll have plenty of time to think about it up in Scotland. Sally will definitely help,' Mum said then. 'It's her fault you got the baking bug in the first place.'

I smiled. 'She will be excited,' I agreed, knowing she'd be so proud if I opened my own bakery. 'I'll talk to her,' I promised.

'I think it'll do you good to go back up there,' Dad said then. 'The Scottish air is excellent for decision-making.'

'I don't know about that – it made me want to marry you,' Mum replied, making us all chuckle.

I watched them smile at one another and my heart ached for what they had.

Chapter Thirty-Nine

When Inverness train station came into view, I felt a weight lifting from me. The countryside and brisk Scottish breeze made me smile as I stepped off the train and onto the platform, clutching my case.

'Emily!'

I turned to see Beth waving madly at me from outside her car down the steps off the platform. I walked over to her, feeling like I had come home.

'Thanks so much for meeting me,' I said as she pulled me in for a long, tight hug. 'You look glowing,' I told her, when we pulled back. She really did. Her hair was loose and wavy over her shoulders, her skin was tanned, her figure as slim as ever. She wore cropped jeans and a white t-shirt and looked as if she hadn't got a care in the world. Whatever it was, I wished I could bottle it up, and drink it.

'Married life suits me, I guess,' she replied with a shrug. 'Anyway, you're the glowing one. I am resisting the urge to touch your stomach by the way,' she added with a laugh.

'I suppose I'd better start getting used to people doing that,' I said. 'Where's Izzy?'

'She stayed over at her friend Daisy's last night, I'm going to pick her up this afternoon.'

We heaved my case into the boot and climbed into the car, setting off for Glendale together. 'So, the honeymoon was wonderful then?'

'It was, although the wedding feels like forever ago. I've hardly been allowed time to be smug about being a new bride, my mother is in full-on wedding planning mode. I mean, talk about Bridezilla.' She rolled her eyes but kept on smiling, showing me she really didn't mind. 'It's nice to see her and John so happy though so I'm putting up with it.' She looked over at me, concern taking over her happy face for a moment. 'We're so glad you agreed to come. Should I ask how things are or would you rather not talk about it?'

I shrugged. 'It's fine, honestly. Greg has gone to rehab and our house is up for sale. It's completely not where I ever thought I'd be when I finally got pregnant but I'm trying to look to the future. I just wish I knew what it was going to look like. It feels like so much is changing... even my job, now.' I told her about Molly's planned retirement and wish to travel the world. 'I want her to be happy, of course, but to say it feels like a rug has been pulled from under me is a massive understatement.'

'I know how much you loved working there,' Beth said, sympathetically. 'Has she said what she'll do with the bakery?'

I explained then about her passing it over to her son and daughter-in-law. 'But that's not all,' I said, telling her that Molly had also offered me a large sum of money so I could start my own bakery. 'I'm still trying to take it all in.'

'Wow.' Beth whistled. 'Life is throwing everything at you, isn't it? But that sounds amazing! And you've done the right thing in coming here. Glendale has a way of making everything seem clear. It changed my life. I think it just might change yours.'

I was about to ask her quite how when we approached Glendale Hall, and I lapsed into silence. We drove through the large iron gates and along the gravel drive up towards the house, and I was happier than I thought I'd be to see it again. It had only been a few weeks since I left but because so much had happened, I felt like a different person now. 'Still as gorgeous as ever,' I said as Beth pulled up in front of the Hall.

'Wait until you see the garden – it's in full bloom now, and it's just stunning,' Beth said, jumping out eagerly. I climbed out too and felt the sun warm my arms instantly.

The front door was flung open and Aunt Sally stepped outside. 'Emily, it's so good to have you back,' she said, holding out her arms. I went over and hugged her. 'You look pale,' she said, giving me a look up and down. 'You've been doing too much,' she scolded, gently.

'There's been a lot to do,' I replied, defending myself.

'Well, we'll soon perk you up, won't we Beth?' She led me by the arm inside the hallway, Beth following, dragging my case behind her. 'Cup of tea?' Sally didn't wait for a response as she led the way to the kitchen.

'I'll put this in your room,' Beth said, heading for the stairs.

'I can do it,' I protested.

Beth snorted and walked off without a response. I smiled at her retreating back. I knew they both wanted to take care of me but I didn't want to be a burden. I was here for a wedding, and I wanted to help. I couldn't deny it though; it felt nice to have people who cared, and the opportunity to have some rest up here was a welcome thought after the past hectic few weeks. It wasn't just physical fatigue from packing up the house; I felt emotionally drained by it all as well. I followed Aunt Sally into the large open-plan kitchen and looked out at the grounds through the open French doors. Beth was right. The flowers in pots along the patio by the side of the house were full of bright colours and the lawn was a lush green, the sun shining down on it from a clear blue sky.

'There's been so much going on here,' Aunt Sally said as she made tea. 'I'll be glad when things quieten down a bit to be honest. Two weddings in one summer is a bit too much.'

'I thought you liked to be busy,' I said, turning back from the French doors.

'I do but I'm not as young as I once was, you know.' She smiled over her shoulder. 'In fact, there is a lot to talk to you about. There's a lot of change happening here as well.'

'I'm not sure I can take any more change,' I admitted. I took the mug of tea that she handed me and we stepped outside into the garden and I sat down on the picnic bench.

'Unfortunately, there isn't much we can do to stop it, is there?' Sally sat down opposite me. 'Before I get to my news though, how are you doing, really?'

'I'll be fine,' I said. She glared at me. 'I promise! It's been really strange sorting out the house and putting it on the market but we had to do it. Greg has gone to get help and I hope it works for him, I really do. I just have to move on now, don't I? But please, tell me your news. I need the distraction from my life right now.'

'Well, as I said, things have been very hectic here lately, and it's made me realise that I'm no spring chicken any more.'

'Don't be ridiculous,' I said, instinctively, but even I could see Aunt Sally did look a little tired. Panic suddenly ran through me. 'You're not ill, are you?'

She smiled, and shook her head. 'No, I promise. I've just been thinking that it would be nice to take things a little easier now I've hit my twilight years.'

I often forgot that Aunt Sally was a few years older than my mother, and that meant she was close to retirement age. Like my mum though, I had never really pictured Aunt Sally actually doing that. But look at Molly. Perhaps I had been in denial about the women in my life. I suddenly felt selfish. 'Well, you certainly deserve to take things easier,' I told her. 'You've worked hard all your life. But what will you do? I mean, I can't imagine you not being here.' The thought of Glendale Hall without Aunt Sally was too much to fathom.

'That's exactly what I said,' Beth said from behind me then, carrying out the mug of tea left on the side for her. 'The Hall is your home.'

Aunt Sally smiled at her. 'Well you and Caroline have certainly been extremely generous.'

'No, not generous at all, just selfish,' Beth said, sitting down next to me. 'We knew there was no way we could cope without you.'

Aunt Sally saw my confused expression, and explained. 'After the wedding, John is going to finally move into the Hall with Caroline, which means his cottage will be empty. Beth and Caroline have kindly asked me to stay on and live in the cottage. I'll still help out around here but I'm going to be stepping down as housekeeper. We're going to find some new blood to take over.'

'God knows how,' Beth muttered. 'Talk about big shoes and all that.'

'Wow,' I said. 'I'm so glad you'll be staying here.'

'It's my home,' she said, simply.

'And always will be,' Beth promised.

'Well, I'm happy that you'll be taking things easy, and hopefully that will mean we can spend more time together. My baby is going to need a great-auntie in their life.'

'Now I feel really old,' Aunt Sally complained but her eyes looked like they were misting over before she hid them behind her mug and took a sip of tea.

'We've sorted Sally out,' Beth said. 'And my mum is finally making an honest man of John so…' she swivelled round to look at me. 'Now, it's your turn.'

'For what?' I asked nervous suddenly.

'For us to sort out, of course.'

'I don't need—' I started to say, as my default positon on people helping me kicked in.

'Oh, yes, you do,' Aunt Sally and Beth said in unison. Despite myself, I couldn't help but burst out laughing at that, and they joined in, and miraculously my troubles seemed to lift just a little bit.

Chapter Forty

'I'm waiting, by the way,' Beth said after lunch as we walked into Glendale village together. I had been right about the weather – there was no sticky London heatwave up here, just pleasant sunshine and a refreshing breeze. And the air was so much cleaner too. Beth had to meet her mum at the Glendale Hall shop and I was excited to see it again, and say hello to Caroline so I went along with her, leaving my unpacking for later.

'For what?' I asked, raising an eyebrow at the devilish grin on her face.

'For you to ask about him, of course!'

I sighed. 'You mean Brodie,' I said, not needing to phrase it as a question. His name still brought a small smile to my lips. Which was too confusing. I wanted to see him and yet I also wanted to run away from having to.

'Yes, I mean Brodie. He's pleased you're back, by the way. I told him you were coming and he said he was looking forward to seeing you again.'

'He's a nice guy, of course he said that,' I replied, trying to ignore my heart lifting inside my chest at her words.

'Why can't you just admit that you like him?'

'Of course I like him but it's pretty complicated, isn't it? We agreed that we're just friends.' I saw her face. 'Seriously, Beth. Who would want to take on another man's child anyway?' I gestured to my stomach. 'Plus, I really don't know what will happen with Greg. Things are so up in the air right now. I just need to keep everything as simple as I can.'

'I know, I know. I'm sorry.' She slipped her arm through mine. 'I just can't help but think you two deserve to be happy. But I won't mention it again. I know it's complicated. Love always is.'

I was about to dispute the fact that this had anything to do with love when Glendale High Street came into view, and I was too eager to see it. Now it was the holidays, the village was alive with families walking around, ice creams in hand, the outside tables of the pub filled with people having lunch in the sunshine, and customers going in and out of the shops.

Glendale Hall shop's door jangled merrily as we walked in. Caroline was behind the counter serving someone. The girl who helped out in the shop when she wasn't at college was arranging honey made from the Hall's beehives in the corner and waved to us when we walked in.

'Look who's back,' Beth said to her mum when the customer had left. Caroline came over and gave me a kiss on the cheek. She wore an elegant linen dress, her skin as tanned as her daughter's, looking more at ease than I had ever seen her.

'How is the bride-to-be?' I asked, able to see the answer for myself.

'A little stressed because the florist just came in to say one of the flowers I wanted just won't be available but other than that… I can't quite believe I'm going to be married again. At my age.' She laughed a little.

'I think it's wonderful,' I told her, sincerely. I left Beth and Caroline to debate flowers, wandering over to look at the shop produce. It was lovely to think that John and Caroline were about to get their happy ever after twenty years after meeting, proving that love really didn't have an expiration date; that you could find it no matter how young or old you were.

My eye was caught then by a teddy bear on the shelf. It wore a jumper with 'Glendale Hall' stitched on it. I realised that I hadn't bought anything for my baby yet. At first, it was all so shocking and then I had so much to deal with, plus the nerves ahead of my first scan but now that had gone well, and everything seemed okay, I felt the sudden urge to start buying things. 'I just can't resist,' I said, taking the teddy over to the till. It would be a reminder of this special place and a promise to bring my baby here with me too one day.

'I'm not taking your money,' Beth said, pushing the teddy back into my hands. 'Ooh, I need to go and collect Izzy from Daisy's house. You want to come?' she asked, coming around the counter.

'I think I'll walk around a bit more. I have missed all the fresh air up here,' I said. 'Are you sure?' I waved the bear at her.

'My first present to my godchild,' she replied. 'That's a big hint by the way,' she added with a smile. I laughed and followed her out. 'While you're walking around, why don't you have a look at the shop over there? In fact…' she pulled out a key from her bag. 'Go inside. See what you think.'

'Think about what?' I asked but she was already walking back towards Glendale Hall. I shook my head and walked down the High Street. There was one empty property still and I looked in the window. It was a wide shop with lots of light pouring in. I unlocked the door and walked in. It was a good space. Walking through, I saw that out the back was an old kitchen. I remembered then that this had been a café when I was growing up in Glendale. They had served excellent cakes and tea.

Running my hand over the dusty kitchen surface, I smiled at how Glendale had returned to the lively, warm village I had known as a kid.

I hoped they would find someone to open the shop again. I took one last look before locking it back up and walking back down the road. I wondered why Beth had wanted me to see it, perhaps to help her decide what to do with it. I thought it could well be a café again. A village always needed a place where you could get a cake, in my opinion. I felt a little daft then, as Beth's suggestion suddenly became obvious. She was shameless, that girl. But despite shaking my head at her, I couldn't help but feel possibility in the air.

'Emily?'

I jumped a little as someone touched me on the arm. I stopped and saw Brodie beside me.

'I called your name but you were miles away,' he said with a laugh.

My cheeks flooded with warmth. Brodie was in his dog-collar shirt with jeans. Looking tanned, and even more handsome than I remembered. He removed his hand quickly from me, and put it in his pocket.

'I'm sorry, I was,' I said, a little breathlessly. I was still startled by his sudden appearance, and how my pulse had started racing at seeing him again.

'It's good to see you in Glendale again,' he said. 'How are you?'

'I'm fine. Good, thank you,' I babbled a little. 'How are you?'

'All well with me too,' he said. 'I was just about to pick up some steak for dinner,' he explained, gesturing to the butcher's behind me. 'Did you just get back here?'

'This morning,' I said. 'Just taking in the village again. I've missed it.' I looked away, wishing I could tell him that I'd missed him too.

'It gets under your skin, doesn't it? Well, I'd better be going...'

'Oh, okay, sure.' I stepped back, a little stunned by him wanting to escape so quickly.

'I'll see you around, Emily,' he said, walking past me.

'Bye,' I said, lamely, but he'd already disappeared into the shop. I hadn't exactly imagined what our first meeting again would be like, but I was certain I hadn't expected it to be so anticlimactic. I waited a beat before turning and heading back towards Glendale Hall, wondering why I felt quite so disappointed.

Chapter Forty-One

Aunt Sally and I walked through the garden towards the towering oak trees that hid the cottage from view until you were right upon it. John had already started moving his things into the Hall and had invited Sally to come and look around the cottage. I had never been in there and Sally said she hadn't for years – John preferring to look after it himself, and not being the entertaining company sort of man – so we were curious to see it.

Through an opening in the trees, we joined the thin path that twisted up to the low, wide cottage. It was made from the same cream stone as Glendale Hall's main house, with two floors, and a pretty patch of flowers either side of the path that took you up to the oak front door. Letting ourselves in, we stood and looked around the cosy, tidy cottage. There were beams across the ceiling and a large fireplace in the living room we stood in. Through the living room was a pine kitchen, perfectly formed with a door that led out to a small garden. Upstairs, there were two bedrooms and a bathroom, all decorated in the same off-white, with wooden floors, and wide windows letting in lots of light.

'It's lovely,' I said when we returned to the living room. I imagined Aunt Sally curled up in the armchair with a crackling fire in the winter, and I knew she'd be happy here. 'It's perfect. A lot bigger, actually, than I thought, too.'

'Me too,' Aunt Sally agreed. 'I was worried there wouldn't be space to cook but the kitchen is a lot roomier than I remembered. And I love how he's marked out a small front and back garden so I can potter about without ruining the wider grounds,' she said with a laugh.

I turned to her. 'Is this really what you want? To retire, I mean?'

'The Hall is too big for me now, and there are too many people here now. Once Beth and Izzy came back to live here, there was so much more to do. I know we have Jo in a couple of times a week but there is still too much for just me. They need someone younger with more energy. And I like helping out in the shop, which I can rarely do now so I will carry on doing that, don't worry. You know me, I will always keep busy but it's time for someone else to take over the Hall.'

'You deserve to start taking things easier, for sure. It's lovely that they don't want you to leave the Hall. You're part of the family.'

She smiled. 'You are too, Emily. Don't forget that. Right, having said all this, I need to get back to the house to serve dinner. We have a few guests tonight, as always now.' She rolled her eyes.

'I can't believe there will be another wedding here so soon,' I said as we stepped back outside into the sunshine.

'It's about time for them,' Aunt Sally replied dryly.

'But never for you?' I said, glancing at her. She had never even thought about finding love after my uncle died.

'I count myself lucky to have had true love once, and that was all I needed.' She nodded. 'You haven't found your true love though, I promise you.'

I hoped she was right. 'Will I know it when I see it?'

She thought for a moment. 'We don't always know it as soon as we see it but that just makes it all the more worthwhile once we finally do realise it.'

'That's cryptic,' I laughed.

'Is it?' She left the question hanging and we lapsed into silence as we walked back to the Hall, both thinking of true love perhaps, and how some people find it, and others just think they have.

When we got back, the Hall was indeed bustling with life. Izzy was home again and Drew had returned from his night shift at the hospital. Rory, Heather and baby Harry were there too, setting up the picnic tables on the patio for dinner.

'Do you want to join us, Emily?' Caroline asked when she saw me, carrying a jug of homemade lemonade over.

'Join you?' I asked, unsure what she was talking about. Aunt Sally slipped past me into the kitchen.

'We're attending the church service tomorrow and then having a quick wedding rehearsal afterwards,' she explained, putting the jug down on the table. 'It's the last service before the wedding.'

I was curious to attend one of Brodie's services, I couldn't deny it. Ever since we met, I had found it hard to picture him as a minister.

'We're all going,' Beth added with a roll of her eyes. I knew she found church boring, a reminder of her youth when her family used to make her go when she wanted to be anywhere else.

'I'd better come too then,' I replied, telling myself she had made the decision for me.

'Emily, you're back, yay!' Izzy said, rushing over to give me a squeeze. 'I knew you couldn't stay away for long.'

'What did you think of the empty unit by the way?' Beth asked, putting down a large bowl of salad. She tilted her head at me. I felt a few pairs of eyes on us then.

'It's a good space,' I replied, casually. 'It was the café years ago, wasn't it?'

'It was. Jean, who ran it, has long since gone, bless her,' Beth said.

'Sit down everyone,' Aunt Sally said then, cutting into the conversation, bringing over a tray of salmon fillets drizzled with lemon.

I climbed onto the bench and poured myself a glass of lemonade. Everyone was smiling and chatting as we handed each other the salmon, new potatoes and salad, and broke into the warm, crusty bread. I tucked in, as hungry as ever, looking at everyone, and Aunt Sally was right; it did feel as if I was part of the family. I knew then that I'd never be alone with this baby, no matter what happened with Greg. I had my parents, and I had everyone at Glendale Hall, and that was so much more than so many people had. I had to start counting my blessings because really, I did have a lot of them.

'This time next week we'll be man and wife,' John said quietly to Caroline beside me.

She picked up her wine glass and clinked it against his beer. 'The best things in life are worth waiting for,' she said.

I saw Beth exchange a smile with Drew and knew she felt exactly as her mother did.

After dinner, Sally dished out strawberries and cream to everyone. I started to think then about Greg, wondering how he was getting on at the treatment centre. Cut off from the world, it must be strange and scary but I hoped the help there would be worth it. I thought of our baby fast growing inside me and how much I wanted Greg to be okay for him or her. I looked at Drew pouring more lemonade for Izzy, and Rory who had Harry on his lap, and hoped my baby would get to experience a father like both those men were, and like my own father was.

'How did you manage, really?' I asked Beth later as we made everyone coffees and teas, insisting Aunt Sally relax with the others. The sun was just starting to dip outside, promising a pretty sunset 'Raising Izzy alone. I mean, I know I was there at the start, but really it was just the two of you. When I came to see you and left you in that tiny bedsit holding the baby, I really didn't know how you were doing it. I was sure I'd never be able to do it on my own like you were. But I think I might have to now.'

Beth leaned against the kitchen counter. 'I guess it wasn't ever a choice, really. I mean, once I was in London away from my family, without Drew, I just had to suck it up and do it. But it was when I held her for the first time that I really knew that I could. She needed me. And I'd never felt love like that before or how badly I wanted to protect her – those two feelings got me through it. It was bloody hard, though. But it's different for you, Em. You're older, wiser, and you have so many people who love you, that will help you. I really don't think you'll be doing it alone. And even if you are, you can do it. Because that baby needs you to do it.' She picked up the tray of drinks. 'You'll think about it, won't you? The shop in Glendale, I mean?' she asked, finally admitting why she'd told me to look at it.

I nodded. It was appealing. Molly wanted to give me the money, and there was a property ready and waiting for me. But it really wasn't going to be that easy, I knew. There was so much to think about. Not only the baby but Greg too. Coming up here would mean taking it away from its father. In the short term anyway. But it would also be offering a lot of opportunities for both me and the baby. I just had to decide what the best thing to do really was.

'You believe me, don't you? That you're not alone, and that you can do it?' Beth prodded as she walked to the door to rejoin the others.

'I'm getting there,' I replied with a smile.

Chapter Forty-Two

Glendale church was almost full. The congregation in Glendale was as healthy as I'd been told it was thanks to Reverend Brodie. With the whole of the Glendale Hall extended family there too, there was barely any pew space free this Sunday morning. A guitar band played as we walked in, very different to services I had attended as a child there, and Brodie was at the front, smiling and waving at people. He nodded at us filing in, and I couldn't tell for sure if he had realised I was there or not as his gaze had quickly moved on to another family walking in, whom he went to greet.

Once everyone was seated, Brodie began. 'Today I wanted to talk about second chances. Next week, I'm conducting a wedding, which I suspect most of Glendale knows about, between two people who have known each other for a long time. People often say that you only get one life, and therefore, only one chance to live it the way you want to, and if you happen to make a mistake during this one, short, life, then it's all over,' Brodie said from the front of the church, his voice clear and loud in the hush. 'But we know that there isn't only one chance. We know that through the resurrection, you can have a second chance. That you can be forgiven; that you can be given the chance to make things right. And if that is the case then think of all the possibilities, all the opportunities that are ours for the taking. We don't need to live with what was, we can instead live with what can be. If you only focused on what you wanted, instead of worrying about what you deserve or what went wrong last time you tried or that it's too hard, then what could you really achieve in this life? What could you do, really do, with this gift of life we've been given? If you took the second chance you've been given, just what would you do with it?'

The band started playing a song then and everyone rose to their feet to join in. It was a newer song, not a traditional hymn and I had no idea what it was but the words appeared up on a screen and I managed to soon join in too. Brodie's sermon rang through my mind. I still didn't think I'd ever have his kind of faith in things like resurrection but it was interesting to think of life as offering you more than one chance to get it right; that there was always hope, always a possibility of doing better, of making your dreams come true, of being the person that you wanted to be.

I really hoped that was true for all of us.

And as the song died down, I wiped away a tear that had rolled down my cheek.

–

After the service, the congregation filed out and our Glendale group remained at the front where Brodie gave us a quick run-through of the wedding service. Caroline said she had only invited family and close friends on Saturday, a contrast I knew to her first large white wedding to Beth's father David, and after the service, there would be food and dancing back at the Hall.

The rehearsal over, I hung back to speak to Brodie, nodding at Beth to go ahead without me, trying to ignore the knowing smile on her face. That woman was impossible sometimes.

'Emily,' Brodie said, turning around and looking surprised when he realised I was still there.

I stepped forward. 'Do you have a few minutes? Can we talk?'

He looked at me for a moment then nodded. 'Of course. Why don't you come to the vicarage?'

'Okay,' I said, wondering if there was any etiquette about going around to a minister's house I should know about.

'You don't need to look quite so worried. I'm offering tea and a chair, that's all,' Brodie said, smiling at the look on my face. 'I don't do human sacrifices until the evening.'

I laughed. 'That's a relief then.' We walked around the church and down a short path to the small, pretty vicarage building behind. Brodie let me in and showed me through the narrow hallway into the kitchen, which had a small round table in it.

'I can't take any credit for how clean and tidy my house is, I'm ashamed to say,' Brodie said, going over to the kettle. He gestured for me to sit at the table, which I did. 'Gloria, my housekeeper, is out for lunch with a friend. She'll be upset to have missed you, she's heard so much about you.'

'She has?' I asked, looking around, curiously. It was kept very clean and neat and not at all bachelor-like.

'Of course. So, how are you really? How is the baby? And everything in London?' he asked, lightly, as he poured out our teas. 'Milk, no sugar, isn't it?'

I smiled, pleased that he remembered how I liked my tea. He brought our drinks over to the table. 'I had my first scan, and everything is going well,' I told him.

'That's great.'

'London isn't going quite as well… We've had to put our house up for sale and Greg… well, Greg is at a treatment centre. He's working hard to get the help he needs.'

'Well, I'm glad of that. And how do you feel about selling the house?'

'Honestly, I'm more upset about it than I think I should be – I mean, it's just a pile of bricks at the end of the day.'

Brodie shook his head. 'Of course you're upset; it's your home.'

'Your sermon today…'

He smiled. 'I can't quite believe you were in my church.'

'Don't expect it to become a regular thing,' I replied, but I smiled back because I didn't think I would actually mind all that much if it did. 'But I found it interesting. There's been a lot of change that I've had to deal with and some of it has made me feel like I've failed in some way, I suppose. And that I don't deserve things to turn around. Does that make sense?'

Brodie stirred the sugar into his tea and took a sip. 'It absolutely makes sense but it couldn't be further from the case. You haven't failed at all – none of this is your fault, after all – but even if you had failed, then I would still say the same thing: there is always a way to turn things around. And they will turn around.' He looked up at me. 'Remember what I told you about my past? My dad said that I'd end up in prison the way I was going. I made so many mistakes. I mean, I turned my back on God! But after my sister got better, I changed. I tried to make things right. And I'm still working on that. I really do believe that we can always make things right.' His voice turned softer. 'But I really don't understand why you think you don't deserve that chance?'

I sighed. 'You say that it's not my fault but how can it not be? I lived with a man that I was meant to love but I had no clue what he was doing. All these things were happening right in front of me but I didn't see it or want to see it. I didn't help him. Before it got so bad. I failed at saving him.'

'Was it really your job to save him? And don't forget that when he finally did ask you for help, then that's exactly what you did. You could have walked away, left him to deal with everything but you didn't. You're helping him now. When he really needs you. That counts for a lot. And if you didn't see it, isn't that because he didn't want you to see it?'

I nodded slowly. Why did everything make so much more sense when Brodie said it? 'I know that he hid things, yes, but I worry that I just had this idea of who he was, and that's who I loved, and he actually wasn't anything like that.'

'Doesn't love blind us all?' Brodie gave a wry smile. 'But also people often let us see only what they want us to see. I had no idea the woman I loved had fallen in love with someone else. I could take the blame for that, and I did for a long time, but I realised that it wasn't really anyone's fault. Some things just aren't meant to be. We don't always understand why at the time but hopefully one day, we will. I understand now that I wasn't meant to be with her.'

I swallowed hard, wondering just who he was meant to be with. Who I was meant to be with. We lapsed into a short silence. Then I decided to tell him about Molly's offer.

'But am I being selfish in even thinking of taking her up on it? I mean, with my baby on the way, I feel like I should be focusing on just that but I keep thinking... I've been offered something I've always wanted but I'm worried that I shouldn't take it now, that it's the wrong time, that I should only be thinking about my baby. That maybe it's greedy to want more than that,' I admitted.

'Who says you're only allowed one good thing in your life at a time?' Brodie arched an eyebrow. 'I think going after your dream is scary, and hard work, and it's probably easier not to do it but wouldn't your baby be proud if they found out one day that their mother made her dream come true, and then maybe they would think that they could do the exactly the same thing.'

'I think what you did was amazing,' I told him then. 'Turning your life around like you did. It's inspiring.' He really was someone to admire. I wondered if I could be someone like that too one day.

'Sometimes I think about what might have happened if I hadn't. If my sister hadn't pulled through that day...' He shuddered. 'But I try not to dwell on it. And you shouldn't either. You should focus on what's ahead — for you, and your baby. And go after what will make you happy.'

I nodded. 'I'm scared. And if I'm honest, I've been wondering if it's easier not to try than to try and fail at something else in my life. What if I just keep on failing? What kind of example would that be for this baby?' I touched my stomach then, wondering how something so small could be causing such chaos in my life already. God only knew what would happen once they actually arrived.

'A brilliant example,' Brodie replied, firmly. He looked across at me, holding my gaze with his own, steady one. 'Who can be proud of someone who never tries? You only really fail when you don't try. Don't you think?'

Chapter Forty-Three

The following day, Beth, Aunt Sally and I stood in the empty shop on Glendale's High Street. Beth had hooked Aunt Sally in to help her mission to try to convince me that it could become my own bakery one day. 'Look how perfect it is,' Beth said as she flung open the door. 'I mean, it used to be a café, so most of what you need is in place already,' she added, walking inside, followed by Aunt Sally and me.

'It's a good unit,' Aunt Sally agreed with a nod. 'There's enough space that if you wanted to have tables for people to eat inside, you could.'

'Definitely. There's plenty of room for a big counter and tables,' Beth agreed, throwing Sally a grateful smile. 'And the kitchen is huge.'

'If anything it's a little large for just a bakery,' I said, looking around again. 'You would need tables but obviously that would be more work serving everyone; you'd need two people working in here every day, I would think.' Molly had always wished that she had enough space so people could have tea and cake inside. I knew her eyes would light up if she could see this place. But I couldn't help feeling daunted by it. I chewed on my lip. 'I just don't know, Beth.'

'You could use Molly's money to set this place up. We would offer you the same structure as the other shops – you only pay rent once you start making money. I mean, you're family, so you don't need to worry about money; we'd just love to see this shop open and we'd love it even more if you were the one running it.'

I smiled. 'I really appreciate that, you know I do. But there's a lot to think about. Not only whether I could make this place successful but it would mean moving up here again, and there's Greg to think about... Plus, soon I'll be really pregnant. Maybe this isn't the best time to set up a business.'

'There's a lot to think about, I know,' Beth said. 'But this could be brilliant, I just know it.'

'I really think you could make it work,' Aunt Sally said, thoughtfully. 'We'd all be here to help you get set up, and find you great staff, and I know the whole community would be excited.'

'What about when the baby comes though? I'd need time off...'

'You'd have us to keep it all going,' she replied. 'I'll have a lot of time on my hands, after all.'

'I don't think you realise how much work it would be.'

'Just don't say no yet,' Beth said. 'Think it over. Talk to your parents, and Molly. And Greg too. It's a big decision, we know that.'

I nodded. 'Okay.' It was tempting but I just really didn't know if I could do it. Or should do it, right now. I took out my phone and snapped a few photos though so I could show it to Molly. As I followed Beth and Aunt Sally out, I couldn't help but glance back and for a moment, I let myself picture what it could look like. The long counter filled with cakes and pastries, a coffee machine, round tables and chairs in pretty colours, a vase of wild flowers on each, and then as I walked away, I looked up and imagined a large sign across the front of the shop: 'Emily's Bakery'.

And a pleasant shiver ran up my spine.

–

'The estate agent has had four viewings this week,' Mum said on the phone to me the night before Caroline and John's wedding. My stay in Glendale was almost up, and I had to admit being here had helped. Aunt Sally had been feeding me nutritious home-cooked meals, of course, and I had rested a lot too. Strolling through the garden in the sunshine, and helping out with wedding preparations had filled my mind, and jotting ideas down in my note-book about the bakery was exciting too. Things felt a lot brighter in my world than they had when I left London.

'Maybe someone will make an offer then,' I said, sitting on my bed as the sun started to dip in the sky outside my bedroom window. I hadn't seen much of Brodie since our chat though, with everything going on at the Hall and him in full-on wedding season, but perhaps that was for the best. Somehow looking into his eyes made everything feel both more confusing and clearer all at the same time, it was quite disconcerting. 'It's so strange imagining strangers walking through my house deciding whether or not they want it.' I was relieved I wasn't there, actually. It was better out of sight, out of mind. I needed the house to sell but I didn't want it to at the same time.

'Fingers crossed someone will want it soon. Is bump doing okay?'

I smiled. 'Bump is fine, yes. I've had my next scan scheduled – the one when they can tell you the sex if you want. I have no idea if I want to know or not.'

'It helps with buying things but I kept it a surprise. I think because I really wanted a girl so didn't want to feel disappointed by knowing in advance,' Mum replied with a chuckle.

'I don't think I mind, really.' I wondered if it would look like me or Greg. 'It's strange not being able to talk to Greg about all of it.'

'Of course it is. Have you heard anything?'

'His mum texted to say the centre had rung them as planned to say he was doing okay. We just have to hope he's getting the help he needs. I want him to be a father to this baby even if we're not together.' I sighed. 'I hate that we failed, you know?'

'I wouldn't think of it as a failure. You loved one another, you've made a baby together, and that will always be special. Sometimes things don't work out but that doesn't mean there was no point, you know? You'll look back on it and realise that it all happened for a reason, I think.'

'Maybe.' I sighed.

'Have you thought any more about the bakery idea?'

I had told her about the empty unit in Glendale. 'I sent photos of it to Molly and she said it was perfect, but it would be such a large undertaking, and I'd be so far away from you guys.' I knew I had Aunt Sally up here and all my friends but my parents and Greg – once he finished rehab – were in London. It was so hard to know what to do. 'What would Greg say about it?'

Mum was silent for a moment. 'You've always been excellent at thinking about other people's feelings, Emily. But, first, you should think about what you want. If this is something you want then you can worry about everyone else later.'

'That sounds a little selfish.'

'Sometimes in life you have to be a little bit selfish. Don't you think you deserve it after everything that's happened?'

This time, I was quiet, letting her question sink in. 'I really don't know what to do,' I admitted then.

'You will,' she promised. 'You will.'

After we hung up, I gazed out at the garden. I thought about how different life could be if you just made one or two different choices. If I hadn't agreed to that first date with Greg or if I hadn't walked into Molly's bakery that day, and asked for a job. Small choices at the time that led to big life changes for me. And were still affecting my life now.

Perhaps if we did realise what a big impact some choices would have, we'd never be able to make them in the first place. Maybe it was better not knowing. The problem was, I knew the choices I needed to make now were big ones, that would impact not only my life but my baby's too, and that was what was so hard. If only you could take a quick peek into the future so you knew where the choice would lead you to a few years down the line... but then again, if you knew the outcome, would it even be a choice in the first place?

I yawned – over-thinking really made me sleepy. It was too early to go to bed but I laid down on the pillow anyway, letting my eyes fall shut. It would be a long day tomorrow with my second Glendale Hall wedding to attend and I hoped that a good night's sleep might make everything seem just a little bit clearer in the morning.

Chapter Forty-Four

Caroline and John's wedding dawned cloudy but muggy. After lunch, I put on a long floral dress which skimmed my bump perfectly, left my hair loose, and added a pink cardigan, clutch bag and sandals to complete the outfit. My week in Glendale, spent so much outside, had deepened my summer tan, and lightened my hair further.

Once I was ready, I joined the others in the driveway where three cars were waiting to drive the short distance to the church. Beth and Izzy, bridesmaids of a fashion, both wore cream dresses, and then Caroline swept downstairs in her elegant cream skirt suit, her hair pinned back, a small hat completing the chic look. She looked a little nervous, which was unlike her, and I noticed Beth chatting away trying to help. John had stayed over with a friend in the village so we would see him at the church.

We set off, everyone in good spirits, to Glendale. Brodie was outside the church waiting for us, looking smart and smiling at everyone. I gave him a little wave as I went inside with Aunt Sally and Drew and we slid into one of the pews close to the front. John nodded at us, looking smart in his kilt, his best friend beside him in his. Looking around, I recognised a lot of faces from the village, people I had known growing up and seen around the village during my trips here this summer. Heather and

Rory waved from the pew opposite. Brodie walked in then, standing at the front, gesturing for us all to stand up. A bag-pipe player started up from the back, and I turned to see Caroline walking up the aisle, flanked by Beth and Izzy, all holding hands.

For some reason, the sight of grandmother, mother and daughter made me feel more emotional than the wedding itself. Perhaps because of my own impending motherhood. I hoped that my own bond with my child would be as strong as the one that the three of them had. I knew they had had their ups and downs but they were a tight unit and I wanted to have exactly that relationship. Wiping away a tear, pleased I'd worn waterproof mascara, I sat back in the pew as Brodie began the ceremony. Caroline and John took each other's hand, smiling, and I knew that theirs was a strong union, created over time, growing from friendship into something more, and that they would be companions for the rest of their days. It hadn't been easy, Caroline had, after all, been a married woman when they met, but they had come through it all still side-by-side.

If only we could all be as lucky as they were.

–

Glendale Hall really was made for weddings. The sun came out and shone down on the garden as the guests arrived, filing into the marquee on the lawn. Caroline and John's marquee was smaller than Beth and Drew's had been – inside there was just the top table and three smaller, round ones. Each had a large bouquet of lilies in the centre, and a wooden floor covered the grass. A harpist provided the music as we sat down for the meal. Beth pointed to my table and I joined Heather, Rory and

Heather's father, Ron. Then Brodie came over, walking with a woman clutching his arm, smiling from ear-to-ear.

'This is Jen,' he said, pulling out the chair for her. She was pretty with layered fair hair, and was wearing a bright blue dress.

'You run the nursery, don't you, Jen?' Heather asked her, pouring herself a glass of wine. 'How do you two know each other then?'

'That's right. I brought the kids to the church so Brodie could talk to them,' Jen replied, smiling a little shyly at him. 'He was so great with them.'

'They're a cute bunch,' Brodie replied. 'I've been thinking of starting up a Sunday school that Jen might help out with,' he added, glancing across the table at me.

I suddenly wished I could have a glass of wine myself. It was so silly but I didn't like the idea that he had brought a date to this wedding at all.

'Beth tells me you're considering taking the empty shop on the High Street,' Heather said to me then, perhaps sensing the need for a change of subject. 'We've loved opening up the farm shop,' she added, with a warm smile.

'I've always wanted to open up a bakery of my own so Beth suggested I use that unit,' I replied, trying not to look at Brodie and Jen again. 'I'm not sure, though... it would be a lot of work, and would mean moving up here too. Well, it's a big decision, you know? There's a lot to think about – especially with the baby,' I said, gesturing to my stomach.

'Oh, you're pregnant?' Jen said, her eyes widening. 'Congratulations! I can't wait to have children. Is your husband here?'

I felt a little sick all of a sudden. 'Um, well, no...'

A tapping of a glass saved me from struggling to form a response, and I turned gratefully to see John standing up at the top table.

Next to me, Heather gave my knee a quick squeeze in solidarity, and I shot her a grateful smile.

As John began his speech, I found myself looking back at Brodie and Jen. She had leaned close to him to say something soft in his ear, and he smiled at her, and I felt my heart break just a little bit.

Chapter Forty-Five

I awoke the morning after the wedding having slept restlessly, to bright sunshine streaming into my room. I had retired to bed before the others in the end. I hadn't been drinking like them, and wasn't in the mood for dancing – especially as Brodie and Jen seemed to be on the dance floor most of the night, twirling in each other's arms to every slow song played by the band. I had felt like a party pooper but I was sure that no one really noticed as they had all been having such a lovely time. Caroline and John had left at midnight in a limo for the hotel they were staying at before their honeymoon trip to Paris. It was clear they had had a lovely day, and it was wonderful to see the pure joy on their faces as they danced as a married couple for the first time. But annoyingly, it had served to make my heart ache just a little bit more.

I climbed out of bed, having to remind myself that I really wasn't alone; that romance should be the last thing on my mind as I prepared to bring my baby in the world… but I couldn't shake the image of Brodie and Jen from my mind. Just why had I had to meet him at such a crazy point in my life? I let myself imagine for a moment what things might have been like if, instead of Greg, I had met Brodie but I quickly dismissed it. I would not be having this baby if that had been the case.

After a quick shower, I pulled on shorts and a t-shirt and my Converse, tied my hair in a ponytail and put on sunglasses to hide the dark circles under my eyes. I didn't want to mope around the house all morning on my last day at Glendale Hall, and I knew that no one else would be rushing to get up so instead, I padded softly downstairs and left the house, stepping out into the warm morning.

Walking towards the village, I enjoyed the feel of the sunshine on my arms and slowly started to wake up. It really was a beautiful morning and that did help my mood but I still felt unsettled.

The High Street came into view, and I realised I was walking automatically to the empty shop. Peering inside, I pictured what it could be like again if it was mine, and I felt another thrill run through me. Finally, it felt like my long-held dream was attainable. Still, though, something held me back from going for it.

It wasn't only my life in London or how Greg would feel about me taking our child to Scotland to live, but also the fact that if I did move here, I would be living around the corner from Brodie. It was fine to say that we were friends but the way I felt when I saw him with Jen proved that we were far more complicated than that. Did I really want to make it even more complicated by becoming his neighbour too?

'Penny for your thoughts.'

I jumped to see Brodie behind me. 'Stop sneaking up on me!' I said, clutching my chest, thanking my lucky stars that he wasn't able to read my mind.

'I'm sorry,' he said, holding his hands up, his eyes crinkling at the corners with his easy smile. 'I was just getting breakfast supplies,' he said, holding up a bag as evidence. 'You're up early too?'

'I couldn't sleep. And I wanted to see the shop again, I suppose,' I explained.

'Can I tempt you to breakfast? I promise that Gloria will make it, not me, if that helps.'

I was surprised that he was alone for breakfast but my stomach rumbled and at the moment there was nowhere on the High Street to help, so I found myself nodding. 'Okay, then.'

He grinned. 'Great.' We set off towards the vicarage together. 'I think a bakery would do really well here,' he said then. 'And I've tasted your cakes so I know you'd do a great job. What's holding you back?'

I frowned a little. 'I've always wanted to do it but I never really pushed myself, I suppose. It's like I know in theory that I can do it but it's still terrifying, the thought of all the work and putting myself out there. But more than that, I want to be a good mother and I'm not sure if I can really do both.'

'You don't think you can work and be a mother at the same time?'

'God, my mum would kill me for even questioning that. She thinks women can do it all and I agree in principle, but I don't know how much Greg will be around. It might all come down to me, and I worry I'm not good enough, I suppose, to handle it. To do it all… well.'

Brodie shook his head. 'I think that if you're the kind of person who worries about not being good enough then you have nothing to worry about. The people who think they can do anything and everything are not always the people you want to be around, are they?'

Once again, he made an excellent point. I began to feel some more of my worries slide away.

We arrived at the vicarage and I followed Brodie into the kitchen where a tall, grey-haired woman was making tea. 'This is Gloria. I couldn't function without her,' he said, handing her the bag. 'This is Emily.'

She smiled. 'I've heard a lot about you, dear. Now, then, you both look in need of a good breakfast.'

'Are you sure you have time before you go to Inverness?' Brodie asked.

'Of course! Sit down, you'll only get in my way otherwise.' She gave him a fond look. 'My sons are both married,' she said to me as she poured out the tea. 'And they really don't need me any more so I'm happy to fuss over this one.'

'Thanks for once again reminding me I'm a confirmed bachelor,' Brodie said.

'Jen might have something to say about that,' I couldn't help but say.

He looked at me. 'I think Gloria would say that a woman would have to put up with too much to be my wife,' he said, breaking into a grin. I was relieved that he took what I said to be a joke. For now, at least. 'But enough about me... we were talking about you,' he said, pointedly. 'What would you do with the bakery, if it was yours?'

I found myself telling him about the sign above the door, the tables and chairs I would have, the cakes I would bake, and the lavender I would place in pots to bring colour and fragrance inside. I could picture it all and I could feel myself smiling as I talked about it. 'I suppose I could even offer breakfast too if people wanted it. Although I'm not sure I could top this,' I finished with a smile as Gloria handed us both plates piled with scrambled eggs, bacon and toast.

'I think your bakery sounds wonderful,' Gloria said. 'You could offer some traditional Sottish cakes as well like dreaming bread.'

'What's dreaming bread?' Brodie asked as I felt my cheeks flush annoyingly.

'It's sweet shortbread with almonds and herbs in it. It used to be broken over a bride's head to bring dreams of love to come, and to provide good luck for all,' she explained. 'Right, I'm off to get ready, eat that up, you two!' She swept out with a smile.

'You looked so animated when you talked about the bakery,' Brodie continued, perhaps wisely choosing not to focus on her dreaming bread idea. 'That passion shouldn't go to waste.'

'I don't want it to,' I said. I did feel excited about it, he was right. 'Moving to Glendale would be a big step though,' I said, glancing at him to see how he would react to that.

'It would,' he agreed with a nod. 'But you'd really be moving back, wouldn't you? You grew up here, right? I suppose you need to think about where you want your baby to grow up.'

I stared at him. I hadn't really thought about that. My childhood in Glendale had indeed been idyllic. Where would my baby be most happy? Here, or back in London? 'My parents though, and Greg, are in London...'

'That's true. You have family here too, though. And nowadays, it's not difficult for them to come here or for you to go down there really, is it?'

I thought about Beth, who had left city life to return home and had thrived as a result, but it wasn't quite the same for me. I didn't have a home here anymore; I'd have to make a new one. But then again, I no longer had one in London, really, either. Soon it would be sold and I'd need a new home for me and my baby there as well. 'And you'd be okay with me being here?' I asked him then, finally. It was the question that had been on the tip of my tongue since he had found me in the High Street. I couldn't look at him; instead I stared at my eggs, my breath hitching in my throat as I waited for him to answer me.

And then I felt him reach across the table and squeeze my hand gently, just for a moment. 'I didn't think you'd need to ask that.'

I looked up then, wishing he hadn't let go so quickly, but also glad that he had. 'Thank you. And for all your advice.'

'What are friends for?' he said then with a smile.

I nodded, my stomach sinking a little even though I knew that was all that we could be.

Chapter Forty-Six

Heather and Rory invited me, Beth, Drew and Izzy over to their farm for dinner on my last night, and I was excited to see it. We drove down the bumpy, gravel track towards the pretty red-brick farmhouse, passing fields of sheep and pens with pigs in, and on the other side, a paddock with two horses in, nibbling at the grass.

'This place is so rustic,' I said with a smile.

'They've been doing a lot of work on it, much needed work,' Drew said, pointing out a new barn that was being built off to the side of the house.

'I can't wait for them to get the goats,' Izzy said. 'They will be so cute!'

'Although they eat anything they can get their hands on,' her father replied.

The farmhouse door opened with a flourish as we pulled up outside and out spilled Heather and Rory, waving madly. Heather held baby Harry in her arms, beaming at us. 'So glad you could make it,' she called as we climbed out of the car. She was definitely an advertisement for Scottish air; her skin glowed and the smile was wide on her face as she gave me and Beth a kiss on the cheek, and wrapped her arms around Izzy.

'Who wants to top up the chicken feed?' Rory asked, taking Harry from Heather and putting him in his pram. Izzy waved her arm in the air.

'I'll come too,' I volunteered. It had been a long time since I had set foot on a farm. I followed them, the other three opting to head inside to the kitchen to help finish dinner. The sun hadn't dipped a lot yet; it had been a long, hot summer's day, which showed no signs of wanting to end. It reminded me of summers when I was young in Scotland, when I was Izzy's age, running around Glendale village, my feet bare, my arms tanned, hoping that I'd never have to go back to school. The summer back then seemed to last for eternity. What was it about time that as you grew, it seemed to keep on shrinking? This summer already felt like it was hurtling past me with so much going on, I hadn't had much time just to enjoy it. And I knew I should. It would be my first, and possibly only, summer pregnant. And that was something that would forever mark it as special.

'Here we go,' Rory said as we walked around the farm-house to the field behind, where a dozen or so chickens roamed. He put the brake on the pram and then picked up a bucket of pellets and gave a handful to each of us. 'You can scatter this for them, they like to forage, and I'll top up their feeders,' he said, walking over to the coop.

'They're hungry,' Izzy said with a giggle as two chickens came right up to us. She scattered some pellets, and they dived straight in.

A chicken approached me and I bent down, holding open my hand. He started pecking at the food.

'That's so cool,' Izzy said, looking over.

'They're a friendly bunch,' I said with a laugh as I started to get a little swarm around me. I stood up and threw the rest on the grass for them. I looked at Harry's eyes widen in the pram as he watched what was going on around him. It would be wonderful for him to grow up on the farm. It got me thinking about my own baby, of course. Plenty of families were raised in cities, but there was a lure out here in the countryside that made me remember how much I had loved my own childhood, and how I would love my own child to have such an upbringing too. I hadn't gone to London until I was fourteen and by then the shops and the abundance of things to do were more important to me than fresh air and countryside but I had missed both and being back once again in Glendale now was reminding me just how much.

'Let me show you my favourite horse,' Izzy said as we strolled back towards the farmhouse. She took my arm and pulled me towards the paddock. I laughed at her excitement. She jumped up on the fence, standing one of the slats, and pointed to the silver pony. She clucked her tongue and it lifted his head.

'Here,' Rory said, behind us. He gave her an apple. She held it out and the pony trotted over immediately. 'Mind your fingers,' he warned and she held out her hand further away. The horse took the apple in one swipe, crunching on it happily.

'I really want my own pony,' Izzy said, reaching out to pat him. 'Mum said I can have riding lessons and then we'll see.'

I smiled. What was it about girls and the allure of ponies? I was pretty sure I'd had a pony dream once myself too. But it was soon replaced by my love of baking.

'Come on, you lot!' Heather yelled then from the doorway. 'Dinner's up!'

We pulled a reluctant Izzy away and headed into the farmhouse, lining up to wash our hands in the kitchen.

'I bet Harry will love living here,' I said to Heather as I picked up a bowl of salad for her.

'It really is lovely seeing him watch the animals – they always make him smile,' Heather said. 'I've never been an outdoors kind of person but it really has grown on me. Not the early starts in winter though, I refuse to help Rory with those, but summer evenings outside are really beautiful. I've been thinking actually that I might need to leave the library. It's so busy here, and with our shop in the High Street, I really feel like I should focus on the family business. I'll miss the books though,' she said as we went outside where everyone was waiting at the picnic table. We faced the rolling fields of the farm, the sun finally starting to dip in the sky, lending a pretty glow to dinner.

I nodded. 'The shop is doing well then?'

'Really well. It's taken a while to build the business back up, you know? But the community is strong, and we have been getting lots of press lately encouraging tourists too. It's going from strength to strength.' She looked at me as she placed the basket of fresh bread down. 'All we need now is a place for coffee and cake,' she added with a wink.

I smiled. 'I think you're right,' I agreed, sitting down next to Beth. It was hard not to look around me at the happy group of friends I was eating with, and not feel like I wanted to join them. It wasn't of course a perfect life, no life is, and Heather herself had just said how hard it could be, but I could see how happy they all were, and I did feel like I could be happy here as well.

'Are you okay?' Beth asked then, noticing that I hadn't tucked into the food like they all had.

'Just thinking,' I said, leaning over to pick up the bowl of potatoes and scoop some onto my plate.

'As long as it's about how you're going to move to Glendale then I'll leave you be,' she said with a laugh.

I shook my head. She really was relentless. My phone rang then. 'I'd better take this, it's my mum,' I said, climbing out from the bench. I answered as I walked towards the field. 'Hello?'

'Hi, darling. Are you all right?'

'I'm fine. What's up?' I leaned against the fence, looking up to the pink sky above me.

'I have some news – some good news. A couple have made an offer on your house, and it's for the full asking price!'

'Oh my God,' I said, slowly, letting that sink in.

'They are desperate for somewhere. I think she's pregnant too actually, and they'd like to move in as soon as possible. No chain, of course. They're asking how quickly you can come down to sign all the paperwork, and discuss a moving date.'

'Wow, okay.' I glanced back at the others. 'I can be back by midday tomorrow.'

'Great. We'll come with you, of course. Soon all your debts will be cleared, and you can put all of this behind you.'

'I hope so. I'll see you tomorrow.' I said goodbye and hung up, looking back up at the sunset. I was pleased the house had sold so quickly although I really didn't relish the prospect of having to go back to London again at all, which seemed to be a sign. Perhaps the sign I had been waiting for.

With a sigh, I pulled myself from the fence and went back to the others to tell them the news, hoping with all my heart that I would be back here again soon.

Part Three

Chapter Forty-Seven

My house was a hive of activity.

Mum and Dad were helping me to pack up the last of my things. After completing all the paperwork, the couple who had bought my house begged me to rent it to them until the sale officially went through. They had nowhere to go after their landlord had found new tenants, and she was heavily pregnant, and the extra money was too much of an incentive for me to turn down. There was an added bonus – they wanted to keep as much furniture as I was prepared to offer them. As I was planning to store everything at my parent's house until I made a final decision on my future, it was fine with me to let them buy what they wanted, and leave with just my belongings. Greg's parents checked it was okay with him through his therapist at rehab, and they were coming over later to pick up the things he wanted to keep.

Now the house was sold, I just wanted for it to be over, to get everything done that needed to be done, and then I could make a fresh start.

'I'll carry that,' my dad said quickly, grabbing a box from my hands as he passed me. 'I keep telling you not to carry anything heavy today,' he added with a stern look.

'I'm fine, Dad,' I told him with a roll of my eyes.

'You need to take care of yourself,' he said, walking through with the box.

I sighed. I preferred to be keeping busy but I was getting a little tired, not that I would admit it to him, so I headed for the kitchen for a well-earned tea break.

'Oh, good idea,' Mum said, following me in. 'Have we got any biscuits left?'

'Definitely,' I replied bringing the tin over to the table. We sat down with two mugs of tea. 'Isn't it weird how you can just pack up your life like this?'

'These are just things,' she said with a dismissive wave of her hand. 'Not your life.'

I nodded but it did feel as if my old life was being put away in a box. I just needed to decide what my new one was going to look like. I was planning to see Molly the next day – it was time for me to make my final decision. 'Greg's parents will be here soon,' I said after taking a sip of tea. I was hoping to both get an update on how his treatment was going, and to also talk to them about Scotland. I knew I couldn't just skip off to Glendale without seeing what they thought about it. I certainly didn't want to do or say anything that might set back Greg's treatment – he was allowed to make phone calls soon, and I had to plan what I would say when he called me.

'Do you want us to stay while you talk to them?'

I shook my head. 'No, you guys have done so much today already. I really appreciate it, I couldn't have done all this on my own. I didn't realise that I had so much stuff.'

'Well, at least it's been a good excuse to have a clear out. You wait until you have to deal with baby stuff as well…'

The doorbell rang, and we looked at one another.

'Greg's parents are here,' Dad called from the hallway. We hastily got up and went out to greet them. Greg's parents were older than mine, and both retired. They lived out in Kent, and we had always got on but it felt a little awkward under the circumstances. There was a round of hand-shaking and cheek-kissing as everyone said hello.

'Right, we'll take everything back to ours now then,' Dad said, turning to me.

'That would be great, thanks. Do you want to go into the living room?' I suggested to Sue and Tom, gesturing behind me. I stepped outside to see Mum and Dad off, their car packed up with my things. 'I'll see you soon,' I said. I would be staying at their house for the time being. I glanced back at the house. It was pretty much ready for the new owners. The end of an era.

Mum patted my arm. 'Onward to bigger and better things, I promise.' She gave me a quick, tight hug, and then Dad gave me a kiss. I watched them drive off, lifting my hand in a wave before taking a deep breath and going back in to talk to Sue and Tom.

After I made a fresh round of tea, I sat down on the opposite sofa to them. 'So, how is Greg doing?' I asked. I had phoned the treatment centre a couple of times but all they had said was that things were progressing well.

'We spoke to his therapist this morning,' Tom said. He looked like Greg, albeit with less muscles and more grey hair. He had been a police officer and I knew he was proud his son had followed him into the emergency services. 'She said Greg has been finding it tough, but that is to be expected. They are happy with how it's going but they did mention that Greg has been asking about the possibility of staying longer.'

I raised an eyebrow. 'Oh, really?'

'She said that he's nervous about how he will cope when he leaves. She asked us to think about whether we might want to keep him there for another month. Obviously, it's a lot of money but if that's what he needs...' He glanced at his wife.

'They said that Greg has particularly been focused on the baby, and how he will cope being a father if he can't get a hold of his addictions,' Sue continued, smiling kindly at me. 'If he needs to stay in longer, we'll find the money.'

'Of course,' I replied. 'I think you've been so supportive... he's lucky to have you both. Obviously, I want Greg to be as strong as he can be for when the baby comes. And if he is going to be there longer then I need to talk to you both about something.' I told them about Molly's offer and the fact that my friend Beth had a shop that I could use for my bakery. 'It's in Glendale, where I grew up, and I don't want to do anything that will set Greg's progress back but obviously I need to think about the future, and what's best for me and the baby too,' I finished up, honestly.

They exchanged a wary look.

'So, you're thinking of moving up to Scotland?' Sue asked, a frown creasing her face. 'Before the baby comes?'

'It would need to be as soon as possible if I have any hope of opening it before the baby arrives. I have always wanted my own bakery and this is such an incredible opportunity,' I found myself babbling a little with nerves at seeing the horrified looks on their faces. 'Not only is Molly giving me such a wonderful leg-up but my friend runs the shops as a profit-share scheme so until I make money, I won't need to pay rent. Plus the rent is far cheaper up there than anything I could find down here. And Glendale is a wonderful place – there's countryside, and fresh air, and such a wonderful community. A lovely place to raise a baby.' As I spoke the words, I realised how much I believed in them. How much I really did want this now.

'But it's so far away,' Sue said. 'This is our first grand-child! When would we see it? And Greg... he'll be heart-broken.'

'I would never stop Greg from seeing our child, or you,' I said, firmly. 'I want you all to be involved. I mean, as long as Greg is capable of being involved. And you both could come up too, whenever you wanted.'

Tom patted his wife's knee. 'It is a good opportunity for you, we can see that, but have you really thought about how Greg will feel?'

'Did he think about my feelings when he gambled away all our money and forced us to sell this house? I know he's getting help but he's put me through a lot,' I said, feeling the tears rising up in my eyes. 'And I'm all alone trying to think about what I can do next. What if he can't get his job back? I'll have to support our baby alone. I need to think about our future. And if that's selfish of me then I deserve to be a bit selfish right now I think!' I sat back, wiping my eyes, my heart beating furiously inside my chest.

'I didn't mean to upset you,' Tom said, gently. 'I know our son has put you through a lot these past few weeks. He hasn't been a good partner to you, we know that. He has a lot of issues to work through, and he needs to focus on that, but you're right that you should focus on our grandchild.'

'Do you promise that we can see the baby whenever we want?' Sue asked then, biting her lip.

'I promise,' I assured her. 'And I'll be moving away from my parents too but this is my one chance to have my own business, to build something for me and my child. I really can't turn this down,' I said. And I knew that was true. It would be hard. I was terrified! But I owed it to my baby to try this. And to myself, too. I wanted to do this. 'You know how you feel about Greg. After all he's put you through, you love him and want to protect him, don't you? He's your son. Well, this is my child, and I have to do the same.' I added, touching my slowly growing bump.

They looked at one another again. 'We understand,' Sue said, finally, even as her tears welled up.

Relief washed over me. 'Thank you. Should I… should I say anything to Greg about it?'

'No,' Tom said, quickly. 'Not yet. It's such early days and it sounds as if he's already concerned about the future. We can talk to his therapist about it and get her advice.'

'Thank you. For everything. I mean that,' I said, fiercely. It felt as if a huge weight had gone. I'd made my decision. It wasn't going to be easy but I was going to make my dream come true.

For both me and my baby.

Chapter Forty-Eight

Molly made us both lunch at her house, and we sat in the bright kitchen, the French doors flung open to her long, narrow garden letting in a gentle breeze. 'My supplier recommended these guys,' Molly said, sliding a business card across the table to me. 'They won't rip you off when it comes to the oven you'll need to install.'

I nodded. 'The kitchen is the top priority. It was a café but obviously not a bakery, so we need a much larger oven.'

'And a new counter, I assume, from the photos you sent me.'

'Definitely, so people can see what's on offer, and shelves behind for the bread,' I said, picking up a piece of crusty bread and buttering it. 'I need to find tables and chairs too but Beth knows a place in Inverness we can try. And the whole place needs decorating. I might try to do that myself to save on costs.'

She frowned. 'Well, you shouldn't do too much. You'll definitely need someone to do the painting.'

'I guess so,' I said, hating that I couldn't just do it all myself but it was probably too much work. 'And the floors need sanding and varnishing too.' I showed her my notebook. 'This is the menu at the moment. I wanted to start off simply and add more once we get a good customer base.'

'That's always a good idea,' she said, looking at it. 'I think the Scottish section is such a brainwave, I know the locals and tourists will love it.'

'I hope so.'

'And you've decided on "Emily's Bakery" for the name, do you think?' she asked, taking a sip of her home-made lemonade.

'I know it's obvious but it's what I always dreamed of.'

She laughed. 'Of course you want your name up there. I think it's simple and perfect. I can't wait to see it for myself. You'll need a killer sign too.'

'I'm going to ask Beth's friend Heather – she's really into art and design. I think she can come up with some-thing great. And I can use the sign-makers the other shops have used.'

'I'm so glad you're doing this,' Molly said, giving my hand a quick squeeze. 'It's so exciting.'

I smiled. 'I've been terrified, to be honest, and I still am, but I am excited now I've decided to go for it. I'm still not sure if I can pull it off but this is something I've always wanted, and I'd be crazy to not try.'

'I'm proud of you. And in that vein…' She held out a cheque. 'I want you to know how grateful I am to have had you working with me the past few years, and for your friendship. I meant it when I said you're like my daughter, and I can't wait to see everything that you're going to achieve.'

'Oh, Molly.' I grabbed her, pulling her into me, squishing the cheque between us. 'You don't know how grateful I am. I don't know how to ever thank you.' I let her go, finally, wiping away a tear as I took the cheque from her.

'No thanks needed. You deserve this. You earnt it. I can now retire, knowing that both my bakery is in excellent hands, and your future is taken care of. I'll be travelling but you can bet I'll be up in Scotland as often as I can.' Molly wiped her own eyes.

'I would love that,' I told her. I held tightly onto the money she had given me, knowing that I was incredibly lucky to have her in my life. 'I never could have done this without you. And I still see it as an investment, not a gift,' I added, sternly. She kept changing the subject when I mentioned paying any of it back once the bakery was on its feet, I knew I would be hard-pressed to get her to accept anything but I was determined to try.

She shook her head. 'You know that I'm just happy that I can be part of it.'

'There will definitely be a cake named after you,' I promised.

She laughed. 'Then I shall definitely order it on opening day.' She held up her glass of lemonade and I clinked it with mine to seal the deal.

–

Nervously, I sat in the hospital chair, my mum beside me, as the sonographer came out and told us to go on through. I had had so much to think about that the idea of the second scan had just been hovering around, I hadn't dwelled too much on it, but now I was there ready for it, I was just hoping everything was still okay.

I laid down as the sonographer started chatting but her words hung around in the air like a fog, not really penetrating through. Then she rubbed on the gel and began the ultrasound. It seemed to take forever for her to smile.

'Well, everything seems to be looking good,' she said. 'The baby is a perfect size, I can't see any problems.'

I exhaled deeply and looked across at my mum who beamed at me. 'That's a relief!'

'Still on track for your due date in February,' she added then.

'And are you able to tell me… is it a girl or a boy?'

'Are you sure you'd like to know?'

I nodded. I didn't think I wanted any more surprises. I wanted to be able to plan properly, to prepare for the baby's arrival, to know who I'd be meeting in a few months. 'Yes please.'

'It's a girl,' she said, easily.

'Really?' I stared at the baby on the screen in wonder.

'As sure as I can be, yes.'

Mum squeezed my hand. 'Oh, Emily, how wonderful.'

I smiled. 'Hi, baby girl,' I said to the screen.

'I'll print you off another photo,' the sonographer said.

'I'll see you soon,' I whispered to my baby girl, hardly able to believe that I'd soon be the mother of a daughter.

After we left the hospital, clutching the scan photo, I pulled out my phone to call Greg's parents. I wanted to tell them it was a girl and also to see if they could pass it on to his therapist. Greg needed to know. They were as thrilled as we were about the news.

Mum and I went back to my parents' house. I was in my teenage bedroom again, but it wasn't going to be for long. I had already told Beth I was coming back to Glendale and everything was on track for me to start work on the bakery. To say she was excited was an understatement. I could hardly wait to get back to Scotland again and make a start on everything. Beth had told me I could stay as long as I liked at the Hall but I wasn't sure if they were really prepared to welcome my baby as well so I resolved to have a think about where I could live when I got there too.

I was also feeling a little guilty, though. 'Mum, are you really okay with me doing this?' I asked, watching as she switched the kettle on. I had seen how her face had lit up when she saw my baby girl on the screen. 'Going back to Glendale, I mean?'

She turned around, and leaned against the counter. 'I can see how excited you are. I know this has always been your dream, and it's such a great opportunity. You must take it. Of course we'll miss you, but we will come up as often as we can, and you know we always talked of retiring back to Scotland. We have a pretty great incentive to follow through with that plan now.' She smiled. 'We just want you to be happy.'

Tears welled up in my eyes as I rushed around the table to give her a hug. She was surprised but wrapped her arms around me. 'I wouldn't believe that I was capable of doing this if it wasn't for you,' I told her through my tears.

'You are capable of anything,' she replied.

When we pulled back, both our eyes were glistening. She hurriedly made the tea, wiping at her eyes, never one for letting her feelings show. I smiled at her back. It really helped knowing they'd always be in my corner. My phone rang then.

'Oh, it's the treatment centre,' I said when I looked at the screen. 'Hello?' I answered, walking out into the hallway.

'Em? It's me. Uh, Greg.'

I sank down onto the bottom step of the staircase. 'Greg? Oh my God,' I said. 'I mean, how are you?' I added, quickly.

'I'm doing okay. My therapist said you had a scan today.'

'Yes! Yes, I did,' I said, wondering why I was sounding so high-pitched. It was just really surreal speaking to him at rehab. 'Everything is good. And we're having a girl.'

'A girl.' I could hear the smile in his voice. 'That's perfect.'

'I'll give your parents a scan photo, hopefully they can get it to you. If you're allowed, that is. Is it — how is it there?'

He sighed a little. 'It's hard. Harder than I thought, I suppose. But for the first time in a long time, I can see some light ahead, you know?'

'That's great, Greg. Really. I'm proud of you.'

'You are?'

'Of course. And our girl is too.'

'Wow, a girl. She'll look just like you, I bet. Mum and Dad said you're going back to Scotland?'

'I am,' I replied, carefully, not sure how much to say.

'Good,' he said. 'You seemed to be happy up there. I'm sorry I ruined that. I'm sorry for so much, I can't even begin to tell you.' His voice turned a little shaky. 'Take care of yourself, and bump, okay?'

'I promise.' I hung up and clutched my phone to my chest. He sounded okay. Like he would be okay. And that's all I wanted. 'Well, looks like it's just you and me for a while longer,' I whispered to my bump. 'But we'll be okay, won't we?'

And I felt it. A flutter deep inside. Like little wings in my stomach.

I smiled. 'Good girl.'

Chapter Forty-Nine

For my third arrival in Glendale of the summer, Aunt Sally met me at the station in her Jeep. 'This is becoming a habit,' she said with a laugh, giving me a squeeze.

'Is Glendale a cult or something?' I joked back, instantly feeling better for being back on Scottish soil.

'I knew you wouldn't be able to keep away for long,' Aunt Sally replied with a smile. We put my bags in the boot and set off for the Hall. 'That bump has grown already since I last saw you,' she said as we drove from the station.

'I can feel her moving,' I said with a smile. 'It's amazing.'

'I'm so thrilled you're having a girl,' she said. 'I'm already knitting.'

'Thanks. I really need to get buying things, I'm feeling quite unprepared.'

'Plenty of time,' she replied. She glanced across at me. 'And how are you feeling about everything?'

'Good. I think. I'm excited but terrified too,' I admitted. I had woken at three a.m. worrying about everything but the sight of Glendale approaching made me smile.

'Of course you are – starting over is never easy but you're not alone. Have you heard anything from Greg?'

I told her about our phone call. 'I think it's likely he'll be in rehab for longer, but I think he'll be okay.'

She nodded. 'And so will you. Greg is focusing on himself and his recovery so you should do the same. Glendale is a wonderful place to raise a family, and this bakery will be a huge hit, I just know it. I'm proud of you, Emily. This has been your dream for such a long time. The past couple of months have been testing and you could have easily just fallen apart but I can see that it's already made you stronger.'

'I think it has,' I said, surprised to find that I thought she was right about that. I had put off my dream for far too long but somehow after everything going wrong lately, I could finally see that I was capable of making it come true. Perhaps you sometimes needed things to fall apart so you could put everything back together.

'I have a suggestion,' Aunt Sally said then as the Hall came into view. 'I have just moved into the cottage and I'd love to have you there. That way, you don't need to worry about your living arrangements; you can just stay with me while you get the bakery up and running, and of course when the baby comes. You know how much I'd love to have you both there.'

'Even with all the noise and chaos of a baby?'

'You're family, Emily. Of course!'

I smiled. 'That's really kind of you, and I would love it. I am worried I'm taking on too much so to have you there would be such a help. If you're really sure?'

'I'm really sure,' she promised. 'Is that a yes then?'

I was relieved. I had been worried I'd be taking advantage of Beth and her family by not only opening a bakery without paying them rent, but staying in their house too, so this was the perfect solution. 'I would love it,' I told Aunt Sally. 'Thank you.' Excitement fizzed up in my chest as we pulled up outside my new home.

My life was certainly not going as I had planned but now, that didn't seem like such a bad thing.

-

I stood in the shop with Bill, the owner of the supply company Molly had recommended. 'So, that's the mixer I'd like,' I said. I had set up a folding table and two chairs in the middle of the empty shop for us to work at while we planned what he would need to order for my kitchen.

'And I think a convection oven would be the best choice,' he said, flicking though the catalogue to show me.

'Yes. That's the one we used at Molly's too,' I agreed. We discussed the options and I chose the one that I felt was the best size and price.

'And then the display cases...' Bill showed me the ones he wanted to install.

'And do you think that would leave enough space still for tables and chairs for people to eat in?'

Bill produced his measuring tape and showed me where the counter needed to be to fit the cases. It seemed to leave enough room for six tables, which was enough for a start. Most customers I was sure would take away their cakes and drinks anyway, and in time I could buy tables for use outside in the summer.

'I'll order all this up then, it usually takes four weeks and then I'll need a couple of days to install it with my boys. When are you planning to open?'

'I was hoping for September,' I said, which would leave me a few months before the baby arrived to get the business going. Aunt Sally had already said she'd be willing to run it for the first couple of months after the baby came but I also wanted to hire two members of staff to help us.

'That's doable definitely,' he agreed, holding out his hand. I shook it firmly, allowing myself a smile. Things were getting on track nicely.

After he left, I organised a local decorator to come and give me a quote for painting and sanding and varnishing the wooden floor. I was hoping to do a lot of the finishing touches myself to save on money, and Beth and I were going to look at furniture later in the week.

Pleased I had organised as much as I could that morning, I let myself out of the shop and walked towards the Glendale Arms where I had booked in lunch with Heather so I could ask her to design a sign and logo I could use for the menus and shop front. As I walked past the church, I saw Brodie climbing out of his car out the front. 'Hi,' I said, giving him a wave.

'You're back again,' he said, stepping forward into my path with his easy smile.

'And quite possibly for good too,' I replied. 'I've decided to open my bakery here. I'm going to go for it.'

'Well, that's great news! I can't wait to come in for tea and cake. If you need any help…'

'Thanks, there will be a lot to do, I just hope I can pull it all off.'

'Of course you can. And you're back at the Hall too?'

'I'm staying in the cottage with my aunt.'

'So, you'll be my neighbour then?'

'I will indeed,' I said, hoping he thought that was a good thing. I was about to ask, when there was a shout behind us. I turned to see Jen hurrying across the road. 'Anyway, I'm meeting Heather for lunch so...' I said, not wanting to stick around to watch them being all loved up. 'Hi, Jen, I'm just off to the pub,' I said, quickly, making a move to go.

'I'm just coming for lunch at the vicarage,' she said, a little breathless from rushing over to us. She shook her head at Brodie. 'This one has been so busy, I had to practically beg him to squeeze me in.'

Brodie gave an uneasy laugh. 'Well, have a good one,' he said to me. 'Let's head inside then, Jen.' She gave me a merry wave and followed him as I set off towards the Glendale Arms, wishing the sight of the two of them didn't affect me as much as it did. My only small comfort was that Brodie didn't look anywhere near as excited to see Jen as she did him, although that made me feel like I was a really bad friend.

I should want him to be happy and find someone, shouldn't I?

Chapter Fifty

Heather was waiting at a table in the Glendale Arms when I arrived. She waved and I joined her in the corner. 'How are you?' she asked. 'I got a jug of juice – it's so muggy today.'

'Thank you. I'm okay, just getting a bit stressed with my checklist, there still seems to be so much to do. And there's only just over a month until I want to open.'

'These things always feel impossible until they're done. We were the same with all the work we did on the Christmas trail but that turned out brilliantly. The bakery is going to be wonderful, don't worry. Especially once I get designing the logo.' She waved a notebook at me.

'Are you sure you have the time for this? I feel guilty with how much you have going on.' I really did admire Heather – she not only was a wonderful mother to Harry but she worked in the library and lived on the farm with Rory, helping out there, and also popping into the farm shop in Glendale when needed as well. She gave me hope that I could juggle motherhood and the bakery although I was certain I wouldn't make it look as easy as she did.

'Honestly, I love designing things. I went back to college to get an A Level in art and design last year, and I designed everything for the farm shop. I love it. I'd like to do more but there's so much going on. So, seriously, this is something I'll enjoy, I promise.'

I smiled. 'Okay, if you're sure.'

'So, what do you envisage for the bakery?'

'I want it to feel cosy and homely. Inviting. Like you've gone into someone's kitchen to have tea and cake. Does that even make sense?' I laughed as I tried to put into words how I had pictured my bakery for years. I took out my notebook and showed her the sketches I had done of how I wanted it to look.

Heather looked at it. 'Perfect. I can come up with something to complement that I'm sure. And I can show you my ideas as I go to make sure I'm on the right track. What about colours?'

'Well, the bakery is going to be lemon and blue mainly, with white walls.' I showed her the colour swatches I had.

'Perfect.' She smiled. 'This is so exciting. I love how we're all going to have a business here.'

I smiled. 'Me too.' I took a sip of juice. 'Can I ask, is it difficult doing it all? All the work you do plus looking after Harry. He's still so young…' I was still nervous about how I was going to handle both the bakery, and motherhood.

Heather nodded. 'It's hard sometimes, yes. I'm tired, like, most of the time. But I wouldn't do any of it if I didn't enjoy it. I've always worked and I really didn't want to stop once I had Harry. I mean, it's a personal choice, I think, isn't it? Like the whole marriage thing.'

I smiled, remembering our conversation about how she and Rory were in no rush to get married.

'You just decide on your priorities, really, and go from there. I have decided, like I said, that something does have to give. I'm going to leave the library in September and focus on the farm and Harry. Then once he goes to school, the plan is to set up my own design business. Creating things like logos for companies – business cards and invitations, too. That kind of thing. I'm going to do a calligraphy course as well. So, lots of plans and that's how I like it. I like trying new things.'

'I think it's great. I was so worried that I couldn't do it – open this bakery and raise this baby – and I'm still really nervous about it, and I think if I didn't have everyone in Glendale around to help, I'd probably run a mile.'

'There's so much support here, that's why I'd never leave. The community is so strong, and so is our family.'

I smiled, liking how she saw me as part of the family too. 'So, you think we can have it all?'

Heather thought for a moment. 'No one can have it all. And that would be really greedy of us if we did, but I think we can have everything we want.'

I couldn't stop Brodie flashing in my mind then. I quickly dismissed it. Heather was right – I had more than enough to be getting on with; I certainly didn't need to add any more complication to my life. But I couldn't shake the feeling that he wouldn't be a complication, that if anything, it felt like he was the missing piece to it all.

That was just crazy though, wasn't it?

–

I had moved into the cottage in the grounds of Glendale Hall with Aunt Sally. She was currently spring-cleaning, although John was very tidy, and was rearranging the kitchen to suit her. I had taken the front bedroom, and through a gap in the trees I could see the main house in the distance, rising up grandly from the lawn. It was even more peaceful out in the cottage than it was in the Hall, a million miles away from my house in London with its neighbours on either side, and road traffic at most times of the day. We either had meals at the main house with the others, or we just sat down the two of us to home-cooked food on our small outside table.

The bakery was taking up so much of my time but I knew that the days were ticking by and once summer ended, the baby would not be far away and I should really start planning for her arrival as well.

Fortuitously, Caroline stopped me after dinner one evening, as I was about to walk back to the cottage, to talk about just that. 'Emily, I was thinking… we have a lot of baby things in the loft. Beth's, and even some of mine. I kept everything for when Beth had a child but obviously, as she went to London, I wasn't able to pass it all on to her.' I saw sadness flash in her eyes. It was still upsetting for her to talk about when Beth ran away to London at sixteen, pregnant with Izzy, even though their relationship had healed and Beth had finally come home ten years later. It was particularly awkward because Beth had lived with me at college at first. Caroline composed herself quickly, however. 'I wondered if you'd like to take a look? Anything you want, you can have.'

'That's really kind of you,' I said. 'I'd love to see it.' I was really grateful she had thought of me, and it showed the past had been as put to bed as it could be. I had always wondered if she felt any animosity towards me for giving Beth a place to stay but I hoped she had been relieved that Beth had been looked after. It had been Beth's decision to leave, after all. I had done my best to support her, as my

Aunt Sally had done too, and all was well that ended well, after all.

She smiled. 'Let's go now then.'

Eagerly, I followed her upstairs and then to the end of the corridor where a hidden staircase led to the long, narrow loft. Caroline switched on the bare overhead light and coughed a little as she disturbed the dust, walking across the floorboards. Plastic storage boxes lined the walls; there were Christmas decorations, piles of old books, a few paintings stacked in the corner and then, at the end, an area covered with thick sheets.

'Here we are,' she said. She reached for them, and I leaned forward to help, pulling off the sheets to reveal a cot and baby's pram. We both coughed then as the dust settled around us.

Once I could see properly, my eyes widened. 'Oh wow, these are beautiful.' Despite the dust, I could see that both the cot and the old-fashioned pram were obviously expensive when bought, and sturdy and solid even after the years spent up here.

'They're probably not the "in thing",' she said, making quote marks with her fingers. 'But they are well made. There's all of this, too.' She gestured to boxes labelled as baby clothes and toys, and a pile of baby blankets.

'Are you sure about this?' I asked. There was so much up here and to be honest, I could have done with it all. What with the bakery costs, it would really help if I didn't have to buy all of it myself, and there was something special about the idea of passing down these much-beloved family items to my daughter too.

'I'd love you to have anything you need,' she said. 'I know that we don't really talk about what happened but

I was grateful, you know, that Beth had somewhere safe when she got to London, and that she had you as a friend. I don't know what would have happened otherwise. You took care of her back then, and Izzy too, so please let me do this for you now. I promised Sally that I'd always take care of her. And I want to do the same for you, and your baby, too,' Caroline said then, not quite meeting my eyes. It still hard for her to shake off their family reserve.

I was touched. 'Oh, Caroline.' I had no such reserve. I threw my arms around her and although she stiffened at first, she hugged me back before pulling away quickly. 'That honestly means the world to me,' I said when I was able to speak. Pregnancy really did make you feel everything more potently, I was sure of it.

She waved her hand, dismissing my thanks. 'I will be pleased to see it all being used again.'

I looked at the cot again. Suddenly it became all the more real that soon there would be a real live baby sleeping in it. My baby. Something I had wanted for so long. I wiped at a tear rolling down my cheek when Caroline couldn't see. I sensed me crying on top of the hugging would have been a little too much for her to handle.

Chapter Fifty-One

July sprang into August without warning, and that meant that there was just a month to go until I wanted to open the bakery. Every day, I was in there working to get everything ready, supervising the installation of the new oven and equipment, trying to find the exact shades of blue and lemon that I wanted for the décor, hiring contractors, making them all tea, and looking at Heather's draft logo designs.

Most evenings, I was at the cottage hunched over a meal Aunt Sally had made, barely noticing it, re-drafting the menus over and over again, and trying out the recipes until everyone at Glendale Hall was sick of cake. 'And that's something I never thought I'd say!' Beth said, after refusing the fifth sample of cake I tried to make her taste.

'You're doing too much,' Aunt Sally scolded when she walked into the kitchen after working at the Glendale Hall shop to find me icing cupcakes.

'There's so much to do,' I replied, somewhat defensively. My feet were killing me though, and I did feel quite weary. 'I'll stop once these are done,' I promised us both.

She tutted and walked past me to the fridge. 'I'm making us something to eat. And you're going to sit down all evening.'

'Okay,' I said a little absently as I started to stick roses on the cupcakes. I had decorated them in blue and lemon, hoping they looked sweet and it wasn't overkill to match the cakes to the bakery décor. Sometimes it was hard not to get a little bit too carried away with it all.

'You haven't even looked at your post after I brought it over from the Hall,' she scolded again, waving a couple of envelopes at me that had been sitting on the table.

'Give me one minute,' I said, focusing on the cupcakes. 'There.' I stood up and looked at the four I'd made. 'What do you think?'

Aunt Sally paused in the act of chopping an onion to look up. 'They're just as perfect as the exact same batch you made last night. Seriously, Emily, sit down now.'

I put them on a plate and sighed, carrying them over to the table. I had to get them just right. She handed me a glass of iced water as she went back to her chopping, muttering something under her breath. I thought it was wise not to ask her what she was saying. I was tired, admittedly. But it was that good kind of tired that came with throwing everything you had at something you loved. I felt a fluttering in my stomach and smiled. I was certain my baby could feel the adrenaline pumping through me. She was getting quite squirmy.

Picking up my post, I saw that along with my credit card statement, there was a hand-addressed envelope for me. 'What's this?' I wondered aloud, opening it up curiously. I couldn't remember when I'd last received an actual letter. I pulled it out, unfolding it and realising that I recognised the writing, quickly scanning down to the bottom to check who it was from. 'Oh,' I said.

'What's wrong?' Aunt Sally asked, turning, immediately alert.

'It's from Greg. A letter from Greg,' I said, looking at her. I was immediately nervous. Why had he written me a letter?

She raised an eyebrow. 'I wonder what he has to say? Why don't you take it outside? It's lovely out there, and I'll bring out the pasta in a few minutes.'

'Okay,' I agreed, glad to have instructions to follow as I was so stunned. Picking up the letter and glass of water, I stepped out of our back door to the small garden and sat down at our white, round table. It was a warm summer's evening and the only sound in the garden was a chorus of birds up in the trees nearby.

Taking a sip of water, I picked up Greg's letter and tried to prepare myself. We hadn't spoken since before I left again for Glendale, although I had rung his mum to find out what she knew. Sue told me that his therapist said his treatment was still progressing well and they were expecting him to remain at the rehab centre until September.

Dear Emily,

We talked in group therapy today about apologies. How reaching out to people that we've hurt through our addictions is really important. How recognising that we've hurt someone is a step towards a time when we won't hurt the people we love. My therapist asked me to go to my room and write down the people that I had hurt so we could talk about it, and the person at the top of my list was you. She asked me what I would say to you if I could and got me to write it all down and then she said I could decide if I wanted to send it to you or not.

317

I wasn't sure at first. But I'm learning that being honest is one of the key ways I can get through this, and I want to be honest with the people I love from now on. And you're still the person who means the most to me. I know that this letter can't even begin to make up for everything I've put you through, but I just hope that it might show you just how sorry I am.

I've lied to you for a long time. When we met, I wasn't in a good place. I know that now. But I pretended that everything was fine. Back then, I probably should have just walked away, waited until I was capable of really, properly making a life with someone but I was selfish. I fell for you the moment I saw you and I didn't stop to think about what was best for you, or whether I actually deserved you. I was already drinking a lot and gambling too but I never told you any of that. I made you think I was this fearless person and that that was a good thing but now I'm not sure it is. I should have had fear. Fear should have stopped me from spending our money, from drinking too much – it should have made me realise I would lose you, and lose my job, but I just became even more reckless. The problem is, the more I drank and gambled, the worse things became, which drove me to do them even more. I kept thinking I'd make the money back somehow, or that one drink would be enough but I was just deluding myself.

I'm so sorry that I didn't tell you what was going on. I knew from the start that I had to hide those things from you. I knew what I was doing was wrong even back then. But I didn't think I was addicted. To be honest it took far, far too long for me to admit that to myself. For a while I got away with it. We fell in love and I want you to know that was real; it always has been real. If it hadn't been for you, I think I would have crashed and burned a long time ago. You kept me afloat without knowing it. I didn't seem to need things as badly if I had you. I could keep things just about under control.

But when we started struggling, when we couldn't have a baby, I started to reach for a gambling fix and the booze more and more. The debts started to pile up but I just kept on ignoring it, drinking more to keep myself in denial, and then borrowing money, telling myself I could sort it out, that it would all be okay.

And then I brought you into it. And I can't even begin to say sorry enough for that. I made my debts our problem, and then when I woke up in Steph's bed…

I had to lift my eyes then. They were blurring with tears. I wiped at them and took a deep breath. It was so hard to read it all in black and white. I could feel his pain, his torment coming through the page, the way his pen dug into the paper at times revealed that anguish, but laying it all bare like this was reminding me of my own hurt too. Composing myself as best as I could, I read the rest.

When I woke up in Steph's bed, I knew I had lost control. I didn't even remember going to her flat from the club. I would never have done that to you sober. I don't know if that's any excuse but I am so ashamed of that night. I hope you know that.

I knew that it had all fallen apart when you went to Scotland. I knew I had to tell you and get myself some help. But I know that I did this too late. I should have told you so much earlier. I should not have kept on denying that I was losing my grip on everything.

Most of all I'm sorry that I'm not there for you during the most important time of our lives. I feel like the worst father in the world before our daughter is even born. When my therapist first told me that you were moving to Scotland, I was angry and full of self-pity. I was upset that you'll be so far away with our child but I know now that I have no right to feel that way. I left you with nothing. Of course you need to grab this opportunity. And I'm proud as hell that you're doing it. That you're going to make your dreams come true. Our little girl is going to have the best mother in the world.

I'm trying, Em. I'm trying so hard to be someone that both of you can be proud of one day. I hope that I can do it. But I know that if I can't, our little girl will be just fine with you.

Take care of both of you. I hope that you'll let me see you both one day soon. When I deserve it.

I'm going to do everything I can to deserve it. I promise.
Greg

Chapter Fifty-Two

Aunt Sally came out then, carrying two bowls of pancetta pasta. She looked at me, tears streaming down my face, and sat down, reaching out to hold my hand. 'That bad?' she asked.

I sniffed loudly in the quiet garden. 'It was just hard reading it, remembering everything, going back to that place when I found out that I didn't know the man I loved. And I feel for him. He hurt me, yes, but I know he was ill. And it's painful to read about how broken he is. He really doesn't know if he'll ever be a good enough father to our baby girl, and I just wish so much, so hard, that he will be.'

She nodded. 'Of course you do. He's getting the help he needs, we just have to hope that it works. It will still be hard for him, though. It will always be hard, I imagine.'

'I think maybe I'm only just realising that. I know it sounds stupid but I saw this rehab as the fix, you know? But reading about how broken he still is, I know now that it'll be a really long road even after he comes out. I find it hard to put myself in his shoes. I've never been addicted to anything, I don't think. I mean, maybe, cake...' We both smiled a little at my weak attempt at a joke. 'But it is a disease and he'll have it forever. Can he be a good dad, do you think?' I picked at the creamy pasta. As usual, it was delicious, but I had lost my appetite.

'If he really wants to be then he will be,' Aunt Sally said, firmly. 'Everyone makes mistakes and I think as long as you do something about them then why can't your children know about them? I think reaching out for help when you need it is something to be proud of.'

'I hope he doesn't blame me for coming up here. That by moving away, I'm somehow saying he can't be a good father to our baby.'

'Well, why don't you write back and tell him that?'

I looked up from my plate at her. 'Do you really think I should?'

'I think it could only help.' She tucked into her food but I continued to pick at mine. Greg's letter was so honest and heartfelt, I did feel as if I should respond to it. If he wasn't up to reading it yet, I knew they wouldn't let him.

'I'm going to do it,' I said, finally.

Aunt Sally smiled. 'Good. Now eat some food. You're wasting away when you should be eating for two. And don't tell me that's a myth, young lady. I'm supposed to be looking after you but I can only do that if you stop being so stubborn and do what I say, okay?'

I shook my head. 'I'm not a child,' I mumbled but I picked up a forkful and swallowed it just to keep her happy.

'You wait until your daughter turns out to be as stubborn as you are,' Aunt Sally said with a sigh.

That did indeed shut me up.

–

It was Brodie that I wanted to speak to about how to reply to Greg's letter. I had long since learnt to both seek and trust his advice, so I went to the church where he was practising his Sunday sermon to the empty building, and walked up to the altar. 'Hey,' I said.

'Oh, hi,' he said, stepping down from the lectern. 'Everything okay?'

'Can I talk to you for a minute?'

'Of course. Come on, let's sit down.' He gestured to a pew and I sat down next to him, feeling weirdly nervous – maybe because he suddenly felt like a minister, and not Brodie, in his dog collar. But perhaps that was what I needed. 'What's up?'

'I've had a letter from Greg,' I explained, telling him briefly about its contents. 'I want to write back but I'm scared of saying something that might, I don't know, halt his progress somehow. I can't say it's all okay, because it isn't. He lied. He hurt me. I'm up here alone, our life together over, you know? And a baby on the way who I might have to raise as a single mother. But I know he's trying. He reached out for help and I want to encourage that. And I want him to know that I do want him to be a father to our baby. If he's up to that.' I sighed. 'It's so hard putting how you feel into words, isn't it?'

Brodie nodded. 'Definitely, especially to people who mean a lot to us. But I really don't think you'll set anything back if you're as honest with him as he was with you. You're obviously a forgiving person. You realise that he was ill and that this disease isn't him, it's a separate thing that made him do things that he's sorry for, that he's ashamed about, and that he's getting help for. That is admirable. And the fact that you'd like him to be in your baby's life is also admirable, and something that can only help him in his treatment, I think. Give him something to strive for perhaps?'

I nodded. I had been hoping that. 'That's what is important, isn't it? Not looking back and blaming him, but letting go of the past and focusing on making the most of this opportunity. And our baby needs her father so I need to support him.'

'And you will. It sounds like you know exactly what to write.' He smiled. 'All any of us can do is try to be better people moving forward than we have been before.'

'That's a nice thought. There's always a second chance; that's what you said in your sermon.'

'I'm glad what I said sunk in to someone.' He chuckled. 'But it's true. I think good people aren't those that have always been good in everything they've ever done, that's impossible. But instead they are the ones who keep trying to do better, to *be* better.'

'Thanks, Brodie.' I stood up. 'I think I'll go and write it now while I know what I want to say.' I smiled. 'I know I told you I'd never met a minister like you before, and I haven't, but I think that's what makes you a great one.'

He looked surprised but pleased as he stood up to let me out of the pew. 'Well, I'm honoured that you think that. I'm glad you've moved to Glendale, Emily.'

I smiled. 'Me too.' I walked out and went straight to the bakery where I sat down and wrote Greg my reply.

Dear Greg,

Thank you for your letter. I know how sorry you are. I just wish you could have told me how bad things had been getting for you sooner. I would have wanted to help you. I still want to help you.

I'm already proud of you. You finally reached out and I know how much you're trying to battle your demons. I know our little girl will be proud of you too. You haven't given up, and I know you won't because of our baby waiting to meet you.

I want you to know that I've moved to Glendale for our baby. To give her the best life I can but I never want you to feel like you can't be part of that. I want you to be part of it. We may no longer be together but we will always be parents, and she needs both of us. Maybe you can come up when you're feeling up to it. I want you to see the cottage she'll be growing up in, and my bakery. I want you to help me get ready for our little girl. Please think about it.

But most of all, I want you to concentrate on the future. The past is behind us both now. We can't change it, we can't erase it, but we can learn from it. Being up here in Glendale, I've learned that the past can make you stronger if you let it. We will both be stronger because of all of this, I know it, and I hope it will make us stronger for our little girl. So, we can protect her and help her not to make the same mistakes. So she can follow her dreams.

Take care of yourself and know that I'm always here for you,
Love, Emily

I posted off the letter straight after writing it in case I lost my nerve, hoping that he would read it and know that I was speaking the truth. That it might help him in some small way.

I really did want him to be part of my life, and our baby's life, and I was sure that he would be if he kept on working on his problems. Our house was sold now, and our accountant was busy paying off our debts. It was a relief to not have all of that hanging over us.

This was a fresh start now, and I hoped Greg would grasp that as tightly as I was trying to.

Chapter Fifty-Three

The next couple of weeks just flew by. August was beginning to fade away, and I was well into panic mode because of it.

'You're up early,' Brodie said, leaning around the open door to the bakery one morning.

I jumped a little at the sound of his voice. 'I needed to start painting so it would dry before the furniture gets here,' I explained, pausing to look over my shoulder at him. The kitchen was finished and the bakery shelves had been installed; the ceiling and walls were freshly painted white, and the floors were shiny but that was it – it was still a shell. I thought all white would make the place bright, which it had, but it also didn't feel as if it had any character. I decided in the early hours, when I was tossing and turning unable to sleep, that what it needed was a coloured wall to bring it to life. So I was painting one of the walls lemon to complement the blue tables and chairs that had been ordered. The sign was going to be blue and lemon along with the menus, so it seemed like a perfect choice.

'Should you be doing that?' He came in, frowning at me on the ladder reaching up to paint the top of the wall. 'Let me help.'

'I'm fine,' I said, dismissively, carrying on. I had to get it done, and couldn't wait for someone else to help. Besides, it was only painting. 'I'm pregnant, not an invalid.' I knew I was being snappy but I was anxious to finish it.

'Well, let me make you a cup of tea at least,' he said, marching into the kitchen before I could protest. I sighed and pushed a stray strand of my hair back into my ponytail. I wiped my brow; it was warm already in the shop and I was beginning to work up a sweat from painting. I already loved the burst of lemon. It had been a genius idea. A bit annoying that it had happened at three a.m. as I really was tired but it would be worth it in the end, I knew.

'Come down and have this, you need a break,' Brodie called then, coming back in with two mugs of tea in his hands. 'Emily, please?' he pleaded, looking up at me.

'Okay, okay,' I said, knowing that I could do with a break really. It was annoying though. I wanted to do things that my body didn't approve of. I climbed down the ladder and when I reached the bottom rung, I swayed a little.

Brodie quickly put the mugs down and took my arm. 'Are you okay?' he asked, anxiously, helping me to put my feet on the floor.

'A little dizzy, that's all,' I admitted. I felt light-headed suddenly and a little wobbly.

'Here.' He pulled out one of the folding chairs from the table and helped me sit down. 'Have a sip of this,' he said, handing me a mug. 'You've gone really pale.'

'I'm okay,' I said but I did feel a little shaky. I took a sip of the tea, suddenly worried that I might faint.

'I'm going to call Drew. No arguments,' he added when he saw me about to protest. He walked away a little bit to make the call and I heard him speak in a low voice to Drew. 'Right, he's on his way. Have you had breakfast?'

Miserably, I shook my head.

Brodie sighed. 'Emily, you need to look after yourself. Stay there. Do not move,' he said, somewhat fiercely, and disappeared into the kitchen again.

I nursed my tea, sipping it slowly, beginning to feel less light-headed. My legs still felt shaky though.

'Eat all of it,' Brodie said, coming back out and handing me a plate with two slices of toast spread thickly with butter and jam. 'How are you feeling?'

'A bit better,' I said, chewing on a piece of toast. I had been so focused on painting, I hadn't noticed how hungry and thirsty I had been. When I had finished up the toast and tea, a car pulled up outside and out toppled Drew and Beth. 'You really didn't need to come,' I said when they came in, feeling embarrassed about all the fuss.

'Yes, they did,' Brodie argued with me, telling Drew what had happened. He and Beth stepped back as Drew sat down next to me.

'How do you feel now?' he asked, in full doctor mode, taking out a stethoscope and blood pressure machine from his bag.

'A bit shaky but not too bad. I hadn't eaten. And I slept badly last night. It was probably that.'

Drew took my blood pressure in silence and then he sighed. 'It's very low, which explains why you felt faint. You're doing too much, and you really need to take care of yourself. Eating regularly and drinking lots of water, and you need to rest more.' He looked at the ladder. 'What if you had fallen?'

I followed his gaze. 'I didn't think, I was just so focused on the bakery,' I said, cupping my bump, suddenly worried. If I had fallen… it didn't bear thinking about.

Drew got up and came back with a glass of water. 'Drink this, and then I'm taking you home. No arguments, you need to rest for the day.'

'But…'

'We can finish this,' Beth said, quickly, pointing to the wall. 'Let us help more,' she added. 'You can't do everything yourself.'

'The baby comes first,' Drew added, pointedly.

'I'm not busy, I can help,' Brodie said then. 'Go home and don't worry about this place, we've got this.'

'I can't ask you to do that,' I protested, but weakly because I really did feel like I just wanted to lie down.

'For goodness' sake, Emily,' Beth said, crossly. 'Just go home. Now!'

I looked at the concerned expression on their faces, and felt a lump rise up in my throat. I really did have great friends. I nodded. 'Thank you,' I said, and let Drew help me out of the chair. I followed him out to his car and he drove me back to the Hall.

Once I got back to the cottage, Drew made me take another glass of water, and watched me go upstairs to my room. I heard him tell Aunt Sally in the kitchen what had happened, and that I needed to rest for the remainder of the day.

I threw open my bedroom window to let in some air and then I laid down on my bed, still in my clothes. I rested my hands over my growing bump. I was exhausted. I hadn't even realised. I hadn't let myself notice. They were all right – I hadn't taken good enough care of myself.

Letting my eyes close, I promised my baby girl I would do better, and then I quickly fell asleep.

Chapter Fifty-Four

At breakfast the next day, I came down to find our small kitchen full of people. Aunt Sally was pouring tea and sat at the table were Drew, Beth, Heather and Brodie; they all stopped talking abruptly at my entrance and turned to look at me.

'What's going on?' I asked, stopping in the doorway in surprise. They all looked so serious.

'This is an intervention,' Beth said, gesturing to the table. 'Come and sit down, Em.' I shuffled over, feeling sheepish. 'We were all so worried about you yesterday so we have a proposal for you – let us help finish the bakery.' She held up her hand as she saw me open my mouth to protest. 'Em, you need to slow down. You are doing too much, and you don't need to. We've all cleared our diaries today, and we'll come with you to the bakery and do whatever you tell us to. We can finish it together. Well, we will finish it and you'll sit down and instruct us from there,' she added, sternly.

'I can't ask you to do that for me,' I said when she let me speak, a lump rising up in my throat.

'You have no choice,' Brodie said. 'We will take no arguments. We want to help, okay?'

'I keep telling you that you're not alone,' Aunt Sally added, kindly, as she passed me a glass of juice and a plate piled high with pancakes, fruit, and honey drizzled all over it. My stomach rumbled on cue. 'Are you sure you all have the time?' I asked, uneasily.

'I can think of no better way to spend my time,' Beth said with a wide smile.

My eyes were now definitely welling up. 'I can't thank you all enough.'

'Wait until we've done it,' Brodie said then with a grin. 'You haven't seen how bad I am with a paintbrush.'

'Tuck in,' Sally said, handing around more plates. 'It sounds like you're all going to need it.'

As I took a sip of my drink, I glanced at my friends eating pancakes, and my heart swelled. I really had made an excellent decision in coming back to Glendale. I wasn't used to leaning on others, Aunt Sally had told me off enough about it, but I realised that for once I wanted to. And it felt good.

After we had all eaten far too many pancakes, we set off in a convoy to the High Street, and opened up the bakery. I was planted in a chair with my copious notes on the bakery and issued instructions to everyone. It was quite a sight, seeing Brodie in scruffy jeans hanging pretty baskets of flowers either side of the door; Heather telling him to straighten them from below, holding the ladder; Beth arranging flowers in vases to place on the tables; Drew rearranging the chairs over and over until he thought they were just right; and Aunt Sally writing the menu up on the chalkboard hung behind the counter.

It was amazing how the finishing touches all came together with everyone pitching in. It was hard sitting back and letting them do the hard work but it was also more enjoyable than I thought, bossing everyone around.

I was soon ticking off everything on my list with a satisfied swipe of my pen.

'And now for the final touch,' Beth said, excitedly, as a van pulled up outside. I was allowed to finally get out of my chair to see this. We all piled outside as two men climbed out of the van, carrying the sign for the bakery. We stood in a line as they climbed on their ladders to attach it above the shop.

'I think we need to say something,' Beth said as they worked. 'Brodie – could you?'

'Right, okay.' Brodie cleared his throat and gestured to the bakery as we all turned to look at him. 'Well, this is an important moment. Emily, you've worked so hard over the past couple of months to get this bakery ready for its opening. It's been a real labour of love. We're so proud of what you've created here. It looks amazing – mostly down to my paintwork, I have to say,' he added with a grin, making us chuckle. 'And I for one can't wait for opening day. I will definitely be putting on weight eating your cakes, as I think we all will. Anyway, here's to making your dream come true!'

The others clapped as I lifted my eyes to look at the sign now hanging above the shop: 'Emily's Bakery'.

The curly, pretty letters were in bold blue against a lemon background, matching the colour scheme inside and on the menus, standing out clearly on the High Street. Even to my own biased eyes it looked welcoming. Especially with the hanging baskets either side full of blue and yellow flowers. I felt my eyes well up. 'I did it,' I whispered.

'You sure did,' Beth said, by my side. She wrapped an arm around my waist and squeezed me.

'We all did it,' I added in a louder voice, smiling through my tears. 'I can't thank you guys enough for today, for all your hard work, and support!'

'Go on through,' Aunt Sally, opening the door with a merry jingle. 'Make sure it's all exactly how you want it.'

I stepped inside, conscious of their eyes on me. I stood in the doorway and looked around. The lemon wall made the room look even brighter and had a sign hanging on it, which read 'There is always time for tea and cake.' The blue tables and chairs were all arranged, each with a yellow vase in the middle with flowers in. A menu stood on each table too. There were lights under the counter now and behind it, shelves ready for baked goods. To the side was a chalkboard with the menu written on it in blue and yellow chalk. I picked up a menu. Heather's logo was on the front and inside was the list of drinks and food in writing to match the sign out front. Every last detail was just right. The wooden floors were polished and the white walls practically sparkling. It looked cosy and pretty and inviting – somewhere I would love to sit down to have a cup of tea and a slice of cake.

It was exactly how I had pictured it.

'Do you like it?' Brodie asked from behind me.

I turned around to face them all. 'No,' I said, shaking my head. They exchanged worried looks. I waited a beat to let them sweat before breaking into a smile. 'I love it!'

'God, you actually had me for a minute there,' Heather said, chuckling.

'Me too,' Beth said, relieved.

'It's perfect,' Brodie said, smiling along with me.

I walked behind the counter. I looked at the new coffee machine, all sleek and silver, ready to be used. Then I ran my hand along the counter. 'It's actually real. I have my own bakery.' And then to my immense embarrassment, I let out a sob.

'Aw, Em!' Beth rushed around the counter and pulled me in for a hug. 'Don't worry – it's pregnancy hormones.'

'Let me thank you all by doing dinner at the cottage for everyone tonight,' I said when I managed to tide the stem of tears. 'I promise I won't cook it,' I added, knowing I was still banned from doing too much. 'But we have to celebrate this.' I gestured around. I turned to Brodie. 'You'll come, won't you? You can bring Jen too,' I said, having to push the words out of my mouth.

He smiled. 'Of course I'll be there. I'm not sure about Jen.' He looked around. 'So, apart from the food, you're all ready for opening.'

I took in a deep breath. 'I am. I've still got to find staff though but Heather said she knows someone. And, of course, everything needs to be baked ready for the grand opening. God, that's a scary thought.'

'No, it's an exciting one,' Brodie corrected me.

'That too,' I said with a laugh. Who would have thought at the start of the summer that I would be not only opening up my own business but have a baby on the way too? I tried to hang on to my giddy, happy feeling, and not to think about the other things that had happened but it was hard not to with Greg miles away, not a part of such significant things in my life as I had always imagined he would be. The silver lining though, I knew, was the people around me.

My baby and I were so lucky to have them looking out for us.

Chapter Fifty-Five

The sky turned an ominous shade of grey as I was changing, and I frowned as I peered out of my bedroom window, sure that I could hear the faint rumble of thunder in the distance. With a sigh, I texted Beth and asked if we could move our dinner to the Hall. There wasn't room in the cottage for everyone to eat; I'd hoped we could be in the garden but that was looking less and less likely. She texted back straight away to say that was fine so I fired off messages to the others to meet at the Hall instead.

Standing in front of my full-length mirror, I twirled a little. It wasn't only my belly that was a lot bigger – my boobs were spilling out of my maxi dress a little bit now, and my cheeks were definitely fuller. My baby fluttered as I twirled, as if she was dancing along with me. I hadn't had a reply from Greg to my letter, not that I had particularly expected it, but I hoped that it had given him a boost. I wanted our baby to know him, and time was ticking along, getting closer and closer to when she would arrive. I was still feeling a little bit overwhelmed about everything that had happened this summer, but I was now a lot less worried about the future. I wasn't doing this alone as I had once believed, that was clear, and I was learning that reaching out for help could be a sign of strength, instead of weakness as I had always imagined.

'Ready?' I called out as I walked downstairs.

Aunt Sally appeared from the kitchen and smiled. 'You look radiant, Emily,' she said.

'I'm feeling so much better, and some of my worries have gone after seeing the bakery finished today. I actually think we can pull this off,' I said, opening the door and slipping outside. A cool breeze wrapped around me instantly, making me glad I had grabbed a cardigan at the last moment.

'Of course we can,' she agreed, closing the door behind us. We set off towards the house, the sky turning blacker above us. 'The garden needs a good soaking. We've had such a dry summer,' she commented.

'As long as it waits until we get inside,' I said, picking up our pace a little bit. 'I know now why you've never wanted to leave here,' I said then. Looking around the beautiful grounds, absorbing the peace, walking towards an evening with people who had treated me with so much kindness, I understood perhaps more than I ever had why Aunt Sally had remained here after my uncle's death, even though my parents and I had moved down to London, and was still here now after she had retired from being the housekeeper at the Hall.

'No place is perfect and there have been a lot of ups and downs here,' she replied. 'But the best times of my life have happened in Glendale. And now you're here, it's just the icing on the cake. I've always said that people make a home and the people here are some of the best I've ever known.'

I smiled. 'Me too.' I hooked my arm through hers and we walked in companionable silence the rest of the way, the cream stone house soon rising up in front of us. I felt a spot of rain on the top of my head as we reached the back door and I hurried inside, followed by Aunt Sally, before the heavens truly opened and rain danced down to the ground.

'Just in time,' Beth said from the kitchen table. Izzy, Drew, Caroline, Heather, Rory and Harry were all there waiting for us. John came in a moment later, leading Brodie inside. I couldn't help being relieved that he was on his own, that Jen hadn't come with him. 'Right, I'll sort out drinks.'

'This is my dinner,' I protested but she waved me away. With a sigh, I joined the table. I had ordered us all pizzas and cookies. When everyone had a drink in front of them, I stood up and cleared my throat. 'So, as we're all here, before the pizza arrives and all hell breaks loose — I know what we're like about our food — I just wanted to say that I know I haven't been easy the past month or so.' They all raised a smile at that. 'I have overdone it but that's only because I want this bakery to do well. I have dreamed about this for a long time. And that dream is only coming true because of you guys. So, thank you for all your help, and for putting up with me. I promise I will take it easier from now on.' The doorbell rang. 'Right, enough of me getting sentimental — the food is here!' I went off to get it, glad I had arranged this. It was a good opportunity to gather everyone together before the opening to show how much I appreciated their help.

When I came back with the food, everyone tucked in eagerly. I was sure the fresh countryside air made you hungrier. The rain outside started to come down in thick, heavy sheets, rattling against the windows, making me shiver. 'So, where's Jen?' I asked Brodie, finding myself seated next to him, eating a slice of the delicious pizza.

'I actually have no idea,' he admitted, glancing sideways at me. 'I suppose she wanted more than I wanted to give so I haven't seen her in a while. She's still going to take over Sunday school but that's it.'

'Are you okay about that?' I asked, wondering what had changed. They had looked pretty close at John and Caroline's wedding.

'It was the right thing,' he said, not giving much away. Caroline asked him something then, catching his attention, and I chewed my pizza, a little frustrated. I was probably being nosy but I just felt like I needed to know what had happened between them.

'I forgot to say,' Heather said then from across the table, drawing my thoughts away from Brodie reluctantly. 'The girl I told you about who comes to homework club at the library, and wants a weekend job, is going to come by the bakery to talk to you. I think she would be good.'

'That's great, thank you,' I said, relieved that I might have found someone. I still needed someone full-time too, but had had a couple of applicants I was planning to interview. It would be tight money-wise but I hoped that with what Molly had given me and what I had left after Greg's debts had been sorted from the house sale, I could manage it because I would need the help once the baby came.

'I have officially handed in my notice at the library,' Heather added, quietening everyone else with her words. 'I am going to be a full-time farm girl,' she said in mock horror.

'And a designer,' Rory added, smiling at her. The love on his face was clear to see.

'The designs you did for the bakery are so lovely,' I said.

'I definitely want to do more of that, when I can. It will be a wrench leaving my books behind. Maybe one day you'll take over there, Iz,' she said with a laugh. Izzy was still a huge bookworm.

'I want to be a writer, you know that,' Izzy said. 'I've written two books already.'

'Well then, maybe you'll be stocked in the library instead, one day,' Heather replied with a smile.

After we had finished the pizza and cookies, the others went into the living room to watch a film but I couldn't deny how tired I was, so said I'd head back to the cottage.

'I'll walk you,' Brodie offered immediately. I would usually have protested, but I didn't want to pass up the chance to speak to him alone.

'Borrow these,' Beth said, carrying two umbrellas from the utility room. 'You're going to need them.' I tried not to notice the smile she gave me when I took one from her.

Opening the back door, I sighed. The rain was still going strong, the grass soggy already, the sky as dark as winter. 'This is not going to be fun,' I said to Brodie. 'Ready?'

He grimaced as he opened his umbrella but nodded. 'Ready.' We set off across the grass, walking slowly as it was hard to see and slippery to walk on. 'You guys need to get golf buggies,' Brodie said loudly, over the rain.

I laughed. 'That would be useful actually.' I slid a little, Brodie reaching out quickly to steady me. 'Oops! It's so hard to see.'

340

'Here,' he said, holding out his arm. I threaded mine through his and we walked closer together, slower, our bodies providing much needed warmth.

I shivered again but I was certain this time it wasn't because of the rain.

Chapter Fifty-Six

When we reached the cottage, we were both wet. The umbrellas hadn't done much to hold back the slanting rain. The bottom of my dress was soggy and Brodie's jeans were damp. I let him in, and we left the umbrellas propped up under the porch, and then took off our wet shoes. 'Do you want something to change into? I'll put the fire on,' I said, hurrying through to the living room. I turned on the fire, the flames bursting into much-needed life.

'I'll be fine in a minute, I think,' he said, going over to perch near the fire.

'Back in a sec then.' I hurried upstairs and pulled off my dress, putting on fleecy tracksuit bottoms and a hoodie, tying up my damp hair, and putting my cold feet into a pair of fluffy socks. Then I went into the kitchen and made us both a cup of tea. 'I'm sorry you got so wet,' I said, handing him one. 'I really appreciate you walking me back through that. I hope Aunt Sally will just stay at the Hall if this rain keeps going.'

'No problem. I'm warming up nicely already.' He looked around. 'It's really cosy in here.'

I smiled, perching on the armchair opposite him. 'It already feels like home,' I said. 'It might get too cosy once the baby comes though, so I won't stay forever, Sally deserves some peace for her retirement but I'm glad I'm here for now.'

'It's a shame there are no flats above the High Street shops – although that would mean you would probably never leave the bakery.'

'True, so it's probably a good thing I can't live there as well. I really did appreciate all your help getting it ready. I think sometimes I forget that I'm not superhuman, I just want to do everything myself. I'm learning though.' I smile.

'Good. I'm glad we could help. We all want to. With the baby too, when she comes.'

'Really?' I caught myself wondering just how much help he meant. I remembered telling Beth that I didn't think it was likely that a man would want to help raise someone else's baby but I knew that if such a man existed, it could well be Brodie.

'Of course. It won't be easy with the business and everything, but we will all pitch in. Do you think… will Greg be helping too?'

I took a sip of tea. 'I don't know. He's still at the rehabilitation centre. He should be out soon though. I want him to be part of her life, if he's in the right place for that. I think it's a case of taking it as it comes. I wish things had turned out differently but as long as this baby is loved then I think that's all that really matters.'

'Definitely,' he agreed with a nod. 'I admire you. So much has happened but you seem to have taken it all in your stride.'

I raised an eyebrow. 'I wouldn't say that exactly, but I'm trying. For this little one.' I rubbed my stomach. 'And as you say, I've had so many people rallying around. And

Molly helping me with the business… I couldn't have opened the bakery without her. It's amazing, isn't it, how people you meet can shape your life so much.'

Brodie lifted his eyes to meet mine. 'The mark that some people can make is something you can never really see coming.'

Another shiver ran down my spine. 'Are you going to tell me what really happened with Jen?' I said, finally asking the question I had been burning to ask him.

'Honestly?'

I hesitated before nodding.

'I started seeing Jen after you'd been down in London for a while. She is a lovely person, but I never felt that real… connection. And when you came back I couldn't deny that to myself any more. Because I felt it again instantly. With you,' Brodie said, quietly, steadily holding my gaze as he admitted how he felt.

My breath hitched in my throat. 'I felt it too,' I admitted. 'Do you wish I hadn't come back?' I asked, my throat drying up a little.

He shook his head. 'Of course not, but I do wish things were less complicated.'

'Me too,' I agreed. It was a relief that he hadn't fallen for Jen but it was also painful because I really didn't know where we went from here. I had wanted him to feel the same as me, and part of me was happy that he seemed to. I thought about how it seemed like everything was perfect apart from not being with him but I realised that there was no such thing as perfect. Life was hard and right now, it was especially hard. How could I add something else into the mix? I took a deep breath. 'I wish we could be together,' I said, and my heart ached to see his eyes light up. 'But even if you would want to be with me too, I have been guilty in the past of putting myself, my life I suppose, second. And I can't do that now. I need to make this business work. And not just for me. But for my baby too. I need to focus on that. And it sounds selfish, I know...'

'No,' Brodie interrupted. 'It doesn't sound selfish at all. That's absolutely what you should do. Your priority is your baby and building the best life possible for the both of you, and that's what it should be. I would never want you to not put that first.'

I nodded. 'I know that. I was so in love with Greg I didn't even see what was happening right under my nose – that the man I loved was broken. I know that you're nothing like Greg, but I'm still me. I think that I need to know that I can do this, that I can make this happen, by and for myself. Does that make sense?'

Brodie got up then and came over to my armchair, kneeling beside me on the floor. He reached out and brushed my fingertips with his. 'I understand. Ever since I met you, I feel like my grey life has been brushed over with coloured paint. Like the lemon wall in your bakery.' He smiled down at me. 'I was content with my faith, with my work, but you've made me want more. I'm not going anywhere. Anything this special, anyone as special as you, is worth waiting for.'

Wow, this man really did have a way with words. I gave his warm hand a squeeze. 'I've never met anyone like you. But I don't want to hurt you. I don't want to get hurt. I wish that things were different, I really do.'

'I know,' he said, gently. 'You are the last person who would intentionally hurt anyone.'

'Are you… are you saying that you'd wait for me?' I asked him then, tentatively. I was torn between desperately wanting him to and thinking that it really wasn't fair of me to ask that of him.

'Are you saying that there's a chance for us? One day?' His eyes were alight, and it was proving very difficult not to lose myself in them.

'What about the baby?' I half-whispered. It was becoming harder to remember why I needed to be alone when he was sitting so close to me, and I hadn't been held in so long. But my daughter needed me, and that was more important. She would always come first.

'She's part of you,' he said, simply. He reached up and kissed me once softly on the lips before standing up. 'I won't mention it again. I understand, Emily. I understand how you feel. I just wanted to make sure you knew how I felt. It's getting late – I'll head back to the village, and I'll see you soon.'

I started to get up but he held out a hand. 'I'll see myself out. Take care, okay? Of both of you,' he said.

I watched him go, so stunned by our conversation that I didn't have a chance to respond. I heard him leave and then I was alone – the only sound the crackling of the fire, and the rain falling outside.

Chapter Fifty-Seven

With the bakery opening just a week away, I met with Lucy, the girl from the library that Heather had recommended, and I was impressed with her politeness. She was keen to save up for a car so I felt confident that she would work hard, and hired her to work weekends at the bakery. I also interviewed the people who had applied for a full-time job, and I ended up taking on a mother of two called Jules who was looking for her first job now her kids were at school. I liked her warm attitude, knowing she'd get on well with customers. They were also both Glendale born and bred, which was always a bonus in making sure the community would be on our side.

I sent out invitations for the launch, and, with Izzy's help, put leaflets through the doors of most of the village. Heather had got a reporter from the local newspaper coming along to do a story on the launch, and Beth had given me some bunting from the Hall to hang across the door, making sure it wasn't me getting up the ladder to secure it.

And then the baking frenzy began. Aunt Sally helped me any spare minute she got, and Izzy was a God-send helping after school as much as she could. I ran through every recipe on the menu to make sure I had it as perfect as I could, forcing anyone I came across to try the products. I then spent all day in the bakery practising using the coffee machine, my two assistants joining me when they could to train themselves too, and made sure we could all work the till.

The days leading up to the launch were all busy although I tried to make sure I rested as much as I could, and ate and drank regularly. Drew kept a close eye on me, and everyone pitched in as much as I would allow. The only person I didn't see as much during this time was Brodie. I don't think we were exactly avoiding one another but it felt like it wouldn't be the best idea to spend a lot of time together alone either. He came to the Hall one night for dinner when the whole group was there, and our eyes kept finding one another across the table, so much so that I thought the others would notice but they didn't. I didn't see him at all after that. I posted an invitation to the opening through his door though, hoping he would come.

I was still sure that I had done the right thing in telling him that I wasn't in the right place for any kind of relationship but my heart just didn't seem to want to get on board, and it ached with missing him. I had to actively stop myself from calling him or walking past the church, and I was sure that he was avoiding the High Street in case we bumped into each other. His words kept going through my mind again and again. I kept thinking, what if I had just kissed him? What if I had said we could be together?

And I knew that I still could, which was why I made sure to stay clear. My resolve was much easier to stick to when he wasn't there in front of me. And there was so much to do and think about that it did keep getting easier.

I couldn't stop myself from hoping though that he would wait for me, even though I felt like I shouldn't. That I should tell him to move on and forget me. And then I worried that he would do just that. Would he really wait for me? Was what we had really that special?

I broke down and confessed all to Beth one night as she helped me make croissants. 'I should have told him that we could never happen, shouldn't I?'

'No, you were honest, that's all you should have been,' she replied. 'Brodie is a grown man, Em. And it sounds to me like he's fallen head over heels for you. Anyone can see that you're right for one another but sometimes the timing is wrong, sometimes life gets in the way. I mean, look at me and Drew. And you're pregnant too – wow, history really does repeat itself.' We smiled at one another in recognition. 'Not to mention how hard you're working on this business. Of course you haven't got the headspace yet to start something with him. And I know you're still worried about hurting Greg. Brodie gets it. I'm sure he does.'

'But how will I know when I'm ready?'

'You will. I think things will work out just fine. You just need to have a little faith, right?'

'I'm sure that's what Brodie would say.'

'Exactly. He believes there's a greater plan, and maybe he's right. All you can do is focus on the now, and everything else will fall into place, I'm sure of it.'

'You didn't used to be this optimistic,' I grumbled a little as I rolled out pastry, working my frustration into the dough.

'I didn't used to have faith that things would work out for me but look how they did.' She chuckled then. 'God, I'm so smug, I hate myself.'

'I hate you a little bit too,' I said but I smiled at her. It was lovely to see her so happy. Life had certainly sent her on a rollercoaster of ups and downs through the years but she had made it out the other end.

I just hoped that I would too.

-

The day before the opening, I moved into the bakery kitchen to prepare the cakes that would be available on the menu at the launch. It was a muggy but grey day and I threw open all the windows in the kitchen, getting hot as soon as I turned the ovens on, pulling my hair into a messy bun, and wrapping an apron tightly around me. The recipes were all fine-tuned but there were still nerves running through me as I mixed up cake batter, hoping that everyone would like them.

I knew from working with Molly that you only had one chance to make a good first impression – if people tried my cakes and liked them then they could well be customers for life; if not, then the whole enterprise could sink.

Usually baking relaxed me but I knew today that was going to be unlikely. I turned on the radio though and tried to stop thinking about the opening and just focus on the cakes. I managed to lose myself in the task enough that when the bell rang in the shop signalling that someone had come in, I only heard it vaguely and stayed where I was, pouring ginger cake mixture into a loaf tin.

'Em?'

I jumped out of my skin as a voice said my name from the doorway to the kitchen. I looked up and only became more startled to see Greg standing there. 'Oh my God!'

Chapter Fifty-Eight

Shocked at Greg's sudden appearance, I continued to pour the mixture and realised I'd poured too much when it overflowed from the tin over my nice new, shiny, counter. I stopped hurriedly and put it down, wiping my hand over my face, smearing myself in cake mixture.

'Are you okay?' Greg asked, stepping further into the kitchen, smiling a little at my flustered reaction to his entrance.

'I'm fine, fine!' I trilled. I grabbed a tea towel and wiped my hands and then my face and then reached over to turn the music down to more of a background volume. 'What... I mean, how are you here?' I asked him, recovered enough to just about form a coherent sentence. I was able to peer at him then, face clean of cake mixture, and noted that he looked thinner than I had last seen him but his skin was tanned, his face was unusually free of facial hair, and his hair was cut a lot shorter, showing off his eyes and the smile on his face. He looked far more relaxed than I felt.

'I got your invitation – I mean, my parents did – and I wanted to come up and see the place, and support you, but I wasn't sure I could deal with a big launch party,' he said. I knew he had left the rehab centre a few days ago and his mother had told me he was living with them and was doing a lot better. But of course it wouldn't be easy at an event with strangers, especially as we were all planning to go for drinks after the bakery shut.

'That's really sweet of you. I didn't expect you to come. I mean, I wanted to see you but I knew it was a long way, and you've only just come home,' I said, babbling still. 'Anyway…' I shrugged out of my apron and went over to him. 'Is it weird if we hug or weird if we don't?'

'I'll take a hug.' He reached for me and pulled me into his arms, giving me a warm hug. When we pulled back, he smiled, looking down at my bump now visible without my apron covering it. 'Wow, you're so much bigger! And blooming. You look great. Are you well? Everything is still okay?' he asked, catching my babbling a little.

'I'm fine. I'm little bit stressed about tomorrow but we're okay,' I replied. 'Actually, let me just…' I turned and put the new batch of cakes I had made into the oven. I set the timer. 'Right – we have about forty-five minutes until they need to come out.'

'This place is great,' he said, walking back into the bakery and looking around. I followed him and smiled at how impressed he seemed. 'It's what you always wanted, isn't it?' he added, turning around to look at me. 'Fancy a quick walk before you need to get back to the cakes?'

'Okay,' I agreed, wondering what he wanted to talk about. I locked up and followed him out onto the High Street. There was a bit of a breeze outside at least to cool me down a little. I was nervous of seeing someone I knew but we walked side-by-side towards the park without bumping into anyone.

353

Walking through the gate, we weaved our way down the path, the green stretching out beside us. A dog-walker nodded hello as he passed by.

'So, how are things?' I asked Greg. It was incredibly strange how you could go from living with someone and sharing a life together, to having no idea what was happening with them, to be reduced to small talk. We reached a bench and Greg suggested we sat down.

'Better,' he replied, once we were seated. 'It's been so hard. I wanted to give up so many times while I was there, and almost did, but somehow I made it through. It does get easier every day, but I think it will always be there. It will always be something I have to work at. Recovery has no expiration date, as my therapist says.' He smiled then. 'God, look at me, quoting my therapist.'

'You definitely seem to be doing a lot better,' I told him. 'I'm pleased.'

He swivelled to look at me. 'Thanks. It means a lot, you saying that. Especially after everything I put you through. Your letter really helped me, Em. It gave me a much-needed push. To know that I was doing this in part for our baby. It got me through some really dark days.'

'I'm really glad it helped. This baby needs both its parents.'

'It's generous of you – you could quite easily have disappeared from my life with our baby, and I wouldn't have blamed you.'

I nodded. 'I want her to know you. As long as you're in a good place, obviously. I will protect her but you know that. You're a good man, Greg. You just got lost somehow along the way, and I didn't notice until it was too late. I should have seen it and made you get help sooner.'

'None of this is your fault, I promise you that.'

'I'm just glad you've got the help you need now.'

'I have. And look at you – your very own bakery. I'm really proud that you've done it.'

'Well, it opens tomorrow, we'll see how it works out. I'm nervous,' I admitted. 'Especially as it's not too long to go before the baby arrives. I hope I can cope with it all.'

'Well, I have no doubt you will,' Greg replied. 'And I can come up whenever you need me. I think I'll stay at my parents for now. I'm still on leave with work, they've been great actually, and it'll take time to rebuild everything. But I'm determined to. When things are better, maybe I can be nearer you both. But I'm not ready yet, I know that.'

I gave his hand a quick squeeze. 'I'm proud of you.'

'So, how are you finding living back in Glendale then?' he asked, looking a little embarrassed by my words.

'I'm enjoying it. I really like the peace and fresh air but… it's the people. They all feel like family already, and everyone has been so helpful with the bakery. I couldn't have done it without them,' I told him.

'You deserve it. It's going to be a big success, I just know it. Your cakes will soon be world famous.' We were silent for a couple of minutes and then Greg sighed. 'When I went into treatment, I still had this fantasy, you know, about you and me, and our baby, how we could be a family. But I know that's impossible, I put you through too much. I lied; I hurt you; I broke your trust. I just want you to be happy now. I want you to have the life you want. You really do deserve that. You're really special, Em. I know I didn't treat you how you should have been treated. I hope that one day you'll find someone who will do that.'

I listened in surprise at his urgent words, my mind involuntarily moving onto Brodie. I knew he would treat me how I deserved. He always had. 'Greg...'

'No.' He shook his head. 'Don't say anything. I just wanted you to know that. I'll always love you, you know?'

I smiled. 'I'll always love you too.' He covered my hand with his and we sat for a few minutes more, holding hands, thinking of the past, and of the future, and how different they were going to be. 'I'd better be getting back,' I said, finally.

'Of course. I'm going to head back on the train soon. I know it's a long way but I had to see you and wish you well. I'll be thinking of you tomorrow.'

'Thank you for coming. You deserve it too, you know. To live the life you want, I mean. And to be happy.'

Greg leaned in and gave me another hug. 'We got one thing right, didn't we?' he said, his hands resting on my bump.

I smiled. 'We did.' I would never be sorry about being with Greg because of that. And I knew he felt the same way. Some things just didn't work out but that was okay, because there was usually a reason for them. Our reason was our baby. And that was a pretty bloody good one.

Chapter Fifty-Nine

I woke up at what felt like the middle of the night still on launch day, nerves and excitement acting like an alarm clock. I jumped up to look out of the window, my heart sinking a little on seeing that it was raining outside. I hoped it wouldn't put people off from coming to the opening. At least it would make people fancy a cup of a tea and a slice of cake. I had to be at the bakery ridiculously early to bake the bread, and Aunt Sally had offered to help me. Jules and Lucy were coming in time to open up with me, and I was glad that they'd all be on hand to help.

Jumping in the shower, I pulled on jeans and a white shirt. I slipped into my Converse and tied my hair up, and then I grabbed my bag and headed downstairs where I made tea and warmed up two croissants. Aunt Sally came down soon after, yawning, and we had a quick breakfast in silence, still both trying to wake up. She drove us into Glendale, which was a ghost town at this hour and we went into the bakery, switching everything on, and pulling on our Emily's Bakery branded aprons.

'How do you feel?' Aunt Sally asked as she started rolling out dough on the counter.

'Like I can't quite believe it's actually happening. Remember when you taught me to bake? Did you ever think we'd be here now?' I asked, sliding the pastries I'd pre-made yesterday into one of the ovens.

She chuckled. 'No, you burnt the first cupcakes you made.'

'Well, let's hope that doesn't happen today.'

Once all the bread and pastries were in the oven, we switched on the coffee machine. Dawn came and the sun rose, pushing away the rain thankfully, and soon the bread was ready for cutting, and the pastries were crispy and warm, and we laid them all out on the shelves behind the counter. We'd made sourdough and rye bread as well as cheesy white bread, and bread with cranberries and cashew nuts in, which was absolutely delicious with cheese. We had croissants and apricot Danish pasties as well as pain au chocolat. I'd made Belgian buns, and we also had scones with jam and clotted cream on offer.

And then it was time to put all the cakes under the counter. I had named them all for the special people in my life to mark today. There was Beth's wedding cake; the cupcakes I had made for Molly, the ones which had got me the job with her; there was carrot cake for my mum, her favourite; brownies for Aunt Sally; the dreaming bread which I couldn't resist adding Brodie's name to, remembering his housekeeper telling us about the wedding tradition behind it; and shortbread for Rory and Heather. Not forgetting chocolate cake for Izzy. I'd also made a Victoria sponge, which had my dad's name on it, and lemon drizzle for Caroline and John.

And then there was the final cake. A traybake of sponge covered with icing, sprinkled with hundreds and thousands. It had been my favourite cake to make growing up. I cut it into chunky pieces, smiling as I labelled it 'for bump'. I couldn't wait for the day I'd get to bake it with my little girl.

'It all smells, and looks, delicious,' Aunt Sally declared as we stepped back to look at our handiwork. I smiled with pleasure. Even my mouth was watering.

Lucy and Jules turned up then, and put on their aprons. We laid the tables with flowers and menus, made sure the chalkboard was written correctly, put on the radio, and made fresh orange juice. We then made up two sample trays for people coming to the launch of everything we had on offer.

Then Beth and Drew arrived with Izzy in tow, carrying balloons, which we hung around the bakery. The bunting was already up above the shop, and we opened up the door, turning the closed sign to open, as the clock ticked towards opening time.

'This is it then,' I said, looking around, unable to see anything glaring that we had missed.

'People are starting to arrive,' Beth said, looking outside. 'Shall we go out then?'

I nodded and led the way. I thought gathering outside would lend more ceremony to the occasion as well as hopefully pulling people just walking by to the event. Plus, if everyone I had invited turned up it would be a squeeze to fit them all inside anyway.

Lucy and Jules picked up their sample trays and followed me. Outside, a small group were indeed gathering, to my immense relief.

'Hi, I'm Steve, from the local paper,' a man said, approaching me, a camera around his neck.

'Thank you so much for coming,' I said, shaking his hand. He asked a few questions and then said he'd be taking a few photos. Heather appeared then with Rory and she led me around, introducing me to anyone in the village I hadn't met yet. She really did know everyone.

'Emily!'

I turned around to see my mum and dad arrive with Caroline and John, who had picked them up at the station. Caroline had insisted that they stay at the Hall while they were up here. I found myself being bear-hugged by my parents so tight, I had to squeal that they were squishing the baby.

'I haven't had dreaming bread since I was a little girl,' a grey-haired woman exclaimed from behind me as she examined the sample tray.

'This shortbread just melts in your mouth,' her friend told her.

'This is the best chocolate cake ever!' Izzy said at my elbow then. I smiled with relief that everyone was enjoying the cakes.

'A great turn-out,' a voice said from behind me. I turned to see Brodie had arrived, along with Gloria, his housekeeper. I opened my mouth to say something but then Lucy called my name frantically, pushing through the group to get to me.

'The samples have all gone!' she cried in horror.

'Right, fill up another tray and then we'll do the speech and try to get everyone inside and hopefully buying some-thing,' I told her in a low voice. There was quite a group outside the bakery now but I was waiting for one more before I officially opened it.

Finally, a car drew up, and out climbed Molly. 'Darling,' she breathed when she saw me, gripping my arm and looking up at the bakery. 'It's perfect.'

'Do you really like it?' I asked, clinging to her a little bit.

She beamed at me. 'It's just how I pictured your bakery. Emily, you've really done it! I couldn't be more proud!'

'It's all thanks to you.' I gave her a quick kiss on the cheek as she protested my words. 'You have to try a Molly's Cupcake,' I said, nudging her towards Lucy and the cakes. I heard her gasp in delight when she saw them.

I went over to the doorway of the bakery then and called out for everyone's attention. Slowly, a hush fell and faces turned to me. Only a month or so ago, I would have been nervous to address people like this. I realised now that I had lacked confidence. I had kept putting off trying to realise my dream because I was scared but I had learned that I was far more capable than I gave myself credit for. I had so much more confidence in my abilities now, but I also had people around me helping me to be more confident. And they were all with me today to celebrate something I had wanted since I was a little girl. There was really nothing to be scared of. There was much to be proud of instead.

'Hello everyone. I can't thank you all enough for coming to the opening of Emily's Bakery today. Don't worry, I'm not going to do a long and boring speech, I know myself that when I need coffee no one better stand in my way.' There was a ripple of laughter at that, and a couple of knowing nods too. 'I just wanted to thank everyone who has helped turn this bakery into a reality. Molly, my boss and mentor, and above all, friend, this is all thanks to you, and I'm not going to look at you because I know if I do, I'll start crying,' I said, turning my head from her. Out of the corner of my eye, I saw her dab at her eyes and I knew I was right to avoid eye contact.

'Thank you to my parents for always supporting me. Beth and Caroline Williams for welcoming me onto the High Street and into this shop, and for everything you've done for me this summer. Heather Douglas for designing such a fabulous sign and logo, and all the menus too; they were just what I wanted. And all my friends who pitched in and helped me get the bakery ready.' My eyes fell on Brodie then and I smiled at him, hoping he knew just how grateful I was for his friendship. 'And, finally, I want to thank my Aunt Sally for teaching me to bake when I was little, and giving me the dream that today is finally coming true! And now I'm going to shut up and welcome you to my bakery. I hope you like it!' I stood back, and everyone clapped. I smiled as people walked inside, ooh-ing and aah-ing in delight. Lucy and Jules rushed behind the counter and were soon taking coffee and cake orders.

'Can I get a shot of you with your family?' Steve asked then, pulling me back outside for some posed snaps with Mum and Dad, and Aunt Sally, and I made sure Molly was included as well.

'Right, I'm in desperate need of a coffee,' Mum said when Steve left. I watched them all go inside but I paused for a moment, looking up at the sign. 'I'll tell you one day about this,' I said in a low voice to my bump. 'How you were with me at the grand opening of my first ever bakery,' I promised her. 'I hope that you're as proud as I am in there.'

'We need more cupcakes!' A frantic call came from within. I smiled, and hurried through the door to help.

Chapter Sixty

By lunch time, we had sold out of bread and cakes, and we were exhausted but happy. I was thrilled with the response, and looked at the empty shelves with triumph. We had really done it.

Beth had arranged a celebratory late lunch back at Glendale Hall so after clearing up, I locked up and Aunt Sally and I drove back with Lucy and Jules. The bakery would be shut on Sundays so I would be back bright and early on Monday for our first proper day, and I couldn't wait.

'There they are!' Beth called as we trooped into the kitchen. The French doors were thrown open and the afternoon promised to be bright and sunny. Everyone was at the picnic table waiting for us. Balloons had been hung by the door and the table was decorated in our bakery colours. I smiled at the friendly faces waiting for us, and the treats on the table. Much needed after our morning.

'Sit down,' my mum instructed me sternly after I'd greeted everyone. I half fell down onto the bench, glad to be sitting, I had to admit.

'What a morning!' Lucy said, taking a drink from Beth.

'It was crazy,' Jules agreed but they were smiling, and I think they had enjoyed their first day on the job.

'Such a good turnout,' Aunt Sally said. 'The whole of Glendale seemed to be there.'

'I can't believe how supportive everyone was,' I said taking a long gulp of ice-cold lemonade. But actually I could, Glendale was such a warm community, and I had high hopes that the bakery would thrive.

'The dreaming bread I had was delicious,' Brodie said. He was sat opposite me in jeans, his shirt sleeves rolled up, no sign of his dog collar. He smiled at me and I blushed, thinking about what dreaming bread symbolised. Weddings should definitely not be on either of our minds.

'I need to steal the recipe for my bakery,' Molly piped up from down the table. 'Oh, actually, no, it's not mine any more,' she added, remembering. 'I'll just take it for myself then.'

I smiled. 'You can have any recipe you like. This is all thanks to you.' I lifted my glass at her. She shook her head, I think she would forever dispute that the bakery was anything other than mine, and mine alone, but I knew I wouldn't be here without her. Or without anyone sat at the table with me actually.

'Right, tuck in everyone!' Beth called out as she carried over a plate of burgers and added them to the vast array of food already on the table. We certainly knew how to do food in Glendale. I was sure half of my bump was from eating too much, and not the baby at all.

After lunch, none of us could face any more cake but we had fresh strawberries grown by John and lashings of clotted cream. The sun came out properly, bathing Glendale Hall in warm light. Izzy rounded up everyone who wanted to play a game of rounders on the grass with her, and I took Molly, Lucy and Jules on a tour of the garden. My parents, who hadn't been there in a long time, and Brodie joined us.

'It's stunning,' Lucy breathed. 'I heard that it was but wow,' she said as we walked alongside the stream sparkling in the sunshine. 'You're so lucky you get to live here,' she added to me.

'I know. I've gone from a tiny back garden in London to all of this,' I replied, stretching my arms out wide. 'I can't believe what a summer it's been.'

'Where's your cottage?' Mum asked. I pointed and they set off towards it. I hung back a little, and Brodie fell into step with me.

'You really did it,' he said, smiling across at me.

I paused, and he stopped too, letting the others go on ahead of us. 'I was so sure that I couldn't do it. I don't think I would have done either, if life, and everyone here, hadn't given me such a kick up the arse.' Brodie grinned at that. 'And now I've said arse in front of a minister.'

'You've said worse,' he replied, dryly.

I chuckled. 'It's a compliment that I can be myself around you. I think.'

'I'm glad you can be yourself with me. I'd never want you to be anyone else.'

We set off again, strolling slowly, enjoying the warmth of the afternoon. I did feel more comfortable with him than I had with any other man before. Even though he was a minster. Or maybe because he was, I wasn't sure. 'Brodie…' I stopped again, and patiently he turned to me again. 'I really didn't know if I could open the bakery, if I could move here, if I could raise this baby… I thought that I didn't have space in my life for anything else. That I had to focus on me and this baby, and I do. And I will. But

I've realised that doesn't mean I can't also be happy. And being without you doesn't make me happy. It just feels like there's something missing. It's not like I need you, like I've needed people before. I know I can do this alone, but do I want to?' I was babbling, and we both knew it. I took a deep breath. 'What I'm saying is, if you still feel anything for me, if you still want to be part of this crazy mess I'm now calling a life then I want you to. It's going to be as complicated as hell. Sorry for saying hell. But maybe life always is complicated. Maybe we should grab our chance to be happy while we can. Only if you want to, though.'

'Emily?'

'Yes?'

'Please shut up.' Brodie stepped closer, and reached out to tuck a stray hair behind my ear. He touched my cheek and then my lips, and I felt my breath hitch in my throat. 'Ever since I met you everything has been thrown into chaos. And I've loved every moment of it. You've always told me exactly what you think and I love that. I love your honesty and your loyalty, and how kind you are to everyone, always thinking of others before yourself. And I've watched you grow stronger with every setback you've had. You are the most capable woman I've ever met. And you're gorgeous too. I haven't been able to get you out of my head from the moment we met. I know that things won't be easy, there's so much going on, but I never want to make things harder for you. I want to make them easier. I want to be your partner, to help you. I want to be there for you and your baby. I already love you. And I want to love you forever.'

I put my arms around his neck, and his hands slipped to my waist. 'I think it's your turn to shut up now,' I said, smiling. I reached up and his lips met me halfway, giving me a long, slow, deep kiss that I felt from my lips right down to my toes. He picked me up then and twirled me around, both of us laughing. When he put me down, he kissed me again. 'Are you really sure?' I asked him, anxiously. 'I'll be a single mother, I mean you're a minister… will people be shocked?'

'I don't know that I always set a good example to my congregation but I try to. If loving someone, if helping someone, if looking after someone, if being loving and honest and kind isn't a good example then I really don't know what is.' He took my hands in his. 'There's no rush. We have all the time in the world. Let's take it slow. As long as I know that you feel the same as I do then that's all that matters. The rest will come in time. When we're ready for it to.'

'What did I do to deserve you?' I said, shaking my head.

'What did I do to deserve you?' As he kissed me, I felt my baby give me a solid kick, and I hoped that meant she was giving her seal of approval to Brodie.

We certainly wouldn't be a conventional family but love was love, and I knew our life would be filled with it, and that was all any of us could really wish for, wasn't it?

Epilogue

One Year Later

I stood at the church altar, smiling at Brodie who was addressing the congregation. Beside me, Greg wore a suit and a wide smile on his face. In my arms, I held my squirming baby girl. Behind us sat our family and friends, and outside the Scottish rain could be heard dancing on the church roof.

'Will the godparents come forward, please?' Brodie asked. I smiled as Beth and Heather stepped forward with Drew. Greg had been happy for me to ask them as they spent so much time with me and our daughter, and had done so much for the both of us.

'People of God, will you welcome this child and uphold them in their new life of Christ?'

We all replied in unison. 'With the help of God, we will.'

We then moved to the font, and I handed Iona to Brodie. She quietened immediately as she always did when he held her. A safe pair of hands, and she knew it. Brodie dipped his fingers in the font water and made the sign of the cross on her head. She stared at him, wide-eyed, wondering what he was doing to her. 'I baptise you, Iona, in the name of the Father, and of the Son, and of the Holy Spirit. Amen.'

The congregation chorused 'amen' in response, and Brodie handed Iona back to me, our eyes meeting over her, a smile on both of our faces. I leaned down and kissed my beloved daughter on the forehead, still wet from the font, and was struck again by the miracle that she was. It had actually been Greg who had suggested a christening. I knew Brodie had wished for it, not that he would say anything, he was brilliant at being there for us and stepping back when he thought it best. I agreed to please them both – the men in our lives.

After the service, we left for Glendale Hall to celebrate. We drove past the bakery which was locked up for the day, and I smiled at it. It was doing really well and I loved coming up with new recipes, and early morning baking with Iona asleep beside me. I leaned on Brodie's shoulder as we drove, Iona starting to fall asleep in the car seat beside me. Brodie squeezed my hand. We had grown closer than I ever thought possible but I still lived at the cottage, and he at the vicarage. Until we got married, that was the way it had to be. We hadn't wanted to rush anything but I was starting to wonder if we were taking things too slow.

At the Hall, I found Greg in the kitchen. 'Want to help me put her down?' I asked. We went into the living room where I put her in her carrycot, tucking her into her blanket. She loved company and always stayed awake when people were there, her bright eyes taking everything in, so it was best to move her in here for a nap. I switched on the monitor and looked down at her. 'She's so beautiful,' I said, my heart bursting with joy as it always did watching her sleep.

'I still can't believe we made her,' Greg agreed, leaning down to give her a little kiss. He smiled at me when he stood up. 'It was a lovely service. Thank you for doing that.'

'Are you sure you won't stay here tonight?'

He shook his head. 'It'll be easier to wake up in Inverness ready for the interview.' Greg had applied to join the fire service in Inverness. He was doing well and it felt like the right time for him to move closer to Iona.

'Are you nervous?'

'A little. I can't wait to be up here though.'

Brodie came in then. 'Oh, sorry,' he whispered, seeing the baby asleep. 'They want to bring out the cake so sent me in to get you guys.'

'I'll never meet anyone who has as much cake as you lot,' Greg said with a grin. He started to walk out then paused and looked back. 'You know, now that I'm moving up here, you both should think about making a change of your own. How long are you going to make us all wait for a wedding? I'm fed up with everyone talking about it.' He strolled out leaving us both a little stunned.

'That was weird,' I said in a low voice. 'Everyone is talking about it?'

Brodie shook his head. 'I love Glendale but people should really mind their own business.' He wrapped an arm around my waist.

'What if they're right?' I asked, looking up at him.

He raised an eyebrow. 'You think?'

'I suppose I'm wondering what we're waiting for. We already feel like a family. I mean – we are a family. I love you two with all of my heart. There's nothing I want more than for us to be together.'

Brodie smiled. 'Me too.' He gave me a kiss. 'Leave it with me then.'

'Leave it with you?' I asked with a laugh.

'Maybe I already have it all planned out.'

'No way. Mr Easy-Going. I'm the planner, not you.'

He sighed. 'Fine. I will plan it all out then. Will that make you happy?'

'You make me happy,' I replied.

'You too.' He reached for me and the kiss lingered so long that I heard Beth calling us. 'Sounds like we'd better go.'

I nodded. 'Cake waits for no man.'

'Ooh, I could hide an engagement ring in a cupcake,' Brodie said as we went out, his eyes lighting up.

'You've kind of ruined that as a surprise. Besides, I'd probably choke on it.'

'It could be a hazard,' he agreed with a grin. 'I'll just have to think of another way to surprise you then.'

'I don't think you can,' I said. I knew him so well, I was sure I'd cotton on to anything he planned.

'I'm taking this as a bet. I warn you now.'

'I really don't think proposing marriage should be a bet, Reverend Brodie. What would your bishop say about that?' I asked as we walked into the kitchen.

'We just won't tell him,' he replied.

'Lying to your bishop!' I tutted at him with a smile. 'I told you when we met, you really weren't like any minster I'd ever met. I still stand by that.'

'Guilty as charged.'

'Never change, Reverend Brodie.'

'As long as you don't, Emily Prescott.'

Beth shushed us then to wheel out the cake and make a speech. I leaned into Brodie, his arm strong and warm around me, and smiled at our family and friends gathered to celebrate my baby girl. I hoped that we'd all never change, but I knew that if life did throw any of us a curve ball again then we'd all be okay, because we had each other.

A Letter From Vicky

Dear reader,

I am so excited to be returning to Glendale Hall! I was so touched by your reviews and messages after releasing *Coming Home to Glendale Hall*, and hearing how many of you wanted to return there. Well, here we are!

This time we follow Emily's story even though we are still very much in the world of Glendale, and hopefully all of your favourite characters from the first book pop up in this one. I knew when I was writing the first book that I wanted to know more about the woman who took Beth in when she was a pregnant teenager, and what her journey looked like. This time it's summer in the Highlands – there is a lot of cake, and a minister that you might very well fall in love with yourself so curl up with a cup of tea and escape again to Glendale. My fingers (and toes!) are crossed that you will all enjoy it as much as your first visit there.

As ever, please do get in touch online to let me know if you enjoy this book, and share your thoughts with other readers by reviewing on Amazon and Goodreads!

Much love,

Victoria

Acknowledgments

It has been such a pleasure returning to Glendale. My biggest thanks is to all the readers who loved book one, who were desperate to know what happened next, and made this such a joy to write. Thank you to all the reviewers and bloggers who spread the word about Coming Home to Glendale Hall – I am so grateful for your support. Special thanks to my Book Squad for being such amazing cheerleaders. And everyone who took the time to contact me online to say they enjoyed the book, your messages make my day every single time!

Thank you so much to Keshini and Lindsey at Hera, my agent Hannah Ferguson, the team at Hardman and Swainson, and everyone who has worked on my books behind the scenes for your hard work, talent, support, and for putting up with this perpetually anxious author.

To my fellow authors for your endless encouragement especially the Savvy Writers' Snug, the Doomsday Writers, George Lester, Kim Nash, Kiley Dunbar, and Mary Jayne Baker. Special thanks to Heidi Swain for your generous support.

As always, a big thank you to my family and friends. And special thanks and love in particular to my long-suffering mum!

Author Biography

Victoria Walters is the author of the bestselling novel *Coming Home to Glendale Hall*. As well as being a writer, Victoria also works as a Waterstones bookseller. She lives in Surrey with her cat Harry (named after Harry Potter). Find out more about Victoria by following her on Instagram at @vickyjwalters, on Twitter at @Vicky_Walters or by visiting her blog at: http://victoria-writes.com/

Books by Victoria Walters

Coming Home to Glendale Hall
Summer at the Kindness Café
The Second Love of my Life